HOPE
OF
AGES
PAST

HOPE OF AGES PAST

An Epic Novel of Enduring Faith, Love, and
the Thirty Years War

BRUCE GARDNER

Publisher's Cataloging-in-Publication Data
provided by Five Rainbows Cataloging Services

Names: Gardner, Bruce E., author.
Title: Hope of ages past: an epic novel of enduring faith, love, and the thirty years war / Bruce Gardner.
Description: Petaluma, CA : Zino Publishing, 2018.
Identifiers: LCCN 2018904022 | ISBN 978-0-9998811-1-8 (pbk.) | ISBN 978-0-9998811-2-5 (hardcover) | ISBN 978-0-9998811-0-1 (ebook)
Subjects: LCSH: Thirty Years' War, 1618-1648--Fiction. | Magdeburg (Germany)--History--Fiction. | Faith--Fiction. | War--Religious aspects--Fiction. | Historical fiction. | Romance fiction. | BISAC: FICTION / Historical / Renaissance. | FICTION / Romance / Historical / Renaissance. | FICTION / Thrillers / Historical. | GSAFD: Historical fiction. | Love stories.
Classification: LCC PS3607.A73 H67 2018 (print) | LCC PS3607.A73 (ebook) | DDC 813/.6--dc23.

To: Nancy, Tina, Jeff, and Maddie

Main Characters

(in order of mention)

Peter Erhart (AYER-haht)
- 1618: accounting aide to his father (in Prague)
- 1629 to 1632: assistant Lutheran pastor (in Germany)

Jakob Erhart (Peter's father)
- Chief accountant for the Holy Roman emperor's Bohemian embassy

Count William Slavata* (Slah-VAH-tah)
Count Jaroslav Martinic* (Mah-ti-NEEK)
- Bohemian provincial governors (Catholic)

Hans Mannheim (MAHN-hime)
- 1618: junior diplomatic aide to his father (Prague)
- 1629 to 1632: major-of-cavalry, Catholic League Army

Baron Albert von Mannheim (Hans's father)
- 1618: Chief military advisor for the Holy Roman emperor's
  Bohemian embassy
- 1629 to 1632: Major general and chief of staff, Catholic League Army

Count Heinrich von Thurn* (TOORN)
- Bohemian noble and leader of the Bohemian Protestant rebellion

Ursula Erhart
- Wife of Peter Erhart
- Vice superintendent of Magdeburg city orphanage

Dr. Heinrich Weber (VEY-buh)
- Senior pastor for St. John's Lutheran Church (in Magdeburg)
- Peter Erhart's supervisor and mentor

Count Albrecht von Wallenstein* (VALL-in-shtine)
- Supreme commander, Catholic Imperial Army (1625–1630)

Christian Wilhelm* (VEEL-hem)
- Lutheran administrator for the archbishopric and city of Magdeburg

*Real historical figure

Anna Ritter (REE-tair)
- Peasant girl from Grünfeld, a small village outside Magdeburg
- Father: Adam – "Vati" (FAH-tee)
- Mother: Frieda – "Mutti" (MOO-tee)
- Sister: Liesa (LEE-suh)

Christian Gilbert de Spaignart* (SHPY-nyart)
- Senior pastor for the Lutheran Church of St. Ulrich (in Magdeburg)

Konrad Fitcher (FEE-chair)
- Assistant pastor for the Lutheran Church of St. Ulrich (in Magdeburg)

Dietrich Ackar (AH-cahr)
- Countryside village rent collector

Otto Gericke* (GAIR-ee-keh)
- Leading member of Magdeburg city council's moderate faction

Reinhard Bake* (BAH-keh)
- Senior pastor for the (Lutheran) Magdeburg Cathedral

Count Tilly*
- Lieutenant general and supreme commander, Catholic League Army

Helmut Schuttmann (SHOOT-mahn), "the Black Knight"
- Major-of-cavalry, Catholic League Army

King Gustavus Adolphus* (goo-STAY-voos uh-DOLL-phoos)
- Lutheran king of Sweden and commander in chief of the Swedish army

Dietrich von Falkenberg* (FAHL-kin-bairg)
- Commander of Magdeburg's combined Swedish–German defense force

Friar Rusche (ROOSH-eh)
- Franciscan monk and rector of St. Matthew's Chapel

Herbert Sturm (SHTURM)
- Leader of Leipzig vigilante gang

*Real historical figure

HISTORICAL PREFACE

Martin Luther never dreamed his bold action on All Hallows' Eve in 1517 would rock the foundations of religious faith and alter the course of world history.

In fact, at the time, Luther—a German Catholic monk and professor of theology—had no desire to disrupt the order and doctrines of the Catholic Church or to dishonor its pope. At most, he presumed the Ninety-Five Theses he nailed to the door of the All Saints' Church in Wittenberg would result in the gradual reform of certain "corrupt" Church fundraising practices.

Martin Luther was wrong. Over the next hundred years, the Protestant Reformation—for better or worse—grew and swept like wildfire through Germany and the entire Western world. Luther's doctrine of "sola Scriptura" (the belief that the Bible alone—as opposed to the pope and his councils—is the final authority for judging all matters of Christian faith and practice) became one of the primary flash points for life-or-death conflict. Cities and towns throughout Europe were thrown into turmoil as Protestant evangelicals struggled to establish a firm footing, while the Catholic faithful sought ways to resist or dislodge them. Several bloody religious wars were fought, resulting in the destruction of cities and the deaths of hundreds of thousands.

By 1618, a tenuous peace prevailed across central Europe. Religious treaties were holding; regional tempers were for the most part controlled.

There was one major exception. In the Bohemian capital city of Prague, serious trouble was brewing . . .

PROLOGUE

The Spark

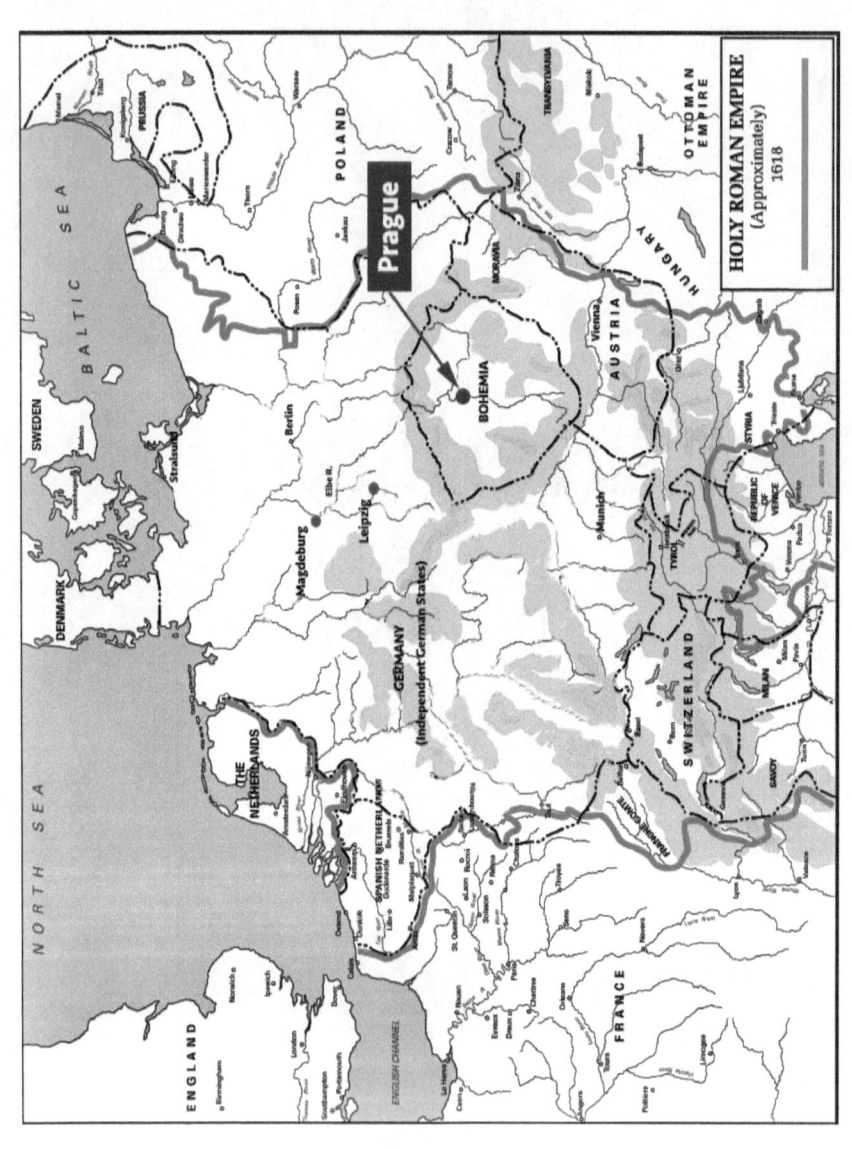

HOLY ROMAN EMPIRE
(Approximately)
1618

CHAPTER 1

Prague, capital city of the Kingdom of Bohemia
May 23, 1618

Peter Erhart clenched his teeth, trying in vain to stop his heart from pounding.

It made no sense. The prospect of another Wednesday morning serving the weekly convocation of Bohemian governors would normally stimulate nothing but a huge yawn. Today, though, Peter sensed something unusual afoot. Something big, possibly threatening. Whatever it was, the sixteen-year-old accountant's aide dreaded facing it.

Striding with his father across the bridge on the way to the nine o'clock meeting at Hradschin Castle, Peter squinted to make out the multitowered behemoth atop the hill on the other side of the river. It was a dreary sight, partially obscured by the unseasonably cold, drizzly rain and fog now blanketing the area—not exactly the view he would have chosen to calm his anxious spirit.

He flinched at a sudden clamor of fog-muffled shouts.

"The antichrists have betrayed us! A hundred years since Luther began the great Reformation, and look how we Protestants still suffer!"

"Yes, the pope's stooges can hide no longer—Matthias and the

Catholic governors have exposed themselves for what they really are!"

"Down with the whole putrid lot of them!"

The angry protests seemed to hail from the foul-smelling tanners' quarter near the west riverbank just north of the bridge, the locale where Prague's expanding horde of Protestant agitators loved to gather every morning.

Peter, a German Lutheran like his father, knew the shouts meant trouble. The agitators had often voiced displeasure with the actions of Matthias, the aging Catholic ruler of the Holy Roman Empire that now embraced most of central Europe, including Austria, Germany, and the Kingdom of Bohemia. But today was different. For the first time, they sounded unleashed, willing to express *anything* that would support their dangerous goal of stirring up anger against the emperor for his latest attempts to interfere with Bohemian Protestant religious liberty.

Even more worrisome than the agitators' shouts was the odd behavior of Peter's father, Jakob, as the two started up the hill toward the castle's main entrance. Herr Erhart had barely spoken a word since leaving their suite at the Imperial Embassy nearly half an hour ago. He appeared to be in a trance, oblivious to the commotion from the tanners' quarter.

Peter could no longer stand the suspense. "Father, what's going on?"

Herr Erhart stared straight ahead. "I fear there's a conspiracy in the making. The Catholic governors may be in real danger. There's a hint of it in that message that was slipped under our door last night."

Peter knew that if anyone was capable of understanding the true threat implied by a small hint, it was his father, the appointed *Rechnungsführer*—chief accounting officer—for Matthias's official embassy to Bohemia. It was an important job, and not just for keeping track of money. The emperor, who resided nearly two hundred miles away in Vienna, had lost touch with the Bohemian situation. Only Jakob Erhart and the emperor's four trusted Catholic governors were now in a position to confirm what had long been rumored: the Protestant governors' disloyalty to the Holy Roman imperial cause.

"May I ask, Father . . . what did the message say?"

"Just two sentences. 'Beware tomorrow—Thurn and his followers intend to act. Don't interfere.' What exactly that means or who left the message is anyone's guess."

Peter flinched at the mention of the name. His father had schooled him well on the notorious Count Heinrich von Thurn, a wealthy former military colonel. Thurn was not a man to be trifled with. Nor was his cause: securing the right of Bohemia's Protestant citizens to worship freely. Already angry with the emperor for a previous personal slight, Thurn was well motivated and capable of converting a peaceful resistance movement into a full-scale armed rebellion. According to Jakob Erhart, the only thing holding the count back from setting the whole cataclysmic process in motion *now* was his determination to wait for the right opportunity.

Peter and his father froze at the sight of two dark shapes emerging from the murky fog on the path ahead.

"Father, who is—"

"Quiet, son. Don't say a word. Let them pass."

Peter held his breath as the black-cloaked, hooded men approached. Each was bent over and carrying what looked like a heavy peddler's sack on his back.

Fewer than three feet away, one of the men paused in front of Peter's father as his partner continued stumbling down the path. The withered face underneath the hood betrayed a lifetime of misery and bitterness. Releasing one hand from the noose of his sack, the man pointed a gnarled finger at Herr Erhart's chest. "I know who you are, oppressor!"

Herr Erhart glared back. "Tell me, then. Who *am* I, friend? And who are *you* to refer to me by that offensive name?"

The man stood motionless, breathing heavily with eyes narrowed. Peter looked warily at his father as the awkward silence continued.

Herr Erhart exploded. "What do you have to say, man? *Anything*? If not, get out of our way. We have pressing business."

The old man took a step closer, his face twitching. "You're the emperor's filthy German Lutheran agent—that's who you are. A traitor to your own faith. Hired by the Catholics to persecute Bohemian

Protestants like me, who ask nothing but to worship as we please. But mark my words, oppressor, your repayment is coming. And it is coming soon."

Herr Erhart lashed out with a swift kick to the sack on the man's back, knocking it out of his grip and onto the ground. "Get out of here, swine! I've heard *enough* of these irresponsible rantings for one morning."

Peter breathed a sigh of relief as he watched the old man flee after his partner like a terrified rat.

"Bohemian scum," Herr Erhart muttered. "Let's go, son. We're already late."

That was it? Peter wondered in amazement. Like the shouts from the tanners' quarter, his father was taking this alarming encounter in stride. Just another minor interruption to his preoccupation with last night's warning.

As the castle wall loomed directly ahead, Peter broached the obvious question. "Father, do you really think Count Thurn will try to make trouble today?"

He shrugged. "Hard to say. We've been able to maintain civility at these weekly meetings up to now. But given that message, we should be prepared for just about anything."

The two men passed in mutual silence through the outer wall entrance and courtyard before arriving at the inner entrance gate. Unchallenged by the guards who recognized them as regular visitors, they walked across another courtyard and entered the main castle tower.

Something wasn't right. On previous occasions, the chatter of provincial governors conversing in the top-floor meeting hall could be heard at the tower's entrance. Today, there was stark silence. Peter glanced anxiously at his father as they ascended the seven flights of stairs.

Inside the hall was another surprise. Only seven men were present, congregated around the administrative desk at the far end of the room. Peter recognized Bohemia's four Catholic provincial governors and their scribe, but the other two he'd never seen before. Like Herr Erhart and Peter, they appeared to be a father accompanied by his teenage son. None of the Protestant governors, numbering over thirty, was anywhere to be seen.

Two of the Catholic governors, Counts William Slavata and Jaroslav Martinic, looked up from the desk and strolled over to shake hands.

"Jakob," Slavata said, "it's good to see you, as always. Our apologies for the sparse gathering this morning."

"The pleasure is ours, counts," Herr Erhart acknowledged. "Where is everyone?"

Slavata displayed a wry smile. "It seems our Protestant colleagues have called their own pre-meeting for some reason. We expect them here at some point, but who knows?"

Strange . . . no mention of last night's message, Peter thought.

Martinic continued with the amiable greeting. "I must say, Jakob, your boy here is becoming a strikingly handsome and impressive young man. It's obvious to all of us how much he's grown in stature and skill over the past year. You must be very proud."

Peter blushed but was nonetheless thrilled with the compliment. It could not have come at a better time. Born and raised in the north German city of Hanover, he had been brought along to Prague last year by his father. His task was to learn the ropes of government financing in preparation for a future career in mercantile accounting. Before leaving Germany, he had tried to remind his father that he had no real interest in pursuing such a worldly occupation—that becoming an ordained Lutheran minister like his beloved grandfather Nikolaus had long been his heart's true desire. But his protests had made no difference. Jakob Erhart was determined that his only son should follow in his own footsteps, starting with an apprenticeship in Prague. Resigned to his fate, Peter knew the time had come to prove to his father that he was actually learning something useful. And what better proof than a personal validation from the highly respected Count Martinic?

"Of course I'm proud of him, my lords," Herr Erhart said, putting his arm around Peter's shoulders. "And I'll be even prouder as soon as he figures out a way to keep our mountainous debt from piling up further." He paused, glanced quickly around the room, then spoke again in a lowered voice. "My lords, I must tell you of a mysterious message I received last night that—"

Before he could complete the warning, one of the other governors hailed loudly from the administrative desk. "Count Slavata, did you forget that you still have some introductions to make?"

Slavata slapped a hand against his forehead. "Oh, where are my manners? Come, and let's introduce you." He and Martinic escorted Peter and his father to the opposite end of the hall, where the two strangers stood observing several large oil paintings on the wall. "Herr Jakob Erhart and son Peter," said Slavata, "allow me the privilege of introducing you to Baron Albert von Mannheim and his son Hans."

Peter locked eyes and shook hands with the slender, good-looking youth who appeared to be a couple of years younger and a full head shorter than himself. The boy's firm grip and friendly, sincere expression were a welcome contrast to the limp handshake and averted gaze that Peter was used to receiving from the other diplomats' sons. He liked Hans immediately.

"Baron von Mannheim is the emperor's newly appointed military advisor for the Bohemian region," Count Martinic explained. "He's here today to inform us all about the latest plans from Vienna for dealing with the Protestant agitators."

Count Slavata gave the baron a conspiratorial smile. "And Herr Erhart here is our resident *Rechnungsführer*, directed by the emperor himself to play another special role in this eminent body's proceedings."

"Oh? And what's that?" the baron asked, eyebrow cocked.

"To monitor and hopefully improve our sloppy methods of financial analysis, of course!" Slavata said, laughing heartily. "Herr Erhart is a highly reputed accountant from Germany. If *he* can't keep us all on the straight and narrow, no one can."

"Really, Count," Herr Erhart protested, "you overestimate my importance. I hardly do more than occasionally report to Emperor Matthias the simple fact that everyone here seems honest and capable of adding two plus two correctly."

"No doubt we all could use some monitoring in *that* area," the baron said. "But I'm curious. Why would the emperor see the need to import an accounting expert all the way from Germany? Don't we have adequate resources right here in Prague?"

Slavata glanced at Martinic before replying. "Our honorable emperor wanted to appease the large Protestant majority of our governing council. But instead of appointing a local Bohemian—who'd inevitably be tainted against us Catholic governors—he demanded we hire a *German Lutheran* acccountant for the task. That way, he reasons, few here in Prague or the entire Bohemian region would ever question the impartiality of the findings."

"Well, Herr Erhart," the baron said, his voice dripping with condescension, "being a faithful Catholic myself, I can't say I'm impressed with your religious credentials. But since it seems you're proving to be a reliable accountant, I suppose we'll have to tolerate everything else. So long as the emperor approves your role here, so must I."

Peter recoiled at the patronizing slight to his father and the Lutheran faith. It wasn't the first time he'd heard an anti-Protestant sentiment expressed. But it was definitely the first time he'd heard it directed so personally by a high-ranking imperial official. He looked at the baron's son, who was now staring at the floor.

Before Herr Erhart could respond, a low murmur arose from the ground floor. Peter and the others exchanged bewildered expressions at the sound of angry voices and booted feet tromping up the stairs.

The meeting-hall doors burst open. Thirty Protestant governors poured in and surrounded the counts, the baron, Herr Erhart, and the boys. Another ten men rushed to corner the other two Catholic governors and their scribe. Peter stood frozen as the glaring Protestants edged closer.

Baron von Mannheim spoke first. "My lords, what is the meaning of this? I'd been looking forward to addressing a normal Wednesday meeting of the honorable provincial governors of Bohemia—all in accordance with the emperor's wishes, of course."

A loud chorus of jeers greeted his query. A tall man with ferocious eyes and a full beard strode slowly forward. It was Count Thurn himself.

Thurn's deep voice resonated with hostility. "That's precisely the problem, Baron. We have little regard for Matthias's wishes anymore. Why should we? The emperor clearly wishes nothing for us Bohemian Protestants except slavery to the abominable curse of Catholicism!"

"But why threaten us personally?" the baron asked.

Thurn's tone softened. "You and Herr Erhart and your sons needn't worry, Baron. You're merely tools of the emperor's ambassadorial staff, and you've done nothing yet to directly interfere with Bohemian religious freedom. Unfortunately, I can't say the same for our Catholic governors here."

Thurn turned to the governors, his face darkening. *"In the name of the true God, seize the antichrists!"*

The mob descended on Slavata, Martinic, and the other two Catholic governors. Wrenching their arms behind their backs, they forced the four to kneel together in the center of the room and hurled accusations.

With all the shouting and commotion, Peter struggled to make out the charges. It seemed that the Catholics were accused of halting construction and imprisoning the pastors of several new Protestant churches in their districts. If true, these actions would be clear violations of the previous emperor's Letter of Majesty guaranteeing freedom of worship throughout Bohemia. But the main charge was personal: the Catholic governors had supposedly helped the emperor craft a recently circulated "open letter" to the Bohemian people. In it, Matthias had threatened the very life of Count Thurn himself.

After a heated discussion, Thurn declared two of the Catholic governors innocent and ordered them freed. Turning next to Slavata and Martinic, he demanded to know if they wanted to deny the accusations. Each man defiantly pleaded guilty as charged.

The mob attacked like a pack of ravenous wolves, mercilessly beating and kicking Slavata and Martinic. In a culminating fit of fury, they lifted both men over their heads, then slammed them to the floor at the feet of the baron and his son. Peter gaped in shock as the blood poured from Martinic's head.

"My lords, won't you at least permit these men an official trial?" the baron protested.

"Baron," a pockmark-faced Protestant governor scoffed, "these two antichrists have proudly boasted of their criminal actions! Who are you, another antichrist, to question our manner of dealing with them?"

"But, my lords, do their crimes call for the severe punishments you're now meting out?"

"Enough of this infernal stalling!" Count Thurn roared. "Mannheim, I'm giving you one last warning: don't get in our way." He pointed his finger at Slavata and Martinic. "What say you, guilty ones? Will you finally now beg for mercy?"

Slavata barely managed to lift his head. He responded in a weak, hoarse voice. "The mercy of Protestants be damned, and may their cursed doctrine of *sola Scriptura* be damned as well. We ask no mercy of anyone except that of the Blessed Virgin and our Holy Father, the pope. We acted in good conscience. Emperor Matthias has the right to halt construction of Protestant chapels on our royal Bohemian lands as he so wishes. And anyone who dares to defy the emperor's wishes deserves what they get."

"Then you have damned yourselves and will get what *you* deserve," hissed Thurn, motioning for his accompanying guards to step forward. "Prepare, counts, to pay the full price for elevating the decrees of your pope and the emperor above the supreme authority of the Holy Scriptures and the natural right of religious liberty for all Bohemians."

Baron von Mannheim tried to block the guards but was struck brutally on the face and shoved to the floor. Blood gushed from his nose and split lip as he struggled to rise to his knees. "Hans, where are you?" he gasped, looking wildly around the room.

"Ho, look at our bold imperial stooge now!" cried one of the Protestants. "Calling for help from his boy! Where, oh where, could that little mouse possibly be?"

Peter struggled against his own father's restraining hands, wanting desperately to go to the baron's aid.

"Stay still, Peter," Herr Erhart spoke firmly in his ear. "Don't interfere. You'll only make things worse."

Peter watched helplessly as the beatings of Slavata and Martinic resumed. He opened his mouth to shout out in protest, but the shout remained stuck in his throat. He had to do something, but what?

The fleeting thought made little sense, but it was something. *Find Hans!* Peter wrestled free from his father's grasp and ran through the wall of ranting, fist-shaking Protestant governors. It didn't take long to find the boy curled up behind the base of a large column at the rear of the hall. He was trembling violently, hands covering his head.

Peter knelt and grasped the boy's shoulder. "Hans, come on! You can't stay here. Your father's calling for you."

Hans grabbed Peter's forearm tightly with both hands, his face a tearful, contorted mask of shame. "Peter, I can't. I ran. I-I let him down. He expects me to become a strong military man like him. I . . ."

"It'll be all right, Hans. It's not too late. I promise. Please, just get up. He needs you, Hans. Let me take you back to him. Don't let *them* find you here."

Hans stared at the floor for a long moment. Finally, he nodded, eyes glistening as he managed a thin but grateful smile. Peter helped him to his feet.

"Well, well. What have we here?" One of the Protestant governors towered above them. "The frightened little mouse thought he'd found a comfortable place to hide, did he? Come, Mannheim, your father calls out for you." The hulking man grabbed Hans by the back of his collar and dragged him toward the crowd.

"*Leave him alone!*" Peter shouted, grabbing the governor's arm. The man batted him aside like a small dog. "Your own father was warned last night to stay out of this, boy. If you don't want to get hurt, I suggest you follow his example."

Peter drew back, allowing the seductive logic of self-preservation to take control. Really, hadn't he already done enough? Why risk getting hurt for someone he didn't even know? Especially for a Catholic boy whose arrogant father had just insulted his own Lutheran faith. He followed behind in cowed distress as the governor dragged Hans back to the fray.

"Count Thurn, look what I found—hiding behind one of the pillars!" The governor shoved Hans to the ground next to the savagely beaten Slavata and Martinic, both of whom were now lying helplessly on their backs.

Silence engulfed the encircling mob as Count Thurn leveled his cruel gaze at Hans. "So, it seems we have a fine young example of Catholic 'courage' in the face of a little danger. Baron, aren't you *proud* to see the weak, weeping face worn by your own seed, the face of a boy too cowardly to come to the aid of his injured Catholic brothers or even his own father? What do you have to say to your father, boy?"

Hans turned slowly toward the baron, his head bowed in abject shame. "Father, please . . . forgive me."

Peter cringed at the governors' laughter and insults that rained down on Hans's head. But he knew that far worse for the boy was seeing the look of deep disappointment and disgrace on his father's face. It was a look that bore no sign of willingness to forgive.

The ordeal wasn't over. Thurn yanked Hans by his collar and forced his head down to within an inch of Slavata's face, making him look directly into the man's terrified, bulging eyes. "This is the price for abuse of authority by Catholic tyrants," Thurn shouted in Hans's ear. "Never forget it, you gutless little piece of dung!" He slapped Hans viciously on the face before flinging him aside like a rag doll.

As if on cue, several of the armed guards stooped and picked up Slavata and Martinic by their hands and feet. They carried them to the end of the hall along with their scribe, who until then had been hiding in a corner. One by one, each man was heaved, screaming, through the window. It was a seventy-foot fall to the cobblestone courtyard below.

Peter fell to his knees and pitched forward, his head buried in his hands.

Later that night, Peter lay on his bed, listening to his father's fitful snores and the pelting of rain on the embassy roof.

Mercifully, in the hours since being released by the Protestant governors and returning to their suite, there had been some welcome news: Slavata, Martinic, and their scribe had all—amazingly—managed to survive their falls. Though badly injured, they'd been helped away by supporters and were now out of immediate danger.

There was disagreement among the embassy staff as to what had saved them. Some said it was the Blessed Mother Mary herself who had arrested their falls, others that they'd simply had the good fortune to land on a heaping pile of moldering manure that someone had forgotten to remove. There was one thing, though, upon which *everyone* at the embassy agreed: the long-anticipated spark for violent rebellion by Bohemian Protestants against the Holy Roman Empire had finally been lit. There would be no turning back now.

Peter tossed on his bed, unable to erase the memory of the pain in the younger Mannheim's face as Hans and his father, bloodied and disgraced, had been led out of the castle. Even worse was the piercing guilt he felt for not having done more on the boy's behalf. It hadn't been enough to gently console him when no one was looking. No, he should have shown the courage of Grandfather Nikolaus, jumped on that Protestant governor's back, threatened to plunge his small dagger into the man's neck if he had to—*anything* to rescue Hans from the degrading treatment he had been about to receive. Instead, he'd hung back like a scared little bird and justified it on the basis of Hans's being Catholic and therefore not worth fighting for. His performance today had definitely not been the way of his grandfather, who'd once jumped through the flames to rescue an innocent Catholic woman from being burned at the stake for allegedly practicing witchcraft.

In a last-ditch effort to fall asleep, Peter prayed with an intensity he had never before known. *Lord, forgive my pathetic effort to help that Catholic boy in danger today. Please don't end my dream of serving boldly in the Lutheran ministry like Grandfather Nikolaus. And Lord, if it is your will, allow me to meet Hans again someday—I promise I will make things right.*

PART I

Shifting Winds

CHAPTER 2

City of Magdeburg, Germany
February 28, 1629

Assistant Pastor Peter Erhart crumpled a sheet of paper with fewer than three sentences and hurled it against the wall of his private study. Would the right words *ever* come? If the news he'd received yesterday from the city councilman was true, they had better come quickly. Christian Wilhelm—the de facto Lutheran administrator for the archbishopric of Magdeburg—was back in town. He'd decided to lead the special delegation charged with evaluating Peter's sermon performance on Sunday, and he was reportedly salivating over the prospect of delivering a crushing blow to Peter's promising ministry career.

In five hours, Peter was scheduled to meet with his supervisor, Dr. Weber, the senior pastor of St. John's Lutheran Church. It would be the last chance for the two to review Peter's special sermon for Sunday, his final test for membership in the powerful Magdeburg Cathedral Council to which Weber had recently nominated him. But if, by then, Peter could not even produce a *draft* sermon that Weber would see as exceptionally well conceived and motivating—without being unduly offensive to the wrong people—there could be only one possible outcome. Weber would have to inform Christian Wilhelm and the other evaluators not to bother attending Sunday's service. Wilhelm, looking for *any* excuse to squelch the moderating influence of St. John's Church on city politics, and Peter's career hopes along with it, would then force Weber to withdraw his nomination. The glorious urban-ministry career that Peter had pursued so vigorously after his father's sudden death nine years ago would be nipped in the bud, with his future church responsibilities limited to Vespers services, pastoral visits, and intercessory prayer. Surely, God intended more for him than *that*.

Peter sighed, stood, and flung open the panels of the lattice window behind his desk. It was an overcast day. He inhaled deeply, immediately wishing he hadn't. The scents of deep-fried donuts and roasted meat combined with the stench of last night's gutter droppings on the narrow street below created a pungent, sickening odor. Disgusted, he closed the window and drew the curtain.

It didn't have to be this way. He should have taken his wife's advice last year and avoided publicly confronting Wilhelm about his crazy church-seating policy for the city. Then he wouldn't be in this tenuous position. In fact, if he'd listened to Ursula's counsel on a number of other things lately instead of pursuing his own headstrong ideas, his professional life would probably be going a lot smoother.

The soft knock on his study door signaled the arrival of a welcome diversion. "Peter, I've got your breakfast."

"Of course, dear, come in."

Ursula entered and placed the platter of pickled herring, cheese, and pieces of honey cake on the small table next to his desk. She glanced at the sheaf of blank papers and flashed a knowing smile. "Having some trouble with this one, aren't you, Pastor?"

Peter grimaced. "More than I'd care to admit."

"My, my," Ursula teased, "when have I ever known the immensely gifted Pastor Peter Erhart to struggle with writing a great sermon? Honestly, Peter, did you forget? You're the grandson of that master sermon-writer, Nicholas Erhart. It's in your blood, for heaven's sake!"

"You *would* have to remind me of *him*, wouldn't you?"

"How else am I supposed to encourage you in your special calling?" Ursula smiled as she drew close and coaxed a small chunk of honey cake into his mouth. Peter pulled her in and embraced her. Immediately, he felt the tension ebb from his body. Lord, what would he do without her?

At twenty-two, she was considered one of the most attractive young ladies in Magdeburg. Not that she was a vain woman. In fact, anyone looking for a model of unpretentious, natural feminine charm and beauty needed to look no further than Ursula Erhart. Tall and graceful body lines, long light-blond hair, clear-blue eyes, high cheekbones, a softly rounded chin, and a wide mouth with thin lips—all combined in an appealing way that bore strong witness to her Swedish ancestry.

But it was not only her physical qualities that had first drawn him to her. When they'd met five years ago at a social function of the University of Strasbourg where he was pursuing his graduate studies, Peter noticed that highly intellectual subjects were not beyond the scope of Ursula Andersen's comprehension or interest. She'd surprised him with her awareness of some esoteric theological writings. Further conversation had revealed that she was the daughter of the university library administrator, raised by her father to respect and appreciate the arts of scholarly reading and literary analysis.

By the end of that very evening, Peter knew he would one day marry Ursula. After two years of courting, he'd asked for her hand and secured her father's approval. The couple had wed in the university chapel and soon after had taken up residence in Magdeburg, where Peter was beginning his internship at St. John's.

It hadn't taken long for Ursula to prove she was just as adept at homemaking as she was at literary analysis. She'd poured herself into creating a comfortable space for Peter to enjoy at the end of each workday. He especially loved their evening routine: putting their two young children to bed; sitting by the cozy fire; sharing the happenings of the day; discussing the Bible and other ancient texts; and talking of their hopes and dreams for the children and each other.

There was no denying it, Peter thought as he watched his wife glide effortlessly about his desk, straightening some loose papers and repositioning the vase of dried flowers. Beauty, intelligence, commitment, and tenderness—in Ursula, God had combined them all into one delightful package. And *he* was the lucky recipient.

"It's Herr Wilhelm who you're really worried about, isn't it?" she continued, snapping him out of his admiring trance.

Peter plopped down in his chair. "Wilhelm and my other detractors in this city, who'll no doubt be attending Sunday, hoping to catch me saying something stupid or offensive. You know how fearful rumors always seem to bring these people out of the woodwork. Especially rumors about the war."

"But Peter, the war's been going on many years now. And we still have yet to see any fighting approach the city gates. Is there something new you haven't told me?"

Peter stared at her. Up to now, he'd tried to spare her from the most frightening stories emerging from the multinational conflict sparked by the incident at the Prague castle he'd been involved in eleven years ago. Ursula had enough to worry about, including managing the household and taking care of their two-year-old son Josef and one-year-old daughter Edith. Maybe, though, it was time to let her in on the latest talk.

"Ursula, do you remember my telling you about that new imperial army led by Count von Wallenstein that invaded eastern Germany a couple of years ago?"

"The one you said the emperor sent to enforce Catholicism throughout central Europe? Yes, I remember. But I thought you also said they'd been contained by our Protestant armies well to the northeast. Has something changed that?"

"Yes, something *has* changed, dear. The city councilman told me about it yesterday, along with the news of Wilhelm's attendance on Sunday. Wallenstein's army has apparently broken out of its winter quarters. It's now heading this way. And word has it that Magdeburg could soon find itself in the center of its path."

Ursula gave him a blank look. "Peter, what does that mean? Do we need to do anything?"

"It's too early to tell. It'll depend partly on whether Emperor Ferdinand is more committed than his predecessor Matthias was to giving free rein to his supreme army commander. But there's no need to panic—these rumors can quickly come and go. The only thing I know for sure is that Christian Wilhelm, the cathedral council, and the city council will be having some serious joint discussions over the next couple of weeks about the threat and what to do about it."

Ursula pursed her lips. "And let me guess. The last thing that Herr Wilhelm will want to hear in the meantime is my darling husband spouting some 'holy nonsense' from the pulpit on Sunday—such as 'God's divine logic' for how the city should deal with this situation. Am I right?"

"Exactly right," Peter said. "Now you can see why I'm having such a time writing this sermon. You know how hard it is for me to keep my words in check when it comes to speaking the truth in love to the likes of Wilhelm."

Ursula walked behind Peter's chair, wrapped her arms around his chest, and kissed him on the cheek. "Yes, Pastor, I do know how hard it is for you. And that's why I *know* you're going to write your best sermon ever. Since when have you ever backed down from a major sermon challenge? Just remember, do what you always do: write to please God. If Herr Wilhelm and the other evaluators are impressed enough to approve you for the cathedral council, so much the better. Either way, you'll have done your best, and we'll know it was God's will. Now enjoy your breakfast and get back to work. I need to check on the children."

Peter laughed. "Are you commanding me, wife?"

Ursula flashed a coy smile from the doorway. "No, Pastor, I'm just loving you." She closed the door behind her.

Turning back to his desk, Peter picked up his quill and dipped it into the inkwell. Within moments, the right words began to flow.

CHAPTER 3

Magdeburg
February 28, 1629

Halfway to the church, Peter was already sweating under his cassock. He wasn't the only one affected by today's unusually mild weather. Even the Schneiders' children had responded, moving their daily game of ninepins out of the sun's glare in the middle of the street to the scant shade offered by their parents' butcher shop. It was a welcome change from the gloomy skies of earlier this morning.

His chest tightened at the thought of meeting with Dr. Weber. But he'd made tremendous progress on the sermon this morning, especially after eliminating any direct references to the rising war threat. Plus, he'd still have some time once he arrived at the church to hone the final paragraphs. Hopefully, Weber would be pleased enough with this draft version to press forward with the planned Sunday delivery.

As he passed by the butcher shop, Frau Schneider came bustling out of the entrance with a small box in her hands. "Pastor Erhart, don't you dare go to the church without our offering!" she exclaimed, beaming proudly.

"What have we here?" Peter asked.

"Didn't you remind us at last Thursday's Vespers that you'd be going to the countryside to visit the Jünger family this afternoon?"

"Yes, that's right."

"I thought they might enjoy a few choice slices of veal, cheese, and rye bread that I baked especially for them earlier this morning. The Lord only knows the misfortunes that poor family has suffered. To think of Herr Jünger losing his dear wife and three youngest children within a week of each other. It's almost too much to bear."

Peter's shoulders slumped. The past year's crop failure and spread of influenza had wreaked havoc on the local population, especially those living outside the city walls. Herr Jünger and his oldest son were the only ones in their family of six to have survived.

"I know our offering is mere chicken feed in the face of disaster like that," Frau Schneider lamented.

"It may be chicken feed to you," Peter said, "but certainly not in the Jüngers' or God's eyes. May the Lord richly bless your generosity."

Frau Schneider blushed. "You're so kind. Now don't let me keep you. I know you've got an important sermon to finish." Peter said goodbye, then resumed his walk toward the church.

A few minutes later, he arrived at the base of the massive eastern city wall. The majestic facade and dual, flanking bell towers of St. John's Lutheran Church stared down at him, conveying lasting peace and tranquility.

Peter quickly mounted the steps to the church's main entrance and waved to the worship director Samuel Scheidt, who was standing in the doorway.

"Hello, Pastor Peter," he hailed. "Would you care to join me in a little bell-tuning operation?"

Peter laughed. Everyone knew that Samuel's "little operations" could easily turn into major productions taking hours. "Not today, Samuel, but I'm glad to see you're carrying out your duties faithfully. We'll need those bells to ring out loud and clear on Sunday, just like your magnificent choir and organ. Don't let me hinder you."

"No trouble at all," said Samuel. "And may God grant you a successful sermon. I know everyone will be listening with eager ears, especially our esteemed Lutheran administrator."

Peter rolled his eyes. He needed no extra reminder of Christian Wilhelm. "Well, I'll just have to resist the temptation to tickle those 'eager ears' in order to advance my own position, now, won't I?"

"Of course," Samuel replied with his usual wide, innocent grin. "We must rely on the Lord for our true advancement. By all means, my dear friend, speak tomorrow only from your heart and according to the word . . . as the Spirit guides."

Peter walked into the rectory office. Elderly Frau Gerda Mittlech, one of the church housemaids, was busy dusting off his desk. Childless and a widow for more than seven years, Gerda was especially fond of Peter. She'd been one of his strongest supporters ever since he'd first arrived at the church three years ago to begin his internship.

"Good morning, Gerda. I didn't mean to interrupt."

"Oh, I'm almost finished. But you know it takes a while for an old woman like me to clear the dust left by a studious young man like yourself. What's in the package?"

"A food offering from the Schneiders for Herr Jünger and his son," Peter said. "I'll be visiting them later this afternoon."

"Bless those Schneiders. They're always thinking of others before themselves. Here, let me take that and put it somewhere out of the sunlight. We mustn't have a spoiled offering." Gerda took the box from Peter and placed it in the shade.

"Gerda," he asked, "how is your family doing? It's been quite a while since you've mentioned them."

Gerda turned to him slowly, her hand to her mouth. He could see she was trembling and trying not to cry.

He walked over and gently put his arm around her shoulders. "Gerda, please, come and sit down." He led the distraught woman over to the chair next to his desk. He helped her sit before taking a seat in his own chair, which he'd placed immediately in front of hers.

Gerda sighed. Her eyes brimmed with tears. "Oh, Pastor, I hate to take up your time. You've got an important sermon to finish."

"It's you who are here right now, dear friend. The sermon completion can wait. Tell me what's going on."

It took Gerda nearly a minute to compose herself. "It's my youngest brother, Stefan. I just found out he was living in sin for the past year with a young married woman from the countryside. It's now become public knowledge. Thank God, he's broken off the affair, and the woman's abusive husband has accepted her back into their home. He says he doesn't plan to press civil charges. But Stefan was still required by his church's pastor to appear before Administrator Wilhelm. And though he confessed his sin, he insisted his feelings of love and desire to protect the woman from her husband's abuse were honorable."

Peter tensed. He'd heard this rationale before in his still-early pastoral career and understood the temptation to think in those terms. "Go on, Gerda," he said softly.

"Even though Stefan begged on his knees for mercy, Herr Wilhelm said he has to be disciplined. So two Sundays from now, public readings of his name and his sin will be made at *all* the city's churches. His reputation will be ruined. And if he still refuses to completely repent of what Herr Wilhelm calls his 'evil attempts to justify his terrible sin in his own eyes,' he'll be excommunicated."

Peter winced. Lutheran church discipline, though intended for the sinner's eternal benefit, could be very severe—especially when dealt from the hand of Christian Wilhelm. "Does Stefan still care about remaining in the church?"

Gerda sobbed. "My brother's been a faithful member of his congregation for over twenty years. He's helped many in need despite his own hardships. And he's well loved by everyone. He knows that leaving the church would mean terrible personal loss and humiliation. But right now, he seems willing to accept any penalty for refusing to confess that his motivations were purely evil. Oh, Pastor, I'm so afraid for him! What, oh what can I do or say to Stefan that will make him change his mind?"

Peter drew a deep breath and let it out slowly. Inside, he was smoldering with frustration at Wilhelm's inflexibility. But he also knew that Wilhelm was acting within his bounds, and that there was virtually no chance the man would ever find it in his hardened heart to grant a reprieve. A descendant of the ferociously Protestant branch of the House of Hohenzollern, Christian Wilhelm brooked no patience for anything less than radical adherence to strict Lutheran doctrine and orthodoxy.

He had to proceed gently. "Gerda, my dear friend, listen to me. I know you love your brother even more than your words could possibly convey. But Stefan has to make his own choice and live by it. You can't impose your will or faith on him. It'll destroy you to think that you can. As long as he's aware of his choices, which it seems he is, then the matter has to rest between him and God. But there's something we both need to do for Stefan in the meantime, and you know what that is."

Gerda managed a weak smile. "Of course, Pastor. Just as Dr. Weber and you have always encouraged us. We pray for him. With all the strength and heart that we have. And we continue to love him no matter what he decides."

"We've taught you well," Peter said. "Now pray along with me, and know that God will hear us. We can't say what Stefan's ultimate decision will be. But at the very least, you'll know that you've loved him through this situation in the best possible way."

Peter prayed with Gerda for some time. At the end, she was visibly more relaxed. Just before leaving, she gave Peter a hug.

"Now don't tell anyone I just did that," she said with an embarrassed smile, "or they'll accuse me of vile things. Imagine someone my age trying to foist themselves on the younger generation!"

"Don't worry," Peter whispered, "your secret is my secret."

He closed the door behind Gerda and returned to his desk with a warm sense of inner peace, glad that he'd done something tangible to relieve her distress.

It took fewer than ten seconds for the familiar voice inside his head to spoil it all. *Well done, Pastor. Go on—take some credit for being such a good shepherd to poor little old ladies who adore you. Oh, and give all the glory to God while you're at it. He'll definitely be impressed with your humility. But just remember, Pastor, all you did was pray for her. If you really want to be a bold Lutheran minister like Grandfather Nikolaus, shouldn't you have done more to help her? Or was the thought of standing up directly to Administrator Wilhelm on her brother's behalf just a little too inconvenient, or possibly . . . frightening?*

The internal, self-accusing voice usually expressed itself in rational sentences, often intruding on his thoughts when he least expected it. He'd sensed it first on that traumatic day eleven years ago with his father in the castle. The voice had continued to torment his mind for weeks afterward that his efforts to help that abused Catholic boy, Hans Mannheim, had not been good enough. He should have done more to protect the boy, put his own life on the line if necessary. Never mind the fact that he'd been only sixteen years old at the time. The voice suggested that he'd completely dishonored his grandfather's legacy. Fortunately, later conversations with his father had helped to dispel such overwrought, foolish notions. But the voice's pattern had been set. It would continue to haunt him over the years. And its arguments were becoming even more sophisticated and difficult to cast aside.

Maybe, Peter thought, the voice was God's way of keeping him humble, especially in view of his chosen path in life. Hadn't he read that Martin Luther himself had struggled throughout much of his early career, his mind tortured by this sort of thing? Anyway, what could he do about it, beyond praying for God to take the voice away? And since God hadn't yet done so, why fight it? Just get on with things, he told himself. Especially knowing he was about to face the biggest test of his professional life yet.

CHAPTER 4

Magdeburg
February 28, 1629

Peter drew a deep breath, gathered his notes and Bible, and went to the church garden. It was nearly noon. His draft sermon was finally ready for Dr. Weber's review.

Just like almost every other aspect of the buildings and grounds associated with St. John's, the garden was well designed and maintained. Peter strolled down the main path, which was bordered by vegetable plots on the left and fruit trees interspersed with yet-to-bloom flowering shrubs and plants on the right. A slight breeze had picked up, carrying the vague scent of honeysuckle.

At the end of the path, Dr. Heinrich Weber sat on a small bench with his head bowed, no doubt engrossed in his daily meditations.

Peter approached hesitantly, not wanting to interrupt.

Dr. Weber looked up and grinned. "Well, here he is. My fellow servant of the Lord, committed to helping me shed God's light on our beloved city. Please join me, Pastor Peter! Are you enjoying our warm weather today?"

"I'm enjoying it better out here than inside, sir." Peter doffed his hat and bowed.

Dr. Weber stood slowly and pointed toward the grove of apple trees on the other side of the garden. "Shall we walk for a bit?"

A short and somewhat portly man with light-gray hair and a lighter full beard, Weber conveyed an impression of gentle joviality. His deep-set, gray-green eyes always radiated cheerfulness, even in the worst of times. Throughout his sixty-three years, Weber had enjoyed excellent health. But his recent fall had taken a toll, and he'd been slow to recover. Peter was glad to see him feeling well enough to suggest the walk.

The two men strolled along the path in meditative silence. At the edge of the grove, they sat down together on a stone bench.

After a short prayer, Weber signaled it was time for the official appointment to begin. "So tell me, Peter. Is your sermon in good shape?"

Over the next half hour, Peter shared the gist of his draft. Weber was clearly pleased. He had only a few minor suggestions for tailoring some of the details and gave his permission to proceed with the sermon's delivery on Sunday. Elated at the reaction of his supervisor and longtime mentor, Peter gave Weber a brotherly hug.

As he was about to leave, a last-minute thought occurred. "Doctor, earlier today I remembered something you said to me once. It had such a beneficial impact on my life, and I don't believe I ever thanked you for it."

Weber chuckled. "I'm always glad to hear that I've actually *helped* someone, my dear young man. I sometimes worry that my supposedly sage utterings over the years may have done more harm than good to those I love most. Please remind me. I'm all ears."

"One evening, you visited my family for dinner. It was just after the Prague castle incident. I was only sixteen then, but I was really worried about where I was heading in life. If you'll recall, I had a strong leaning to become a Lutheran minister like my grandfather. But my father had other ideas in that regard."

"Yes, Peter, I do remember that evening," Weber said with a deep sigh. "Those were the days, sitting around the table with you and Jakob, reminiscing about the heroic exploits of my old friend Nikolaus. Oh, how I so miss both of them!"

"After dinner, you took me aside," Peter said. "You told me that I shouldn't rush my decision. You said that becoming a Lutheran minister was *not* something to pursue just to imitate someone I admired, or even because of my great interest in the doctrine and writings of Martin Luther. You said that it was first and foremost a matter of the heart. That without a true heart of compassion for the people I'd be shepherding, my ministry would be nothing but an empty shell."

Dr. Weber nodded. "I'm impressed. You remembered my advice well."

"Yes, sir, that I did," Peter said, looking down at his lap. "Though I have to admit, your suggestion to wait for God's direction bothered me a lot. After my father died and I no longer felt bound by his wish for me to become an accountant, those first two years at the university were agonizing. I really sensed that I wanted to be a pastor, but I didn't yet feel that inner conviction of truly caring about others."

"But that waiting time was well spent," Dr. Weber observed, "wouldn't you agree? Pursuing a course of study like you did in the field of anatomy and medicine wasn't a pointless undertaking. I keep hearing reports from our desperate Protestant military commanders. They're always calling for more barber-surgeons capable of treating the new generation of battlefield wounds."

"Yes, that's true," Peter said. "But all my medical studies happened before my 'spiritual lightning bolt' struck in the middle of that unforgettable night five years ago. I woke up with a certainty I'd never known before. No more worries as to whether I was compassionate enough. I don't know how the Lord did it, but I knew right then with every fiber of my being that my time had come to minister to others through the power of Christ."

Dr. Weber smiled. "Timing is important, isn't it?"

"Without your wise encouragement to wait, sir," Peter replied, "I wouldn't have entered God's service with the right spirit driving me."

"So now you're poised to see exactly where God plans to take you next," Weber said. "And your ministry to our congregation and this city along with you—hopefully without the need for another lightning bolt! My compliments to you. You've done very well, Peter. Only one more major hurdle."

Peter blushed at the praise. "Thank you, sir."

After a moment of silence, a frown darkened Dr. Weber's face. Weber reached over and grasped his forearm. "Peter, I want you to be ready for something when you're speaking on Sunday."

"What's that, sir?"

Dr. Weber hesitated, as if debating with himself whether to bring up the subject. "You're no doubt already aware that Administrator Wilhelm and the other evaluators will be sitting front and center in the congregation."

"Yes, sir," Peter replied. "That I am."

"What you may *not* know is that Wilhelm is on another new warpath. He's told the cathedral council that he's finally had it with 'waffling and vacillation' when it comes to defending the city against Wallenstein's Catholic army. He's also insisting our defense strategy should include allying with any foreign power he can convince to help him restore his own personal fame and fortune in this region."

This much was nothing new. Wilhelm's penchant for seeking foreign alliances had long been a bone of dissension across the city. It was one of the main reasons that the cathedral council, in a close vote, had forced him out of his official position last year but had allowed him to continue functioning in an acting capacity until a suitable replacement could be found.

"The new twist," Weber continued, "is that Wilhelm says he'll no longer tolerate the preaching of any Lutheran pastor in this city that even hints of opposition to his latest pet project."

"Which is . . . ?"

"Forging a military alliance with the Swedes to help face the threat from Wallenstein. He threatened to remove any pastor who opposes this."

Peter's jaw dropped. "Seriously, sir? *What* in heaven or on earth, may I ask, is giving Wilhelm the gall to take such a stance? He's not even our formally sanctioned administrator anymore."

Weber flashed a bitter smile. "Not *what*, Peter, rather . . . *who*."

"All right. Then *who*, sir?"

"Spaignart and his band of radical followers."

Of course, Peter thought. *Who else?* Christian Gilbert de Spaignart, the senior pastor for the Lutheran Church of St. Ulrich on the western edge of the city, was a fiery orator second to none in the entire region. His bombastic style and use of apocalyptic imagery to warn of impending divine judgment on those who would compromise the "true faith" of Lutheranism had already attracted quite a following among Magdeburg's citizens.

"Even now," Weber continued, "I hear Spaignart's preparing a special sermon for his own congregation on Sunday. It's going to condemn St. John's and some other city churches for our stance against Wilhelm's foreign alliances. Sad to say, he'll probably convince many in this city who hear him that Wilhelm's way is 'the Lord's way' and that any who oppose it are allied with the devil.

"My point in telling you all this, Peter, is to prepare you for any eventuality on Sunday. With fanatics like Spaignart promoting his crazy schemes, Wilhelm's been known to stand up and walk out on any pastor's sermon that casts even the slightest negative light on his political stances. I should know. He walked out on one of my own several years before you arrived, and I almost lost my position. My advice is this: if Wilhelm acts out his displeasure on Sunday concerning anything you say, simply bow, beg his patience, and politely request a meeting with him after the service. I'd be happy to arrange the details myself and attend with you."

"Thank you for the suggestion, sir," Peter said, trying to sound as nonchalant as possible despite his growing queasiness. "I'm sure everything will work out."

Weber grinned. "Well then, enough forebodings from this rusty old spigot of doom. I seem to recall you have some work to do this afternoon! Just be careful you don't wear yourself out ministering to our countryside brethren. We can't have you less than your best for

Sunday's special audience of smug, self-righteous critics of anything connected with St. John's!"

"Critics like . . . Administrator Wilhelm?" Peter asked with a knowing grin.

Dr. Weber shook his head and smiled resignedly. "God help me. I *must* strive harder to stop slandering those who make my life difficult and instead practice what I'm always preaching: love your neighbor! Love even your enemy."

Peter knew of no one who tried to practice what they preached more than Dr. Heinrich Weber. But the personal grudges that Christian Wilhelm continued to nourish against any city pastor who'd ever dared to challenge his policies were reaching the boiling point. And depending on his reaction to Peter's sermon on Sunday, the whole situation could become quite ugly for everyone.

The afternoon view of distant blue mountains and the fragrance produced by early-blooming wildflowers rejuvenated Peter's spirit. His horse, one of the church's stable mares, seemed to be enjoying the country scents as well. It was good for both to get out beyond the city walls once a week, away from the stale air and constant haranguing of street vendors.

As he approached a junction about a hundred yards ahead, Peter noticed two people walking huddled together along the crossing lane. They appeared to be staggering. He drew nearer, and the couple came into clear view. A peasant girl, seemingly in her late teens, was doing her best to support an older man who was struggling to keep from falling.

"Good day, Fräulein," Peter said, stopping his horse just before the intersection and allowing them to cross as he lifted his hat. "May I be of some assistance?"

The girl stared at him for a long moment. "Thank you, sir, but we're very capable of handling things ourselves," she answered finally.

The basket under her arm started to slip. The man's legs suddenly buckled, and the girl lost her grip on his arm as he sank to his knees. Peter dismounted and ran to help. Stooping down beside the girl, he reached out to help her keep the inebriated man from falling over sideways. As he did so, his hand pressed hers against the man's shoulder. She looked at him, her attractive, diamond-shaped face only inches away. Fighting off his pastoral inclination to avert his eyes, Peter looked back and smiled at her. The girl's concerned frown softened before she shyly lowered her eyes and returned her gaze to the man. Still, she did not remove her hand from under Peter's. With a concerted effort, they finally managed to restore him to his feet.

"It looks like you'll need some help getting him home," Peter said, finally taking his hand off of the girl's.

"No, sir. Please. We'll be fine. Don't let us delay you."

"Of course, Fräulein. But please, I can see that your basket is going to get in your way. I'd be more than glad to—"

"As I told you, sir," the girl insisted, her voice taking on an irritable edge, "we can manage on our own. You don't need to be concerned. This is my father. He's not feeling well now, but we only have a short way to go. Thank you anyway."

The pair continued awkwardly across the road and down the crossing lane. Smoke rose in the distance, presumably from the chimney of the girl's cottage. "It was good to meet you!" he called after them. "May I ask your name, at least?"

The girl looked over her shoulder and shouted back, "Anna Ritter! And this is my father, Adam!"

"Well, praise God for both of you, Anna and Adam Ritter. My name is Peter Erhart, and I'm the assistant pastor at—"

"*I know who you are!*" the girl interrupted him again, before turning with abrupt finality to proceed on her way.

Peter scratched his head. *That was certainly strange*, he thought. She sounded almost angry at him. And she knew who he was? How could that be? And yet . . . there was something familiar about her. The voice, the pretty face, the long dark hair falling behind her bonnet—even the name: Anna Ritter. Yes, something very familiar. What was it?

After a few moments, Peter gave up trying to make the connection and gently kicked the flanks of his horse to move on. The Jünger family badly needed his service.

CHAPTER 5

Countryside west of Magdeburg
February 28, 1629

"Vati, stop fighting me. I don't have enough strength left to get us both home!" Anna Ritter was doing her best to keep her drunken father Adam from falling over, but he wasn't making her job any easier.

"Girl, just let me be," he growled. "I'll walk home when I'm good and ready."

"Oh, Vati, you know you'll just pass out and lie here on the lane all night. Mutti won't stand for it."

"Who does she think she is?" her father protested. "Does your mother wear the breeches in our house now? I'll decide for myself where I spend the night." He pulled himself free, twisted to the side, and leaned over, retching violently.

Disgusted, Anna pulled a cloth out of the basket and tried to help him wipe the mess off his mouth and chin. "Vati, enough nonsense. Now take hold of my arm, and let's get home."

"Oh, all right."

"Vati, what *is* that red blotch on your cheek?"

Her father hesitated. "It's nothing, daughter. Don't trouble yourself about it."

"But it looks like a bruise. Did you get into a fight with those two men at the tavern?"

"I said don't trouble yourself now, girl," her father snarled. "It's none of your business! Now just lead us home like I already said. Or was it *you* who said it?"

Anna knew there was more to this story but decided not to press. She struggled to guide her father down the lane for another quarter of an hour. Exhausted, she breathed a sigh of relief when they finally reached the path to the modestly sized cottage that had served as home to her family for the past nine years.

"Anni, Vati, you're home!" Anna's eight-year-old sister Liesa cried from the yard, where her mother Frieda was hanging clothes to dry. Liesa rushed up the path. Arms stretched open for a hug, she halted at Anna's feet. "Vati, what's wrong?"

"Nothing, child. Go back to your mother. We'll be there in a minute."

Anna and her father approached the rickety fence in front of the family's vegetable plot. Her mother, facing the clothesline, kept her back turned to them.

"Now remember, daughter. Not a word to your mother until I speak about this whole thing first."

"All right, Vati."

As Anna and her father passed by, her mother gave them both a stern sidelong glare—confirmation that this would not be a pleasant homecoming. They'd all been through this experience together too many times before.

Anna set down her basket and helped her father through the doorway and across to the staircase. It was all she could do to get him up the stairs and into the loft room, where he collapsed facedown across his bed. After helping him to reorient so that his head was on the straw pillow, she leaned over and whispered the all-too-familiar refrain in his ear. "Now, sleep it off, and don't come to supper until you've washed up."

She started to kiss him on the cheek but once again noticed the bruise, now blackish-blue. Someone had clearly struck him. She kissed him as gently as she could, though it hardly mattered. He was already sound asleep.

Before leaving the room, Anna picked up the washbasin with the intent to fill it with fresh water. Her father would need that to make himself presentable for supper. As she passed her mother and Liesa on the way to the well, Liesa ran over and asked to help. Frieda once again stared at Anna coldly as she continued to hang the wet clothes in a jerky, annoyed manner.

"He's sleeping now, Mutti, but he'll be ready for supper. I'm sorry we were so late. I had trouble finding him."

Frieda laughed bitterly. "That doesn't surprise me. It's a miracle you found him at all. Every time seems to get worse. Did he find out anything about the rent situation? Or did he ever get around to that?"

"He didn't say. He wanted to talk about it with you first."

"That means no. I should have known!" Frieda picked up her empty clothes basket and stalked toward the door in disgust. Just before entering, she turned around, her face now lined with worry. "Is he all right?"

Anna thought better of mentioning the bruise on her father's cheek. "Yes, Mutti, he'll be fine by suppertime. Don't fret about him."

Frieda slammed her basket down. "How can you tell me not to fret, child? He's all we have. What'll we do if he fails to settle our debts, or just decides to leave us? And why are *you* so calm about everything? You think you can catch a husband anytime you want, some noble knight who'll sweep you away to a magic castle. Well, let me tell you, O daughter so appealing, it isn't all that simple."

Liesa started to cry and hid her face against Anna's apron.

Anna gritted her teeth, fighting the usual urge to scream something disrespectful back at her mother. It wasn't easy. Mutti was becoming more prone lately to strange expressions of annoyance over one thing or another concerning her elder daughter's looks or interests.

After a moment, Frieda grabbed her basket and stomped through the front entrance.

Anna, still steaming over her mother's tongue-lashing, walked to the well with Liesa and drew up two bucketfuls of water—enough to fill the washbasin half full. Together the girls managed to carry the basin by its handles into the cottage, then up the stairs to the bedroom. After checking to see that their father was still snoring soundly, Anna shooed Liesa outside and returned to the main room, bracing herself for more complaints.

Thankfully, Frieda had calmed down. She was tending to a pot of stew in the large black-iron kettle over the fire, humming one of her favorite tunes.

Anna took a deep breath. As usual, *she* would be the one expected to break the tension. "Mutti, that smells delicious, like always."

Frieda managed a tight smile. "Here, take this spoon and ladle yourself a little."

"Ooh, that is *so* good."

Her mother sighed. "I'm glad you still like *some* things I make. Now, child, go look after Liesa for a while so I can get some rest. We'll be ready for supper in about three hours. Let's hope your father will be able to join us by then."

"I'm really tired myself. I'll see if I can get Liesa to take a nap with me. And really, Mutti, I don't think things are quite as bad with Vati as you think."

"I certainly hope not. All right, child. Go take your nap."

Anna went outside to find Liesa absorbed in her favorite game with the three family geese, prodding them with her little stick to march in orderly fashion around the yard.

"Liesi, will you *never* stop pestering those poor birds? Why don't you let them rest awhile? Put them back in the cage, and come take a nap with your sister."

After securing the geese, Liesa ran and jumped up into Anna's arms. She was small and light for her age, and Anna had no trouble supporting her.

"Will you still play marbles with me after supper tonight?" Liesa asked.

"Of course, princess. But first let's get some rest so we'll be fresh for later on, shall we?"

Anna breathed a huge sigh of relief after carrying Liesa up the staircase and lowering her onto the straw pallet in the smaller loft room they shared. Before lying down on her own, she opened the window shutters wider.

A breeze had picked up outside, and it was cooling down quickly. Resting her elbows on the sill, Anna breathed deeply and took in the view toward the east. About five miles away through the unusually clear air, she could just make out Magdeburg's western wall. Rising behind it were the twin steeples of Magdeburg Cathedral, the city's largest and most famous Lutheran church. Four miles to the southeast was the small farming village of Grünfeld, where she had gone earlier that day to find her father. The surrounding landscape was mostly flat, much of it set aside for farming and pasture. Two hundred yards down the lane to the north was the large, fenced-off plot of wheat, rye, barley, and other crops that her father tended for Freiherr von Schwarz, a local landholder.

Anna loved the beauty of the rural scenery but at times wished she could see more signs of the city from her window. The Ritters' cottage had been built on the edge of a thickly wooded area that extended several hundred yards in all directions behind them. The nearest cottage belonged to the Schiffers, a half mile to the north. If outside help were ever needed in times of distress, it would be a *very* long time coming.

Drowsiness finally overtook her. Before lying down, she checked on Liesa.

The little girl at first appeared sound asleep, but then she suddenly opened one eye and smiled mischievously.

Anna laughed. "You little pretender! What're you still doing awake?"

"Watching you," Liesa replied with a coy grin.

"Well, stop spying and go to sleep."

Liesa giggled, then turned over and covered her head with the pillow.

Anna took off her bonnet, apron, and outer dress. She made to lie down on her own pallet, now totally exhausted. Finally, a little sleep. Or so she thought.

"Anni," Liesa asked, "why does Mutti always get so angry with us?"

Great question, thought Anna. She sat down on the edge of her sister's pallet and brushed a lock of hair out of the little girl's eye.

"Liesi, she gets tired. Think of all Mutti does for us. Cooking all our meals, baking, taking care of you, hauling water from the well, feeding the animals, milking the cow, sowing and weeding the vegetable garden, washing and mending our clothes, keeping the house—it's a lot!"

"But you help her sometimes," Liesa countered.

"Only when I'm not running errands to the village or helping Vati in the fields." Anna knew she was a great help to her father, working alongside him during the planting and harvesting seasons, and performing all but the heaviest tasks. Having borne no sons, Frieda didn't object to offering her elder daughter's services to her husband in that regard. But it took away from the help that Frieda herself would have greatly benefited from.

"Try to understand. It's not easy for Mutti to do all she does and be in a good mood all the time. We just have to try to be patient and kind to her."

"All right, I'll try," Liesa conceded. "Anni?"

"Yes, Lies?"

"Will I ever be as pretty as you?"

Anna couldn't avoid this label anymore. Not that she really wanted to. Now eighteen, she felt she *was* deserving of a little special notice, especially after enduring all those giggles and mocking nicknames whispered by supposed friends in her awkward younger years. By age fifteen, her physical features had become the barely disguised envy of many a former taunter. And it wasn't just her waist-length, dark reddish-brown hair, or her angular face with high cheekbones and captivating jade-green eyes. The tallest of her friends, wide-shouldered, and lithe of figure with a proportionate bosom and trim waist, Anna knew that men looked at her in a certain way. Not that she would ever dream of bragging about it, though. The virtue of self-effacing modesty had been drilled into her by her mother long ago. "Never flaunt your beauty, daughter—it'll only bring you trouble, mark my words," Mutti had warned more than once.

"Who said you're not as pretty as me already?" Anna asked, laughing.

"Nobody. But yesterday I heard Vati tell Mutti that a lot of men in the village thought you were beautiful, and Mutti got mad at him again."

Anna rolled her eyes. Vati could be so clueless sometimes. She knew her mother would misinterpret Vati's innocent compliment as proof that Anna was deliberately provoking the men's attention. Or worse, as some kind of hidden message that Vati intended only for her, like: *Frieda, you just aren't as attractive to me as you used to be.*

"Vati was just trying to make Mutti feel proud of her children. Sometimes she takes things the wrong way. But don't you worry, princess. I think you're just as pretty already, and you're even smarter than me. I could never get those geese to follow me the way you can!"

"At least they like me," Liesa allowed.

"And I like you too. Now go to sleep, goose-face!"

Anna returned to her pallet and stretched out on the thin blanket covering the straw. Reaching under the pallet, she pulled out the large, old, worn book that Vati had brought home along with other souvenirs from his soldiering days with Count von Mansfeld's Protestant army earlier in the war. It was a fifteenth-century German translation of *Aesop's Fables*, complete with woodcut illustrations. One of Vati's soldier friends, an educated man, had patiently spent long evenings with him by the campfire in winter quarters, teaching him how to read the fables and parts of the German Bible. He'd given the book to Vati as a gift to share with his family.

Anna could still remember the evenings several years ago sitting by her father's side in front of the hearth. As he read the fables, Vati would point to the illustrations to help connect the word meanings, and then ask her to try recognizing and pronouncing the words herself. He'd been amazed and near bursting with pride at how quickly she had caught on. Within only a month or two, she'd been able to read many of the stories without his help, even managing to read a few that he had never before attempted.

"This girl's going to make a name for herself someday, just you watch!" Vati had exclaimed to her mother after one especially successful reading session. "I always knew she was smarter than the other girls around here. Speaks more clearly and makes more sense than others her age—and even a lot of adults. She's going to go places."

"'Pride comes before a fall,' Herr Ritter," Mutti had reproved him. "Just remember our family's station."

"*Hmmph*," Vati had retorted. "I predict that one day this girl's going to impress *kings* with her wits and speech."

"Come down from the clouds, Herr Ritter!" Mutti had said, the irritation in her voice unmistakable. "It's quite enough that your daughter is able to impress *you* with all her talents!"

Anna had been thrilled by her father's encouragement. Ever since, she'd made every effort to practice reading regularly from Aesop as well as the family Bible that he kept on the main room's shelf. She often didn't understand the words, especially some of those in the Bible, but she kept at it.

Anna opened the book and turned to her favorite fable, "The Tortoise and the Hare." She laughed to herself as she reread the story and recognized how well the tortoise depicted her own experience of life so far.

Slow but steady, just like the tortoise, she thought contentedly. *Sooner or later, it seems to win the race.*

CHAPTER 6

Countryside west of Magdeburg
February 28, 1629

S leep didn't come as fast as Anna expected. She tossed and turned, still feeling wound up from helping Vati home from the tavern and the memory of Peter's hand covering hers.

Why didn't he remember me?

And looking back on it now, why was she so *annoyed* that he hadn't? After all, they'd only met briefly once following a sermon he'd delivered at the Grünfeld village church three years ago. Having accepted an internship at St. John's in the city, Pastor Erhart had been invited to be the guest preacher for the village church's midweek evening service. He'd made quite an impression on Anna and two of her friends, seated in the back row of the congregation . . .

꧁꧂

"Hilde, what are you doing?" Anna was on the verge of tears from laughing at the antics of her friend Hilde Kerner, who was seated to her left on the wooden bench in the back row of the church.

"Herr Geier's head is too big," Hilde whispered back in mock despair as she weaved from side to side, attempting to see around the obstacle presented by the huge gentleman seated in front of her.

Anna leaned over, pretending to be the voice of authority. "Really, child, stop your nonsense. You are disturbing those around you!"

The girls broke into barely suppressed giggles, drawing the inquisitive smile of Anna's longtime best friend Barbara Saller and the reprimanding stare of Hilde's mother. Barbara, along with Hilde's parents, was seated on Anna's right. Frau Kerner now probably wished she'd chosen to sit *between* Hilde and Anna, rather than let them be together and indulge in mischief.

It was unusual for all three girls to be in attendance and seated together. Normally, Anna would sit separately with her own family. Barbara, who was Catholic, would be attending Mass with her mother at the small parish church farther out in the countryside.

Illness had disrupted things. Anna's mother had come down with a cough, providing the perfect excuse for her father to miss church— "obviously" he needed to stay home and care for his wife and Liesa. Barbara's mother, widowed two years prior when her husband had unexpectedly died of heart failure, was visiting a sick acquaintance who lived alone in another village. Frau Kerner, knowing both families, had offered to chaperone Anna and Barbara along with her own daughter Hilde at the midweek service and to have them both stay overnight at the Kerners' house in the village. The girls' mothers had both accepted the kind suggestion. Frau Saller had been especially grateful. She was not rigid in her Catholic practice, at least not according to Barbara, and had actually encouraged Barbara to go see what a Lutheran service was like.

Having finally composed themselves, Anna and Hilde sat up properly in their places. It was time to focus their attention for the climactic part of the service: the one-hour sermon from Pastor Tiedeman.

According to Anna's father, if there was ever a Lutheran preacher who loved to contrast the radiant light of the Christian gospel with the dark terrors of hell, Pastor Ernst Tiedeman was the man. In years past, Tiedeman's sermons had balanced warning with hope, judgment with grace. But he was now nearing seventy, and his body had begun to wear down along with his patience. Lately, his preaching seemed to dwell almost incessantly on the horrible eternal punishments awaiting unrepentant sinners.

After the scripture reading by one of the deacons, Tiedeman lumbered stiffly to the lectern. He peered out at the congregation with his usual scowl.

Leaning over, Hilde cupped her hand around Anna's ear. "Brace yourself, girl. Another message of doom from 'Old Wagon Wheel.'" Anna closed her eyes and put her hand over her mouth, her chest and shoulders shaking from barely repressed laughter.

"Good evening, brothers and sisters in Christ," Pastor Tiedeman said after an unusually long pause. "May the peace of our Lord be with you."

"And with you also, Pastor," the congregation replied in unison.

"Tonight I have the honor of introducing an aspiring fellow-minister of the Lord's grace. We're greatly blessed to enjoy the presence of Herr Peter Erhart."

Anna and Hilde exchanged puzzled glances.

"Herr Erhart is now performing his internship as junior pastor for St. John's, our sister church in the city," Tiedeman continued. "Their senior pastor, my good friend Dr. Weber, highly recommended him as an occasional guest preacher for our village church. I was happy to accept the offer, especially as it would provide a deserving young minister of God the chance to develop his oratory. Herr Erhart has prepared a special sermon for us this evening. I hope you'll find it as commendable as those I myself have delivered from this very same pulpit over the past thirty-five years."

Anna and Hilde looked at each other with arched eyebrows and tightened lips, trying their best to contain their mirth. Pastor Tiedeman just didn't seem to have a clue concerning his own vanity.

"In any case," he concluded, "please join me in welcoming Herr Erhart to our church."

Until Herr Erhart approached the lectern, Anna had been unable to see him sitting behind a column at the front. After shaking hands with Tiedeman, he turned to rest his hands on both sides of the lectern. He smiled warmly at the congregation. "Good evening, my Christian brothers and sisters of Grünfeld church, and may the glory of God shine upon you. Thanks be to him, to you, and especially to your kind pastor for allowing me the opportunity to speak to you this evening."

Anna's heart leaped. She gazed with rapt attention at the twentysomething man facing the congregation. He was of medium height and build, good-looking but not overly so. He conveyed an air of confident energy balanced with humility, as if recognizing the sacred duty he'd been entrusted with. And there was something special and soothing about his kind face and the sound of his medium-deep voice that expressed great care for the congregants receiving his message tonight. Anna glanced at Hilde and then Barbara. Obviously enthralled like Anna with the new scenery in front of them, neither girl's head turned in response. *This should be good*, Anna thought.

Over the next hour, Herr Erhart delivered one of the most heartwarming sermons that Anna had ever heard. Instead of contributing yet another lecture to Pastor Tiedeman's dreary, three-month-long series on the Book of Ezekiel, he spoke from the gospel of John about the story of Jesus's encounter with the Samaritan woman at the well. For the first time, Anna felt a surge of true excitement as she considered the sermon's implications. The divine Son of God had been willing to extend his tender love and power even to the outcast of society, offering peace in place of worry, "living water" that would never run out. It was such a wonderful vision. If only she could learn to have a deeper trust in her loving Lord, to reach out for him, to reach out to others as he had done. No one had led her to experience such feeling for the Lord as Herr Erhart had done that night.

As inspiring as the sermon was, though, Anna recognized that her emotions had not been focused completely on the beauty of Christ alone. Up until now, she'd never really been interested in men. Only fourteen-year-old Johann Braun had been able to briefly break the ice when he'd dared to plant a hasty kiss on her lips one day last year, while they'd been helping her father in the fields. Nothing had ever come of that. But watching and listening to Herr Erhart had aroused something new deep inside, something she wanted to yield to but desperately felt the need to hide—even from herself. It just didn't seem right to have such thoughts about a minister of God.

Following the final hymn, the congregants filed out of the church. Most walked over to the reception line in the yard outside to welcome Herr Erhart and congratulate him on his sermon. The three girls were among them. After deliberately allowing the other two to greet him first, Anna stepped forward.

The close-up view of Herr Erhart took Anna's breath away. Black hair, lightly bearded face with impossibly large dark-brown eyes, the kindest smile she'd ever seen from a man—she could do nothing but stare.

"Good day, Fräulein . . . ?" Herr Erhart took her hand. His touch was warm and gentle, yet firm.

Anna felt as if she were about to melt on the spot. "Oh! Yes . . . uh . . ." she finally managed to sputter. "Fräulein Ritter, sir . . . Anna Ritter."

Much to Anna's disappointment, before she could respond further, Frau Kerner approached and pulled the three girls away from the line. She apologized to Herr Erhart, explaining that they needed to get back to the house without delay. A late supper needed to be prepared, and the girls were expected to help.

Anna craned her neck as discretely as possible to look back at Herr Erhart as she walked away with the others. She was ecstatic—exactly the way she desperately wanted him to be feeling as well. *He saw me for only a few seconds, but I hope . . . No, the way he looked at me and held my hand, I'll even dare to think . . .*

Later that evening, Anna, Barbara, and Hilde gathered together in the living area, two large candles illuminating their faces as they sat on stools around the family worktable. Each was engaged in a mutual project to hand-sew a quilt for one of the town's elderly widows. Their discussion jumped from one thing to another, but it all served to make the work less tedious.

Hilde glanced at Barbara and winked. "Well, at least *I* for one was glad for the change of pace at the service tonight. What did you think of the new preacher, Anna?"

Barbara started to giggle but bit her lip and looked back down at the quilt piece she was sewing. "I thought his sermon was wonderful," Anna replied. "It . . . it really made sense and meant a lot to me."

Hilde cocked her head. "Oh, and pray tell us, Queen Anna the Pure, did you not find the new pastor to be slightly *different* in manner and looks than what we've gotten used to? Maybe in a way that was, well, rather exotic and pleasing?"

"Well, certainly. I . . . I . . . he . . . well, yes, I . . ." Anna flushed beet-red.

Hilda's eyes widened with glee, and her hand flew to her mouth. "Ooh, I knew it! She likes him. No, she's *crazy* about him! Barbara, our friend is head over heels in love."

Anna couldn't maintain her pretense of composure any longer. "As if the two of you weren't gawking at him too!"

All three girls burst out laughing.

"Anyway, it's not like I'd ever have a chance with someone like him," Anna finally said. "There are plenty of other girls around who are prettier and smarter than me."

"Oh, Anni," Barbara countered, "you know full well if any girl in this town ever had a chance to land someone like that, it would be you."

Anna could think of little else over the next several weeks. Her imagination ran wild. She pictured herself newly married to Peter, proudly watching him deliver his sermon from her reserved seat in the front row of the St John's women's section. At home, sitting together at the table after the evening meal, enjoying the sound of his gentle voice as he shared funny stories about his workday. Later, lying with him in front of the hearth, completely releasing herself to his passionate kisses and caresses. Life together with Peter would be a pure joy—*nothing* like the dull, resigned union that her parents had turned their own marriage into.

There was only one small obstacle. Anna and Herr Erhart had

barely spoken one sentence to each other. But that was nothing to be concerned about. Wouldn't he be visiting Grünfeld church once every month to deliver the guest sermon? Surely she would have many more opportunities to talk to him and expose him to her irresistible charms!

A week before Herr Erhart's next visit, Anna ran across an acquaintance visiting from the city. The friend told her it had been announced at St. John's the previous Sunday that Herr Erhart was now engaged to be married next month. The lucky woman was Fräulein Ursula Andersen, a beautiful nineteen-year-old from another city. Herr Erhart had apparently known her for some time and had courted her during his studies at the university. The wedding date had been set, and invitations were being sent out.

Anna was crushed. How *could* he? Her first love, and he hadn't even given her a chance! A beautiful city woman. Obviously, stupid fifteen-year-old country peasant girls like Anna Ritter didn't stand a chance with the likes of the highly educated, well-spoken Herr Erhart. Well, she would show *him*. There was no reason for *her* to attend any of his guest sermons at Grünfeld church anymore. He could just enjoy the rest of their wonderful congregation. Let *them* admire him. There were plenty of other young men waiting for an opportunity to court her. She merely had to cast a slight glance, to say a tiny word. And surely, they would all be falling at her feet.

⁓⁓

Anna's last thought before drifting off was how reasonable her plan had seemed three years ago. By avoiding church on the evenings of Herr Erhart's guest sermons, she had thought she would neatly and quickly get over her infatuation and the sting of "losing" him. But, to her surprise, the memory of that first encounter and occasional daydreams of romantic involvement with him had never died. In fact, no other man had even come close to occupying her thoughts like Peter Erhart had since then.

No wonder she'd felt unsettled when encountering him again at the crossroads today. The moment he'd innocently covered her hand with his, she had realized the disturbing truth—her powerful attraction to him was even stronger than before.

CHAPTER 7

Countryside west of Magdeburg
February 28, 1629

Frieda's shrill voice jolted Anna awake. "Daughter, will you get down here and help? How many times do I have to call?"

Suppertime. Another chance for Anna's father to explain his behavior earlier that day.

"Coming, Mutti," Anna replied.

She woke Liesa, then put her ear against the separating wall. She heard the sound of water splashing in a basin. Good. At least Vati was up and awake.

Downstairs, her mother was at the hearth, ladling into bowls Anna's favorite stew of beer, potato dumplings, and small pieces of mutton. Selected as first-prize winner in the food contest at last year's village fair, it was a recipe of which Mutti was quite proud. "Here, girls. Take these."

Anticipating that their father would be joining them, Anna and Liesa placed four bowls filled with stew on the table, where spoons had already been laid out. Frieda brought over a large slab of warm black bread and set it on the table. The three women sat down and waited for Adam.

Within moments, the familiar sound of heavy footsteps on the staircase announced his arrival. Passing behind Frieda on the way to his stool, he placed his hand lightly on her shoulder. She reached up and patted it but said nothing.

Adam sat down and offered a short grace on behalf of the family. "Frieda, you've outdone yourself once again. This looks and smells wonderful!"

Same old Vati, Anna thought. *Acting as if things are perfectly normal, as if nothing at all needs to be addressed. How does he recover so quickly from his drinking bouts? A couple hours of sleep, a little cleaning up, and he's as good as new. No hangover, no lingering bad temper. How does he do it?*

"Thank you, Adam," Frieda responded icily.

Anna shifted uncomfortably. This time it wouldn't be so easy for her father to carry on as usual.

Liesa broke the tension. "Vati, can we all go to the village fair next week? Anni said there'll be special games for children. And can we take one of our geese and enter it in the race?"

Adam chuckled. "Well, I think that's a great idea, child. Hopefully one of those crazy birds is capable of doing more than just laying eggs. Besides, I'd love to see what new inventions the city merchants are hawking at the fair this year. As long as your mother agrees. What say you, Frieda?"

"I'll need to think about it and talk with your father some more. We've many spring-cleaning chores that need to get done around here. And besides, it's not as if we have extra money to be spending on luxuries."

The comment had its intended effect. Adam's face flushed and he bowed his head. Not able to afford the small fee for admission to the village fair? Clearly, her mother was targeting him.

The rest of the meal proceeded in awkward silence until Frieda broke it.

"Adam, what did you find out today about the rent? Do we have a chance? And what in heaven's name is that bruise on your cheek?"

Anna's father put his spoon down firmly on the table and glared at his wife. "Frieda, you know I will not discuss such things around the children."

"When, then, Adam? You never want to discuss it anytime, anywhere, with anyone, including me!"

He slammed his fist on the table. "I *said* I will not discuss this in front of the children."

"Very well, as you wish," she said curtly. "Anna, take Liesa upstairs and play with her while your father and I talk."

"Yes, Mutti."

Anna and Liesa cleared the table, put the dishes into the washing tub, and then went upstairs. Anna knew they wouldn't be out of earshot from her parents. The waist-high wall at the open end of the girls' loft room allowed voices to drift up from the living area almost without obstruction. But Anna made no attempt to remind them. While trying her best to keep Liesa occupied with a game of marbles, she strained to hear the conversation below.

"If you'd just let me explain, Frieda. I told them that come this Monday, I'll be taking on more work in the afternoons helping Herr Lang clear the woods on his property. And with that I'll definitely have all the back rent we owe saved up by the end of next month."

Anna gasped. Had her mother already known this and not told her? It was hard to imagine her father taking on more work—and a major task at that—in his present condition. It wasn't just the drinking. Vati's left arm, injured in the war, had become weaker over the years. It was hard enough for him to perform his regular work cultivating Freiherr von Schwarz's field. But on top of this was the added requirement of twenty days per year of unpaid bound labor, hauling supplies and other tasks levied by the powerful regional landowner Baron von Leitzge on all his countryside tenants. Vati had said that this system of required labor was supposed to help keep the rents down. But, in fact, it stole from the time and energy he needed to work the field for his own family's needs.

And now Vati, in his weakened physical and mental condition, would be tied to yet *more* work, leaving him only late evenings and Sundays to recover from his extra labors.

Anna felt a surge of tenderness for her father. When faced with similar circumstances, a number of other men in the village and countryside had simply given up. They had left their families to follow one of the roving gangs of army deserters, had become beggars in the city, or in a few cases, had even committed suicide. Her father was proposing to make a huge effort for his family, and he deserved credit for that. Now, if only he could control the drinking.

"Who was it that you talked to, anyway?" her mother asked.

"One of them was that new collection agent hired recently by von Leitzge. His name is Dietrich Ackar."

"Gracious Lord!" Frieda exclaimed. "Isn't he the man who threatened to kill Herr Garver for accidentally making him spill his ale in the tavern a few weeks ago?"

"Yes, one and the same. No one seems to know where he's from or even where he lives. He just shows up unannounced at different places and tries to scare people. He talks funny—has a foreign accent and uses fancy words like he thinks he's smarter and better than everybody else. The other man I'd never heard anything about before today. A huge brute. Looks like he could be one of those Catholic army deserters roaming the area. Ackar probably hires him to come along and help frighten the wits out of humble folk like us."

"So Herr Ackar is the man we're supposed to pay our rents to now?"

"I'm afraid so," Anna's father growled. "And count on the fact that the amount he's demanding is at least ten percent more than what Baron von Leitzge's asking for. Nothing like a little profit at the expense of people who're struggling."

"Can't you demand to see a bill signed by the baron showing the right amount?"

"Frieda, I have no power to make any demands of these people, especially with the amount of back rent we owe. I can only ask them to be reasonable."

"So did they agree to delay our payment one more time?"

"Well, they did, but not before . . ." Adam's voice trailed off suddenly.

"Oh!" Frieda cried. "Poor husband, did that cruel man strike you?" Her tender heart for Anna's father had obviously returned, if only briefly. "Let me put some salve on that."

"It's nothing to worry about, dear. I'll manage, and it'll be all right."

"But how did it happen? Why did they do this to you?"

Adam drew a slow, deep breath. "When I got to the tavern, Ackar and his friend had already been drinking for a while. They were friendly enough at first. Offered to buy me a drink, but I refused. When I asked about delaying the rent, Ackar suggested we step outside. 'Let's get some fresh air,' he said. So we walked around back, and I sat down on a log near the supply shed. Ackar pulled out an old stool, plopped it down right in front of me, and sat, all while his brute dog of a friend slowly circled behind me."

Anna's heart raced.

"I knew something bad was coming," her father continued, "but had no idea what. Ackar asked me to repeat my request, which I did. He seemed sympathetic when I told him about our problem and my plan to work it out. But as soon as I finished, the dirty weasel just smiled and pulled a weighted leather strap from his vest pocket. Whacked me hard on the cheek. After I recovered, I lunged at him, but his friend grabbed my waist from behind."

"Oh, dear God!" Frieda gasped.

Trembling, Anna drew Liesa in close.

"Thank God they didn't abuse me any further," their father said. "But Ackar told me he wasn't playing games. Especially with 'pretentious peasants' with the gall to be living in a nice two-floor cottage like ours. He said I was to get him the back rent, in full, by the end of next month— or much worse would be done to me. Then he became apologetic. Said he knew I was an upright man and hoped he wouldn't have to discipline me again. His friend fetched a barrel of ale from the shed, and Ackar suggested we share a few mugs." Her father sighed. "I'm ashamed to say I accepted the offer. I didn't want to rile him any further."

"Oh, Adam," Anna's mother said between sobs. "Adam!"

"Frieda, I swear by the living God that gutter-dog will live to regret what he's done to cow me and our family."

Frieda was silent for a moment. "Husband, please don't take this upon yourself to seek revenge. You know that's in the Lord's hands."

Anna flinched upon hearing the loud thump and her mother's cry. She recognized the source of the noise—Vati had heaved his mug of beer against the wall. He'd done this before when aggravated enough by something, but it never failed to shock her.

"What? Would you have me 'turn the other cheek'? This side hurts bad enough! Frieda, I'm sorry. I just can't love this particular enemy like Christ commands. At least not when he's so ready to abuse all of us, not just myself."

Liesa cried softly as the girls sat together hugging each other, wondering what would come next.

"Adam," Frieda pleaded, "I'm only suggesting . . . don't let your anger get the better of your wisdom. Herr Ackar *did* say we could have until the end of next month to pay, didn't he? Why not just do as he says? Don't resist, and put this all behind us."

"I suppose you're right." Adam's voice sounded calmer but weary. "Hopefully, if we pay up, this crook will get off our backs. But we probably should start thinking about what to do for the longer run. Who knows when something like this might crop up again?"

"As you think best, husband," Frieda said. "And thank you for being so honest with me. Now, let me take care of that bruise. Come over here by the fire."

After a few more minutes, Liesa was sound asleep in Anna's arms. Anna laid her on her pallet and then walked over to the half-wall, leaned over, and peeked down at the hearth below.

For the first time that she could remember since childhood, her parents were touching each other with tender affection. Her father lay with his head on her mother's lap and was reaching up to lightly stroke her neck and back. She dabbed at his bruise with a damp cloth. After gently applying some salve, she cradled his head in her hands and kissed him on the lips.

Anna drew back and lay down on her pallet, tears dampening her cheeks. She let out a huge sigh.

Everything will be all right, she consoled herself. *Whenever Mutti and Vati have made up before, haven't things always turned out just fine?*

CHAPTER 8

Magdeburg
February 28, 1629

D arkness set in as Peter approached the city gate. Only a one-
mile ride through the now-quiet streets separated him from
a peaceful evening with Ursula and the children. It would
be a welcome relief after the countryside visit with Bernhard Jünger
and his son. The young boy had a fever and was starting to complain
of aching in his armpits and groin—possibly early symptoms of the
dreaded plague. Peter had done the best he could to support Bernhard
and his son with prayer, comforting verses from the Psalms, and the
food offering from Frau Schneider. But he couldn't deny how terribly
inadequate these had all seemed, considering the horrific loss the
Jünger family had already experienced.

"Ho, Peter!"

Peter strained to identify the man holding up his hand and walking
toward him out of the shadows. It was Dr. Weber. *What is he doing here
this late in the day?*

Peter stopped his horse. "Hello, sir. Shouldn't you be home by now?"

The light from one of the lanterns illuminating the gate's massive
archway revealed the distressed look on Weber's face. "I hate to

interrupt your plans for this evening, Peter, but there's trouble afoot."

"Trouble, sir?"

Weber glanced to either side to make sure neither of the two gate sentries were within earshot. He spoke quietly in short, rapid bursts. "Archdeacon Beckmann stopped me on my way out of the church. New rumors are spreading. Emperor Ferdinand is supposedly going to announce something soon. It's big, Peter—some kind of new imperial edict. Beckmann says the emperor's gone berserk. He wants to force all of Magdeburg to convert back to Catholicism! He's committed Wallenstein's army to besiege the city if we refuse. Some of the radical riffraff among our citizens opposed to the emperor have gotten wind, and they're already up in arms. They're threatening harm to 'imperialist sympathizers and compromisers,' and St. John's seems to be included on their list. Beckmann urged us to come up with a plan to protect our church property and people from any radical troublemakers—by tonight, if possible!"

Peter eyes widened. Magdeburg had managed to avoid the war's terrors for eleven years. Were things really now coming to *this*? And yet Josef Beckmann was a reliable source of information. If anyone could be trusted for a clear-eyed view of the situation, it was him.

"But, sir, what can we—"

A man ran toward them, shouting frantically and waving his hands wildly. It was one of the church's groundskeepers.

"Dr. Weber, Pastor Erhart! You need to return to the church. There's a mob gathering in front. They saw our organist Samuel locking the doors for the night. Now they're giving him a hard time, calling St. John's an 'agent of the emperor's schemes' and making other terrible charges. Samuel's trying to hold them off, but he's all alone."

Peter stared at Dr. Weber in dismay, grabbed his proffered arm, and, with the other man's help, managed to swing his mentor up on the horse behind him. With the old stable mare now carrying a double load, he knew it would be at least ten minutes before they could arrive at the church. *God, please protect Samuel.*

"Wouldn't come any closer if I were you, Preacher."

From the sound of his voice, the drunk and disheveled young man had no intention of turning tail and running off as his two companions had just done. Even so, Peter breathed a sigh of relief. The groundskeeper's "mob" report had been exaggerated. Only three men had gathered to spread their mischief, as opposed to the twenty or more that Peter had feared. But the remaining man's threat sounded serious. He had a drawn dagger pointed at Samuel, who stood with his back pinned against one of the church's front-gate columns.

Peter and Dr. Weber dismounted at a respectful distance.

"Samuel!" Peter called. "Are you hurt?"

"No, Pastor," Samuel replied in a strained voice. "I'm all right. They haven't hurt me."

Peter and Weber slowly approached the pair.

"I *said*," the man shouted, "don't come any closer!" He pointed the dagger toward Peter and Weber, who stopped about ten feet away.

Weber held up his right hand in a gesture of peaceful intent. "Friend, please, we mean no harm to you. May I ask why you've come here tonight?"

Unsteady on his feet, the man groped for a response. "W-why, to teach you compromisers a lesson, Preacher—just like that other preacher Spaignart suggested in his speech at the tavern a little while ago. It made a lot of sense to me and my pals from the fish market."

Spaignart's speech at the tavern? Was that fearmonger now spreading his message of divine intimidation and terror beyond the confines of his own congregational district? Peter gulped and looked at his mentor.

Dr. Weber's face was livid. "Friend," he asked, "what's your name?"

"Markus, Preacher. What of it?"

"Tell me, Markus," Weber said, "what reason did Pastor Spaignart give for 'teaching compromisers a lesson'?"

"He said the Catholics are coming, that the emperor's about to pass a new law that'll let his army enter our city and take our money and women. They'll force everyone to convert. Spaignart said the only way to face things is to stand firm, just like Administrator Wilhelm. Show the Catholics we mean to fight to the death. He told us God wills it. And if we're true Lutherans, we'll *do* it if we want to see heaven someday. He also said we should get some practice in defending ourselves before the Catholic army arrives by standing up to 'traitors and weak-willed cowards' in this city."

"And what does this have to do with St. John's, Markus?" Weber asked calmly. Peter was amazed at his mentor's self-restraint. "Did Spaignart identify us with these so-called traitors and cowards?"

"He didn't say so directly. But when somebody suggested the leaders of St. John's and Magdeburg Cathedral as two perfect examples of these, Spaignart just threw back his head and laughed. Like he couldn't agree more. So my friends and me, we decided to come here, ask a few questions to see for ourselves. But your organ boy here hasn't been too willing to give us any answers."

Hot anger rose in Peter's gullet. Spaignart was now targeting his irresponsible rantings at the poorest of city folk, at fishmongers like Markus with no sense of how to draw the line between faithfulness and overreaction.

"Markus," Peter began, "can't you see that—"

Weber put a hand on Peter's arm and then started calmly walking toward Markus.

"Stay back, Preacher!" Markus screamed, raising his dagger. "I already warned you once!"

Weber stopped a mere two feet in front of Markus, easily within striking distance of the knife. Peter held his breath and steeled himself to jump to his mentor's aid in the next split second.

"Markus," Weber said, "you didn't come here tonight to do us harm, did you?"

"What? Well, no, well . . . y-yes, of course I did, Preacher."

"No, you didn't, Markus. Do you know how I know that?"

Markus hesitated, now swaying slightly from side to side as if a sudden dizziness had come over him. "How?"

Weber smiled. "Because, Markus, though you could easily have chosen to run away like your two cowardly friends, *you alone* chose to remain standing here. Even though you saw it would now be three against one. I know there's a reason why you made that choice. And so do you."

Peter looked on anxiously. Where was Dr. Weber taking this?

"Yes, you're exactly right. I *am* standing here alone!" Markus yelled. "With my dagger drawn and ready to plunge it into your face. What are you getting at?"

"Markus," Weber continued, his voice now barely audible, "put it down. Just put it down now, and tell me why you're still standing here all alone without any of your friends. Why aren't you at home with your family tonight?"

A violent trembling overtook Markus. Peter rushed to Dr. Weber's side, preparing to catch Markus's arm before he could hurt the older man, but the effort was unnecessary. Markus dropped the knife and sank to his knees, head buried in his hands and sobbing profusely.

Weber dropped to his knees next to Markus. He put his arm around the young man's shoulders and motioned for Peter and Samuel to draw close. "Son, what is it?" he whispered. "Tell me."

It took a few moments before Markus could bring himself to choke out the words. "They paid us, Preacher."

"Paid you?" asked Weber. "Who paid you, and to do what?" Peter suspected his mentor already knew the answer.

"A couple of men from Spaignart's church. They stayed behind in the tavern after his speech, and then came over and talked to me and my friends. Said they knew we were hurting for money and that they had a little favor to ask of us. They gave us each fifty heller and told us they'd give us another hundred if we'd agree to 'cause a slight stir' at St. John's tonight. Hassle one of the workers. Find some small shed on the church property to burn down. Anything to 'give those compromisers a scare,' as they put it."

Still weeping heavily, Markus reached into his cloak pocket and produced a small moneybag. "Here it is, Preacher. You take it. Give it to your congregation. I don't want it. Guess that's why I stayed behind. I knew you were the preacher, and I wanted to confess. I know I've done wrong. My wife would kill me if she ever found out. But I was just desperate, trying to help out with our little girl being so sick and hungry all the time. Preacher, can you forgive me? Will God forgive me?"

Peter's chest tightened. Was this just another sob story from a lazy vagrant looking for a handout?

"God forgives you," Weber said. "And so do I, Markus. You've confessed, and I believe you're truly repentant. And here. Take the money. Use it well to support your family as God would wish you to do."

"Preacher," Markus said in disbelief, "how can I ever repay you?"

Dr. Weber gripped him firmly by both shoulders and met his gaze. "Honor God. Never again take a bribe from anyone, especially Spaignart's people. And one other thing."

"Yes, Preacher?"

"How about coming to our worship service with your family on Sunday? I'd like you to hear what I know will be a great sermon delivered by a magnificent speaker!"

"We'll be there, Preacher. I promise!"

Peter exchanged glances with Samuel. Neither man could hold back his tears. Dr. Weber certainly had a special way with people.

It was a short walk to Dr. Weber's private quarters adjoining the rectory. After bidding Samuel good night, Peter helped his weary mentor up the three entrance steps and into the small front living area.

Weber collapsed into his favorite chair and lit his pipe, while Peter poured him a mug of watered-down wine. The two men spoke briefly of what had just happened and, since there'd been no damage or injury, agreed it might be wiser for now not to alarm the congregation about the incident. Weber said he had no desire to ignite an internal war between the Lutheran churches of Magdeburg, especially in view of the growing Catholic threat.

At the end of the conversation, Peter walked over to Weber's chair and knelt beside him. "Doctor, there's one other thing I meant to tell you earlier today, and I'm even more convinced of it after tonight."

"What's that, Peter?"

"Sir, no man has taught me more than you what it truly means to demonstrate the love of Christ to others. For that, I can never thank you enough."

Dr. Weber, who was childless and had lost his wife to influenza several years earlier, looked down at his lap. He bit his lip. "Peter, you've been like a son to me. I'm so very proud of you, and I know you're going to be a shining light for our congregation and others in this city. Especially after you pass your big test Sunday."

"It's largely due to your personal care and efforts on my behalf, sir," Peter said, "that I received the training I needed to prepare myself."

Weber looked at him fondly. "Your training and preparation for ministry have been very important. But, Peter, promise me one thing. Promise me you'll never allow the finer points of your religious thinking and practice to obscure Christ's two greatest commandments: 'Love the Lord your God with all your heart, soul, mind, and strength; and love your neighbor as yourself.' Always strive your best to follow these, Peter. Measure your every thought and action in their light."

Peter couldn't help but smile. *Leave it to Dr. Weber to set the bar high and personally demonstrate the way to reach it*, he thought. "I can't imagine a better goal for which to strive, sir."

"And one final thought." Weber gently grasped Peter's forearm with both hands. His eyes had never appeared so intensely focused. "When hard trials come your way—as you know they surely will—always remember this: God loves you. He's always watching over and caring for you. He'll never forsake you, Peter. Even in your darkest hour, when all your hope in him seems lost. *That* is the most important truth about your life in Christ that I could ever wish to impress upon you."

Even in my darkest hour, when all hope seems lost. On his way home, Peter kept thinking about Dr. Weber's reminder. It was nothing new, nothing he hadn't heard many times since childhood and strived to convey to others over the years.

The memory of that awful scene in Prague eleven years ago returned unbidden. Certainly it would have been the darkest hour for Hans, that poor Catholic boy who Peter had tried to help. Had Hans experienced any sense of Christ's comforting presence at the time? How had he fared afterward? Was he still alive and well today?

And what about that peasant girl, Anna Ritter? Was her father's drunken state but a sign of a much greater darkness about to descend upon their household? It was hard to imagine. The girl had seemed so responsible. Her hand had felt warm to his touch and, when he'd first looked into her eyes, he'd been so astonished by their innocent beauty and—

Enough. Don't go there. It was the end of a long and hard day, the time when tempting thoughts tended to prowl around Peter's mind. Time to get home. He would be late, and Ursula would no doubt be annoyed. But he would explain, and she would fawn all over him, just like always. It was one of the reasons he loved her so much.

CHAPTER 9

Magdeburg
March 4, 1629

I n their bedroom, Ursula Erhart reached up to adjust her husband's ruff collar. "Don't forget to grant me the favor of an occasional glance during your sermon. And *please* don't rub your eye or scratch your nose while you're speaking. It's a terrible habit."

Peter laughed. "But, lovely wife, what if my nose truly itches or my eye tears up? And what other major annoyances would you like me to avoid while I'm at it?"

"Just keep your hands away from your face," Ursula chided, "and I'll be perfectly happy. Honestly, it makes you look like a little child sometimes." One more flick of a speck of dust off Peter's shoulder, a lingering kiss on his cheek, and she appeared finally ready to release him for today's special test of fitness for the Lord's service.

Peter smiled and kissed her back, desperately trying to project some confidence. He didn't want to admit to her what he feared the most—that Administrator Wilhelm's desire for personal revenge against him and Dr. Weber would bias his judgment of Peter's performance today. And if the vote was close, Wilhelm's negative opinion could easily sway the final result—just as Weber's vote last year had swayed the cathedral council to depose Wilhelm from his formal position.

"So, my love," Peter said, holding her closely, "this is the point to which God has brought us, is it not? And where would I be, had not the beautiful Ursula Andersen been willing to accompany this ragamuffin altar boy so faithfully along the entire journey?"

"Oh, Peter, stop your blathering. You'll make me cry." Ursula's face beamed. "Now go, so I can make myself presentable for your adoring congregation."

Peter kissed his wife goodbye once more then walked down the stairs and out the front door. As he rounded the corner at the end of the street, he smiled, thinking of his wife's preparations for the eleven o'clock service. In about forty minutes, Frau Metzger and Fräulein Schuler would be arriving to accompany Ursula and the Erharts' children on the walk to St. John's. Normally, Ursula would need only about half of that time for washing, dressing, and grooming. But today was a special occasion, and Peter knew she'd be grateful for the full forty minutes, wanting to look her very best for him. Spotting the St. John's bell towers rising majestically above the rooftops in the distance, Peter thanked God for what he had so clearly and generously provided: the ideal marriage to the ideal wife.

A truly wonderful sentiment. But admit it, Pastor. Something still troubles you about your "ideal marriage" to that "ideal wife" of yours, doesn't it?

Peter stopped, glancing in every direction. There was no one in the vicinity except a young man purchasing a bouquet of flowers from Frau Gärtner's small shop, one of the few permitted by the city to do business on Sunday mornings. Yet Peter was sure that for once he'd actually heard it audibly: the voice—confronting him at the worst of times.

The young gentleman completed his purchase and turned toward the street. Seeing Peter, he smiled and tipped his hat.

Suddenly feeling faint, Peter barely managed to respond in kind. He took a deep breath and forced himself to carry on. Determined not to let self-accusatory ideas distract him from his vital mission today, he said a quick prayer asking God to silence the voice. But God, apparently, wanted him to continue wrestling with it a little longer.

She just hasn't quite enjoyed you as fully as you'd like, has she, Pastor?

Maybe it was Ursula's upbringing in a Swedish household ruled by a dedicated though prudish father. But whatever the reason, she had rarely been able to fully relax and enjoy her intimate relations with Peter. As she'd once confided to him, a certain sense of impropriety, unreasonable though she knew it was, always seemed to interfere. To make matters worse, she seemed unable to rid herself of the imagined presence of her scowling father standing next to their bed, pointing at her with an accusing finger. Peter had tried hard to be sympathetic and as gentle as he could. But despite Ursula's great physical beauty, he'd often been silently frustrated with her lack of responsiveness.

That's right, Pastor. Ursula's lack of responsiveness. Quite unlike that other pretty young thing you still can't get out of your mind, correct? You know—that girl who seemed to crave every part of you, not just your marvelous intellect and your pastoral tenderness.

The voice knew exactly where to strike: at the most vulnerable memory plaguing Peter's conscience. The event had nearly proven to be his undoing, both as an upright pastor and as a faithful husband.

It had all started so innocently about a year and a half ago . . .

⁂

His first child, Josef, had just been born. Peter was making a charitable visit to a widowed mother and her seventeen-year-old daughter living in one of the poorer districts of Magdeburg. The daughter was ill with some unknown malady. It was only the third ministerial visit of Peter's internship phase and a happy time for him—his career progressing well, his marriage to Ursula so far proving to be a great delight.

Receiving no response to his knock, Peter opened the front door of the small house. He announced himself and entered. Someone was lying covered on a pallet against the far wall. The sick daughter? He saw no sign of the mother. Peter approached the bed and asked if the girl was awake and how he could help. The girl turned over on her side, lifting the blanket to reveal her nakedness. She smiled invitingly, held her arms out, and beckoned Peter to embrace her. He knew he should leave immediately but didn't. Captivated, he sat down beside the girl, allowing her to take his wrist and guide his hand downward along the smooth contours of her body. Just then, the sound of footsteps on the upper floor of the house startled him into action. He bolted for the door and ran down the street.

It took a full two weeks before he finally confessed his action to Dr. Weber. Weber told him that he believed his story and that he hadn't heard any complaints from the girl or her mother. He then counseled Peter to simply ask God for forgiveness and resolve not to brood on the matter any longer—and, of course, to learn the lesson about entering unfamiliar homes.

Peter had tried to put the incident behind him. But the memory of the girl's pleasing figure and inviting posture had not died so easily. Lustful thoughts would often intrude, especially on those evenings when Ursula was tired and particularly unresponsive. With the passage of time and much personal prayer, the memory had subsided but had never completely disappeared.

The voice spoke again. *You know your little sin of lustful malingering with that girl is forgiven by Christ, Pastor. But the natural consequences remain. As wonderful as Ursula is, you'd still love to have that girl even now, wouldn't you? Not to mention that other pretty treat for the eyes who you met last week, Anna Ritter. Imagine, you of all people—a happily married assistant pastor—allowing yourself to dwell on such things. And just look at you now, getting ready to preach to others about their need to repent of such sinful thoughts, to instead follow God's command to "be perfect as I am perfect"! Do you know what the Lord calls those who don't practice what they preach, Pastor?*

Peter knew what he had to do: just keep walking toward those beautifully carved church doors up ahead. *Get behind me, Satan!* he thought. He would deal with the nagging voice some other time. Today, he had a critical test to pass.

CHAPTER 10

Magdeburg
March 4, 1629

T he twin-tower bells of St. John's rang in joyous anticipation of the special Sunday service. Peter, trying hard to calm his nerves, peeked through the side door leading out to the dais. It was five minutes before the hour. The church nave was already packed to near capacity, and the honored dignitaries and guests were now arriving.

Administrator Wilhelm waited for the other evaluators from the cathedral council to seat themselves, then strode majestically forward and took his own reserved seat in the center-front pew next to the aisle. It was the best seat in the house, only ten feet from the pulpit.

Peter swallowed hard as he watched Ursula and the children being escorted up the aisle and seated next to the Erharts' good friends Otto Gericke and his wife Margarethe. It was the perfect arrangement, given how fond Ursula was of them both. Their mere presence would help relieve her anxiety for Peter today.

At precisely eleven o'clock, Samuel Scheidt finished the organ prelude. Then, to the rousing strains of Martin Luther's epic hymn, "A Mighty Fortress Is Our God," the congregation stood and the St. John's choir filed solemnly into the chancel from a side entrance. The choir was followed by Dr. Weber and Peter, both of whom knelt at the altar to make their confession together. After the confession, they stood in front of their designated seats. Facing the congregation, Peter struggled to keep his knees from knocking together. His throat had gone dry. Still, he was confident in his message and eager to deliver it.

After the liturgical hymns, prayers, and scriptural readings, it was finally time for the sermon. Dr. Weber stood to give Peter a short introduction and wish him well. All eyes turned toward the pulpit.

Peter surveyed the congregation. A stern frown with arched eyebrow from Wilhelm. A shy wave from Frau Schneider's young son. Encouraging smiles and slight nods from Otto and his wife. A tender gaze from Ursula—she'd never looked so radiant.

"Good morning, my brothers and sisters. I greet you cordially in the name of the Lord. May the Lord be with you."

"And with you also, Pastor," the congregation said in unison.

"Let us pray . . ."

If the body language of the St. John's congregation was any indication, Peter sensed that his message was hitting the mark. The vast majority, including most of the evaluators, were nodding vigorously in agreement with his bold statements. He brimmed with confidence and heartfelt compassion for the congregation as he drew toward the climax.

"And so, fellow believers, I challenge you with the same question I'm constantly asking myself: Where in your life today might you be misplacing your confidence in human intelligence, innate special talent, great wealth, or other fortunate circumstance? Where might you be depending on the wisdom and strength of man, while neglecting to consult with God through prayer and the words of scripture when making your important decisions? Are you relying on man's abilities alone to improve your life or to rescue you from a coming disaster?

"We would all do well, brothers and sisters, to remember the words of our Lord in the Book of Isaiah: 'Woe to the obstinate children,' declares the Lord, 'to those who carry out plans that are not mine, forming an alliance, but not by my Spirit, heaping sin upon sin; who go down to Egypt without consulting me; who look for help to Pharaoh's protection, to Egypt's shade for refuge.'

"Yes, beloved, the scriptures tell us clearly that we must depend ultimately on the wisdom and power of God, not on that of man alone, for our direction and well-being. And it is my fervent prayer that, whatever our station in life, whatever our calling, each of us will come to accept and apply this principle more and more faithfully in our daily lives!"

Peter paused to let his words sink in. His entire audience appeared to be mesmerized.

All except Christian Wilhelm.

He scowled and crossed his arms, indicating significant displeasure with Peter's last few statements. *What on earth*, Peter wondered, *could have possibly set him off?* Peter had avoided controversy, had merely spoken what God had put on his heart to say. Had he somehow said something that would forever ruin his chances for membership in the cathedral council, thereby consigning his future ministry to the backwaters of obscurity and irrelevance?

A slight movement in the back of the nave caught Peter's eye. Someone had discreetly risen from their seat on the aisle and was now quietly exiting the front door of the church. Peter had spotted the handsome young man earlier during the course of his sermon. He'd been sitting in the back row, appearing to watch Peter closely and listen intently to his every word. He hoped that his message hadn't led the man, whoever he was, to leave in a state of disgruntlement or confusion. Having Wilhelm to deal with in that regard was more than enough for one day.

Peter offered his closing remarks and benediction. He'd done his part the best he could. The rest was in God's hands.

Two unofficial reception lines formed in the church narthex following the conclusion of the three-hour service. Peter headed the men's line and Ursula headed the women's, while Fräulein Schuler and Frau Metzger graciously tended to little Josef and Edith. Ursula waved at Peter from across the room and patted her hand over her heart. Regardless of the still-awaited decision by Wilhelm and the evaluators, who were now meeting in the rectory, it was all the confirmation he would ever need that he'd delivered a powerful message.

Peter grinned and blew his wife a quick kiss before turning to greet those in his own line with relieved cordiality, thanks, and encouragement. He was grateful when only Dr. Weber and Otto Gericke remained.

Peter reached out to shake the elder man's hand, but Weber brushed it aside and simply embraced his protégé. "My boy, you've done St. John's justice today. I sense that the Lord is well pleased! And you know that *I* am very proud of you. I can't imagine anything but a unanimous decision in your favor by the evaluators."

"Well, my good friend," Otto said, "allow me to join your chorus of admirers. That was a well-crafted and well-delivered piece of inspired oratory. Excellent sermon, Peter. Even my wife, who you know loves to critique such things, agrees."

This compliment was one to be treasured. A newly appointed Magdeburg city council member with special talents and strong educational background in mathematics and physics, the twenty-four-year-old Gericke was already well known and respected in German university circles. His opinion on any substantive scientific, political or religious matter was highly regarded by all who had the privilege of knowing or working with him. Peter could not have been more delighted by his reaction.

"Thank you both," Peter said. "I must admit I was surprised that I—"

Peter caught sight of Christian Wilhelm walking briskly toward them. He had obviously waited until the line had cleared to make his grand entrance. It could only mean one thing: the evaluators had reached their decision.

"Good day to you, sir," Dr. Weber offered. "We're pleased to have you at our service today."

"Yes, well, thank you," Wilhelm said with a haughty smirk. "I'm here today because I had a special job to do, as you well know. Though I must admit, I should probably attend more often. How else am I going to keep all you naysayers honest, Weber? But at any rate, allow me to express the joint decision of the evaluators in regards to Pastor Erhart's candidacy for the cathedral council."

Peter held his breath. This was the big moment—the one that would determine the course of his future. Recalling Wilhelm's apparent displeasure with the sermon's climax, he braced himself for the worst.

The administrator drew himself up to full height, pulled a sheet of paper from his pocket, and began to read:

> "In view of the fine performance by Pastor Erhart in his sermon delivery today, and considering that he has met all other requisite qualifications, it is the decision of this board of evaluators to approve the nomination of Assistant Pastor Peter Erhart to the Cathedral Council of the Archbishopric of Magdeburg. He is herewith designated a full member and is requested to attend the council's next meeting."

Peter stood in stunned silence as Dr. Weber and Otto erupted in a chorus of joyful shouts and backslapping.

An unsmiling Wilhelm stuck out his hand. "My compliments to you, young man. Your delivery was thorough and clear, the tone pleasant, and the content was for the most part quite edifying."

"Why, thank you, sir," Peter said. "You're most kind." He was enormously relieved. Apparently, he'd misinterpreted Wilhelm's earlier reaction.

Now warmed up, Wilhelm launched into the personal needling for which he was so well known. "All in all, I predict that one day soon this young man will be giving you a good run for your money, Weber!"

"I couldn't agree more, Herr Wilhelm," Dr. Weber responded evenly. "There'll certainly come a time when my service to the Lord in this capacity will no longer be needed. Until then, count on me to do my very best. And in the meantime, I can't imagine anyone I'd rather be preparing for that day than Pastor Erhart here."

"You do seem to have made a good choice in that regard," Wilhelm acknowledged. "Well, I must be returning to the business of keeping this city functioning, even on the Lord's Day. Good day to you all."

Wilhelm spun on his heel and started to walk away. He then turned back and looked at Peter, his face darkened with a frown. "Oh, by the way, young man, if I may be so bold as to offer one piece of advice?"

"Of course, sir," Peter replied.

"Your message today spoke about depending ultimately on God and not on man. While that's certainly true at the personal level, the situation is far more complicated when it comes to civic affairs."

"How is that, sir?" Peter asked, feeling his pulse quicken.

"I mean that you're going beyond your station as a pastor when you hint at your personally preferred solutions to complex political issues."

"But, Herr Wilhelm," Dr. Weber protested, "how exactly did Pastor Erhart 'hint' at anything like that?"

"Oh, Weber, please don't feign ignorance on this. What I'm referring to is Pastor Erhart's use of Isaiah 30:1–2 to substantiate his claim that reliance on the power and good intentions of other men will always lead to God's displeasure and disaster."

"Again, sir," Weber asked, "what's the harm in Pastor Erhart's using a quote directly from scripture to help make a point?"

Wilhelm rolled his eyes and scowled. "The harm is this, Weber. If not explained in the proper context, which Pastor Erhart unfortunately failed to do, that particular passage might well lead those with less discerning minds to believe that God disapproves of *any* alliance that this city might undertake with foreign powers to secure its safety. And, as you well know, the vast majority of our populace have very limited formal education and are highly vulnerable to manipulation."

So that *was Wilhelm's real issue,* Peter now realized. He should have known. Just yesterday, Dr. Weber had warned him once again about Wilhelm's vested interest in the opinions of ordinary Magdeburg citizens regarding foreign alliances. Weber had recalled how three years ago—and against the advice of the Magdeburg city council— Wilhelm had raised a private army and entered into an alliance with Denmark to stop Wallenstein's initial advance into Germany. But Wilhelm and the Danes had suffered a terrible defeat at Dessau Bridge, and Wilhelm had been lucky to escape with his life and temporarily retain his official position. Weber said this experience was considered by many on the present city council to bode ill for Wilhelm's latest effort to obtain similar help from the Swedish king. And as shaky as his position now was with that same council, he clearly didn't want the common citizenry stirred up as an additional source of opposition. *No wonder he's angry with my choice of scriptural verses,* Peter thought.

"Sir, if I may," Peter said, "I didn't intend by using those verses to imply that *all* foreign alliances are necessarily bad. I—"

Wilhelm held up his hand. "You might not have intended it, young man," he said, his voice rising, "but unless you're very clear that you're using this passage only as a metaphor for behavior at the *personal* level, your congregation may well be tempted to apply it literally in every situation. They could easily use it as an excuse to undermine the Magdeburg civil government's strategy for the survival of our city. They might claim that 'God doesn't approve of *any* foreign alliances' or some such nonsense."

Dr. Weber frowned. "Herr Wilhelm, *please.* Of course the context for any scriptural passage is important to communicate. But you're greatly exaggerating—"

"I exaggerate nothing, Weber! I merely point out the truth whenever I perceive it."

"Gentlemen!" Otto Gericke said, trying to diffuse the heated conversation. "This is an important topic, but I'm not sure this is the best time or place to discuss it. May I suggest we defer the issue of foreign alliances until the next city council meeting?"

Wilhelm relented. Gericke's was the only opinion at St. John's that he seemed to respect. "Well, at least *someone* around here has the good sense to propose an end to useless chatter. My congratulations again to you, Pastor Erhart. You indeed performed extremely well, for the most part. But in your new position on our council, please know that I'll expect you to refrain from wasting everybody's time by challenging me on trivial points of no consequence as you've done in the past. I simply won't tolerate it." Wilhelm made a quick about-face and marched away.

Peter, Weber, and Gericke exchanged glances, all speechless.

The elder man finally broke the silence. "Well, Peter," he said with a rueful smile, "welcome to the world where religion and politics collide. Before long, you'll learn firsthand how hard it is sometimes to love your enemies—even when they're supposedly on the same side as you. But don't let all this ruin your evening of celebration with your lovely wife. You were superb today, and the evaluators' decision proved it. There's not one thing I would have said differently."

Despite Weber's reassurance and his own relief and joy at today's victory, Peter couldn't suppress a disturbing realization. Wilhelm's personal hostility toward him had, if anything, increased. It was a development that portended a rocky road ahead.

After putting the children to sleep, Peter and Ursula curled up together on the blankets and feather-stuffed cushions that she had arranged by the hearth.

"You must be exhausted, darling," Ursula said, rubbing the back of Peter's neck.

"I definitely am. Though I do feel very good about how things went— except, that is, for Wilhelm's complaint."

"Peter, don't let that man's self-centered agenda cause you guilt or doubt about the direction the Lord gave you for your sermon. Anyway, the board overall said it was a fine effort. So why not just let Herr Wilhelm's silly quibbles go?"

"Yes, my lady. You're right. Enough worrying over that." Peter smiled and then reached for his wife's hand. "Ursula, there's something I want to tell you."

"What's that?"

Peter gazed at her with all the tender affection and appreciation he'd been wanting to express since spotting her in the congregation that morning. "You've made my life a joy. There's no one on earth I'd rather spend my time with, no one I feel more at peace with or better understood by. I only hope I make you feel as loved as you make me feel."

Ursula slowly sat up and undid the knot in her hair, letting it fall down to frame her comely face that glowed in the soft candlelight. "Oh my," she said with an inviting smile. "I think I just might have to retire early for the evening. You won't be studying long tonight, will you, Pastor?"

Peter grinned. "I think now most definitely not."

After a few minutes, Peter climbed into bed with Ursula, who was waiting for him without any of the usual armor of layers of underclothing.

She snuggled up close. "I saw all those pretty young women in the center section staring intently at you today, Sir Peter," she teased.

Peter laughed. "I'm sure they were all concentrating hard on my message."

"I'm not sure that was *all* they were concentrating on," Ursula whispered. For the first time in what seemed like ages, Ursula was able to abandon herself completely to Peter's embrace.

CHAPTER 11

Magdeburg
March 5, 1629

P eter hardly noticed the knock on the rectory door. It was Monday, and Gerda had no doubt arrived with the usual midmorning refreshments.

"Come in."

The door opened and then closed softly. Peter didn't bother to look up. The audacious new draft order from the cathedral council captured his attention.

"If this is a bad time, Pastor, I can come back later."

Peter stared in surprise at the tall, well-built man standing with hat in hand in front of his desk. There was something familiar about the handsome face, especially the deep-set eyes and angular jaw. Yes, he looked vaguely familiar, but where . . . ?

The man grinned. "I don't suppose you'd remember that day you tried to shelter this cowering little mouse from the wrath of the Protestant governors, would you now?"

"*Hans*! Hans Mannheim from the Prague castle!" Peter shouted, bounding from behind his desk to grasp Hans's hands in both of his. "I can't believe it. Is it really you? You must have grown at least three feet!

How did you . . . ? What are you doing here?"

Hans chuckled. "After seeing the city announcement that you'd be preaching, I attended your sermon yesterday. I wanted to come and pay my respects today, especially after so rudely leaving the church just before your benediction. My apologies for that—I had an urgent appointment that I needed to attend."

"So *you* were the culprit! Not surprising, considering we ran a half hour longer than usual." Peter laughed and shook his head in disbelief. "I hadn't forgotten you, Hans. I often wondered what had become of you after Prague. Please, sit and tell me your story."

Hans removed his cloak and settled into the small armchair that Peter offered him.

"Actually, Pastor, it's not a particularly exciting one. After the Prague incident, my father, at his own request, was honorably discharged from the emperor's service. He purchased a number of salt mines near Salzburg, and it turned out to be a very successful venture. He financed my education at the University of Ingolstadt and then took me on as manager of operations for his expanding business interests. I married five years ago, and I now live in Munich with my wife Marie."

Peter smiled. "And let me guess. You're now visiting important European trade centers like Magdeburg, looking for opportunities to increase your father's profits."

"Nothing more earthshaking than that, I'm afraid. And look at *you* . . . assistant pastor for St. John's Lutheran Church! What in heaven's name got a hold of you, Pastor? I thought you were destined to become an accountant like your own father."

"I was—before my father died. But then God reminded me of my original dream to follow in my grandfather's footsteps, and the love of my life finally convinced me that ministry was in my blood."

"The love of your life being . . . ?"

Peter picked up the small portrait that he'd commissioned shortly after the birth of his second child and handed it to Hans.

"My wife, Ursula. That's my son Josef beside her, and Edith whom she's holding."

Hans stared intently at the image. "I can see why you allowed yourself to be persuaded. She's stunningly beautiful, Pastor, as are your children." He handed it back with a strange, wistful glint in his eye. "What I'd give to be done with my constant travels—to take up a permanent job in Munich, enjoy my own lovely young wife, become a father. It seems that the ministry life has afforded you all of those delightful benefits."

"Those, along with the thousands of headaches that always seem to disturb my lush, comfortable lifestyle." Peter grimaced, picking up the document he'd been reading earlier. "Such as this new proposal from our Lutheran administrator. Christian Wilhelm is requiring every pastor in the city to sign a pledge to refrain from using the pulpit for promotion of 'personal political views.' Obviously, he wasn't pleased with some things I had to say yesterday, and he has no intention of allowing any views but his own to be voiced in Magdeburg churches from here on. I doubt he'll secure approval for this outrage from the full council. But its tone and intent are alarming."

Hans's eyes narrowed as his entire face took on a cold, stony expression. "Pastor, I—"

"Please, Hans, no need for formality among friends. Call me Peter."

"Peter, I don't know if you're aware, but this city is in big trouble."

"Are you talking about the new imperial edict that's been rumored?"

Hans shook his head and sighed. "I wish it were only that. I just heard from my business associate who has close contacts with the imperial court in Vienna. The emperor's in a murderous rage over Wallenstein's failure to capture the Baltic port of Stralsund after three months of siege last summer. He's told Wallenstein that with France, England, and Sweden all now sending their mercenaries to resist imperial advances in Germany, he has no time or patience for any more 'cowardice or buffoonery' on the part of his own army's supreme commander. If Magdeburg fails to accept all terms of the new edict once it's passed, then Wallenstein is not to waste any time. The emperor expects him to *level* the city at once—setting an example for any other north German Lutheran strongholds that might think about resisting."

"With that report, it seems we have little choice but to sit here and accept our God-ordained fate," Peter said with a tinge of sarcasm. "Honestly, Hans, do you really think Magdeburg will cave that easily to Catholic threats? After all, we've successfully resisted imperial sieges in the past, and Wilhelm is actively recruiting foreign support from—"

"Wilhelm is a loud-mouthed, pompous turd. He has no idea how to combat a fully equipped, properly trained Catholic army backed by heavy artillery and cavalry. Any attempt to resist Wallenstein by force is doomed to failure and will mean suicide for this city."

Peter sat back in his chair, rattled by Hans's vehement, almost arrogant tone. It was the voice of Hans's father at Prague, who'd been so quick in mixed company to tout the superiority of his own Catholicism over Lutheranism.

"I won't pretend to have a different opinion of Wilhelm than you, Hans, but he *has* been successful in stiffening the back of many in this city who long ago might have given in to imperial interests."

"It will be to their ultimate regret if they resist the emperor, I assure you."

"Well, my friend," Peter said with a helpless shrug, "you've delivered what I know is a well-intended warning. But I'm only an assistant pastor in a city that worships not only our triune God but also its own glorious past as a bastion against the Catholic 'antichrists.' Many of our most prominent citizens have become enchanted by Wilhelm's call to once again rise to our reputation. And there's little I can see to do about it, especially given his personal animosity toward me."

Hans leaned forward. "Actually, Peter, maybe there *is* something you can do."

"And what's that?"

"You've earned an appointment to the cathedral council, correct?"

"Yes, that's true, but I'm only a—"

"Listen to me, Peter. I have it on good authority that Wallenstein may be open to a personal bribe to spare the city, if it's substantial enough. If you can somehow communicate that possibility to your more senior council members and get them to start considering it, I believe it will bear much fruit when the time is right."

"A *personal bribe*?" Peter asked incredulously. "But how then would Wallenstein justify his sparing of the city to the emperor? And besides, how is it, Hans, that *you* have come across all this information and wish to share it with me?"

Hans looked at him sharply. "I can say no more. On both questions, Peter, you'll just have to trust me, as I cannot reveal my source."

Peter eyed him suspiciously. "Trusting you is one thing, Hans. Convincing others on the council to believe that *I*—of all people—have somehow obtained 'secret' information about Wallenstein is another matter altogether."

Hans said nothing for a long moment. "Yes, well, it was just a thought. Do with it as you think best." He glanced at his timepiece. "How time flies! I must let you get back to your work and be about my own." He rose abruptly and extended his hand. Peter rounded the desk to escort him to the door.

Despite his reservations as to the credibility of Hans's story, Peter didn't want to seem ungrateful. "Thank you, Hans. I will definitely take all you've said under advisement."

Hans nodded. Just before reaching the door, he paused. "Peter, I do have one question that has been troubling me lately. It's been nagging at me ever since completing one of my theological classes at the university."

"Yes?"

"Let me state it completely and formally. How is it that you Lutherans can justify trusting in *sola Scriptura*—the Bible alone—as your final authority, the only infallible rule for Christian belief and practice? How can you do that while you reject the official Church—the Catholic Church—which the Bible itself has ordained as the authoritative earthly agent for interpreting, spreading, and teaching God's divine revelation to man in the form of *both* written Scripture and unwritten tradition?"

Peter laughed. "You expect me to address one of the most important issues that divides Protestants and Catholics in five seconds on your way out of here?"

"What better opportunity to give a brief defense of your Protestant faith to a humble Catholic businessman—one who respects and desires to know your opinion?"

"In that case," said Peter, "I'll speak for myself. Let's just say that my own trust in the Bible alone isn't based on what other human authorities—whether Protestant or Catholic—*say* about it as much as my own personal experience of its truths. The more I've devoted myself to its study and have striven to put into practice what it commands— and the more positive results and inner peace I've gained from doing so—the more I'm inspired to trust it as my final authority. Like Dr. Luther, I simply can't place that level of trust in the pope and his councils, who've so often permitted terrible abuses and nonbiblical practices, like the sale of indulgences, to run wild within the Church.

"There. You asked a formal question and I've given you a formal answer. Have I convinced you?"

Hans smiled. "Spoken like a theologian with a heart. Dr. Luther would be proud of you. I'll also take what you've said under advisement. And maybe someday, Peter, you can teach me how to discover your holy grail, your mysterious 'personal experience' of biblical truth. I think I would like that very much."

"It would be my privilege to do so, my friend. And in the meantime, Hans, I'll forever be thankful that the Lord has answered my prayer of long ago—that I'd meet you again someday and make things right. I've felt so badly about not doing more to help you that day at the castle."

Hans grabbed his forearm. "Peter, no one could have spared me from what I deserved after disgracing my father like I did. You did what you could, and the care you showed in trying to help me that day meant everything. There's nothing more you need to do to 'make things right.' Any misplaced guilt on my behalf should no longer burden your heart."

Peter swallowed hard and placed his hand over Hans's. "By the way, if I may ask, how *are* things between you and your father?"

Hans's expression suddenly darkened, accompanied by a slight twitching of the left side of his face. "Passable. He's never quite gotten over the humiliation of Prague, but his business activities and my expanding role in them are definitely helping him to move on."

The men embraced, and Hans turned to exit into the hallway. Peter called after him. "Hans, I hope you'll be returning to Magdeburg sometime soon. I'd love to have you meet my wife and children the next time you're here."

Hans stopped and grinned. "Why, of course, Dr. *Luther*. I'd be delighted!"

CHAPTER 12

Magdeburg
March 7, 1629

Major of cavalry Hans Mannheim, special attaché to the general staff of Count von Wallenstein's Catholic Imperial Army, sat by himself in the dim, smoke-filled tavern.

Hans knew he'd washed down as much ale as he could handle for a Wednesday evening. Unfortunately, it hadn't erased his despairing mood. Almost six months had passed since he'd last enjoyed the sweet, intimate embrace of his wife, Marie. And after one whole month alone in this rabidly Lutheran city, his special covert mission still hadn't produced any useful results. Would it *never* end?

True, his meeting two days ago with Peter Erhart had not been a total waste. Hans had delivered the unofficial message from Wallenstein, while successfully feigning his own identity by using the made-up "salt-mining businessman" story. But it wasn't clear that Peter had taken the bribe suggestion seriously. And even if he had, would he be able to convince the other, more senior members on the cathedral council that Wallenstein could possibly be bought off?

Complicating matters, Emperor Ferdinand had just yesterday announced in Vienna his new "Edict of Restitution." If fully implemented, the edict would mandate the transfer of power and property from the local Protestant gentry back to the Catholic Church and legitimize the forced conversion of *all* Magdeburg citizens to Catholicism.

The timing of the edict's announcement couldn't have been worse. It was bound to further stiffen the backs of the already rebellious Magdeburg populace and their leaders. Surely the last thing on their minds now would be the idea of offering a cowardly bribe to Wallenstein to spare the city. If only the emperor had delayed the volatile announcement a few weeks longer to coordinate with the arrival of Wallenstein's army! Then the city leaders would have had more time to quietly discuss the bribe idea in a less poisoned atmosphere, increasing its chances for approval. But that had not happened.

It was all just another indication, Hans feared, that Wallenstein was not consulting with the emperor about his own private plans concerning the bribe. It was a recipe for confusion. Possibly even for future disaster. And Hans was stuck in the middle of it all, with a job that no sane person could possibly want.

"More, sir?" the shy tavern barmaid asked as she held the pitcher over his half-empty mug.

Far too young and innocent-looking to be working here, Hans thought. *I wonder where the usual wenches are flaunting their goods tonight.* "Thank you, but no, Fräulein," he said softly.

"Please just let me know if you'd like more, sir." The barmaid smiled before turning to the next table. "Or just ask someone for Gisela—that's my name."

Gisela. She probably belonged to one of those peasant families that had recently arrived in the city from the countryside, all trying to find shelter from the soon-expected onslaught of Wallenstein's army.

As well they should, Hans reflected grimly. *Once Wallenstein's forces flood this area to enforce the new edict, peasant families outside the city walls will especially be at risk. Who would know that better than me?*

The mere recollection of his primary purpose in the city was enough to tighten the growing knot in Hans's gut. Spying on the meetings of the Magdeburg city council? That would be considered an unglamorous and even ignoble task by any self-respecting young Catholic army cavalry officer. But for twenty-five-year-old Major Hans Mannheim, one of several young rising stars within the emperor's combined military forces, it was no less than a mission from hell. A mission that only the devil or Baron von Mannheim, Hans's father, could have possibly devised and suggested to the emperor that Hans was the right man to personally carry it out. And, true to form, the baron had done just that.

His reasoning had been quite simple. He had seen yet another opportunity to advance Hans's military career—not to mention his own. Successful performance of this special mission would pave the way for an extremely important Catholic takeover of Magdeburg. It would earn the respect and gratitude of the emperor, both for Hans and for his father. Besides, Hans's absence from his own cavalry unit operating under Count Tilly's command in northwestern Germany could be spared until the spring offensive.

Hans knew he had to stop grousing and just pay the piper. He'd already disgraced his father eleven years ago in Prague and, contrary to what he had told Peter, the baron had never come close to getting over the incident. And after all his father had done since Prague to promote Hans's military career, how could he refuse to support his elder's latest scheme?

"Oh, pardon me, sir!" The curvaceous hip of the tavern's other barmaid brushed against Hans's left shoulder as she walked past.

After setting down four full mugs in front of the rowdy customers and successfully avoiding their roving hands, the barmaid returned down the aisle toward Hans with one full mug still on the tray. She stumbled slightly, and the mug and tray together went crashing to the floor at Hans's feet.

"Oh my, how clumsy!" the dark-haired girl exclaimed with a laugh that exhibited no hint of embarrassment whatsoever. She batted her eyes at Hans.

Hans glanced around cautiously. No one else in the noisy tavern seemed to have taken notice.

The girl knelt down and began to clean up the mess, her low-cut dress revealing her ample, well-formed bosom. He knew it was all on display for his personal benefit. Try as he might, he couldn't avert his gaze from the tempting view.

She patted the floor dry with a cloth she'd produced from her dress pocket. Once finished, she lifted her head and locked eyes with Hans, smiling seductively. "Now I *know* it's getting late. I can't even walk straight!"

A real beauty, especially for this place. And not so innocent-looking like Gisela. Strange that I've never seen her here before tonight. He gave himself a quick shake of the head. *Enough, Mannheim. Stop staring. Just politely nod, and then get back to downing your ale.* He couldn't take any chances on alluring diversions. Besides, she didn't hold a candle to his sweet wife Marie. *Well, maybe a short one.*

Hans didn't offer to help. He merely smiled and nodded. The girl got the message, rose, and walked away. *Thank God.* Thoughts of Marie were proving once again to be a strong antidote to his natural desire for erotic adventure.

Hans shook his head in wonderment as his mind drifted to the previous Sunday. He had heard just the day before that Peter would be delivering his special sermon, and he couldn't resist the chance to see him in action. It had turned out to be a good decision. After observing and listening to Peter, he knew he had found the right Magdeburg citizen with whom to plant the idea of Wallenstein's openness to a bribe and had made the decision to go see him the next day in the rectory. But besides the obvious benefit for his covert mission, hearing Peter speak had brought Hans an unexpected personal surprise.

What a man Peter has become, Hans marveled. *An articulate Lutheran preacher, no less! Holy Mary, Mother of Christ, please forgive him for imploring and teaching others to follow his Protestant heresy! Who would have predicted it eleven years ago in that cursed Prague castle?* But then again, who would have predicted that *he*—Hans Mannheim, cowardly youth and betrayer of his father's honor—was destined to soon become one of the most highly reputed cavalry officers in the emperor's service?

The aftermath of the castle incident had certainly been a whirlwind: Count Thurn's unlikely success in raising a large Protestant army; the Protestants' near annihilation of Emperor Matthias's forces in battle; Matthias's death and succession by Ferdinand II. Most surprising of all had been the new emperor's summoning of Baron von Mannheim to serve as major general and chief of staff for the newly commissioned Catholic League Army, commanded by Count Tilly. The baron—determined not to waste all his effort and expense in having his son Hans trained from an early age in the skills of horse-mounted swordsmanship—had immediately recruited him as aide-de-camp.

Over the next nine years, Hans had more than proven himself in battle. Early on, his leadership of a daring Catholic cavalry charge had aided the destruction of the Bohemian Protestant rebel army at White Mountain near Prague. And later, after the emperor had directed the separate Catholic armies of Tilly and Wallenstein to invade Germany to "punish" the German Protestant nobles for lending their support to the Bohemian rebels, he had once again performed brilliantly. Tilly had rewarded him with promotion to the rank of major.

Yes, he had come a long way since the Prague debacle. There had been only one strike against his record—his inexplicable tendency to go soft on surrendering enemy soldiers in the heat of battle. Especially frowned upon was his habit of taking them as prisoners instead of immediately dispatching them with sword or pistol. He'd even been known on occasion to dismount and offer a drink or perform other small kindnesses for the severely wounded.

Unfortunately, cavalry officers in the heat of a mounted battle had little time for that kind of merciful behavior, especially as it could put their own men at risk. It was a pattern that had caught the negative attention of Hans's superior officers, especially his father. The baron, of course, had no desire to be reminded further of any hints of softness associated with his son.

Hans would never forget the evening after receiving news of his promotion, when his father had summoned him to his private quarters. Standing in front of the blazing hearth, the baron had not even turned to acknowledge Hans as he entered.

"Congratulations, son," Baron von Mannheim had said darkly, arms akimbo and his tall, black silhouette framed by the flames. "Now the real work of proving yourself begins. You know what the Protestants did to us in Prague. Never forget that you ran and hid when your father needed you most. Never forget the sound of those governors' taunts. And never forget that there is only one way to erase those memories completely."

"What is that, Father?"

The baron slowly turned to face him. "*Show them no mercy.*"

"But, Father, they are already dead. They no longer—"

"They are *never* dead, major. They live on in the minds and bodies of those today who insist on worshiping the Bible alone as their 'true God,' on calling the Pope 'the Antichrist,' on perverting the meaning of Holy Communion and demeaning the power and holiness of Mary and the saints. These Protestant scum—whether Lutheran, Calvinist, Anabaptist, or other heretical sect—are all *anathema*. We must eventually eliminate them from the face of the earth. And in your new position, you will be at the tip of the spear."

"Father, you know I will always fight for the Church that you raised me in. In fact, I will give my life to it if required. But is it never possible to extend the slightest mercy even to those who—"

"*Enough!* You always were a weak-willed, soft little boy at heart. Spoiled by your mother and doted upon by your older sisters despite my warnings to them. The result showed at Prague. But it's time to put that aside. You've demonstrated the skills that I paid dearly to have you learn, and you have now received your reward. Now step up to your new commission. You know I went to extra lengths with Tilly to secure it for you in the face of your competition and all those negative stories about your battlefield 'mercies' to surrendering enemy soldiers. Do not let me down, major. That is all."

The recollection of that conversation burned like a hot iron poker thrust into the pit of Hans's stomach. No matter what he did, no matter where he went, the bitter memory was always there to plague him— just like the memory of Prague. Just like those other terrible memories of when his father had berated him as a youth for failing to "act like a man." The worst of it was, Hans believed in his heart that everything his father had said about him was true. Underneath the surface bravado and accomplishments, he was an undeserving weakling. And he would forever be in his father's debt.

Hans lifted his mug to drain its remaining contents. Enough self-pity. It was time to finish this crazy mission once and for all. He'd already surveyed and mapped the Magdeburg city walls and other defensive structures. Tomorrow night, an emergency city council meeting would be held to discuss ways of resisting the new edict. Hans had been granted a pass by one of the clandestine Catholic sympathizers on the council to observe the meeting as a spectator. All he needed to do was show up and sit in the back. Keep his head down and his ears open. Let that idiot Christian Wilhelm and his radical followers show their cards. Report back to his father and Count Tilly, who would no doubt have the necessary information conveyed to Wallenstein's army. Eventually, Hans would be rewarded with a furlough in Munich with his wife. And maybe someday down the road, once the war ended, he could come back here and reacquaint himself with Peter.

Yes. Time to get this whole thing over with.

Two hours and three mugfuls of beer later, Hans slapped the coins for his fare down on the table and stumbled out of the tavern. His mind was reeling, his head splitting. He felt the need to retch but couldn't.

As he turned the corner to retrieve his tied-up horse at the end of the short alleyway, a soft, inviting voice called from a nearby dark doorway. "Sir, in here. Please. In here."

Hans immediately recognized the voice as belonging to the raven-haired barmaid he'd brushed off earlier. He understood the implications but no longer tried to employ his better judgment. He walked unsteadily to the doorway and entered.

Closing the door and grabbing his hand, the woman gently led him up a short flight of stairs and into a small room that was illuminated by a single candle and furnished with only a table, two chairs, and a bed in the far corner. The woman helped Hans to remove his cloak and sword. Pulling out one of the chairs, she helped him to sit down, then took the other chair for herself. She rested her elbows on the table with her hands folded under her chin, smiling demurely at him.

Hans tried to keep his words from slurring. "Didn't I meet you in the tavern just a couple of hours ago? It hasn't closed yet, so why aren't you still working? And why haven't I seen you there before—are you new, or only there sometimes?"

"Sir, you ask too many questions. Especially in your condition. But I'll try to answer. Yes, you did meet me a little earlier. And yes, I have served there before, once in a while. My father's one of the owners. But he's away tonight, and I am very lonely."

Prior to his marriage, Hans had encountered this kind of situation before. He was no stranger to the little dance that it called for. In the old days, he would have wasted no time taking the lead. Satisfy his loins, pay her for the privilege. He knew she would welcome the money. No doubt a young child somewhere to feed.

Tonight, however, was a different matter. Instead of the usual lust, Hans was feeling his earlier overwhelming sadness return in force. He looked over blankly at the wall and felt the urge to leave, as a vision of his wife flashed suddenly before his eyes. Seeing his distraction, the girl stood up. She was wearing a revealing chemise, and she was very desirable. She sauntered over and kneeled down beside him, took his face in her hands, and kissed him softly on the lips.

It took only a few more moments for both to see that he would be unresponsive to her intimate caresses. Standing up, she asked plaintively: "Do I not please you, sir?"

Hans looked up at her. "Fräulein," he said quietly, "I have no business being here—I'm married."

The girl became incensed. "Get out! Get out now, you pervert! Who do you think you are? Just because you're a handsome rogue doesn't give you the right to talk down to me!"

"What makes you think I was talking down to you?"

"Oh, stop pretending. I can hear it in your voice. You're just like all those other married knaves who come to see me. The only difference is they don't stay *soft* like a little boy!"

With one motion, Hans stood up, grabbed his sword, and unsheathed it.

"You wretched whore!"

The girl stood transfixed with her hands over her mouth as Hans raised the weapon, preparing to cut her through from top to bottom. At the last second, he turned at the sound of her shriek. The sword crashed down, not onto the girl's head but into the wooden table just beside her. Seething with rage, Hans extracted it and jammed it back into its sheath.

The girl was still half-screaming and half-sobbing as Hans grabbed his cloak and stalked through the doorway. On a sudden impulse, he stopped and pulled out several coins from his pocket. He threw them toward the girl, who then slammed the door shut in his face.

Ten minutes later, a light rain had just begun to fall as Hans staggered up to the door of his rented room and placed his hand on the knob. Suddenly, the realization of what he had almost done to the barmaid hit like a sack of heavy stones. Turning around, he leaned back against the door and slid wearily down to the ground. He wrapped his arms around his knees and turned his face upward to receive the cool drops. He closed his eyes, allowing the scene in the girl's room to replay in his mind.

Soft. That's what she had called him, just like his father had. If *something* hadn't caused him to turn at the last second, the girl would have paid a horrible price for stoking the ever-burning memory of the baron's accusation.

Soft. Weak. Less than a real man. Maybe they were right. The fear that it could be true had long plagued him. Tonight, it had nearly destroyed his soul.

CHAPTER 13

Grünfeld, a small village southwest of Magdeburg
March 8, 1629

"We'll be able to *slide* our way to the village if it keeps pouring like this!" joked Barbara Saller.

After nearly four weeks of dry weather, a late-winter storm had dumped torrents of cold rain since yesterday evening. The deluge had combined with the poor drainage features of the surrounding fields to turn the country lane leading to Grünfeld into a slick, muddy quagmire. The rain had let up in intensity over the last two hours, tapering off to a steady drizzle. But only a few minutes ago, the heavens had once again opened up.

Anna, walking between Barbara and Frau Saller, did her best to stretch a wide cloth over everyone's head as shelter. "As soon as we get to the market," she said, "I promise you I'll take this old sheet and throw it in the garbage. Fitting end, for all the good it's doing us."

Anna was in high spirits despite the weather. Any time she could spend with her best friend, regardless of the circumstances, was always time well spent. Today being Thursday, Barbara and her mother were making their weekly journey into the village. There, they planned to exchange Frau Saller's latest hand-sewn clothing articles for some necessary food items and other supplies that Herr Denzel, the market proprietor, would have held in reserve. As usual, Anna had met up with them at the crossroads to accompany them and purchase a few items at the market for her own family.

Reaching the village boundary, they proceeded down the deserted main street to Herr Denzel's general store. *At last*, Anna thought, *a chance to rest and dry off.*

As she entered, she wondered why there were no customers.

"Hello!" Frau Saller called out. "Herr Denzel! Is anyone here?"

After a few moments—longer than it should have taken—Herr Denzel responded from his counter at the rear of the store, beyond the intervening rows of tall barrels filled with grain and foodstuffs. "Yes, I'm back here. What is it that you want?"

"Oh, good," Frau Saller replied. "I'll be there in a moment, sir."

Frau Saller told the girls to start picking out their desired items from the crates stacked against the walls. She herself would go back and talk with the owner, ask for some cloths to dry off with, then give him the newly made clothing items in her basket.

After only a few minutes, Frau Saller returned with a crushed look on her face. She handed the girls dry cloths, which they gratefully put to use.

"Well, what did he say, Mother?" Barbara asked.

Her mother frowned. "He hardly offered a word. I had to drag everything out of him. He looked confused and worried. At first, he didn't want to accept my new clothes, but finally he grabbed them and thanked me in a very odd voice. After he handed me our supplies, he just stared hard at me for a few seconds, and then he walked away to talk to some people sitting at a table in the back room. I couldn't really see who they were."

It didn't make sense. Herr Denzel was a gracious man. A bit cautious, maybe, always on guard for tricksters, thieves, and the like. But Anna had never known him to treat anyone with disdain, especially Frau Saller, whom he'd always welcomed so warmly in the past.

Sinister laughter from the rear of the store caused Anna to flinch.

She huddled close together with the Sallers at the sound of heavy footsteps. Someone was walking down the aisle on the other side of a line of tall barrels.

"Guess you set old man Denzel straight, boss!" a man said in a gruff, deep-throated voice.

A second man spoke in a far more melodic and higher-pitched tone with a cultured, distinctly foreign accent. "Yes, yes. They just never seem to take us seriously, do they, Schmidt?"

Anna held her breath and grabbed Barbara's arm. She knew she'd heard those voices before—but where?

The men headed for the door, hopefully never to be seen or heard from again. Abruptly, the footsteps halted.

"Schmidt, can you smell that sweet fragrance?"

"No, boss. Can't say that I can."

"Well, I definitely can. And I'm sure that its source lies just on the other side of these barrels. Shall we *investigate*?"

The two men rounded the end of the line of barrels and stood with arms crossed. They were the same two who'd abused Vati at the tavern only a week ago. Anna still remembered their mocking leers when she'd arrived and picked up her drunken father to take him home.

"Greetings, beautiful ladies!" said the thinner, shorter, and far more intelligent-looking of the two men. His dark cloak and black, wide-brimmed peasant hat somehow seemed at odds with his cultured speech and genial smile. "We didn't mean to frighten you. Please allow us to introduce ourselves. My name is Dietrich Ackar, and this is my good friend Herr Schmidt." Ackar doffed his hat and bowed, prompting his partner to do the same. "And may we have the pleasure of knowing *your* names?"

"Oh, of course, sir," Frau Saller said in a relieved tone. "My name is Gretchen Saller. This is my daughter Barbara, and this is—"

Anna gripped Frau Saller's forearm to stop her from finishing her sentence.

"This is . . . ?" Ackar smiled. "My, I must say you somehow look very familiar." He peered at Anna with unconcealed pleasure.

She could almost consider Ackar handsome: thirtyish and of medium height; thin, well-formed facial contours; shoulder-length dark hair; pointed, well-manicured beard and mustache framing a wide mouth with full lips. Yes, almost handsome, but not quite. It was his eyes that disturbed her. Set close together and almost black in color, they had an eerie, piercing quality that would set anyone on edge.

"Ritter, sir," she said at length, a tinge of bitterness in her voice. "Anna Ritter."

Ackar replaced his hat, tilted his head, and stroked his goatee, eyeing her up and down.

"Ritter. Ritter. Hmm . . . I know I've heard that name somewhere. Oh, yes, of course! Have I lost my senses? You're the lovely daughter of Adam Ritter, the gentleman Herr Schmidt and I had the privilege of sharing a couple of drinks with a few days ago. A very nice and honorable man, your father."

"Oh, yes," Anna hissed. "So 'nice and honorable' you decided to clout him on the cheek with your infernal leather strap!"

"Dear God!" Barbara and her mother whispered as one. Anna had never told them about the incident.

Ackar narrowed his eyes and shook his head sympathetically. "Ah, that. Yes, it's sad that at times certain unfortunate actions cannot be helped. But I believe your father has now learned his lesson. It need never happen again, so long as he conforms to the terms of our little agreement for payment of his long-overdue rent." Ackar's broad smile returned, and he spread his arms wide as if to welcome Anna home to the fold. "But Fräulein Ritter—Anna, if I may—why should one little incident prevent us *all* from becoming good friends? Really, we'll all be needing each other's mutual protection and support in the coming weeks and months, won't we?"

"H-how do you mean, sir?"

"Dear girl," Ackar replied, pausing to glance up at his towering comrade, who was displaying a barely disguised smirk, "haven't you heard? The Catholics are coming to Magdeburg! Yes, the emperor's new edict announced two days ago has given the signal that Wallenstein's army has been waiting for."

Anna shook her head. "I don't know what that means, sir. Out here in the countryside, we don't usually hear all the—"

"Oh, Anna," Ackar interrupted, "I completely understand. You shouldn't feel at all inferior. Let's just say that Count von Wallenstein and his powerful Catholic army will be arriving in this area in the near future. And when they do, *no one* will be safe from their thievery, their pillaging, or their raping and torture. Especially poor folk like you three living out in the isolated countryside. Just ask Schmidt here. He used to be one of them. Didn't you, Schmidt?"

"Yes, boss, but that was before I saw the error of my ways," Schmidt replied with a strange laugh. "And glad I am now that I decided to quit Wallenstein's band of murderers and come work for you, an honorable and decent man."

"There!" Ackar said. "You see, ladies? That's why it's so very important that we all become good friends and stick together. We have to protect ourselves from these Catholic army vagabonds who'll be crawling all over this area soon. Now, Anna," he continued with a smile as he took a cautious step in her direction, "if you'd just permit me to kiss your lovely hand as a simple gesture of friendship and good will toward you and your family, I'd be—"

"Don't you come any closer, sir." Anna cringed and fell back against Barbara and her mother.

"But, Fräulein, I—"

"I said stay back!"

Thump! Thump! Thump!

Anna could scarcely believe her eyes. There, at the end of the aisle, stood none other than tottering, scowling, sixty-nine-year-old Pastor Tiedeman from Grünfeld's church. He rapped the floor three more times with his walking stick and then glared at Ackar and Schmidt, as if pronouncing final judgment on their sins. "Are these men disturbing you, ladies?"

Ackar allowed them no chance to respond. "Of course we aren't disturbing them, Pastor Whoever-You-Are," he replied breezily. "Are you accusing us of ill-intended tomfoolery?"

Tiedeman's scowl deepened. "I'm not asking *you* that question, sir. I'm asking the ladies here. Fräulein Anna, once again . . . are they disturbing you?"

"Sir, they haven't harmed us in any way," Anna said quietly, "but we do wish they'd leave us alone."

Tiedman rapped his stick on the floor once again. "Well then, gentlemen, I must demand that you respect the ladies' wishes and depart from their presence here."

"Ah, but, Pastor," Ackar said, "may I ask what gives *you* the right to command us to leave these premises?"

Anna was shocked to watch Tiedeman's scowl transform magically into a confident smile.

"An excellent question, sir. And the answer is simple. These ladies belong to *my* church. And as their pastor, I'm obligated by God to watch over and protect them. Yes, to lay my life down for them if that is what's required. And I guarantee you both, gentlemen, at my age I'm more than prepared to do just that. Now, as I've said already: depart from these ladies. *Now!*"

Anna held her breath, anticipating a violent reaction from Ackar and his friend.

To her surprise, Ackar remained calm and collected. "Oh, Pastor, of course, of course. My friend and I have no desire to disobey a command from God himself, whom I'm sure you feel you're speaking for. Come, Schmidt, we mustn't trouble these beautiful ladies any longer with our unwanted presence today."

After once again doffing his hat and bowing with an unctuous smile, Ackar made for the door with Schmidt just behind.

Ackar stopped and turned back to face Pastor Tiedeman and the women. "Fräulein Anna," he said with narrowed eyes, his voice taking on a much deeper and more threatening tone. "Remind your father I'll expect him to deliver on his back rent when I next see him. And ladies—all of you—*please* don't hesitate to call on us if ever in the future we can be of some service to you. Times are changing, and so perhaps should your misguided perceptions of us. We truly all need each other! Good day, my ladies and pastor." He and his sidekick left.

The three women rushed over to the old gentleman, who looked ready to collapse.

"Pastor," Frau Saller exclaimed, "we can't thank you enough for what you just did! And to think you spoke of my daughter and me as belonging to your church, even when you knew we're Catholic! Oh, sir, I'm overwhelmed by your generosity."

The pastor smiled and took the lady's hands in his own. "There are times when Christ's church must embrace its universal intent, especially when dealing with the likes of those two godless characters. It was my honor to stand for you. Thanks be to God that he brought me here exactly when he did. And now, ladies, I suggest we return to our original purposes in this store. The day grows short, and I don't want you returning home in the dark."

Anna and the other two women waited outside for Pastor Tiedeman to complete his purchases. After he came out with his partially filled bag slung over one shoulder, Anna accompanied him to the horse he'd ridden from his home. She took his free arm and looked tenderly at the man with a new sense of respect and admiration. "Pastor Tiedeman, thank you for the protection and love you extended to me and my friends today. I've never been so proud to belong to our church—or to have *you* as my pastor."

The elderly man said nothing, but Anna could tell he was deeply touched. Just before mounting his horse, he turned to her with an ironic smile and amused twinkle in his eye. "Anna, my dear girl, you see, even an 'old wagon wheel' like me can occasionally offer something besides gloomy sermons to those we love."

Anna flushed beet-red, knowing she and her friend Hilde had been among Pastor Tiedeman's worst critics in that regard. He had obviously picked up on their joking and gossip somewhere. She hoped he wouldn't hold it against her forever. *"Do not judge,"* she scolded herself, *"or you too will be judged."*

"Yes indeed, sir," she said as innocently as she could, "I always knew that."

"Oh, and Anna—I notice we don't see you in church on those evenings once every month when Pastor Erhart, our guest speaker from St. John's, delivers our sermon. I know it's difficult listening to less experienced preachers who haven't yet mastered the finer points. But I hope you'll consider coming on those evenings as well. After all, the Lord expects it. And if I might admit it . . . I, for one, very much miss having you there."

Anna caught her breath. Unwittingly, Pastor Tiedeman had just reminded her of her own adolescent foolishness. Really, it was all so silly. Staying away from church so she wouldn't have to confront her romantic feelings toward Peter? Feelings that had been lingering for more than three whole years?

As he rode off, Anna rejoined the Sallers. During the trek home, her mind drifted once again to her awkward encounter with Peter at the crossroads last week. She wondered how he was doing these days. Was his marriage to the beautiful Ursula Andersen working out well for him?

CHAPTER 14

Magdeburg
March 8, 1629

P eter groaned, his frustration building. Tonight's emergency joint meeting of the Magdeburg Cathedral Council and the city council was on the verge of chaos. The heated speeches, angry glares, and fierce mutterings revealed the obvious: hopes of city unity over how to deal with the emperor's new edict were fast dissolving.

Even the seating preferences of individual council members and their supporters reflected the growing partisan divide. Positioned along the right side of the long rectangular table in the center of the hall were the "radicals," led by the inimitable Pastor Spaignart of St. Ulrich and his assistant Konrad Fitcher, who demanded a hard-line stance against any and all compromise with the agents of Catholicism. Dominating the left side were the "imperialists," led by Reinhard Bake, senior pastor of Magdeburg Cathedral, who generally supported acceptance of the Catholic emperor's decrees and policies. At the foot of the table sat the "moderates," led by Dr. Weber and including Peter and Otto Gericke from St. John's—all firmly committed to treating each issue on its own merits.

To Peter's chagrin, the radicals were having no problem making their opinions known with the aid of their champion, the acting administrator Christian Wilhelm, who was seated at the head of the table along with the mayor. Together, the two shared official responsibility for setting the council's agenda and moderating discussions. But as always, Wilhelm's dominating presence and personal priorities took precedence.

"Gentlemen!" Wilhelm stood and pounded the table with his fist, his eyes distended with apoplectic fury. "I've heard quite enough of these tortured ramblings from the imperialists. We're wasting precious time. I demand that from here on we address the *only* non-trivial issue before us today: how to respond to the threat of Wallenstein."

Pastor Bake—chief spokesperson for the powerful imperialist lobby that included many of the city's wealthy patricians—didn't hesitate to object. "With all due respect, Herr Wilhelm, these supposedly 'trivial' issues we've been discussing have great bearing on the Wallenstein matter."

"Explain yourself, sir," Wilhelm retorted, slowly taking his seat again. "With Wallenstein's forces threatening us, our first priority should be planning this city's defensive strategy—fortifications, recruitment, weaponry placement, and the like—*not* how much to tax new applications for citizenship!"

Bake held his ground. "On the contrary, sir. Isn't it obvious to you what's happening? With the increasing threat from Wallenstein, we'll be deluged with applications for citizenship, not only from peasants in the immediately surrounding areas but also refugees from other towns in Wallenstein's path. The level that this council establishes for the citizenship fee will determine how much financial reserve we'll be able to offer Wallenstein as ransom for sparing the city."

Peter held his breath. Yesterday, he had told Dr. Weber about his meeting with Hans Mannheim and about Wallenstein being open to a bribe. Weber had expressed his own doubts but had nonetheless decided to mention it to Bake and other sympathetic council members as something to put forth at tonight's meeting. If nothing else, it would serve as a counterweight to more aggressive ideas by Wilhelm and the radical faction.

"*Ransom for sparing the city?*" Wilhelm shouted. "Have you and your cohorts already decided to sell out our glorious Magdeburg to preserve a dubious peace with the emperor and his forces? Where is your backbone? I won't stand for it! Why cave at the outset when we know we have adequate resources and battle know-how to effectively resist—at least until outside help from wisely chosen foreign alliances can arrive?"

Good, Peter thought. Wilhelm might not yet be ready for the ransom idea, but at least he'd just stated the underlying issue.

Bake pressed on. "Herr Wilhelm, we've all witnessed the result of overconfidence in foreign alliances and our own military prowess. We need only recall your unfortunate alliance with the Danes, resulting in the disaster at Dessau, to destroy any optimism along those lines."

Wilhelm sprang to his feet in a sputtering rage. "How dare you, a man never tested on the field of combat, attempt to insult my—"

"And as for your claim concerning Emperor Ferdinand's plan to subjugate Magdeburg, allow me to suggest that *you yourself* may be forcing his hand. You continue to provoke him by entering into yet another new alliance—this time with Sweden—despite the objections of the majority of our council. What else should we expect from him, given your own spirit of rebellion and noncompromise?"

Wilhelm sat back in his chair, temporarily silenced but steaming with rage.

A solitary figure among the agitated radical faction leaned back in his seat at the table, casting a bemused smile on the entire proceedings. *The one and only Pastor Spaignart*, Peter thought cynically. He was the ideal complement to Wilhelm for promoting the goals of the radical faction—Spaignart providing the divine vision and sanction for Wilhelm's soldierly resolve.

Spaignart raised his hand and immediately received Wilhelm's permission to speak. Rising slowly, he clasped his hands together below the large brass cross suspended by a chain around his neck. Exceptionally tall and thin with a pointed nose jutting from his craggy face, Spaignart fit perfectly Peter's notion of a self-appointed oracle of heavenly judgment and wrath. All eyes were now on him.

"If I may, Pastor Bake, allow me to briefly educate you and the others regarding the true motivation behind our *un*-Holy Roman emperor's recent actions. As you're no doubt aware, I've devoted much of my life to studying the history of the Catholic Church and the Protestant Reformation with respect to their impacts on our beloved city. I understand what drives this latest Catholic menace, and I know full well that of which I am about to speak. With your permission and that of the council, of course . . ."

Bake nodded reluctantly. Wilhelm displayed a smug smile, clearly pleased at the prospect of his opponents' imminent humbling. Peter shifted uncomfortably in his chair. He'd heard one too many of Spaignart's harangues on previous occasions.

Spaignart began quietly. "Gentlemen, many of you here either do not understand or are deliberately deceiving yourselves. Can you not see that Emperor Ferdinand has but one ultimate goal in mind with this demonic new edict? It has *very little* to do with its *claimed* intent, merely to 'restore lands legitimately belonging to the Catholic Church,' based on the Augsburg treaty. No, the truth is this: Ferdinand has issued this edict for his sole underlying purpose of spreading the Catholic Church's Counter-Reformation and his own Habsburg family's power throughout all German Protestant territories. He has no intention of allowing cities like Magdeburg to continue directing their own religious affairs. Make no mistake, gentlemen. This emperor will not stop harassing our city until he has successfully *obliterated* the practice of our beloved Lutheran faith, forcing every citizen's knee to bow and every tongue to confess that the pope is Lord!"

Spaignart paused, allowing his audience's suspense to build. His resonant voice then began to rise gradually in a mighty crescendo. "Fellow citizens, listen to me. I tell you the truth. The winds of this cursed war have shifted . . . in an unfavorable direction. The emperor's Edict of Restitution has changed everything. And the disunity, the disloyalty evident in this room must end tonight. Herr Wilhelm is absolutely correct in his judgment: there must be no ransom. No compromise. We must aggressively oppose Ferdinand and his lapdog Wallenstein with the help of wisely chosen alliances. We must prepare the military defenses of our city without delay. In short, my friends, we must do as the scriptures command us: 'Be on your guard; stand firm in the faith; be courageous; be strong.'" Spaignart pointed to the rafters. "Thus says the Lord, and thus say I!"

After a few seconds of stunned silence, Spaignart's assistant, Fitcher, shot out of his seat. "*Praise be to God!*"

At that, the entire radical faction rose with one accord to deliver thunderous applause, shouts of approval, and thanks to God. Most of the imperialist and moderate representatives sat with stony expressions, no doubt boiling with resentment at the harsh accusations leveled at them. To his surprise, however, Peter noticed a few nodding their heads and conferring with each other as if an entirely new and worthy perspective had been revealed. Wilhelm, of course, beamed with appreciation for the assistance provided by his favorite weapon, Pastor Spaignart.

Peter looked at Dr. Weber and Otto Gericke in consternation. It seemed that Spaignart had just pulled the rug from under Pastor Bake's ransom suggestion.

Weber allowed the noise and commotion to subside before politely raising his hand.

"Ah, my good friend Dr. Weber," Wilhelm said with a triumphant grin. "You've been strangely quiet during our proceedings so far. I know we're all looking forward, as always, to hearing your moderate, middle-of-the-road views on our best way forward. Please, by all means proceed."

Weber stood and bowed in Spaignart's direction. "On the one hand, Pastor Spaignart, I know all of us here can appreciate the motivation for strong defensive works. On the other hand, I'm not so sure that rushing headlong into a massive, military building project is the very first thing to undertake."

"*Good God, man!*" Wilhelm exploded. "Must you *always* straddle the fence when you speak? Does it not eventually cause discomfort to your intimate body parts? State your point."

Some in the radical faction erupted with uncontained laughter. But the vast majority of council members grimaced at this coarse insult to Dr. Weber, whose deep intelligence and graceful wit were highly esteemed by practically everyone present.

Weber continued on in a calm, measured tone. "My point, Herr Wilhelm, is this: building up our defensive works will require a huge expenditure—far more than our current reserves will allow. It's irresponsible to launch into such an effort before we've properly counted the cost and considered the best ways to offset it. We should delay the defense works construction until we've created a plan that can adequately finance it, very possibly through raising the citizenship tax such as Pastor Bake has proposed."

Weber sat down to strong, sustained applause from the imperialist and moderate factions. Bake's broad smile and nod conveyed his deep appreciation.

"So: more discussion, more delay," Wilhelm grumbled. "More time for Wallenstein to prepare his onslaught and less time for our city to prepare our resistance. Honestly, Weber, I'd hoped you would have something more creative to suggest." Wilhelm suddenly sat up straight in his chair. "But I see that our newest council member, Peter Erhart, is with you today. Perhaps Pastor Erhart could offer us his enlightened views on our way forward."

Peter felt like dropping through the floor. He certainly had plenty of opinions on the issue, but in no way had he prepared to share them with so eminent a gathering.

Wide-eyed with uncertainty, he turned to his mentor. Weber merely stared back and mouthed the words: *Do not doubt.* Otto's reassuring smile and nod provided the final boost needed.

Peter drew a deep breath and rose from his chair. "What I've observed and actually find disturbing, Herr Wilhelm, is that a number of proposals has been offered for dealing with Wallenstein's approach. And yet, not once have I heard anyone on this council mention what I consider to be our greatest mutual threat."

"What threat is that, Pastor?" Wilhelm asked, his impatience already evident.

"Our greatest threat, sir, is the obvious lack of *spiritual* unity that is so sadly evident in this room tonight. It's one thing to point out and denounce our lack of *political* unity, as Pastor Spaignart has so effectively conveyed. But it's another thing altogether to work toward achieving the kind of unity that will most please God as we strive to address the physical threat facing us."

Wilhelm rolled his eyes. "God save us all. How much more naïve, wishful thinking from St. John's must we bear tonight?" He stared at Peter, his face twisted in a massive scowl. "And just *how* would you propose we go about increasing our *spiritual* unity, young man?"

Peter had yet to think through his idea, but somehow the words came of their own accord. "Herr Wilhelm, a rote prayer to open the proceedings of this assembly—as was done today like always—is fine. But isn't it possible to be more diligent in seeking the Lord's help in determining our course of action? Wouldn't it be possible for you, along with the mayor and the key members of each faction represented here today, to convene privately together on a more frequent basis? To devote that time to deeper, *mutual* study of the Scriptures, to spiritual encouragement and intense prayer? Wouldn't there be a greater chance that God could then grace this body with the kind of unified response to Wallenstein that I believe we're all seeking? What I'm suggesting, in my humble view, should take priority over the drawing up of plans and the taking of specific actions."

Peter took his seat, light-headed with relief at having made his point without faltering.

This time, virtually the entire assembly rose in applause and shouts of agreement. Wilhelm remained seated, glancing furtively at Spaignart, who refused to join in the general acclaim. Peter thought he detected a slight shake of the pastor's head in response to Wilhelm's look.

After the noise subsided, Wilhelm responded. "Well said, Pastor. Perhaps in the next few days we can look into an arrangement of the sort you suggest. But our time today is drawing to a close. And, as usual, it seems we'll have to defer a final decision on our response to Wallenstein until someone can suggest a concrete, mutually agreeable way forward from here."

Otto spoke up. "Herr Wilhelm, if you and the council will allow it, I'd be pleased to volunteer my services to work with others in this city over the next week to produce a compromise solution. We can present it for a final discussion and vote at our next meeting."

Wilhelm stood up and grinned broadly. "Otto, as usual you've made my official life easier. That's an eminently worthy suggestion. I move that we take a vote here and now on whether to adopt Herr Gericke's proposal."

After discussion of a few minor points of procedure, the vote was taken and the result unanimous in favor of adopting. The grateful administrator declared the proceedings closed.

On the way out, Peter was besieged by council members expressing their appreciation for his short but bold speech. Many expressed their sincere hope that Wilhelm would follow through on his recommendation.

The last man to approach him was Konrad Fitcher. It was amazing, Peter thought, how closely Fitcher's facial features and mannerisms resembled those of his supervisor and senior pastor, Spaignart—they could easily be mistaken as father and son.

"You spoke eloquently tonight, Pastor Erhart. Your sentiments were obviously appreciated by some. But I must caution you on one thing. If you desire to succeed in your ministry in this city, *never again* say or do anything that compromises the orthodox principles of our Lutheran faith that have been handed down to us by our forefathers. Especially the principle that it is only the truth of God's Word as unambiguously written in scripture—*not* your 'mutual study and prayer sessions' or anything else—that can be allowed to dictate our decisions." Without waiting for a response, Fitcher turned and walked away.

Peter stood in simmering silence. How dare Fitcher—barely two years older than him and nearly as new to the council—address him like an ill-intended heretic who had no real understanding or respect for the great Protestant doctrine of *sola Scriptura*?

Dr. Weber had overheard the exchange. He strolled over and clapped Peter on the shoulder. "What Fitcher meant, Peter, was: 'Don't ever interfere or say anything to outshine my senior pastor's sermons!' Don't let that man keep you from pursuing your clearly expressed and God-honoring recommendation."

Peter sighed. "If only God would *always* make my recommendations and words as clear as he did tonight, it would be so much—"

"He'll make them clear when they need to be made clear," Weber interrupted. "Trust me, Peter. As Wallenstein draws closer, you'll get more than enough practice in making your recommendations and words clear."

CHAPTER 15

Count von Wallenstein's imperial army headquarters
August 18, 1629

(Five months later)

"Only five more minutes now, sirs!" the coach driver yelled above the clomping hooves of the escorts' horses.

Really, Peter groused, staring blankly out the coach window. Did it take *fifty* of Count von Wallenstein's personal bodyguards to ensure the safe arrival of only *two* Magdeburg city councilors at his headquarters camp west of the city? No doubt, Wallenstein wanted to create a certain impression for his special visitors.

Otto Gericke's friendly pat on the knee roused Peter from his trance-like state. "See anything interesting out there, my friend?" he inquired with a chuckle.

Peter turned to his co-rider seated on the small bench next to him. He was glad to see Otto looking so relaxed. At least one of them needed to convey an air of self-assurance in their upcoming encounter with the supreme commander of the Catholic Imperial Army.

Peter smiled tepidly, offering only a shrug. What else, at this point, was there left to say? They'd already rehearsed what they planned to communicate to Wallenstein. Now it was in God's hands.

The count and his army had arrived in the Magdeburg vicinity in April to enforce the emperor's new edict. The city council had refused to accept the terms offered. In response, Wallenstein had imposed a severe economic blockade on the city and surrounding area over the past four months. Thankfully, from what Peter had been told, the situation for the countryside peasants had not been nearly as bad as originally feared—Wallenstein had apparently ordered his men to refrain from mistreating them.

But within the city itself, it was a different story.

Magdeburg's merchants were going broke, and its common citizens were going hungry. The city council was still resisting, and Wallenstein was growing impatient. Under intense pressure from Emperor Ferdinand to "humble that blasphemous haven of Lutheran pride once and for all," he was threatening to pull the trigger on Magdeburg any day now.

Everyone knew it would take a superlative diplomatic effort to convince Wallenstein to desist from launching an all-out siege and sack of the city with his formidable force. The council had selected Otto Gericke as its civic representative. No one in Magdeburg was more gifted with the raw intelligence, verbal proficiency, and diplomatic skills needed to impress the notoriously arrogant count. The decision had been made much easier due to Wilhelm's absence. He was in Sweden, trying yet again to solicit foreign support.

Peter's selection as the clerical representative, on the other hand, had come as a shock to him. True, the elimination of potential candidates like Bake and especially Spaignart had been predictable, since both men had reputations for expressing far too bluntly their vehement opinions. Also, Dr. Weber's declining health had precluded his own participation. Still, Peter was astonished that his own short speech at the March city council meeting was remembered with such fondness and respect that the council had voted to select *him*. Spaignart had been the only dissenter, vowing that "the Lord's vengeance shall fall upon any vacillating negotiators who cave to Wallenstein's demands."

"Just around the bend, sirs!" the driver called. "Almost there!"

Peter's stomach churned. His mouth had gone bone-dry. Otto appeared unfazed. *I should be the more relaxed one,* Peter chided himself. Gericke was the one holding the cards for this encounter.

The coach lurched to a stop in the middle of an open field. After a long pause, one of the camp sentries opened the door.

Peter and Otto stepped out into the sunshine. It was not a comforting first impression. The escorts had dismounted and stationed themselves with their long pikes in parade-rest position along both sides of the rock-strewn path leading from the coach to a large circular tent about fifty yards away. Dozens of off-duty soldiers from the countless smaller tents surrounding the larger one were now swarming toward the path, jeering and shouting unsavory threats at Peter and Otto.

"Pay us well, Luther-boys. You better pay us well!"

"Yeah, or we'll be enjoying the insides of your nice city houses before long!"

"And enjoying your pretty wives and daughters too, you scum!"

"Holy Mary, look at those two idiots! *These* are the proud city's representatives?"

Peter's legs nearly buckled under him. This gauntlet had clearly been orchestrated ahead of time. Mercifully, the end of the path was reached a few feet in front of the large tent's entrance. The escorts closed ranks in a double line behind Peter and Otto.

The camp sentry turned to face them. "You will wait here until Count von Wallenstein is ready to receive you."

"Sir," Otto said, his face red with indignation, "would it be possible for us lowly vassals to have a cool drink of water to soothe our parched tongues?"

The sentry looked at him with obvious contempt. "You'll be given ample refreshment once you're in the count's presence. Until then, I suggest you do your best to contain your physical urges."

Peter glanced at Otto. This was a far worse reception than anything he had imagined. Perhaps Spaignart's doom-filled predictions concerning the Catholic army's nature and intentions had not been so far off the mark, after all.

They waited under the blazing sun. Peter breathed a sigh of relief when the large tent's flap opened at last. An immaculately uniformed lieutenant smiled and beckoned Peter and Otto to step inside.

The blast of cooler air that greeted them from the shaded interior was itself a blessed relief. But it was the wondrous sight in front of him that lifted Peter's spirit for the first time this morning. In the middle of the space was a six-foot-long table, spread with a sumptuous banquet of meats, cheeses, vegetables, breads, and small cakes, accompanied by a decorative flask of wine and a large pitcher of beer.

The lieutenant indicated for Peter and Otto to take their seats on two plain wooden stools that faced the near side of the table. Facing them on the other side was an unoccupied, plushly cushioned armchair flanked on each side by two only slightly less ornate wooden chairs. Peter could already see from the arrangement how the protocol for this meeting had been rigged in Wallenstein's favor.

"Herr Gericke and Pastor Erhart," the lieutenant announced, "Count von Wallenstein welcomes you both. He requests that you take refreshment from the generous bounty that he is pleased to offer you today. The count and his advisors will be joining you after you've dined and refreshed yourselves. He's looking forward to a fruitful discussion today."

Peter was about to reach for the pitcher of beer but stopped himself just in time after sensing Otto's hesitation.

"Lieutenant," Otto protested, "we humble representatives of the Magdeburg city council would not dream of partaking of this feast without the count's presence."

"Herr Gericke, the count is attending to some important business," the lieutenant replied with obvious surprise and annoyance. "He'll join you when he's ready."

"Then we shall wait for him," Otto said. "We desire no special accommodation."

The lieutenant stared at him coldly. "Suit yourselves." He spun around and briskly exited the tent.

Within seconds, two other attendants appeared and removed the tempting board of food and drink from the table.

Peter stared bleakly at his friend.

"Trust me, Peter," Otto whispered. "This is all a big show designed to confuse and soften us up. Stay focused, and don't act intimidated. Someone's probably watching us through some hole in the rear wall even now."

Peter nodded and did his best to appear relaxed. He tried to swallow, but his dry mouth and throat made it nearly impossible. How long was this farce going to last?

At least another ten minutes passed before the rear tent flap was opened and held aside for Count Albrecht von Wallenstein and four men Peter guessed were his senior advisors.

Peter and Otto stood and bowed.

Wallenstein took his seat in the plush chair, after which his advisors seated themselves on either side. The count's appearance matched the portraits Peter had seen: tall and well-built, thin face with high forehead, neatly cut short hair, mustache and pointed goatee.

To Peter's great relief, an attendant placed three tall mugs of watery beer in the center of the table.

Wallenstein hoisted one of the mugs and proposed a toast. "Councilors of Magdeburg: to your city's survival. And to that end, may our discussions here today be short and productive."

Peter and Otto, too thirsty to do otherwise, lifted their mugs in acknowledgment before proceeding to drain them to the last drop.

Wallenstein waited for them to finish, peering at them with an amused smile. "So, councilors, I trust you've been treated well by my people?"

Otto smiled back. "Oh, quite definitely, sir. The escort you provided was very kind to prevent the rest of your men from lynching us on our way to your tent. You have our deepest appreciation for that, I can assure you."

Wallenstein frowned and leaned forward. "I only wish to know one thing from you both today, Herr Gericke. Give me one good reason why I should refrain from leveling your city, starting tomorrow morning.

My patience is at an end."

"I believe we can put forth at least two good reasons, Your Excellency," Otto said.

"Then speak, man," Wallenstein growled.

Otto folded his hands in his lap. His voice was calm and measured. "First, sir, we believe it may not be in your own best interests to 'level' us."

The count sat back in his chair, his right eyebrow cocked in suspicion. "Oh? And how would *you* possibly know what constitutes *my* best interests?"

Peter tensed. This was the crucial first step. If Wallenstein didn't buy what Otto was about to say, there was little hope he'd accept anything else.

"Sir," Otto replied, "our council is well aware of the amazing string of successes you've achieved on the battlefield over the past five years. It's also known to us that there's only one obstacle now that prevents you from realizing that personal goal you've long sought on behalf of the emperor: total and complete control of all maritime trade in the Baltic Sea."

Wallenstein stiffened, his eyes narrowing. He said nothing for a moment and then turned to speak quietly with his advisor on his immediate right.

Peter worried that Otto might have spoken too boldly for the count's taste.

"And what does your wise council perceive that obstacle to be, Herr Gericke?" Wallenstein asked. "How would they know? Have they been consulting the stars lately?"

"Not the stars, sir," Otto said. "Only our sister cities along the north German coast, which, together with Magdeburg, constitute the Hanseatic League. Think of it. The league may no longer enjoy the economic clout it had in centuries past. But our sister cities still have the financial means and naval ships to help the emperor secure Baltic trade routes against further damaging encroachments by the Scandinavians or the Dutch. Now if, in return, the emperor could but guarantee the league's cities some special Baltic trading privileges, then everyone would benefit! But, sir, we ask you: how could you possibly expect to secure the league's approval for such a wonderful arrangement should you decide to destroy Magdeburg, one of its most beloved and respected member cities?"

Brilliant, Otto! Peter wanted to jump up and pound his friend on the back. The emperor's wish to see the new edict enforced in Magdeburg was of little concern to Wallenstein. The notoriously self-serving count would be far more interested in gaining total control of the Baltic trade routes.

Peter held his breath as the count, having apparently made up his mind about something after a whispered conversation with his advisors, turned back to them. His face appeared more relaxed.

"Your argument makes sense, Herr Gericke. But, I must remind you, Emperor Ferdinand is furious over your city's refusal to accept the edict. How could I possibly risk his disappointment, should I fail to enforce this?"

Otto reached into his doublet pocket. He pulled out a rolled sheet of parchment and handed it to the commander. "Perhaps, Count, *this* will serve to make your risk worthwhile."

The count untied the binding string, unrolled the document, and perused it.

"One hundred fifty thousand reichsthaler?" the count sneered. "Your council considers *this* a sufficient amount for convincing me to withdraw my forces and risk incurring the emperor's wrath?"

Peter looked sharply at Otto. That was only *half* the amount that the city council, after months of hand-wringing, had finally approved for this purpose. Why was Otto holding back?

Wallenstein threw it down on the table. His face had turned florid. "You'll need to do better than this, Gericke."

Otto revealed no sign of surprise or dismay. "It's the best we can offer, Count. Your blockade has indeed hurt. Our city merchants are virtually broke, and our coffers nearly empty."

Wallenstein rose to his feet. "Don't blame me for your city's plight, Gericke. If this is all you have to offer, prepare to accept the consequences."

"Sir," Otto shot back, "I fear you've underestimated your own consequences, should you attempt to force your way into our city and fail to take it."

"How could I possibly fail to take it? I have thirty thousand soldiers at my disposal."

"Because, sir, as Pastor Erhart here will surely confirm, the resistance you can expect to encounter from our civilian populace will be even more formidable than that of Stralsund, which your army failed to take last year."

Peter, despite his shock at suddenly being drawn into the dialogue, took the hint from Otto. "It's true, Count. The zeal of our citizens for the preservation of our Lutheran heritage and the right to govern ourselves has been stirred to a fever pitch by this whole affair. They know they've successfully resisted Catholic onslaughts in the past, and they believe God will help them to do so again. I can guarantee, sir, the struggle you would face in Magdeburg would make Stralsund seem like a pleasant outing in the woods."

It was a pathetic attempt at a bluff—nothing but ludicrous bluster of the kind that someone like Pastor Spaignart would deliver. With no outside support like Stralsund had received from the Swedes, there was simply no way that Magdeburg would be able to withstand an all-out Wallenstein push into the city. Peter felt like sinking through the floor.

The count plucked the ransom document from the table, turned to his advisors, and signaled for a private huddle together in the adjoining room. "Wait here," he commanded.

"Otto, *what* were you thinking?" Peter hissed. "That was only *half* the ransom amount that we were authorized to offer!"

Otto grinned and surreptitiously opened his doublet to reveal the top of another rolled parchment poking out from the inside pocket. "And here's the other half . . . if we still need to offer it!"

Peter was stunned. Otto Gericke, the master negotiator, had deliberately refrained from playing the city's last card: the other half of the ransom. It was a significant sum of money. If it didn't have to be forfeited, the city would benefit greatly.

Only five minutes passed before one of Wallenstein's advisors returned to the room and announced the count's decision. "His Excellency wishes to inform the Magdeburg city council representatives that he has decided to *accept* their ransom offer. In return, he agrees to end the blockade and to withdraw his forces from the immediate region. He expresses his regards to all the cities of the Hanseatic League, of which Magdeburg is a member, and hopes they will look kindly upon his generous action in this matter." The advisor offered what appeared to be a forced smile. "That is all, gentlemen. You are dismissed. Your coach and escort await you."

The advisor left them staring wide-eyed at each other. Their mission had succeeded. The blockade was over! Wallenstein's force would be leaving. Magdeburg's survival had been bought at a relatively small price.

"Well, my friend," Peter exclaimed, "we can plan on attending a huge celebration in our beloved city tonight!" It was a pleasant thought. He could already imagine himself lifting a toast in spirit to his good friend Hans Mannheim, the original source of the ransom idea.

Otto smiled weakly. "Yes, celebration's in order tonight. But don't get too comfortable, Peter. Magdeburg is too big a prize for the emperor to just forget about. They'll be back. It's just a question of when."

In the adjoining room of the headquarters tent, Major Hans Mannheim saluted and stepped forward to receive the grateful hand of Count von Wallenstein. It was a wonderful feeling. All the time and effort he'd devoted five months ago to that ridiculous Magdeburg spying mission had actually paid off. Thanks to the idea for the bribe that Hans had planted with Peter, plus the information he'd uncovered the next evening by spying on the city council meeting, Wallenstein's negotiations with the city councilors had turned out exactly the way the count had hoped.

"I must say, Mannheim," the count gushed, "I'm glad Count Tilly sent you here in time to support this negotiation. Your crucial advice this morning concerning the likely positions that would be taken by Gericke and Erhart was invaluable. I would have overreacted without it—insisted on a ransom they could never afford and invaded the city without heeding the warnings about the league's reaction or the citizens' willingness to put up a fight. As it is, we've obtained some reasonably good money, avoided a bloodbath, and preserved our options for future dominance of the Baltic trade."

"It's my pleasure to have been of useful service to you, Count," Hans replied with a broad grin. "I know Count Tilly expected nothing less of me, and I'm eager to report back to him that you appear satisfied."

Wallenstein laughed. "'Satisfied' is putting it mildly, Mannheim. I'll inform Tilly myself that I was *delighted* with your help, as I'm sure Emperor Ferdinand will be also, as soon as he hears the news."

"Thank you, sir." Hans gulped. He was not so sure how pleased the emperor would actually be once he got word. Even if Wallenstein were to faithfully forward all of the ransom received to the imperial coffers in Vienna, it seemed unlikely that the emperor would be satisfied with his supreme commander's failure to achieve full subjection of the city as he had originally demanded. Clearly, Wallenstein's personal priorities were not identical to the emperor's.

"Well now, Mannheim, it's time for you to be on your way back to Tilly's headquarters," the count concluded. "Please send him my regards, and best wishes to you for future battlefield success."

On his way out of the headquarters tent, Hans counted his blessings. No more need to keep running back and forth as a liaison between Wallenstein and Tilly. No more worry that the count might think his service had been inadequate or even irrelevant. And, thankfully, no more concern that Wallenstein's army would obliterate the city where Hans's Good Samaritan Peter Erhart lived—very possibly along with Peter himself.

Yes, this never-ending war's winds have shifted yet again, thought Hans. Magdeburg had managed to avoid what almost certainly would have been a fatal strike. For Peter's sake, he was glad. But the long-term prospect? That was another matter altogether. Despite Wallenstein's personal decision to call off the siege, Hans knew that Emperor Ferdinand's tolerant dealings with the city had become a thing of the past. Sooner or later, his patience would completely run out. And once that happened, the very survival of Magdeburg and its people would be at stake.

Hans pushed the disquieting idea out of his mind. It was time to celebrate.

At last, this city-spying nonsense is over! It was furlough time—to be enjoyed in the loving arms of Marie. Then back to the life of a highly respected, hard-fighting cavalry officer for Count Tilly.

PART II

Approaching Storm

CHAPTER 16

Magdeburg
October 5, 1630

(Fourteen months later)

T he distant sound of drums, horns, and clanging cymbals was faint but growing stronger.

"Peter, what *is* that?" Ursula asked, clearly annoyed that something might interrupt one of her rare shopping expeditions to the city's bustling center square.

Peter knew his wife valued these outings, which were conducted with the children safely at home and under the care of the nursemaid. "It's nothing, dear. Probably just drunken revelers out celebrating a wedding."

Ursula rolled her eyes and shook her head before resuming her examination of linen fabric on the tailor's display shelf. "It's a mystery to me, Pastor, why so many people in this city seem to carouse and drink themselves silly these days. You'd think they would be paying more heed to the possibility of the Lord's return at any moment."

Peter, believing that no one was watching, grasped his wife's waist from behind and leaned over to kiss her on the cheek. "I'm glad to hear my sermons on that subject have at least been taken seriously by you, beautiful lady."

"Well, that may be, but when I keep thinking how close our whole city came to disaster just months ago, I . . ." Ursula's voice trailed off, overtaken by shouting from the street just outside the store.

"*He's done it!* At long last! Wilhelm has secured our city's salvation! Look! He's coming this way!"

Peter whirled to face the street. Outside the door, people were running every which way, seemingly confused as to the administrator's whereabouts. He paid his respects to the tailor, grabbed Ursula's arm, and hurried outside.

Down the street, a group of burly men in strange clothing were erecting a wooden platform. Citizens tried to press close to the platform's edge, pushing and shoving each other to obtain the best viewing positions. An even larger mob streamed toward a row of flags approaching from the opposite direction. All around, street vendors continued to hawk their foods and wares.

"Look out, you dimwitted commoners!" cried one drunken man who was staggering along while sloshing a full mug of beer in one hand and holding a huge dripping leg of mutton in the other. It was difficult to hear him above the increasing din of drums and various instruments. "Wilhelm's done it!" the man shouted. "He's brought the Swedes back with 'im. Make way, make way!"

Peter peered down the street toward the flags, hardly believing his own eyes and ears. The much-ridiculed rumor had apparently proven true. After months of travel and effort, the administrator had finally succeeded in securing military support for Magdeburg from Sweden's King Gustavus Adolphus, a devout Lutheran. And having bullied the council into restoring his full official powers last July, Wilhelm was obviously now taking advantage by orchestrating some type of gaudy city parade to celebrate his latest grand accomplishment.

Peter strained on tiptoe to see over the heads of the crowd. He could barely make out the heads and shoulders of multiple columns of soldiers dressed in an unfamiliar style of uniform. Some of the soldiers marched on foot and carried long pikes in an upright position, resting against their shoulders. Others were on horseback. At the head of the column and just behind the row of flag-bearers rode two men who were clearly the focus of the mob's attention. Peter was quite familiar with one of them.

"Ursula, let's move toward the platform. That's where he's going to make his speech."

"*Who* will be making his speech, Peter?"

"Christian Wilhelm, dear. Who else?"

The sight of Pastor Spaignart and Konrad Fitcher mounting the platform sent a shiver down Peter's spine. He put his arm around Ursula's shoulders and drew her closer to his side.

Spaignart walked deliberately to the front of the stage. He paused to survey the crowd as Fitcher stood next to him, clutching a large Bible against his chest. As he swept his gaze slowly from left to right, his eyes discovered and locked onto Peter's. He smiled condescendingly and nodded before returning his attention to several soldiers in the advance guard who were surging toward the platform, politely pushing any intervening citizens aside.

"Clear a path! Clear a path, please! Step aside, sir! My lady, please! Clear a path to the platform for your returning administrator!"

At least, Peter thought, *these strangely dressed soldiers appear disciplined and well-intentioned.* If they were indeed Swedish, this would all bode well for the city's future.

After a narrow pathway had been formed down the street's center, the pastor raised his arms.

The drumming and horn-blowing ceased, and a stark silence fell over the crowd.

"Citizens of Magdeburg," Spaignart bellowed, "it's been a long and trying wait! But God has rewarded you. Our beloved Lutheran administrator—who you know has worked feverishly for years to secure this city's survival in the face of the Catholic menace—now brings us great tidings. Nay, not just that. He brings us tangible aid of the kind that will ensure our security for decades to come. But allow me not to steal his glory in telling you the story. Citizens, I present to you: *Christian Wilhelm*. Let us all welcome him with praises and thanksgiving!"

Tumultuous shouts of joy erupted as the drumming and horn-blowing resumed. All eyes turned toward the two men riding slowly together through the cleared space toward the platform. Wilhelm grinned and waved his hat vigorously to the crowd. He appeared gratified—even somewhat surprised—at the enthusiastic reception. The identity of the second man remained a mystery. But from his military garb, erect posture, and stern countenance, Peter suspected he had some important role in connection with all the strangely dressed soldiers who were following just behind.

At the platform, Wilhelm and the other man dismounted and climbed the side steps. The military man stood deferentially to the side as Wilhelm walked to the front to receive the embraces of Spaignart and Fitcher. The crowd's cheers grew louder and continued unabated as the three men consulted briefly with each other.

Wilhelm glanced in Peter's direction with what appeared to be a sneer.

"Pastor, why do they keep looking your way?" Ursula asked in a concerned tone.

Peter shook his head. "God only knows. I should be the least of their concerns today."

Wilhelm raised his hand, and the crowd quieted. "My friends. You'll recall that over a year ago, I left my beloved city to secure its long-term future in the face of increasing threats from Emperor Ferdinand and his Catholic army. Sadly, there were some on the city council who mocked my efforts at obtaining foreign aid, who tried to impose ridiculous delaying tactics. Yes, it's true. And some of them are standing here in this assembly even today, though I shall refrain from pointing them out."

Wilhelm stared directly at Peter as a loud chorus of boos rose from the audience. Necks craned to see who the administrator was looking at.

Peter felt the blood rising to his face as Ursula gripped his arm with both hands.

"Despite their hindrances, my friends," Wilhelm continued, grinning broadly now, "a marvelous result has been achieved. As you all know, four months ago the great Swedish king, Gustavus Adolphus, disgusted by the Catholic emperor's demonic Edict of Restitution, finally decided to enter the war on the side of us German Protestants. In July, he landed a formidable fighting force along our Baltic coast. And, since then, the king has greatly solidified that force's foothold to the point where they are now capable of protecting Magdeburg, should the Catholics ever again threaten our city!"

Raucous cheers again erupted from the crowd as the mood continued to grow more upbeat—aided, Peter noticed, by small jugs of brew that several men with canteen wagons were freely distributing to the crowd. After a few moments, the din subsided once again.

"But that's not the best of it, fellow citizens." Wilhelm's voice had grown strangely quiet, almost reverential.

The crowd strained to hear.

"After much diligent effort, your faithful administrator was able to convince the Swedish king that Magdeburg would be a useful ally in the king's future military operations in Germany." Wilhelm paused to let his words sink in before crescendoing to a full-throated roar. "And as a result, he agreed to send us an advance contingent of two hundred of Sweden's best soldiers and cavalrymen! Yes, you see them here before you today. As you look upon them, I think you will have to agree with me: no Catholic army commander will ever again be able to force this magnificent city to grovel at his stinking feet!"

The crowd responded with tumultuous whoops, shouts, backslapping, and hugs for each other and for any Swedish soldiers who happened to be nearby.

"Praise be to God!"

"Hurrah, Wilhelm! Hurrah! The Lord bless you!"

Peter was mystified. *Two hundred Swedes?* Even given the highly reputed Swedish military discipline and fighting spirit, that seemed like a pitifully small addition to the current city militia force of fewer than twenty-two hundred regular soldiers. Hadn't Wallenstein previously threatened the city with nearly *thirty thousand* Catholic soldiers? What was Wilhelm thinking?

The accolades continued for several moments before Wilhelm raised his arm once again. "And now, my fellow citizens, it is my distinct privilege to introduce to you the noble man personally designated by King Adolphus to direct this superb fighting force along with our own city's militia: Colonel Dietrich von Falkenberg!"

The military man who had humbly stood at the side of the platform stepped forward. This man projected something entirely different from the other three. No exaggerated, grandiose gestures. No mocking smile or other hints of deviousness. Only resolute determination and strength. He declined Wilhelm's invitation to speak, but blew a kiss to the crowd and raised both arms in greeting and salutation.

The administrator resumed his speech. "Well, my friends, this has indeed been quite a day to celebrate. And with that in mind, I suppose we shouldn't let the sun go down before paying tribute to the men most responsible for our city's survival of the blockade. Indeed, I see one of those men standing among you today—Assistant Pastor Peter Erhart of St. John's Lutheran Church."

Peter smiled sheepishly and bowed in acknowledgment of the strong round of applause directed his way.

"Pastor Erhart," Wilhelm called, addressing him directly with an arch smile, "perhaps you can now share with all of us the secret that allowed you and my good friend Otto Gericke to succeed in your negotiations with Wallenstein."

All eyes turned toward Peter.

"Secret, sir?"

"Oh, yes, the secret that allowed the two of you to succeed, where other councilors would surely have failed had they been sent instead."

Peter struggled to discern Wilhelm's real intent behind this strange challenge. He had to say *something* in response. "The secret, sir, is what everyone here has free access to at any time: diligent prayer to God and the humility to consult with other believers in discerning God's will for our decisions. That's exactly what Otto and I did in working with the city council to prepare for the negotiations."

The polite smattering of applause and nodding of many heads jolted Pastor Spaignart into action. He grabbed the Bible from Fitcher's hands and stepped forward.

The crowd once again grew silent.

"That's all well and good, Pastor Erhart," Spaignart said, smiling and nodding in derision. "But I'd like to remind you and everyone else here that it's *not* diligent prayer or consultation with other believers that must reign supreme. It is only God's Word—the Holy Bible—that must reign supreme in making decisions for our city and our personal lives. Everything else, by comparison, is useless chaff." He raised the tome high above his head with both hands. "Never forget: *sola Scriptura!*"

The crowd's enthusiasm could no longer be contained.

"Yes, *sola Scriptura!*"

"The Holy Bible alone! It will save us from the devil's schemes!"

"And from the Catholic antichrists!"

"The Lord bless you, Pastor Spaignart. May God protect you, Herr Wilhelm!"

"Long live Magdeburg!"

Simmering with indignation, Peter took Ursula by the arm and carefully led the way through the boisterous crowd. Even though Spaignart's doctrine was sound, his exploitation of that doctrine for his own political power play was obvious. Just before turning the corner at the end of the street, he looked back at the platform. Wilhelm, Spaignart, Fitcher, and Falkenberg stood with arms raised high and hands clasped together in unity.

CHAPTER 17

Countryside west of Magdeburg
October 12, 1630

Anna opened the shutters to greet the day. It was sunny—quite a change from the chilly overcast of the past few days.

"Liesa, get up! We need to help Mutti get breakfast ready. She and Vati want to leave early while it's still cool."

Anna was feeling especially lighthearted today. The Ritter family would be making the seven-mile trek to the annual fair in the town of Hohenstadt. The plan was to meet up with Frau Saller and Barbara along the way.

Anna could hardly believe how much the mood had brightened in the Ritter household over the past year and a half. Her father had recovered far better than expected from the incident at the tavern with Dietrich Ackar and his crony. He'd successfully performed the temporary second job for Herr Lang, earning the extra income needed to pay off the back rent owed to Baron von Leitzge. Even Ackar had seemed surprised and reasonably satisfied when he'd come to collect the money. On top of that, her father had managed to stop his excessive drinking and was showing a new spryness in his daily fieldwork. It was clear to Anna that he was intent on restoring his integrity, both with his family and with his landlord. No longer was he dwelling on his mistreatment at the hands of Ackar.

There was just one little problem. Anna's mother had only yesterday confided that Vati would be unable to make the rent payment due on the first of November. It wasn't his fault. As he'd explained just two days ago to Ackar at the tavern, some issue with Schwarz's city business dealings was preventing him from paying all his workers this month. Ackar had scolded Vati but in the end had agreed to wait until the first of December—so long as Vati promised to make the double payment plus interest. Her father had left the meeting greatly relieved, confident that everything would work out.

Liesa sat up, yawned, and wiped the sleep from her eyes. "Anni, can we enter more than one goose today?" The upcoming goose race at the fair was all Liesa had been able to think about for the past week.

"No, princess." Anna laughed. "You're only allowed to enter one goose. So you'll have to pick the one that has the best chance. Now, hurry up. We have to help Mutti."

Liesa dressed quickly and bounded down the stairs, followed by Anna.

"Mutti, can I have a piece of bread?" Liesa asked.

"No, child. Not yet. Wait until your father comes down and we're all seated at the table."

Frieda's stern voice belied her sunny countenance. Anna had not seen her mother look so calm and happy—or be so productive—in weeks. She had already finished cooking breakfast and was darning some socks for her husband.

"Now, you and Anna go fetch me a little more milk from Irmina," Frieda said.

"Oh, Mutti, really?" Anna loved Irmina, the family cow, but the beast always resisted the best efforts to draw her milk this early in the day.

"Hush, young lady. You know what happened to the Israelites who complained in the desert. Now do as you're told."

"Come on, Liesa," Anna said.

She opened the latch on the door and held it open for Liesa, and the two walked through it into the adjoining animal pen.

"Liesi, why don't you go into the geese's stall and make your choice for the race, while I get Irmina set up outside?" Anna had learned long ago that the cow never wanted to perform her duty while confined to the pen.

After putting the halter on Irmina and picking up an empty bucket, Anna led the cow toward the rear door. She couldn't help but smile as she passed the last stall, which contained an untidy mass of gardening tools and rusty old weapons that her father had retained from his soldiering days. "Vati's Little Armory," as Anna's mother often called it.

Mutti never could see the point in preserving such an exotic collection of items useful only on the battlefield, especially in their current state of disrepair. Vati, of course, saw them differently. They were sentimental keepsakes, for one thing. Protection against home invasion, for another. Some of the weapons, like the assortment of pistols and different-sized pikes and swords, might someday prove helpful.

Anna laughed to herself as she recalled the time about a year ago when her father had decided to give her an unexpected lesson in the art of pike thrusting. One day, while her mother and sister had been away visiting the Schiffers, he'd set up a simple braced frame in the backyard and attached to its center a thick, circular wooden disc about two feet in diameter. Anna had watched as Vati had lunged again and again at the disc with the seven-foot-long half-pike he'd managed to find buried among the other old weapons in the stall. When Anna had asked if she could try, he had laughed and gently ridiculed her request to "perform a soldier's task." After several aborted attempts and some corrective instruction from her father, Anna had tried a charging lunge from twenty feet away. Much to the surprise of both, Anna had delivered a dead-center jab so strong that it had caused the disc to separate from its attachments and fall to the ground.

A heated discussion had occurred that evening between her father and mother when Vati had bragged of Anna's accomplishment. "Well," Mutti had groaned, "maybe Anna should now join one of the Protestant armies and put her new soldiering skills to use!" To Anna's chagrin, Mutti had never since allowed her to practice pike thrusting with her father.

"Liesi, come out here and help me with Irmina."

Liesa walked over and knelt down beside Anna, who was pretending to milk the cow but deliberately failing.

"Did you pick out your goose for the race?" Anna asked.

"Yes, I think Greta will win. She always beats the others in our marching game."

"Well, that settles it. You'll need to ask Mutti to get you a basket to carry her in. But before you go inside, can you look a little closer here? I don't understand why milk isn't coming out of Irmina."

Anna waited until Liesa had poked her head under the cow's underbelly. The setup was now complete.

"Got you!" Anna shouted as she squirted Liesa in the face with the cow's first offering of the day.

"Oh, you . . . stupid sister!" Liesa gasped, then started laughing along with Anna as she tried to wipe the milk off with the hem of her dress. "You're in trouble. I'm going to tell Mutti!" she shouted as she ran back to the house.

After five more minutes of effort, the bucket was half full and Anna led Irmina back to her stall. It was shaping up to be a fun day.

⚓

The long walk to the Hohenstadt town fair had been a joy, especially with the Sallers joining the Ritters for the last three-quarters of the journey.

For the first time since Frau Saller's husband's death, she wore a huge smile. It was hard to believe this was the same woman who for so long now had been living under a dark cloud of depression.

"My son Werner is coming home!" she'd said in a joyful voice when greeting Anna and her family. "We got the message late last week when we were in the village. After running away from us seven years ago, he's still alive and coming back. He should be here any day now!"

Despite the great news, Anna wondered what Werner had been up to during his absence. If indeed he'd been serving in Wallenstein's Catholic army as had been rumored, there could be backlash from some local Lutheran residents who wouldn't take kindly to such activities. But that was a question for another day.

Once the group arrived at the fair, they were swept along the town's center street by a huge tide of people. All manner of society were present: wealthy landlords, foreigners, shop owners, artisans, farmers, prostitutes, petty thieves. Everybody crammed together in the narrow streets and alleyways as they moved from one stall to another. Anna could barely stomach the mixed odors of animals, fish, unwashed bodies, flowers, herbs, and perfumes. Vendors were everywhere displaying their wares, ranging from food, wine, and cloth to tobacco, elixirs, musical instruments, books, toys, leather goods, and furniture.

Along a side street, Anna and Barbara lagged behind to watch some activities taking place on a large, raised stage. Several acrobats and jokers were performing on one-half of the platform. On the other half, a wrestling match was taking place. Anna stood enraptured, enjoying the spectacle until her mother appeared and informed both girls to hurry on—the goose race was about to begin, and Liesa needed help getting Greta ready for it.

Well after lunch, having their fill of the fair's attractions, the two friends obtained their parents' permission to make the familiar trek to the tree-lined bend in the brook two hundred yards beyond the town limits. Within easy shouting distance of the town carpenter's house, it was a reasonably secure and private spot for the two to catch up on each other's lives, while cooling their feet in the clear water.

The sun had broken through and warmed the air by the time they made their way along the brook's embankment to their favorite location. Underneath the shade of the huge overhanging oak tree, they sat on a little grassy patch, removed their shoes, and dangled their bare feet into the rapidly running shallow water.

"You and your mother must be thrilled that Werner's coming home soon," Anna said.

Barbara sighed as she gingerly patted the chain of rosary beads around her neck. "Oh, Anni, you can't imagine how long and hard we've both prayed to the Blessed Mother for this. And now she's answered us!"

Anna smiled affectionately at her friend. "Barbara, why is it that Catholics pray to Mary and the saints and not directly to God?"

It wasn't an accusation. Anna was simply curious. Baptized as an infant and constantly reassured by her devoutly Lutheran mother, she felt secure in the knowledge that she would one day go to heaven—so long as she maintained her faith in Christ Jesus during her lifetime. And as Pastor Tiedeman had so relentlessly drilled into his congregation, a major part of that faith needed to include the belief that nothing and no one should come between the prayers offered by any individual directly to God. So why was it that Catholics should think differently, she wondered—differently enough, obviously, that Catholics and Protestants often felt compelled to kill and maim each other?

Barbara laughed. "There you go again, Anni, asking one of those religious questions that only you, out of all our friends, would care enough to ask." She closed her eyes and thought for a moment. "Our priest says the saints reign together with Christ and offer up their own prayers to God for men. And because Mary is the first and holiest of the saints, she has the best chance of obtaining divine favors for us from Jesus."

"But wouldn't it be so much easier to just ask God directly for help, rather than going through someone else?"

"Sometimes I do pray directly to God," Barbara replied, "and our priest encourages us to do that. For instance, when I say the Lord's Prayer. But, Anni, there are times when it's just easier for me to pray to Mary. I feel like, being a woman, she really knows and understands me. And she also knows Jesus better than anyone and can explain to him what I really need much better than I can. Somehow, I feel greatly comforted when I think of her helping. I don't think God would be angry at me just because I asked him through the Mother of his Son."

Anna thought about Barbara's response. It was hard to argue with. "Well," she said at last, "I really don't understand or agree with you about praying to Mary and the saints. But I guess it's nothing I'd feel like killing you over."

"And I guess it's nothing I'd want to kill you over for *not* accepting," Barbara retorted with a weary smile. "So how many more crazy questions do you have for me today? Why don't you ask your favorite pastor from the city, Herr Erhart or whatever his name is? I'm sure he'd be quite capable and happy to explain all these things to someone as smart and pretty as you. By the way, did you ever see him again after the guest sermon he delivered at your church that time I attended with you?"

Anna tried to hide her embarrassment. "Oh, *him*. I'd completely forgotten about him," she lied. She had no intention of telling Barbara about her brief encounter with Pastor Erhart at the crossroads a year and a half ago and the unseemly effect he was still having on her even now.

Anna stood up. She lifted her dress and undergarments all the way to the tops of her thighs and waded into the brook. "Come on in, Barbara. It feels good."

Barbara followed suit, and the two girls tentatively walked down the stream, watching out for sharp stones.

A sudden sound of hooves clomping along the other side of the line of bushes above the embankment caught their attention. The clomping stopped suddenly and, a few moments later, a man pushed his way through the bushes and emerged only about twenty feet from the girls.

It was Dietrich Ackar.

Ackar doffed his hat and bowed with arms outstretched. "My ladies, it's my great pleasure to see you again."

In unison with Barbara, Anna quickly pushed her dress back down to cover her bare legs, no longer concerned that the hem was now in the water. She glared at Ackar. "What is it that you wish, sir?" She regretted the stupid question the moment she asked it.

Ackar straightened, returned his hat to his head, and broke into a wide grin. "Now *that's* a question that deserves a careful answer on my part! But let me assure you my intentions are honorable. In fact, seeing the two of you here alone and perhaps in need of assistance, is there anything I may do to help *you*?"

As before, there was something about Ackar's goatee and piercing black eyes that made Anna imagine the devil himself trying to strip off her clothing and foist his insatiable lust all over her body. "I assure you, sir, we're in no need of help from anyone today," she replied, turning to walk back to the spot where the girls had left their shoes on the bank. "Come along, Barbara. We need to be going now."

As the girls retraced their path in the water, Ackar sidled along slowly, parallel with the bank. "But, my ladies, surely you'll at least allow me to help you dry your feet and put your shoes back on? Did not the Christ himself stoop to wash and dry his disciples' feet?"

"Sir, you are *not* Christ," Anna said, "and we are most certainly not your disciples."

It had become almost a slow race to see who could reach the shoes first. Finally, Ackar backed off and allowed the girls to come out of the water. While they put their shoes back on, he tried another approach. "Indeed not. But perhaps, if not for yourselves, I could offer my assistance in some way to your wonderful parents. Mend your cottage's crumbling fence, perhaps, Fräulein Anna? Or maybe provide security from night prowlers for you and your mother, Fräulein Barbara? All I would require is a place in your animal pen to lay my poor, tired head at night until I can find more permanent work to supplement my meager income from Baron von Leitzge."

Anna could not believe her ears. Ackar sleeping at night in her family's animal pen, puttering around the cottage during the day while Vati was away in the fields? Did he take her *entirely* for an idiot? She could stand this polite mockery no longer. "Herr Ackar, don't think for a minute that I've forgotten how you abused my father last year!"

Ackar's face darkened, and his eyes turned to slits. "Oh, yes, Fräulein. But recall that he and I parted as good friends. And I was so impressed with his prompt payment of the back rent shortly after that unfortunate incident. My only concern is that, once again, he's begging me to delay his rent payment. I'm happy to do so for an extra month. But it might be nice if just once people like your father and the mother of your pretty friend here would reward my good intentions and consider me worthy of their trust and respect." He removed his hat, smoothed back some stray locks of hair from his forehead, and casually looked up at the sky. "You know, it never ceases to amaze me how so many people could benefit themselves by simply accepting the good services that I offer them. But all too often they willfully refuse, and it makes my own life difficult."

"Sir, please leave us alone," Anna said softly.

Ackar replaced his hat carefully and leveled his piercing gaze at her. He smiled and then placed his hand on the hilt of the long sword attached at his hip.

Barbara stifled a scream.

Anna, though nearly as panicked as her friend, managed to maintain her outward calm. "Sir, please leave us *now*, or I swear to you I'll shout for help from the carpenter's family right up the way there."

"My lovely young maiden," Ackar said with a sigh, "I swear to you that I passed their place and saw no one there today. They must be at the fair." He broke into another one of his wide, friendly grins. "But, my ladies, there's no reason for any of us to become distressed today. After all, the town fair is now at the peak of its activity, and I for one would enjoy partaking of it." He once again doffed his hat and bowed deeply. "Dietrich Ackar, at your service, my ladies! And remember, my kind offer of help to your parents still stands."

As he rode away, Anna and Barbara collapsed with relief into each other's arms.

"Oh, Anni, who *is* that creature . . . *really*?"

"I don't know, Barbara," Anna murmured.

Actually, she *did* know. The devil had visited them today. And she was certain she had not seen the last of him.

CHAPTER 18

Countryside west of Magdeburg
October 14, 1630

P eter held his wife's hand a little tighter.

Monday-morning walks with Ursula in the countryside never failed to replenish his spirits. He basked in the glow of her undivided attention and affections. He could think of no better way to enjoy his one-day respite from required church duties. Especially since Ursula, too, had been granted Mondays off from her recently acquired post as vice superintendent for the Magdeburg city orphanage.

But there was an additional reason that Peter felt content. It had been announced yesterday that Christian Wilhelm had finally received the formal written promise he'd long been seeking from King Adolphus. The Swedish king's main army would come to Magdeburg's aid, should Colonel Falkenberg's city defense force alone prove insufficient to ward off any future threat from a Catholic army. Given Adolphus's impressive military feats in other parts of northern Germany, his written promise was no small prize.

True, all this good news had seemed to vindicate Wilhelm's dangerous obsession with foreign alliances as well as Spaignart's insistence that Peter's idea for "special council prayer sessions"—

which Wilhelm had never approved—would only be a waste of time. But personal reservations aside, the city's prospects for eliminating the Catholic takeover threat now seemed very bright. A pleasant walk in the countryside with Ursula seemed the perfect way to celebrate.

He had set out today with no fixed destination in mind. He was happy to let God reveal where to stop to partake of the food basket that his wife had prepared for lunch.

Predictably, it didn't take long for Ursula to express her concern over his lack of a clear direction. "So, Pastor, where is it that you're leading your innocent little lamb today? Not to the slaughter, I hope!"

The couple had taken a remote cross lane and were now about two miles northwest of the city wall, far from the main country road. The farther the better, in Peter's mind.

"Fear not, my queen!" Peter joked. "Just a little farther and I'm sure we'll discover yet another private paradise. You know—one of those sheltered places where our conversation slows, eating begins, and afterward . . . afterward . . . well . . ."

Ursula laughed. "Oh, Pastor, you should be publicly flogged and locked in stocks for such obscene thoughts! To think—a man of your reputation and position," she teased, no doubt entertaining similar ideas herself. "Peter, are you sure we're not getting too far outside the city wall? I thought we weren't supposed to wander unescorted and beyond the reach of help from our city militia—you've said so yourself to the congregation."

"I don't consider this to be an 'unescorted' situation, Ursula." He peered at her with a sly grin. "After all, it is *I* who am escorting you, is it not? And who would be foolish enough to challenge someone of *my* amazing spiritual skills and mental insights?"

"Let's just hope you don't have to put those marvelous skills and insights to the test, Sir Peter," Ursula said with a resigned smile. "And along those lines," she continued, "I have a question that I'll wager will tax even *your* superior mind."

Peter looked at her, eyes arched in anticipation. "Please ask, dear one."

Ursula hesitated for a moment, as if unsure whether this was a proper subject to raise. "Well, last Friday, Aloise, one of our orphanage assistants, shared something personal with me. She'd kept it bottled up inside for over five years. When she was only fifteen, her older brother raped her. She prayed for God to protect her from his continuing abuse, and soon she discovered she was with child. She thought this was God's answer to her prayers and told her brother. But instead of leaving her alone, he kept on abusing her and threatened to kill her if she told their parents. Months later, she bore the child—a girl—much to the disgrace and anger of her parents. They allowed her to remain with them, but . . ."

Peter waited patiently for his wife, obviously distraught, to compose herself.

"Aloise loved that child so deeply," Ursula continued, "but she suffered terribly from her family's rejection and physical abuse of both her and her daughter. One day she was returning home from her work as a housemaid and found her daughter lying dead in the gutter of an alley. She'd been savagely beaten and strangled. Her family claimed innocence. They insisted the little girl must have been abducted by some unknown intruder while taking her nap. Aloise never believed them, but she had no evidence to prove they had anything to do with it. And now having even more reason to fear her brother, she felt compelled to leave home and go live with strangers in the poorest part of the city.

"Oh, Peter, I can tell this whole thing is still tearing Aloise apart. She's *furious* with God. She feels that he abandoned her and her innocent child. I want so much to reassure her of God's love for her. But I just don't know what more I can say, what more peace I can give her—I've already shared with her every comforting psalm I know. And really, Peter, how could *anyone* expect Aloise to keep on trusting and believing in God after all the evil he's allowed her to suffer despite her constant prayers?"

Peter thought for a long moment before answering. He was well aware of his wife's anguish over losing her mother recently to an excruciatingly painful illness. He also couldn't help but remember poor Herr Jünger, the peasant farmer he still ministered to, whose family had been killed off by disease within the space of one week.

"Ursula," he said finally, "remember Job?"

Ursula looked at him dubiously. "The Old Testament prophet? Of course. But I hope you're not going to suggest that Aloise's situation is somehow—"

Peter put his hand on her arm. "Just listen to me, dear. Look at all God allowed that man to suffer at the hand of Satan despite his innocence and love for God: all his sons and daughters killed; loss of possessions; affliction with a terrible skin disease. And yet, remember how far he was willing to go in trusting in God's power and goodness, even when he was still complaining about the injustice of it all and maintaining his own innocence?"

"I suppose you're going to remind me, aren't you?"

Peter put his arm around her shoulders and drew her close. "Job said, 'Though he slay me, yet shall I hope in him.'"

Ursula bit her lip. She looked on the brink of crying. "I knew you'd come up with yet another lofty, fine-sounding principle from the Bible to answer my question. But Peter, that verse isn't very comforting. How can God really expect us to keep on boldly proclaiming our *hope* in him when he tears our innocent loved ones away from us, allows them to suffer horrible pain and death, and then refuses to *ever* give us any comforting explanation? I know Job somehow managed to do it. But it all seems so . . . cold and impossibly unfair to tout that verse as the expected model for someone in Aloise's situation."

As the couple continued to walk in silence, Peter struggled to stifle his frustration. Ursula had asked him a difficult question. He'd responded with the best answer he believed anyone could muster . . . the Bible *was* the Word of God, wasn't it? What other spiritual encouragement could she possibly be expecting to offer to Aloise?

Still, he had the strong sense that something was amiss in his response to his wife. And the more he thought about it, the more that response now rang strangely hollow in his own ears. Not that he'd *said* anything wrong. But it went beyond that. It was almost as if *he* were not the right man to be answering his wife's heartfelt question. But then again, who indeed *was* the right man? If not himself, an ordained Lutheran pastor who sincerely loved God, then who?

A soft whinnying noise sounded from the wooded glen immediately ahead. Three men on horseback emerged from the shadows of the overhanging trees. They walked their horses in single file across the path just ahead of the Erharts before turning to face them. Cavalrymen. Judging from their appearance and insignia, they were officers for one of the invading Catholic armies.

Ursula cried out, stepping behind Peter.

His heart pounding, Peter placed the lunch basket on the ground. He tried his best to remain calm. "Good day, sirs. You seem lost. May I give some directions or help you in any way?"

The men exchanged glances before bursting out in laughter.

After collecting himself, the soldier in the middle—who from his distinct, black-colored chest armor and feather-plumed, tricorn hat appeared to be in charge—grinned in amusement. "And good day to you, sir. Forgive our intrusion. We just didn't know where to proceed next. But now that the two of you have appeared, our way is now very clear."

"How is that, sir?" Peter asked, becoming more alarmed by the moment.

The good-looking young officer looked left and then right at his subordinates with a quizzical smile.

"Go ahead, Major Schuttmann," one of the men said. "Enlighten them."

The officer named Schuttmann sighed and dismounted. He casually approached Peter and Ursula before suddenly drawing up short.

Peter had drawn a small dagger from his inside pocket, the one he'd sworn to himself he'd never produce except in the direst of emergencies. He held it with a trembling hand, praying silently for God's protection.

Schuttmann stared at the dagger for a long moment and then looked back at his subordinates, who were trying to contain their laughter.

Schuttmann grinned, produced a large pistol from his belt, and pointed it at Peter's face.

Ursula grabbed hold of Peter's waist, huddling behind him and crying softly.

Schuttmann's voice was calm. "Your little dagger against my pistol. Hmm . . . I wonder who enjoys the advantage here! I'll make a bargain with you, Pastor, for I see from your cassock and ruff collar that you are a man of God. Not exactly the God of the Blessed Virgin that *I* worship. But I'm willing to forgive that in the interests of Christian charity. Just hand over the knife, and all will be forgiven."

"Don't think I'll allow you to take my wife under any circumstances, sir. It will only be over my dead body."

Schuttmann smiled. "Pastor, who said anything about taking your wife? We here are Catholic cavalry officers. Why, we wouldn't dream of such infamy! All I demand is this: just put your knife back in your pocket. Then allow me to take a peek into that basket of yours to see if there might be something to relieve the hunger of my famished men. I mean no disrespect to your wife by choosing the basket over her. In fact, from the little she'll allow me to see of her, I must compliment you on your taste in beautiful women. Now, let's put that tiny knife away, shall we?"

Peter hesitantly complied.

"There," Schuttmann said and lowered his pistol. "You see? You and your lady have nothing to fear from us." He opened the lid of the basket and rummaged around. Finally, he pulled out a small bag containing four hard-boiled eggs. "Perfect! These should keep us alive for another fifty miles back to our own lines. Do you agree, men?"

"If you say so, sir," said one of the subordinate officers.

"And see, Pastor? We've still left you the rest of your meal to enjoy together. As I've said, we're Catholic officers, sworn to chivalry. We permit ourselves no plundering, except the absolute minimum needed to survive."

"Thank you, sir," Peter said guardedly. "My wife and I greatly appreciate your mercy and kindness."

"Major!" one of the subordinate officers shouted. "Someone's coming—fast!" As Schuttmann stood, the sound of galloping horses grew quickly in volume, a dust cloud behind them.

Schuttmann doffed his hat to the couple. "Well, my friends, it seems that our pursuers are closing in. May God watch over you both—and maybe one day convince you that Martin Luther had it all wrong. *Long live the pope!*"

Schuttmann mounted his horse just as the loud crack of a pistol sounded from down the path. All three soldiers wheeled their horses and took off at a frantic pace toward the shelter of the nearby woods.

Within seconds, seven mounted Protestant militiamen from the city reached Peter and Ursula, now holding each other closely by the side of the path.

One of the troopers pulled up beside them while the other six raced off in pursuit of the Catholic soldiers. "Were you hurt?"

"No, sir, we're both unhurt," Peter answered. "They were officers, and they treated us civilly enough, all things considered. And it seems we're now safe, thanks to you and your men."

The trooper frowned. "I would use the word *safe* with some hesitation, Pastor. May I ask, what in the name of heaven did you think you were doing this far out from the city wall, *unescorted*? You were lucky to have come across a gentlemanly band of officers as opposed to the more typical set of rogues we've been trying to track down lately."

"What have these rogues done, sir?" Peter asked.

"Two days ago, a Lutheran pastor in one of our small outlying towns had his hands and feet cut off by Catholic plunderers. They were angry because he couldn't produce their required ransom. They left him bleeding on the altar, a sacrifice to his Protestant God. Supporters soon came to his aid, and his life was saved. But just barely."

Ursula grimaced and turned her face away.

"Forgive me, my lady. My only purpose in telling you this sordid story is to discourage you and your husband from future ventures this far from safety. Pastors and their wives are not immune to the dangers. There's simply no way you can be adequately protected."

"We certainly take your point, sir," Peter said, "and thank you for educating us."

"Well, I need to rejoin my unit, so I won't be able to accompany you back to the city. Did you make out any special markings or hear any conversation from the cavalrymen that might help us identify them?"

"Their leading officer—his name was Major Schuttmann or something to that effect—was wearing dark-black chest armor and sported a fiery-red plume in his hat."

The trooper's eyes widened. "*God in heaven!* Pastor, do you know who that is? That's Helmut Schuttmann, the Black Knight—the best and most feared cavalryman in the entire Catholic League Army of Count Tilly!"

Peter was puzzled. "But I thought Count Tilly's army is off quartered somewhere to the northwest? I thought we only needed to worry about Wallenstein's army in this region. And now that *he* has pulled out—"

"Perhaps you haven't heard the news, Pastor."

"What news is that, sir?"

"Emperor Ferdinand has fired Wallenstein. He was furious over his decision to accept the ransom offer from the city council. The emperor will no longer allow Magdeburg to 'get away with it,' as he put things. He's now placed Count Tilly in charge—not only of his own army but of Wallenstein's as well. Tilly is now the supreme commander for *all* the Catholic imperial armies, and Magdeburg will no doubt be one of his first targets."

Peter stared at the trooper in dismay, his earlier sense of elation over the city's prospects having been shot from under him. Wallenstein's blockade had been difficult enough to withstand and finally break. But Count Tilly and his army? From everything Peter had heard, Tilly would be relentless in following through on the emperor's demands for Magdeburg's total submission.

"So what were Major Schuttmann and his men doing out here all alone?" Peter asked.

The trooper thought a moment. "They were probably on a special scouting expedition—trying to see if conditions near the city are ripe for Tilly's army to come and pick up where Wallenstein left off. Who knows? At any rate, this is a prime opportunity for us to capture or kill that cursed Black Knight. Please pray for us troopers, Pastor. You know we desire to do the Lord's work in disposing of these Catholic villains. And best regards to you, my lady. May God protect you both." The soldier wheeled his horse around and galloped off to rejoin his comrades.

Ursula hugged Peter closely. He could feel her trembling. "Dear, what is it?"

"Peter, we *will* be all right, won't we? I mean, Colonel Falkenberg and his Swedes will keep us safe from the Catholics, won't they?"

Peter hesitated to answer, not wanting to alarm his wife. She'd had enough to deal with for one day. "Of course, Ursula. Christian Wilhelm and Pastor Spaignart have guaranteed as much, haven't they?" he said without much conviction.

Whether that guarantee would prove to be an empty one remained to be seen. At this point, Peter knew only one thing was certain: the ultimate test for Wilhelm's "Swedish solution" was coming, and it was coming soon.

CHAPTER 19

Countryside west of Magdeburg
October 31, 1630

"All right, Liesa," Anna declared. "It's time for you to finally do some work around here. Now, go get Irmina. It's getting late, and Mutti will be wondering where we are."

"Oh, Anni, you always have to spoil our fun," Liesa complained before turning to retrieve the family cow on the other side of the hill.

Anna settled back on the grassy slope with her arms folded behind her head. She had only a few more minutes left to enjoy the beautiful autumn sunset and crisp evening breeze in peaceful solitude. Normally, she and Liesa would have been back home at this hour, helping Mutti prepare for supper and putting out food for the geese and pig; Vati would have just finished up his fieldwork for Freiherr von Schwarz and would retrieve Irmina himself on his way home. But today—All Hallows' Eve—Vati had felt ill after his work in the morning and earlier afternoon. Mutti had insisted he take a break and stay home: it would give him some much-needed rest, and Anna and Liesa were certainly capable of retrieving the cow before sunset.

As she gazed up at the sky, Anna noticed dark clouds gathering near the horizon. The light of the setting sun was playing off them and casting spectacular shades of indigo, amber, and orange. Dazzling beauty amidst the gathering darkness. She suddenly thought of Barbara and wondered how she and her family were doing.

Barbara's brother Werner had finally returned home just two weeks ago after his seven-year absence. He confessed his reason for running away: an obsessive belief that his now-deceased father was always disapproving of everything he did. After three years of service with Wallenstein's army, Werner had received an honorable discharge and had taken on a well-paying position as a carpenter's assistant in Würzburg.

Now the co-owner of a nice farmhouse on the outskirts of that city, Werner had convinced his sister and mother that he had the means to support them there, if they were willing to move immediately. They had agreed that it would be a wise move, especially in view of Frau Saller's increasing sense of isolation and loneliness since her husband's death.

Werner had appeared one day last week with an oxcart that some of the local Catholic parish members had donated for their journey to Würzburg. The next morning, Anna had shown up to help load the cart and say goodbye . . .

"Anni, will you promise never to forget me?" Barbara asked tearfully.

"Oh, Barbara, you already know the answer to that," Anna whispered as the two girls held each other in a long embrace.

"Anni, I want you to have something." Barbara reached into her pocket and pulled out a delicately carved and painted six-inch wooden figurine of the Virgin Mary. Taking Anna's right hand, she placed the figurine in her palm and closed her fingers around it. She enfolded Anna's hand with both of her own and locked eyes with her. "I know this isn't something you could ever show openly around your house."

"You're right about that," Anna replied. "Vati would kill me. He's not a devout Lutheran, but you know he's definitely anti-Catholic."

Barbara smiled sympathetically. "I'm not asking you to convert. I'm just asking you to hide this away and look at it in secret every now and then. To remember me and who I am. And to remember everything we've shared—good and bad."

Tears welled up in Anna's eyes. "You know I'll treasure this as long as I live. Just like my love for you, Barbara." She wiped her eyes with her sleeve and drew back, pointing toward the loaded cart where Werner and Frau Saller were waiting. "Now go—before I decide to lie down in the middle of the lane in front of your cart and dare you to run me over!"

As the cart approached the crest of the nearby hill, Anna cried out, "May God love and protect you, Barbara Saller! I pray we'll meet again soon!"

Barbara waved back one final time before the cart disappeared over the rise.

❧

Anna realized she had dozed off. The bottom half of the sun had already dropped beneath the horizon.

"Liesa, *what* is taking you so long?" Anna called as she stood up to wipe the grass off.

Finally, Liesa appeared at the top of the slope with Irmina.

"Hurry up," Anna pleaded, "or Mutti will give us both a tongue-lashing. Especially me. I can hear her now!"

The sisters started their trip home in mutual silence, moving as quickly as possible down the lane with the cow in tow. Anna took the halter rope from Liesa and turned Irmina onto the small dirt path leading directly to the front of the cottage. They'd taken only a few steps before Anna stopped short. She clamped her hand on Liesa's shoulder.

"Wait!"

A voice was coming from inside the house through the partly open window. It was a voice she'd hoped she would never hear again.

"What's wrong, Anni?" Liesa asked in alarm.

Anna's mind raced. Ackar! What was he doing here? He wasn't supposed to show up until the first of December. So why was he here a full month early?

Her mother's piercing scream, followed shortly by a long, loud groan—Vati?—jolted Anna into action. She knelt down and grabbed Liesa by the shoulders.

"Liesi, listen to me. Don't cry. Don't say a word."

"Anni," Liesa whimpered, "what's happening to—"

Anna pressed her hand over her sister's mouth.

"Keep quiet and do exactly as I tell you! Take Irmina as fast as you can back up the lane just a little ways. Tie her to the fence rail. Then run and hide in the woods behind our cottage. Don't come out until I come calling for you. Do you understand?"

Liesa nodded. "But what if you don't come for me?" she whispered frantically.

Anna took Liesa's face in her hands. "Don't worry. I *will* be back for you, princess," she whispered. "Just stay put. Even if it takes awhile. Now go—quickly!"

Liesa took Irmina's halter, walked her back up the dirt path, and then turned into the lane.

Once Liesa was safely out of sight, Anna crouched low and ran to the window near the front door. The left shutter was ajar. It offered a clear view of the right half of the cottage's interior, including the hearth. Anna cautiously raised her head above the sill and peered inside. She nearly fainted at the sight.

Her mother was kneeling and sobbing quietly on the floor beside the hearth. Her hands were clasped in supplication—apparently to no avail. Anna's father was standing on a stool beside her, facing Anna's direction. His hands were tied behind him, and his arms were bound tightly to his body from shoulder to waist. His face was bruised and bloodied. A noose had been placed around his neck, with the other end of the rope cast over a crossbeam and tied to the handle of the hefty iron kettle next to the hearth. The rope was taut enough that any attempt by her father to step off the stool would undoubtedly seal his fate.

Standing behind her father next to the fire was the ogre of a man Anna recalled from the encounter last year at Herr Denzel's market: Schmidt, Ackar's half-witted, gargantuan lackey. He would be a formidable obstacle for anybody to overcome.

Anna watched with horror as the brute carefully stuck one of the iron pokers into the blazing hearth. After a few seconds, he withdrew it, red-hot. He grinned devilishly at Ackar, who was sitting in a chair near her mother, his right foot propped casually on the family dining table. He was dressed in the costume of a wealthy man: tricorn hat with plume, shiny knee-high boots, ruffled white shirt, colorfully brocaded outer jacket, and what appeared to be a necklace containing dazzling gems. It was a far cry from what he'd worn the other times she'd seen him. *Where,* wondered Anna, *has he come across all this finery?*

"Ready for the next round, boss?" Schmidt asked.

Oh God! Anna looked wildly behind herself, hoping beyond hope to discover some divine rescuer standing there. None appeared. Her heart now in her throat, she forced herself to look back at the ghastly drama unfolding before her.

Ackar's voice had a tone of amusement. "Well, Schmidt, I suppose we should at least allow our good friends one last chance to repent. Confession is good for the soul as well as for avoiding painful discipline, is it not?"

"You know exactly how to put things, boss!" Schmidt said, chuckling as he placed the poker back in its holder for the time being.

"Sir, why must you torture us so?" Frieda Ritter pleaded. "What have we ever done to offend you? Why, oh, why? Please, sir, we . . . oh, please just tell us *why!*"

Anna trembled at the pitiful sound of her mother's plea. Mutti was on the verge of hysteria.

Ackar stared at her sadly, almost tenderly, for a few long moments without replying.

Anna could barely choke back her own scream as she watched him draw a long rapier from its scabbard lying on the table.

Holding the slender sword in his left hand, Ackar positioned the pointed tip under Mutti's chin and delicately lifted her terrified face to look directly at him. "Frau Ritter, don't you realize to whom you're speaking? If you did, there'd be no need for such foolish questions."

"I-I beg your mercy, sir, but I know only what I've heard: that you're a collection agent for Baron von Leitzge."

"Ha!" Ackar tossed his head back and laughed. "Schmidt, she thinks me nothing more than a mere tool of that fat little idiot who has the *gall* to consider himself a member of the noble class! When will these people ever learn?"

"Only when they're forced to look at themselves. Right, boss?"

Anna breathed a tiny sigh of relief as Ackar slowly pulled his sword away from Mutti's chin and placed it back on the table.

"Allow me to clarify some things for you, Frau Ritter. You and your husband should be under no mistaken impressions as to my pedigree. For, you see, I myself was born into a line of royalty that would put von Leitzge's pretensions to shame. Yes, I am he! A son of—can you believe it?—the first cousin of Ferdinand the Second, the Holy Roman emperor himself."

"Y-you're related to th-the emperor, sir?" Mutti stuttered.

"You heard correctly, Frau. Does that surprise you?"

"Well, yes . . . no, sir. B-but then why aren't you . . ."

"I know where you're going with your question, Frau. Allow me to explain why I am not now at court in Vienna, merrily satisfying my stomach and loins with the tastiest of royal treats."

Ackar's expression suddenly took on the look of an innocent, hurt boy. "You see, there is a slight flaw in my lineage. My mother happens to be my father's clandestine French mistress, not his wife. But, oh, how that slight flaw caused such grief for my childhood. 'Disown that silly, effeminate little bastard!' the family true-bloods would shout at my father. 'How dare he show his face before this noble court!' Their constant taunts and physical abuse of both me and my mother were something I swore I'd never forgive or forget.

"My weak-willed father yielded to the pressure of those cruel mockers," he continued, his voice now quivering and his face contorting with rage at the memory. "He refused to see me or my mother ever again. To relieve his own guilt, he arranged for my private tutoring in Paris. Even had me enrolled in the imperial French School of Fencing. No doubt he thought I would squander the opportunity. But I surprised everyone. I graduated only two years later with the coveted title of Master Swordsman of the First Rank. And ever since, I've wandered throughout Europe as an enlightened journeyman, putting my talent to good use in the service of others deserving my help."

A sickening wave of nausea passed over Anna. Now it all made sense: Ackar's foreign accent, his fancy words and mocking tone, even the expensive clothes. Clearly, he was seeking revenge against anyone whom he judged to have taken advantage of him, including now her own poor parents.

Ackar stared plaintively at her mother. "Oh, may I give you a little demonstration of my special skill, my lady?"

Frieda nodded miserably. Ackar reached over to pick up his sword and then stood and walked to the center of the room. He bowed deeply, first to her and then to Adam.

The next full minute was devoted to a whirling, ducking, slashing, jabbing display of expert swordsmanship against a mock opponent. Anna would never have thought it possible had she not seen it herself. For a fitting conclusion, Ackar performed one final full-body rotation that ended with arm fully extended and the tip of his sword lightly touching her father's forehead. He tweaked the sword's tip and drew blood. It was not a serious wound, but it was enough to cause her father to yelp in pain and her mother to scream. Ackar's mastery of his chilling art was beyond any doubt.

"Was my performance to your satisfaction, Frau Ritter?" Ackar asked.

Mutti was sobbing once again, unable to answer.

Ackar brought his fist down on the table. "*Speak to your superior, woman—before I completely lose my patience!*"

"Oh, y-yes, sir. It was a very impressive show. But, s-sir, what does this all have to do with us? What have we done to deserve this treatment?"

Ackar's voice dropped to a threatening baritone. "I'll tell you what you've done. You've made me a stench in the nostrils of Baron von Leitzge. By not making your rent payment on a very nice cottage that is obviously above your station and ability to afford, you have incurred the baron's wrath. And when the baron is angry, his first targets are his unfortunate collection agents like myself, whom he accuses of being 'too soft.' Tonight, I must collect immediately—or be disbarred from his service."

"But, sir, didn't you tell my husband that he had until the first of next month to make the double payment with interest? There are still thirty-one days left, and my husband is certain to receive more than enough money to meet your demand by then."

"Ah, that's the rub, Frau. The baron is now requiring me to provide him with the full balance of your payment for last month's rent by tomorrow morning. Exactly why, I know not. All I know is that my job and livelihood depend on my faithfulness in this matter. And so I must insist on receiving this payment in hard coin before we leave tonight."

Full payment in hard coin—by tonight? That's an impossible demand, Anna thought.

"Of course," Ackar mused, "my options might not be so limited if you had not arrogantly refused the kind offer of my services two weeks ago to mend your fence in return for temporary lodging. In that case, maybe I wouldn't be so reliant now on employment by von Leitzge."

Schmidt grinned. "If only these stupid peasants would get it through their thick skulls that you're only trying to help them."

"Yes, yes. They keep suspecting my motives and refusing my kindnesses—and now look where it gets them and their friends! I'm forced into performing acts that are far beneath my station."

"Oh, dear God!" Mutti cried.

Ackar appeared to have reached the limit of his patience. "But we digress from my main reason for being here tonight," he said. "And so, Herr and Frau Ritter, I'll ask you politely only one more time: where are you stashing your treasure? Certainly you've stored enough reserves somewhere to satisfy my light demand? Under a board or buried somewhere in the yard, maybe?"

"Sir," Mutti said, "we've already told you there's nothing here beyond what you can see for yourself. You're free to take it all, if you must. Even our animals."

"You lie, evil wench," Ackar hissed, his eyes narrowing. "And nothing but hard coinage will satisfy the baron's demand. But in my mercy I shall offer you a possible alternative."

"What is that, sir?"

"You said that your two daughters will be returning soon with your family cow. In exchange for a pleasant time alone with the older, pretty one—Anna, correct?—I'd be willing to forgo my monetary demands until thirty days from now and somehow find a way to keep von Leitzge at bay in the meantime."

Anna turned away from the window, her mind and stomach recoiling at the prospect of Ackar forcing himself upon her.

Adam, until now barely able to move or even speak with the noose tight around his neck, could take no more. "No! Frieda, don't assent to this! You rat from hell—I'll kill you!"

Anna forced herself to peer inside again. Ackar's face was contorted with barely controlled rage.

"Well, Schmidt, I take this obstinate answer as yet another refusal of our kindnesses. Do you agree with me that it's time to remind our good friends of *their* station?"

Schmidt smiled, his eyes widening in anticipation. "I'll get it ready again, boss." He picked up the poker and held it over the hearth.

"Hmm," Ackar said, "we'll need to be careful not to let him misstep. Wouldn't want his neck to snap prematurely. How about I hold his legs while you apply your little kiss of hot passion to the side of his neck?"

Ackar grabbed Vati's legs tightly as Schmidt brought the tip of the red-hot poker close to his face. "One more time, Herr Ritter. The money or your daughter?"

"You can rot in hell!"

Anna couldn't bring herself to watch what happened next. But neither could she bear hearing the agonizing shriek of her father and her mother's wail as Schmidt applied the blazing hot poker tip to his neck and held it there for a full five seconds.

Panting from the horror of it all, Anna forced herself to consider the options: turn herself over to Ackar as a ransom for her parents' lives or . . .

The soldier's half-pike!

The one that Vati had let her practice with last year, making Mutti so upset. Yes, it was a long shot. Whether she chose to resist and fail or to simply surrender without a fight, Ackar was going to have his way with her and her parents. The only faint hope was to somehow surprise one of the men, taking him quickly out of action so the other could be faced alone. The pike was her only chance.

But where was it? Then she remembered. Vati had tossed it onto the pile of garden tools behind the animal pen after their practice session.

After listening for a few more moments to the conversation inside, Anna slowly rose and then ran to the rear of the pen. She dug through at least ten tools that had since been thrown on top of the pile. Finally, she grabbed the handle of the half-pike and yanked it out.

She returned to the window and peeked over the sill once again, this time to get a better sense of the positioning of Ackar and his crony.

Pike in hand, Anna crept toward the front door of the cottage. *Please, God, let the inner latch be unlocked.* Once in front of the door, she clutched the weapon's long handle with her clammy palms—just the way her father had shown her. Now the timing was up to Ackar.

Don't panic. Wait . . . wait . . .

CHAPTER 20

Countryside west of Magdeburg
October 31, 1630

"So it all comes down to this, Herr and Frau Ritter," Dietrich Ackar said. "You will stop delaying and reveal the hiding place for your treasure, or you'll agree to grant me the pleasure of your lovely daughter's company for the remainder of the night. Otherwise, Schmidt will be forced to deliver another hot kiss to the other side of poor Herr Ritter's neck. So which will it be?"

Vati gave no response.

"You refuse me, you low-class swine? Well, then, let's have some fun, Schmidt . . ."

Now! Anna placed the sole of her left foot against the door and kicked with all her might. The door flew open. Holding the pike above her shoulders as Vati had taught, she rushed toward Schmidt who was fewer than fifteen feet away. Big and slow in addition to being surprised, Schmidt didn't even have time to raise his poker in self-defense.

Stumbling forward at the last moment and almost losing her grip on the pike, Anna made her final lunge. Her aim was off-center, but it was close enough. Schmidt watched in amazement as the pike's sharp blade pierced his right side. The extra force of Anna's stumble caused the blade to penetrate through his liver and out his back.

He let out a terrible groan as blood gushed from his mouth and his eyes rolled back in his head. He staggered forward two steps, then fell on his side to the floor.

Ackar, recovering from his shock, stared at Anna, who lay collapsed on the floor near her mother. "You'll pay dearly for this, pretty one!" he snarled. He strolled over to his crony. Not bothering to see if the man was still alive, he placed his boot on Schmidt's abdomen, grabbed the pike's handle, and yanked it free. He started toward Anna.

"Daughter, in here!" Mutti shrieked, holding open the door that led directly into the animal pen. "Come now!"

Anna scrambled toward her mother and jumped through the doorway. Mutti slammed the door shut and quickly threw the inside latch into place. A savage kick from Ackar failed to budge it.

The women knelt on the floor of the pen, weeping quietly. Anna could hear Ackar in the main room screaming, cursing, and kicking every loose object in sight. After a few moments, the frightening outbursts were replaced with an eerie silence. Anna held her mother tightly, still too terrified to move or speak. What was Ackar up to?

Anna held her breath and put her ear to the door. She listened in horror as Ackar picked up where he'd left off with Vati.

"Well, Herr Ritter, I suppose the sight of your daughter impaling my disgraceful slug of an accomplice gave you hope that salvation was near. But let me assure you, sir, your purification by pain has just begun. And do you know the best part of it? Now your daughter, in addition to your wife, will be able to enjoy your howls of agony!"

Before Anna could stop her, Mutti let out an earsplitting shriek. "No! You can't! Please, please!"

Ackar erupted in a fit of cruel laughter. "Well, Herr Ritter. It seems that at least one of your women would prefer a different outcome."

"Herr Ackar," Anna's father cried out in a broken voice. "Please, sir, you're right. I'm an undeserving dog who has offended you, and I'm totally at your mercy. Do what you will with me. But I beg you, in the name of God himself, to spare my wife and daughters."

"Herr Ritter, I'm afraid it's a little late for hypocritical pleas for mercy. Did your daughter demonstrate mercy to my poor friend Schmidt over there? I think not. So, are we ready to get started?" He walked to the fire, reaching for the poker.

Anna struggled to repress her mother's panicked sobs. The thought of Vati being tortured again was too much. She had to act now. Do something—anything! But what? Tears mixed with sweat clouded her eyes.

"Ah, looks like this is getting nice and warm. Just another minute or so, and it'll be white-hot. Patience, Herr Ritter, patience!" Ackar's voice had once again taken on a tone of merry anticipation.

Anna looked around frantically. There was nothing useful in sight. She glanced down the row of stalls, her eyes trying to focus in the dim light. Out of nowhere, an idea hit her. Anna pulled herself free from her mother's arms and ran to the stall at the far end of the animal pen. She returned in less than a minute.

"Daughter!" Mutti whispered hoarsely, her eyes wide with terror. "You can't. You'll—"

Anna clamped her hand over her mother's mouth.

Ackar's voice oozed through the crack in the door. "Oh my, Herr Ritter. What part of your proud head shall we experiment with this time? Let's see how your right eye responds to my special treatment!"

Anna stood and steeled herself to unfasten the door. She knew there was virtually no chance her idiotic scheme would work. But there was no other choice.

Just as she took hold of the latch, she froze, unsure of herself.

Ackar spoke again. "Sir, what am I doing? Wouldn't it be far more enjoyable for your right eye, before I burn it out, to witness the spectacle of me ravishing your wife and daughter in turn? To watch them writhe in ecstasy as I satisfy their deepest longings with my special skill? After all, I *am* the master swordsman, as you'll recall. Let me see if they might be interested in this option as well."

Within seconds, Ackar was kicking furiously at the door.

Anna grabbed her mother's arm and led her toward a dark corner.

The two huddled together, waiting for the inevitable.

When the door wouldn't budge, Ackar began hammering away with some other heavy object. The top half of the door began to splinter.

Mutti let out another scream.

After a few more strikes, Ackar had created a hole large enough to thread his arm through. He lifted the latch and gently pushed the door open.

"Lovely Anna, your Dietrich has come looking for you. Where are you hiding, my love?"

After a few moments, Ackar, struggling to adjust his eyes to the low level of light in the pen, discovered the object of his search. Mutti was on her knees, her hands once again clasped in supplication. Behind her crouched Anna, relying on the shield of her mother's protection.

Ackar grinned and bowed. "Well, now. How perfectly quaint. Mother hen sheltering her young."

"Please, sir," Mutti sobbed, "we beg you to let us live and leave us alone."

"Move over, hag. You are spent and undesirable. It's the young, brazen beauty behind you that I desire."

"But sir, I—"

"I said *move over—now!*" Ackar took two threatening steps toward the women, raising his sword above his head.

Mutti screamed and fell away to the side, leaving Anna exposed.

"And now, my beauty, it's time for you to fully reveal yourself to me. Stand up!"

Slowly, Anna stood to face her tormentor. Tears streamed down her face as she trembled uncontrollably. "God, help me," she whispered.

"What's that you say? Did I just hear you mention the name of the Almighty?"

"Y-y-yes, sir. You did."

"Ho, ho! Having always been forced to fend for myself, I have utter contempt for hypocrites who try to hide behind the false prop of religion. But perhaps I'm dealing here with a true believer. Very good. I've waited a long time to put such a rare species to the ultimate test."

Ackar stepped toward Anna. Just six feet away, he raised his sword and positioned the tip on her left cheekbone just below the eye. He expertly flicked the blade tip, making a slight cut that drew blood.

Anna winced. She bit her lip hard and turned her head to the side.

Ackar placed the tip of his sword under her chin. "Now, pretty Anna, let me see you 'turn your other cheek' to your enemy."

Anna turned her face and looked straight at Ackar.

Slowly, he moved the tip of the sword to the top of her right shoulder. Another delicate flick, and he'd ripped through the cloth of the dress, exposing her bare shoulder.

Anna gasped but maintained her posture. *Please, God . . . For Vati. For Mutti. For Liesa.*

"And now it's your turn, my lovely. You'll begin by lifting your dress and exposing those delectable thighs!"

"S-s-sir, I'm sorry, b-but I can't do that," Anna stuttered as she stared at the floor.

Ackar exploded. "What is that you're saying to me, you craven slut? Do you presume even now to refuse my kindnesses?" He dropped his sword, reached inside his tunic, and produced a long, serrated hunting knife. "Prepare, Fräulein, to have your beating heart cut out!"

Ackar moved in. He paused as he noticed Anna's hands clasped beneath her black apron.

"Ooh, now this is indeed interesting," Ackar snarled. "Not only a true believer, but a *praying* true believer. Tell me, girl, do you *truthfully* believe that your God will save you now?"

Seemingly out of nowhere, Anna felt the rush of an overwhelming calm deep within. No longer was she afraid. No longer did she care about anything but allowing this strange new peace to control her actions. She raised her bleeding, tear-smeared face to meet Ackar's gaze. Her voice was quiet but firm. She was not even sure it was her own.

"*Truthfully*, sir, I know my God—and he has already saved me."

Ackar's face clouded with fury. He raised his knife to strike.

In one smooth, deliberate motion, Anna raised her clasped hands to the level of Ackar's face. One final prayer.

Ackar froze. "What the—"

A blinding flash preceded the explosion. The round lead ball flew straight through Dietrich Ackar's gaping mouth and burst out the back of his skull. He slumped to the floor, blood and brains spilling from the mortal wound.

Anna dropped her father's pistol to the floor and ran to her mother, who was screaming hysterically on the other side of the room.

⤶

Two hours later, the Ritter family was curled up together in blankets before a blazing fire. Anna lay next to Mutti, her head resting on a straw pillow. Liesa was asleep, nestled in Vati's arms. Mutti couldn't restrain herself from leaning over every minute or so to alternately kiss Anna, then Liesa, and then Vati.

The threatening clouds that Anna had seen earlier in the evening had finally burst, dumping torrents of cold rain. Fortunately, the storm had held off long enough for Adam to move the bodies outside and for Frieda to clean up the blood in the main room and animal pen while Anna retrieved Liesa from her hiding place in the woods. Adam, though badly shaken and pained by the burn on his neck, had managed somehow to "properly dispose of the enemy corpses according to army regulations," as he'd put it.

Anna, totally spent, closed her eyes and listened to the wonderful music of her parents conversing tenderly with each other.

"Adam, dear husband," Mutti gushed, "I was so proud of you. You did everything you could to defend us and were ready to sacrifice your life for us. And for all the effort you've put into trying to restore our family's reputation and fortune over the past months, I am so grateful."

Vati kissed his wife and smiled ruefully. "I wish I'd done more to prevent this in the first place. But in any case, my efforts tonight pale in comparison with Anna's."

"Adam, what'll we do now?" Mutti asked.

"No one will notice the disappearance of Ackar or his crony for some time. I don't believe Ackar's claim that Baron von Leitzge is waiting for our rent payment by tomorrow. But to be on the safe side, we should move into the city, where no one will ask questions. Would your sister take us in for a while? I'll start looking for work there starting tomorrow."

"Oh, Adam!" Mutti exclaimed. "That's just what I was hoping you'd decide. We've spent enough years in this lonely place—and nearly paid for it tonight with our lives. I know we'll feel a lot safer inside the city walls."

The city! Anna thought. *Shelter from evil like we experienced tonight. A chance for a brand-new life.*

Vati grinned at his wife. "Well, one thing I'll say in my own favor about the way I set up that animal pen: it seems that 'Vati's silly inside latches' and that last stall containing 'Vati's Little Armory' of useless weapons certainly came in handy tonight. Especially that old wheel-lock pistol I showed Anna how to load and use. Weren't all those the very same things I recall my dear wife so harshly criticizing?"

"Husband," Mutti said, kissing his forehead, "you know perfectly well it wasn't your inside latches, your old weapons, or even your brave daughter who saved us tonight. You know perfectly well it was God who saved us."

Anna smiled. "Thank you, Lord," she whispered to herself just before falling gratefully into the soundest sleep she'd ever known.

CHAPTER 21

Countryside east of Magdeburg
April 20, 1631

B y five o'clock in the evening, the mounted scouting party of eight Catholic League Army cavalry officers had nearly completed its mission. Only three more miles stood between the men and their headquarters.

Major Hans Mannheim glanced at his mission co-leader, Major Helmut Schuttmann—the Black Knight. *No doubt*, Hans thought, *Count Tilly will be happy to hear our assessment of the situation.* With Magdeburg now virtually surrounded, the assessment would show that Tilly was finally in position to do the job Wallenstein had failed to complete.

"So Hans," Schuttmann asked, "what should our conclusion be for Tilly regarding the city's defenses?" Before Hans could reply, Schuttman pressed his own case. "I'll tell you what I think. Those enemy fortifications on the islets in the middle of the river below the eastern city wall will be the first obstacle. Capturing those will give us access to the bridgeworks leading to the main city gate. We can also use them to position Tilly's artillery and rain down a barrage from hell against the entire eastern wall. I'd be surprised if anything's left standing by the time we're ready to launch an assault across the causeway if things come to that. And personally speaking, I'll be delighted to lead that charge—be the first to plunge my sword through Wilhelm's big mouth and down his gullet!"

Hans nodded. Typical Schuttmann battle plan—punch your enemy in the gut, then count on him to bend over and present his chin for a finishing uppercut. Schuttmann had definitely earned his reputation for ruthlessness in battle.

"Sounds logical, Helmut. Still, I'm not so sure a frontal assault on the main eastern gate would be the best point to start the attack."

"So what would be *your* recommendation, Herr Supreme Commander?" Schuttmann asked in his familiar mocking tone.

"Think about it," Hans retorted. "Tilly's second—General Pappenheim—has already sent his artillery units across the Elbe. They're now lying in wait just north of the city. All they'd have to do is move south through those lightly defended suburbs, and they'd be in great position to shell the northern section of the wall. You know that section's not nearly as well fortified as the eastern one. Pappenheim's artillery alone should be enough to poke a hole in it for his cavalry and infantry to charge through. They'd be impossible to stop. *That's* where I'd concentrate the initial effort. Then right after that, launch the main assault with Tilly's troops across the causeway against the eastern gate. Once they're inside the walls, Tilly's and Pappenheim's units can then link up, surround any surviving defenders. Kill the resisters, spare those genuinely requesting mercy."

Schuttmann's eyebrows rose in response to this last suggestion.

"My only concern," Hans went on, "is how long we can afford to wait before pulling off a full-scale assault. Right now, we can bring over twenty-four thousand imperial troops to bear against probably no more than twenty-six hundred city defenders. But if we wait too long, hoping in vain for a surrender offer from the city council, we could be in big danger from the main body of Adolphus's forces. If they're willing to make the effort, they could approach our rear from their current positions to the east. Everything depends on how long the Swedes would take to come to the rescue. Assuming, that is, they would attempt to come at all."

Schuttmann touched the tip of his hat in an admiring salute. "Sometimes you amaze me, Mannheim, with the elegance and breadth of your strategic thinking. And, in this case, I agree with you completely." Schuttmann grinned impishly. "Of course, I'll have to refrain from stealing your glory by telling Tilly the truth—that I myself had thought of that exact scenario three days ago."

Hans sighed. Schuttmann's joking never ceased. Still, it felt good to receive the Black Knight's admiring approval.

The scouting party departed the rough dirt lane and proceeded through a wooded glade. They had two miles to go before reaching the edge of the Catholic army encampment. Hans was eager to reach the camp before sunset.

Suddenly, Lieutenant Richter, riding in the point position, stopped his mount and held up his hand.

The entire party came to a standstill. Everyone fell quiet.

After what seemed an interminable length of time, Hans called out irritably, "Richter, you've held your hand up now for a full minute! What in the name of Lucifer draws your interest?"

Richter turned in his saddle. "Sir, I thought I saw something moving just ahead."

"Probably a deer. What else would be rummaging around this godforsaken spot?"

"Sir, I—"

A loud boom preceded a single musket ball that pierced Richter's right eye, dropping him stone-dead beside his horse.

Within seconds, a volley of musket shots rang out from behind the surrounding trees. One of Schuttmann's junior officers was cut down immediately. Two more shots struck another young officer's horse in its flank. The animal reared up and threw him from the saddle.

A musket ball nicked Hans in the right shoulder, forcing him to dismount and run for the limited shelter of a nearby boulder.

Major Schuttmann and the remaining four cavalrymen dismounted.

Immediately, they spread out to locate the musketeers. There would be at most a thirty-second lull before their reloading was complete.

Moments later, Hans heard several simultaneous skirmishes. The triumphant whoops of familiar voices and the absence of any more musket fire up ahead were good signs. Schuttmann's men must be having success either killing or chasing off the enemy assailants. Hans stood up from behind the boulder and began running carefully toward the trees ahead, where the voices appeared to be coming from.

Four enemy soldiers emerged from behind the trees. They raced toward Hans, eager to finish him off with their swords and wooden partisan poles tipped by fearsome metal spearheads with protrusions on the sides. All were dressed in the yellow pants and long coats of the Swedish infantry—no doubt part of Falkenberg's city defense force.

Hans drew his pistol. He fired off a shot, striking one soldier in the right thigh and removing him from the charge. The other three closed in. Alternating between parries, thrusts, and whirling slashes with his saber, interspersed with quick turns to run backward for several steps, Hans drew the Swedes gradually closer to the sounds of his own men's voices.

Finally, one of the enemy soldiers knocked Hans's sword from his hand and forced him to the ground. The three Swedes stood over him, gloating. He closed his eyes and prayed for his death to be quick.

His prayer was answered, but not the way he'd anticipated. Creeping up behind the Swedes, the Black Knight struck with the fury of a raging cyclone. After using his left hand to fire his pistol into the back of one man's head at point-blank range, Schuttmann swung his saber with his right hand. The blow severed the second Swede's arm at the shoulder. The third man lunged with his partisan at Schuttmann's exposed side. He was too late. Schuttman fell back to avoid the blade. A quick scramble to his feet, followed by a straight jab of his sword into the off-balance third soldier's back, brought the mismatch to a quick end.

Schuttmann paused with hands on knees to catch his breath. He glanced at Hans, still staring in disbelief from the ground. "Well, Mannheim, it looks like I've bailed you out once again!" he said, laughing. "Now what have you got for me?"

The Swede that Hans had shot in the leg lay on the ground on his side, writhing in pain.

Schuttmann walked over and picked up the partisan that the man had dropped. He straddled the Swede's waist and glared down at him. "Do you wish now to beg for mercy, soldier?"

"Please, sir," the man pleaded. "I beg you to spare me! I swear I'll devote my life and future service to the emperor's cause."

Schuttmann stepped on the man's left shoulder to force him onto his back.

No doubt sensing his simultaneous peril and opportunity, the Swede tried to thrust the small dagger he'd hidden in his right hand at Schuttmann's groin. The ruse didn't work. The dagger glanced harmlessly off Schuttmann's upper-thigh tasset armor as he hopped backward and to the side just in time.

In a rage, Schuttmann kicked the dagger away and once again straddled the Swedish soldier—this time with the tip of the partisan pointed at his chest. Schuttman shook his head slowly. "My regrets, Herr Swede, but I can't allow your sin of faked surrender to go unpunished. Please convey my regards to Martin Luther when you meet him in hell."

Schuttman raised the partisan with both hands and plunged it into the man's heart. After pulling it out, he stepped away from the body and hurled the bloody weapon dead-center into the trunk of a nearby tree.

Turning to face Hans and the others, Schuttman stood with hands on hips, his eyes gleaming. "What are you all staring at? Shouldn't we be getting back to camp now? I'm famished!"

"Helmut," Hans said, "I don't mean to spoil our victory, but aren't you forgetting something?"

Schuttmann surveyed his surroundings in confusion. "Please help me remember, Hans. We'll be sending someone back to bury our own men later."

"That Swedish soldier over there whose arm you cut off . . . he's still alive! Barely so, but alive, nonetheless. And obviously in horrible pain."

"And what would you like me to do about it, Hans?"

Hans hesitated, knowing what he was about to say would raise an unwelcome subject. "You could put him out of his misery," Hans said quietly.

Schuttman looked at him incredulously, then spat on the ground. "The man attacked us and was about to take *your* life, Hans! I did what was necessary to save it. Not only that, you saw what that other fool nearly did to me when I offered to spare him. Let this man suffer his well-deserved agony before the devil takes him home. We're under no obligation to help him. Come on. Enough of this nonsense. Let's get back to headquarters." Schuttmann mounted his horse and set off with his men.

Hans couldn't stop himself. "Lieutenant Enns, hand me your pistol."

Hans took the pistol and knelt beside the wounded Swede. The man was frothing at the mouth, his eyes glazed and his breathing shallow. Blood oozed from his horrible wound. Hans met the soldier's gaze. The man muttered something in Swedish, his voice barely audible. Hans knew exactly what he was requesting: a merciful, quick death.

After taking the man's hand in his own, Hans placed the muzzle of his pistol against the man's forehead and pulled the trigger.

Hans and Lieutenant Enns mounted their horses and soon caught up with the others.

Major Schuttmann smiled and shook his head sadly. "Ah, Major Mannheim, you have such a kind heart—one of the many reasons I admire you so. I just pray you'll never be put to shame for it by those who despise such things. But don't worry. I promise I'll never mention to your father what you just did."

Hans looked away. He knew exactly what the Black Knight was thinking: his reputation for softness with injured enemies could eventually cost him his military career. He returned his gaze to the path ahead and said nothing. He'd have to process the events of today on his own.

Within a few moments, Schuttmann's jubilant mood had returned in full force.

"Well, men, I can't imagine a more fitting end to our near-perfect little battle—with Major Mannheim administering the coup de grâce. Congratulations to all!"

It would seem, Hans thought with weary amazement, *that this has been an immensely enjoyable day—at least for the Black Knight.*

CHAPTER 22

Magdeburg
May 3, 1631

P eter recoiled from the window. The sounds of digging and construction punctuated by gunfire could be heard outside the northern city wall. The latest rumors suggested that General Pappenheim's artillery crews were preparing positions and clearing the surrounding suburbs for their siege batteries to begin blasting away whenever the order came.

The threat against the eastern wall was even more frightening. Anyone standing on the ramparts at night could see thousands of Catholic League Army campfires dotting the landscape across the Elbe River. Fires also burned on the captured fortified islets surrounding the bridged marsh leading to the main Kröcken Gate.

But it wasn't just the Catholic army's intimidating presence that troubled Madgeburg's citizens. Other German cities and towns had faced similar situations during the war—and survived. But as Peter and the other city leaders well knew, this time was different. Emperor Ferdinand had made it clear to Count Tilly that he expected the wealthy city to be *taken*, exploited for Tilly's own use in replenishing supplies for his depleted army and for countering the Swedish invasion. This time, full conformance to all imperial mandates would be required. Ransom was not an option. The city faced two choices: agree to surrender on Tilly's terms or face an all-out assault.

Magdeburg's economic prosperity was an additional concern. In the event of assault, the potential for plunder and pillage was tremendous. Churches, merchants, municipal treasuries, and wealthy citizens would serve as prime targets, especially in the eyes of Tilly's hordes of mercenaries, the vast majority of whom were known to be dealing with severe shortages of pay and food.

What worried Peter the most, though, was the physical threat to the unarmed citizens. Especially the defenseless women and children. It was all well and good for Wilhelm and Falkenberg to state their confidence in the city's ability to hold out until help could arrive from the Swedish king's main army. But, in reality, the odds were terrible. And should the city defenders fail, there was no guarantee that the unleashed Catholic mercenaries would respect the bodies or lives of individual Protestant citizens—whether man, woman, or child.

The citizens' increasing sense of panic, alternating with bright flashes of hope for imminent rescue by King Adolphus, had swelled the number of church attendees across the city in the last few weeks. Almost every church was now filled to overflowing on Sunday mornings. Even people who'd previously considered God to be no more than an afterthought were now turning out in force. But if raw fear was what it took to bring more citizens to their knees in true supplication to the Almighty, Peter thought, so be it—as long as they eventually learned that faith during hard times only was little better than no faith at all. In fact, that premise would be the very subject of the sermon he'd be delivering tomorrow morning, and he was anxious to get to the rectory to finalize his notes.

As Ursula was quick to remind him, though, he also had some other important responsibilities to consider. "Pastor, can you *please* spare just a few minutes from your heavenly meditations to play with Josef while I tend to Edith? I can't handle both of them at once, and I've already asked you twice!"

"Certainly, my wife of noble character," Peter replied with more than just a hint of annoyance. "As you beckon, so must I *immediately* respond."

Stifling the urge to hurl something against the wall, Peter sighed deeply. He said a short prayer, asking for patience and offering thanks for his wife and children. What a tremendous blessing they were! So many other families in the countryside and city had been decimated by plague, birthing trauma, and demise by a myriad other causes. To have a wife, four-year-old son, and three-year-old daughter all in excellent health was not something to be taken for granted.

Peter emerged from his study.

His outstretched arms brought a relieved smile to his wife's face. "So here he comes, Josef—out of his cave and ready to take you on your 'horsey ride.'"

The small boy waddled happily over to his father.

Peter scooped him up in his arms. "All right, brave little knight. Your horse is ready. Up and onto my shoulders!"

"Peter!" Ursula said. "Please be careful with him. He's only four."

Now properly mounted, Josef squeezed his thighs into the sides of Peter's neck and began pounding on his head. "Go, horsey!"

Peter hopped into his study, doing his best to keep the happily squealing Josef upright on his shoulders. After a few minutes of romping around the room chasing imaginary enemy soldiers, he finally lifted his son off his shoulders and sat down in his desk chair with the little boy in his lap. Josef put his tiny arms around Peter's neck and laid his head against his chest.

"One day, son, I have a feeling you'll grow up to be a real knight. But I think maybe God will make you a *white* knight instead of a black knight. What do you think of that?"

Josef smiled, took one hand away from Peter's neck, and placed his thumb in his mouth. He'd been up since early that morning. It looked like a nap was imminent.

After making sure Josef had fallen asleep, Peter carried him over to the bedroom, where Ursula was already laying Edith down in her crib. "Did we wear them out for an hour at least?" Peter whispered. "I need to be getting up to the rectory and finishing my sermon notes."

"Yes, darling, thank you!" Ursula whispered back as she took Josef and laid him down on his small pallet. "But before you get back to that, there's something we should discuss."

"Can't it wait until this afternoon?" Peter asked.

"No, Peter, it can't."

Chastened, Peter escorted his wife to the living area and sat down at the table across from her. "What is it, dear?"

Ursula's eyes welled up with tears. "Peter, I'm so terribly frightened. The Catholics could attack any day now, and the cathedral council still has no plan for protecting or even hiding all the children at our orphanage. Even worse, *we* have no plan for me and our own children to find you if an attack happens during the day when we're apart."

"*What?* Do you mean to tell me the orphanage superintendent hasn't received *any* instructions from Wilhelm's aides? Isn't that one of Wilhelm's main duties—to oversee church- and charity-related city functions, especially in times of crisis?"

"Herr Wilhelm's been asked several times for his instructions, but the man continually puts it off. He keeps saying, 'You don't need to be concerned. Colonel Falkenberg and our city defense force will keep us perfectly safe until help arrives from King Adolphus.'"

Peter leaned across the table and grasped his wife's hands. "Ursula, listen to me. We can't rely on Wilhelm's optimistic predictions. You're right. We need a plan—now—to shelter the orphans. I'll speak to Dr. Weber and Pastor Bake tomorrow after our prayer meeting. We'll approach Wilhelm together with a recommendation that we'll demand he approve or improve on immediately.

"And as for you, Josef, and Edith, if an attack starts during the day, just stay at the orphanage until I can get there. It's a good distance from the city walls, and you'll be as safe there as any other place in the city."

"But, Peter, what if you're delayed in getting there or . . . even worse . . . ?" Ursula broke down, unable to continue.

Peter held her face in his hands. "Ursula, that'll be part of the plan I'll work out with Dr. Weber and Pastor Bake tomorrow. Please try not to panic over this. It's still very possible that Wilhelm and Falkenberg will negotiate a settlement with the Catholic army and avoid an attack. But regardless, you know God will show us the right way to respond."

Ursula nodded. "I'll just have to do a better job of depending on God and not on man, won't I, Pastor? Didn't you deliver your test sermon for the council on that subject?"

"You have an excellent memory, dear. And don't forget: you'll have somebody else to help you. Won't Katrina be with you at the orphanage? She's a smart girl and should be able to help you keep Josef and Edith safe and secure until I can get there."

Katrina—the part-time nursemaid hired more than three years ago to help Ursula through her difficult pregnancy with Edith—had stayed on as Ursula's personal assistant at the orphanage. Her main function there was to watch over Josef and Edith, allowing Ursula to tend to the needs of the other children.

"Yes," Ursula agreed, "Katrina's certainly a blessing. But promise me that if an attack starts, you won't delay too long, trying to get everything in perfect order at the church."

Peter could feel his wife trembling despite their close embrace. "I promise," he said.

❧

"I presume you've heard the news?" Dr. Weber asked, leaning back in the chair next to Peter's desk.

Peter was pleasantly surprised to find Dr. Weber at the rectory office. The elderly pastor's appearances at the office were becoming less frequent due to his bad hip. "I've heard all manner of news lately, sir. Almost all of it bad. Which news are you referring to?"

"Our 'brilliant' city leaders have once again rejected Tilly's latest reasonable demand for an honorable surrender of the city. This one would require only that we admit a limited imperial garrison and allow the city to be used as a staging area for Tilly's fight to push

Adolphus and his Swedes out of Germany. We'd turn over some lands to the Catholic Church, but there would be no forced conversion of our citizens to Catholicism. Unfortunately, Wilhelm and Colonel Falkenberg balked at the idea. So Wilhelm sent Tilly a counterproposal yesterday demanding the mediation of some north German towns and princes—those claiming to be neutral in the fight between the emperor and the foreign forces from Sweden."

"Are they insane?" Peter protested. "How many more offers from Tilly are they expecting? At some point, even *I* would lose patience with their obvious delaying tactics!"

"Such is the arrogance and self-delusion of those in this city who allow themselves to be swayed by the rantings of our radical brother in Christ, Pastor Spaignart. They insist that yielding in any way to the emperor and Count Tilly would mean renouncing faith in our Lord. They claim that we merely need to wait 'one or two more days' for Adolphus's forces to arrive and deliver our hoped-for salvation."

"And meanwhile," Peter lamented, now seeing the picture clearly, "Tilly's anger builds over the city's continuing refusal to accept his terms. His fear grows that the king *will* arrive soon and threaten the rear of Tilly's own forces. At some point, you know Wilhelm will force him into playing his hand. And when that happens, Doctor, I hate to think of the peril to our civilian population. Especially, selfishly speaking, my own wife and children. Do Wilhelm, Falkenberg, and Spaignart *ever* consider the consequences of their stance?"

Weber shook his head. "If they do, you'd never know it from their rhetoric."

The senior pastor prayed with his protégé and then stood to leave. Peter noted how exceedingly tired and frail he looked. The strain of the past few days was clearly affecting him.

"Doctor, we've discussed my own family's plans but not yours. What will *you* do if the Catholics attack and break through?"

Weber managed a weak grin. "After securing the church, I'll do like I always do in times of personal crisis. Pray and hope for the best. Unlike you, I have no family to worry about. The Lord will show me what to do if and when the time comes."

It sounded incredibly naïve, Peter thought. He started to protest, then checked himself. He knew his mentor. Once Dr. Weber became convinced that "the Lord will show me" something, any argument to the contrary was useless.

Peter rose and shook his hand. "Let's just pray this will all blow over and that we're making a big to-do out of nothing."

CHAPTER 23

Countryside east of Magdeburg
May 3, 1631

The order to report to Count Tilly's headquarters a half mile up the road had reached Hans only a few minutes ago. No reason had been given, but he knew it was something important.

Upon entering the main tent, Baron von Mannheim approached and pulled him aside. "Son, brace yourself. We have a difficult situation on our hands."

"What is it, Father?"

The baron's face was scarlet with horror and fury. "Falkenberg's Protestant demons have sunk beneath the lowest depths of depravity. Late yesterday afternoon, one of their raiding parties from the city decided it was not enough to do honorable battle with our imperial soldiers. No, the cowards decided instead to unleash unspeakable acts against innocent civilians—*Catholic* civilians, few though they are in this region these days."

"Where did this happen?"

"A small country parish church about three miles from here. Four parishioners were celebrating Mass with the priest. Five raiders arrogantly rode their horses directly into the chapel. Told the priest to immediately produce the entire church treasury or face the consequences. The man pleaded that the treasury was depleted to virtually nothing. They became furious and forced the parishioners outside behind the church, tied everyone up, and made them sit and watch their next devilish act."

"Which was?" Hans asked, noticing his father's scowl and hesitation.

"It's almost too disgusting to describe. The soldiers tied the priest to a bench and forced a funnel into his mouth. Made him swallow a whole bucketful of a horrid mixture of unspeakably vile ingredients. They called it the 'Swedish Drink,' and they'd obviously come prepared to administer it. After that, two of the villains pressed and rocked a heavy log against the priest's bloated stomach for several minutes. The poor man died when his heart gave out from the trauma of it all.

"If the raiders hadn't been stopped, the other parishioners would almost certainly have suffered the same fate. But by the grace of our Savior, a troop of Pappenheim's cavalry happened to pass along the road in front of the church and heard the cries beyond. They raced to the scene and captured the raiders as they tried to run away."

Hans had never failed to experience a deep sense of rage when hearing tales of the wanton abuse of innocent civilians, and this incident was among the worst he'd heard. "A case open and shut. I assume the raiders have already been tried and dealt with according to Tilly's system of justice?"

"That's where things get a bit complicated, son. It's the reason you've been summoned here, along with four other officers specially selected by the count himself."

Hans felt his stomach drop. "What exactly are you saying, Father?"

"Tilly's determined to use this atrocity to set an example—not only for Falkenberg's devils but for our own people as well. He wants our whole company of officers and senior enlisted men assembled on the drill field in three days, along with representatives from our civilian camp followers. All five captured raiders are to be executed—beheaded by sword. And it'll be *you* and four others who are assigned to personally perform the executions."

"But, sir, why us?" Hans nearly shouted in exasperation. "Why not our provost officer and his subordinates? Isn't that their job? Aren't *they* the ones who're trained for this sort of thing?"

The baron shook his head grimly. "All I know is that Tilly wants his select field officers to be the ones to help him deliver his hard message about the incident. It's a message he'll explain in the speech he plans to deliver to the assembly just before the executions."

Hans looked down. He despised the whole idea.

The baron gripped him by the arm. "Major Mannheim, look at me. You *will* carry out this task, unpleasant though it may be. The emperor expects it, Count Tilly expects it, and I expect it. Those men deserve far worse than what they'll be getting. This is no time for those weak emotions of yours to interfere with your duty. I'm proud of what you've accomplished in the army so far, son, and so you should be. You've risen in the ranks, honored your family's name. *Do not* imperil everything I've invested in you by making some feeble attempt to get out of this."

Hans saw the steely glint in his father's eyes. He knew the moment had arrived to make up for his cowardly behavior in Prague. Squelch the perception of softness. Prove to his father and others once and for all that he'd truly developed the inner fortitude needed to be a high-ranking career officer in the Catholic League Army. Prove to them that nothing would stand in his way when required to mete out appropriate justice in defense of the holy Catholic faith.

"Of course, sir. You need have no worries on that account."

Hans walked over to the table where three of the other officers had gathered and were now heatedly discussing the situation. Only Helmut Schuttmann, the Black Knight, seemed unperturbed. He sat with eyes closed on a bench against the wall, as if finally getting a chance to take a long-delayed nap.

Hans joined him and tried to pick up snippets of the other officers' conversation. According to one of them, all five prisoners had been convicted and sentenced the previous evening. There was only one messy issue to resolve. It concerned the fifteen-year-old Protestant "soldier" who'd been assigned to guard the horses and four parishioners while the priest was being tortured. Three of those he guarded claimed that the boy had been laughing and taunting them throughout the terrible sequence, telling them they were next in line. But the other one, an elderly peasant woman, defended him. She said the boy had been highly distraught, crying at what was taking place, and at one point had screamed at his cohorts to stop.

Why there should have been such a stark difference in the witnesses' accounts was anyone's guess. What *was* indisputable was that the boy was the only one of the five who hadn't attempted to flee when the Catholic troopers arrived. Instead, he'd thrown himself at their feet and pleaded for mercy. But after a great deal of deliberation, the trial officials had decided in favor of the account of the majority and had declared the boy just as culpable of a war crime as their other prisoners. In the end, Tilly himself had given approval to the boy's execution along with the others.

"Men!" the provost officer bellowed, interrupting the officers' conversation. "We need to figure out who will be responsible for dispatching each of the five prisoners. Step up to the table and draw your lot."

Hans drew the number five.

CHAPTER 24

Magdeburg
May 4, 1631

The basement of St. John's overflowed, reflecting the huge attendance at the Sunday service that had just concluded. Friends, well-wishers, socialites, and dignitaries gathered together in their compatible circles. The two reception lines—the men's headed by Peter and the women's by Ursula—stretched much farther than usual. Each swelled with congregants seeking an extra measure of pastoral comfort and reassurance concerning the city's imminent peril.

Peter's sermon had been generally well received, though at the end a few of the visiting city councilors had made their displeasure known.

Dr. Weber, standing in the reception line along with Otto Gericke, couldn't resist condemning their behavior. "Otto, did you see the reaction of those councilors who hardly ever attend our services? The moment Peter began to pray for the council to simply be open to God's leading as far as their dealings with Count Tilly, they got up and stalked out of the church!"

Otto nodded. "It seems that Peter's message on 'Faith in God for Hard Times' for them translates to 'Faith in the King of Sweden for Hard Times.' Wilhelm and Spaignart have developed that philosophy into a new form of religion."

Peter, in a lull between congregants wishing to shake his hand, started to join the men's conversation but was interrupted by Ursula. "Pastor," she whispered in his ear, "there's someone over in my reception line I think you should meet."

Peter asked Weber to take over his greeting role for a few minutes.

He walked arm in arm with his wife across the room, approaching two women and a child with their backs to him. They appeared to be admiring one of the large murals on the narthex wall. Based on their plain clothes, he guessed they were not well-to-do. One of the women had plaited, reddish-brown hair framed by a lace head covering. Peter stared at her. Was this someone familiar?

The three turned to face him.

"Peter, please greet our newest assistant at the orphanage. This is Fräulein Anna Ritter. She's here tonight with her mother Frieda and her little sister Liesa."

Peter could barely contain his surprise. He'd never expected to encounter Fräulein Ritter again, much less here in the city. "Ladies, it's an honor to meet you."

All three curtsied.

Anna was the first to speak. "Hello, Pastor Erhart," she said shyly. "It's good to see you again."

An awkward silence followed, finally broken by Ursula's gracious reassurance. "Pastor," she said with an easy laugh, "you don't need to pretend you've never met this beautiful and talented young lady before. She's already told me she'd had occasion to meet you before she and her family moved to the city. I certainly don't take offense."

Peter relaxed, relieved to know that Ursula was aware of the innocent explanation for Anna's recognition of him. He'd heard too many stories of pastors whose marriages had failed due to unwarranted jealousies nurtured silently by their wives.

"Fräulein Anna." Peter smiled, bowing slightly. "Indeed, I still remember crossing paths with you and your father on one of my ministry visits to the countryside."

Anna blushed. "Yes, sir. You very kindly greeted us and tried to help, and I'm afraid I didn't exactly respond as I should have. My father wasn't feeling well, and I wasn't in the best of moods."

Peter chuckled. "You certainly don't need to apologize, Fräulein. Trust me, I've had to deal with far harsher responses to my clumsy attempts to help someone!" He hesitated. "And by the way, I hope that Herr Ritter is well."

"Oh, yes, Pastor," Frieda replied. "He's never felt better. I only wish he'd pay as much heed to feeding his soul. He's a believer, but he's never seen much value in attending church."

Peter could see that Frau Ritter was distressed over her husband's lack of religious discipline and tried to reassure her. "Not all of God's children respond to him in the same way and at the same stage of life, my lady. Perhaps the Lord has another time in mind for drawing your husband to worship with his fellow believers."

"Thank you, Pastor. That's just what I needed to hear to ease my own mind. And thank you, sir, for your excellent message today. I know my husband would also have appreciated it very much, if he'd been here with us."

"I'll thank the Lord for the message. But I'm glad that you found it helpful. And what about you, young lady? I'll wager you'd rather be somewhere else right now, wouldn't you?"

Ten-year-old Liesa Ritter smiled shyly.

"Answer him, child!" Frieda said, gently cuffing her daughter between the shoulder blades.

"Y-yes, sir. N-no, sir. Thank you, sir."

Peter knew he was right. Liesa obviously would have preferred to be elsewhere with others her own age. He laughed and patted the little girl on the head. "She's been very patient. I suppose we shouldn't keep her in agony much longer. But tell me, Anna, when did you start working at the orphanage?"

"About four months ago, sir. Your wife was kind enough to recommend my hiring to the orphanage superintendent. She did that knowing only what I'd told her about my limited experience as a housemaid and before that as a field worker helping my father. And ever since, Frau Erhart has been nothing but a wonderful mentor and friend to me."

"Oh, nonsense, Anna!" Ursula protested. "You are too modest. Peter, this young lady has been the greatest help. Everyone agrees. Her willingness to pitch in to clean, straighten up, and even decorate our cluttered play and sleeping areas is priceless. And the children all love her. I don't know how we ever got along without her."

Peter gave her a puzzled look. "I have no doubts. But, Ursula, why did it take four months and Anna's personal appearance here for you to tell me about her? Especially if you knew of our mutual acquaintance."

Ursula flashed a coy smile at Anna.

"Allow me to explain, sir," Anna offered. "When I realized just after my hiring that Frau Erhart was married to you, I told her that I'd seen you preach once at our village church—and that three years later you'd tried to help me and my father at the crossroads. But I begged her not to tell you about me because I was afraid it would irritate you to recall me."

Peter was astonished. So *that* was where he had first seen her, *years* before their crossroads encounter. Now it all came back: his first guest sermon in Grünfeld and meeting Anna and her friends in the reception line afterward. "Irritate me? Why on earth would it irritate me?"

"Because I was rude to you at the crossroads—and the fact that I never was present for any more of your sermons at our church. I feared you might think that I'd stayed away on purpose, that maybe I hadn't liked your preaching."

"So what allowed you to finally overcome your fears and visit with us today?"

"The kind invitations from your wife—and all the good things I'd been hearing from others in the city about you and your church. And," she admitted, blushing, "I started thinking how silly I'd been to avoid you for such childish reasons."

Peter laughed. "Well, I must say I'm ecstatic that all of you are here. I hope—no, allow me to be bolder and say *I'll expect*—to see you all here in the future. Maybe even with Herr Ritter in tow."

"And I'm sure, daughter, that your new fiancé would enjoy this church as well!" Frieda gushed.

Anna glanced beseechingly at her mother.

"Pastor!" her mother continued excitedly as Anna rolled her eyes and shook her head. "Did you know that my daughter will be getting married three months from now? Her fiancé is the son of the blacksmith my husband now works for. He's a wonderful boy—serves on the city defense force. My husband and the boy's father will be signing the papers next week and . . . and . . ." She stopped mid-sentence and began to weep.

Anna and Ursula put their arms around her to console her.

"There, Mother, it'll be all right," Anna said, seemingly without much conviction. "Joachim will make it through this city crisis safely, just like the rest of us. I know he and I will have our special day together and make you and Father the happiest people alive."

Frau Ritter nodded as she composed herself. "You're right. And I'm making such an embarrassment of our family. Imagine, standing here and whining about things over which I have no control. Pastor and Frau Erhart, we're delighted to have met you today. I hope we'll be able to visit your church again very soon!"

Peter bowed and kissed the woman's hand. "A pleasure, Frau Ritter. Your entire family is always welcome here. And Anna, best wishes to you and your fiancé for your upcoming marriage!"

"Thank you, sir. He wishes—I mean, *I* wish—the best for it also," Anna replied—rather awkwardly so, Peter thought.

As he gazed at Anna one last time before she turned to follow her mother and sister toward the exit, Peter couldn't help but be struck by her captivating features. She had a different kind of beauty than Ursula's. Ursula: the classic blonde Nordic goddess. Anna: a mysterious, darker blend of exotic lines and angles, exquisitely proportioned. The slight scar beneath her left eye only added to her compelling allure, and he wondered where it had come from.

The voice was even more inquisitive. *Even prettier than the last time you met her at the crossroads, isn't she, Pastor? Can you imagine what it would be like with her? Remember how you used to enjoy constantly recalling that enticing seventeen-year-old "sick" girl who almost seduced you? It's been a while since you've thought about such things, hasn't it?*

This time, Peter shook off the voice's taunts without too much effort. *Thank the Lord for Ursula,* he thought.

CHAPTER 25

Countryside east of Magdeburg
May 6, 1631

M ajor Hans Mannheim stood at attention. The executioner's sword was in his right hand, its blade resting against his shoulder.

The four other Catholic League Army field officers did the same. In front of each officer stood his assigned prisoner.

"I *would* have to draw the final lot, wouldn't I?" Hans muttered to himself. He hoped he hadn't been overheard by Major Schuttmann, who stood in identical posture only five yards to his left.

Hans did his best to avert his gaze from the fifteen-year-old boy standing restrained in front of him. How was it, he thought bitterly, that lot number five just happened to be associated with by far the youngest and least guilty of the prisoners? Was it pure coincidence? Something orchestrated by God himself? Or was it something that his own father or even Count Tilly might have prearranged in order to put Hans to a true test of fortitude?

Hans tightened his grip on the handle as he fought back his growing sense of revulsion. At least, Hans thought, being last in the sequence would afford plenty of opportunity to observe how four other committed officers were willing to obey any order given them. Hans prayed that the proceedings would go smoothly, that he would perform resolutely and flawlessly.

If only Tilly would just get on with it, he thought. Twenty minutes had already passed. During that time, he had stood under the hot sun in this excruciating posture, waiting for the supreme commander's grand arrival.

A loud and sustained drum roll announced the end of the wait.

"Special Detail, about-face!" the provost shouted, undoubtedly relieved to be absolved today from having to carry out the terrible duty normally assigned to him.

Hans and the other four spun counterclockwise in unison to face the small wooden stand erected in the middle of the drill field.

Count Tilly mounted the steps in regal fashion, followed in order by General Gottfried von Pappenheim and Baron Albert von Mannheim.

"Special Detail, present arms!"

Hans, never having wielded an executioner's sword before, found it difficult to hold the long, heavy weapon in a rigid, upright position with the hilt in front of his nose. Thankfully, the handle was long enough to allow a two-fisted grip.

Tilly and his subordinates turned to face the large assembled company. More than a thousand soldiers and civilians now gathered between the stand and the grassy knoll where the prisoners and their executioners stood. Tilly walked to the front edge of the stand and gazed out upon the crowd. All stood at attention.

Tilly at seventy-two was still an imposing figure to behold, even at a distance. True, some doubters felt he'd shown signs of weariness in directing recent campaigns. General Pappenheim was supposedly among those who would occasionally challenge his decisions even in front of other officers. But there was no sign of fatigue or passivity in Tilly's appearance today.

The supreme commander began with his usual salutation. His voice boomed with confidence. "Officers, soldiers, and civilian followers of the Catholic League Army . . . in the name of the Blessed Mother of our

Crucified Savior, I command that you take your ease."

A hush fell over the assembly. Hans gratefully spread his feet and rested the tip of the heavy sword on the ground. Tilly paused, obviously desiring the crowd's sense of righteous outrage over the atrocity to build.

Finally, he spoke. "For months—*months*—we've all been hearing the praises sung by the heretical followers of that blasphemer, Luther, in the city we besiege. 'Hail to the Swedish king!' they cry. 'All hail, King Gustavus Adolphus, the Lion of the North, the Protector of Protestantism, the Deliverer of Germany!'" Tilly straightened his bent frame, raised his arm, and shook his fist at the sky. "Blind, stiff-necked idiots!" he roared. "Let them continue in their defiant self-delusion. Before long, the lapdogs of Adolphus who now cower behind Magdeburg's walls shall drink the bitter poison of God's wrath, administered by the grace of God through his earthly instrument, our Catholic League Army. Unless, of course, they should cease their stubborn delaying tactics and accept the only offer for survival under honorable terms that we shall ever make to this city: *Surrender now!*"

The assembled crowd let loose an earthshaking roar of approval that rose to the skies. "Hail Mary! Bless you, Father Tilly! Bless you!"

Tilly waited for the noise to subside. "But military considerations aside, we have the current matter to deal with. These five Adolphus-sucking worms deserve the worst punishment devised by man. Alas, our military code permits me to call for nothing worse than to hang the bastards by their necks. But it occurred to me there was a much better way to send Falkenberg and his city defenders an important message. By ordering our leading young field officers to personally decapitate these devils, thus granting them a far quicker and more honorable way to die, we confirm that we, the Catholic League Army, are *above* the filth and degradation that Adolphus seeks to impose on the German population. We testify that *we* are the faithful agents of our crucified and risen Savior, determined to defend his Church, his pope, and his emperor with our lives, yet merciful to every extent possible in our treatment of his enemies."

Most in the crowd nodded to each other or raised their weapons in approval.

So there it was, Hans thought. He and the other four officers had been commissioned to demonstrate a higher standard of behavior and a more honorable method of execution for convicted torturers. Perhaps this supposedly noble action would even convince the citizens of Magdeburg that an honorable surrender to a "merciful" foe like the Catholic League Army would be in their best interests! Why should Hans complain about his designated role in such a high-minded effort? Hadn't Tilly just made his job easier to accept?

"And with that, I hereby order the execution of these thugs to begin!" Tilly shouted.

The crowd unloosed a deafening roar as they shook their fists and weapons at the five prisoners awaiting their final punishment.

"Special Detail, attention! About-face!"

Hans turned once again to face his assigned prisoner. He saw that things weren't going to go easily. The boy was weeping softly, the only one of the five to show any sign of fear or remorse. The others bore expressions of defiance, even disdain for the "honorable" final punishment they were about to receive.

Hans felt his hands sweating heavily on the sword handle as the first prisoner in line was forced to kneel. The restrainer drew his head forward by the hair, making for an unobstructed presentation of the back of his neck. The provost read the execution manifesto. The drum roll began. The executioner stepped forward, positioned the heavy sword against the man's neck. He lifted the sword with both hands, then swung downward in a smooth but deadly arc. The result was a clean separation of head from body. The drums fell silent. The crowd bellowed its satisfaction.

The second prisoner was dispatched in identical fashion, but the third wasn't so fortunate. The officer's first swing somehow failed to completely sever the man's head. Aghast, the executioner stood staring at the twitching, dangling mass. It was a full ten seconds before the crowd's jeers finally spurred him on to finish the job.

Hans cursed under his breath. This was the inevitable result of requiring amateurs to perform such a brutal yet delicate undertaking.

Major Schuttmann's prisoner was next. Hans knew the Black Knight would experience no such trouble. He was right: another perfectly clean separation of head from body. Mission accomplished.

It was Hans's turn.

The young prisoner was forced to kneel. The execution manifesto was read. The drum roll began as the restrainer extended the boy's neck by the hair.

Hans stepped up to position the sword. *Help me, Mary. By the grace of the Savior, help me to do this right!*

"Sir, this is a travesty!" someone in the crowd suddenly cried to Count Tilly. "The boy does not deserve this! I was there! I saw his reaction to the whole thing! He wasn't—"

"Silence, woman!" Tilly shouted. "We've already been over this. You've had your say, as have the others who've contradicted you. I've made my final judgment, and we shall proceed accordingly. Carry on, Major Mannheim!"

Hans nodded. He tightened his hands on the sword handle yet again.

The drum roll resumed.

Hans looked at the boy whose head was bowed before him and on whose neck the blade of his heavy sword now rested.

Suddenly, as if in a split second, a heavy curtain had been lowered and then raised again upon an entirely new scene, Hans no longer saw the boy. He saw himself, being forced by Count Thurn to kneel and look into the terrified eyes of the bloodied governor thirteen years ago in Prague.

Hans stood transfixed. His heart pounded and his mind raced. He was unable to lift the sword that now felt like it weighed a thousand pounds.

The crowd murmured.

Realizing he couldn't complete the task, Hans backed away.

The murmur turned into shouts of disbelief and rage.

"Mannheim, what's the delay?" cried Hans's father. "Perform your duty!"

Hans barely heard him. He stared at the ground, bewildered and oblivious to what was going on around him.

The drummer boy stopped his death roll, obviously unsure how to proceed. The boy prisoner was now sobbing uncontrollably, and his restrainer struggled to keep him in position.

Major Schuttmann dropped his own bloodstained sword and approached Hans.

The crowd fell silent.

The Black Knight grasped Hans gently by the left arm and gazed into his downcast eyes. "Mannheim, what is it? The boy's youth? His lesser crime? What?"

Hans looked up slowly and returned Schuttmann's gaze. "It's everything, Helmut. This whole thing. I just can't . . ."

Schuttmann placed his right hand on Hans's forearm and his left on the sword handle that Hans was still gripping with all his might. "Hans," he said quietly, "let me have your sword."

Hans stared at his fellow officer.

"Please, Hans, my good friend, just let me have it."

Hans released his grip on the handle.

The Black Knight spun to face Count Tilly and the rest of the assembly, sword held in the present-arms position. "Sir, request permission!"

"Carry on, soldier!" Tilly responded.

The Black Knight approached the prisoner and positioned the sword. One quick, smooth motion and it was all over.

This time, dead silence from the crowd.

Within five minutes, the entire assembly had dispersed along with Major Schuttmann and the other three executing officers. Only the decapitated prisoners, the burial detail, and Hans remained on the knoll.

Two subordinates of the provost stepped up and seized Hans by both arms.

It was cold and damp in the cellar of the farmhouse that was serving as a temporary jail for Catholic League Army officers accused of lesser crimes. At this point, Hans was uncertain whether his "crime" would be considered minor or major by Count Tilly. All he knew was a sense of complete devastation. He had failed as an officer and a man, especially in his father's eyes. Sick to his stomach at the thought of what lay ahead, he pushed aside uneaten the meager meal that had been provided to him.

Baron von Mannheim entered the room.

Hans stood and saluted but couldn't bring himself to look at his father.

The baron didn't return the salute.

"Father, I beg your—"

The baron slapped him hard across the face with his gloved hand, knocking him to the floor.

"Major Mannheim, you have committed a grave error in refusing to carry out your assigned duty. You are a disgrace to your unit and to this army. It's a wonder that Count Tilly, in his mercy, has decided not to have *you* beheaded for insubordination in front of his entire assembly. Fortunately, his gratitude for your commendable service and his great respect for your fighting skills have given him pause. As it is, he's relieved you of your command for the duration of this operation in Magdeburg. You are confined to this jail until appropriate, long-term disciplinary measures can be decided upon."

Hans was overwhelmed with despair. Tears flooded his cheeks.

"And for what, Mannheim? Your misguided sense of guilt and softheartedness not only embarrassed your supreme commander, it caused needless suffering by prolonging that poor prisoner's agony. God only knows that Tilly went beyond the pale in allowing those men an honorable method of execution. And you couldn't even follow through to help him in accomplishing that.

"Hans," he continued, his voice softening slightly, "you're still my son. Nothing will ever change that. I'll ensure that you remain well treated and provided for here. I'll do whatever I can to restore your commission. But you must know that your performance today has disgraced us both."

"Father," Hans sobbed, choking on his words, "I know full well how I failed you in Prague. And here yet again. Can you ever forgive me?"

Baron von Mannheim sighed heavily, then turned and walked toward the door.

"*Father!*" Hans cried desperately. "I swear with every bone in my body: I will make amends to you and to the army! I'll never fail you again! I beg you and Count Tilly for just one more chance!"

The baron paused at the door, turned, and looked at him sadly. "We shall see."

Hans watched his father close the door behind him as he left. *I've disgraced him yet again*, he thought bitterly through his tears. *Just like at the castle. And this time, no Peter Erhart with me to soften the blow.*

CHAPTER 26

Magdeburg
May 17, 1631

Anna plunked down onto one of the wooden stools beneath the apple tree in the far corner of the Ritters' small backyard. After peering cautiously over her shoulder to make sure Mutti and Liesa were inside the house and out of earshot, she leveled her gaze at her fiancé.

"Joachim, why won't Mutti allow me to make just one small decision about the ceremony? I'm not six years old anymore. When will she and Vati finally realize that?"

Joachim's eyes widened. "You speak so ungratefully toward them, Anna! Think of all they've done to help make our wedding possible."

Anna buried her face in her hands. Why was Joachim always so determined to defend her parents and make her feel like a heartless, spoiled child?

Maybe, she conceded, her annoyance with her mother's overbearing tendencies of late was unfair. It hadn't been easy for anyone in the Ritter household since they'd moved to the city in early November and squeezed together in the back of her aunt's house. After a long search, during which her father had remained sober and had secured a decent job as an assistant blacksmith, they had moved into a one-floor house with a single loft in the southwestern part of the city. Her mother had taken on morning work as a seamstress while Anna worked part-time in the afternoons—at first as a housemaid and later as a city orphanage assistant—to help with the rent. The adjustment to city life had been especially hard for Mutti, who'd never been comfortable with changes to her normal routines. But still, couldn't Mutti be just a little more considerate of her daughter's wishes for the most important day of her life?

Anna lifted her head, her eyes brimming with angry tears. She blinked them back, not wishing to provoke Joachim into yet another misplaced defense of her parents.

"Really, Anna," Joachim said, easing himself onto another stool next to Anna and taking her hand in both of his. "Why are you making such a big thing of this? Isn't the fact that we'll be together soon the only thing that matters? Your mother won't have the final say over your decisions after that."

Anna jerked her hand away and crossed her arms. "Ha! That's what you think. You obviously don't know Mutti like I do."

Joachim was quiet for a moment. "Well, at least I'm thankful for your mother's good sense on *some* things."

"Such as?"

"Such as the fact that if she and your father had left you to your own devices, you might have been lured away into a miserable life. Just think. If they hadn't introduced you to me, you might have run away with that idiotic Swede from Colonel Falkenberg's bodyguard unit. You know— the one who started panting after you the moment you moved here." He grinned devilishly. "Or who knows? Maybe you'd have frittered your life away as a spinster, keeping your nose in all those high-minded religious pamphlets and books you've become so obsessed with."

Anna rolled her eyes. Joachim always exaggerated when trying to make a point.

Twenty-four-year-old Joachim Kappel, the son of the blacksmith for whom her father worked, had begun courting Anna three months ago.

Joachim was nice, good-looking, and well-intentioned. Especially in the eyes of Anna's parents, who hadn't hidden their eagerness to secure a comfortable life for her. Thrilled by the prospect of her marriage to such an honorable young man, they hadn't objected that it had taken so little time for Joachim to state his intentions.

Though she liked and respected Joachim, Anna had at first resisted the idea. But she had finally succumbed to her parents' pressure. After two months of courting, she'd surprised even herself when she'd agreed to marry Joachim. When she had told her parents, they'd shouted with joy. It had almost seemed they'd taken Anna's decision as some kind of validation for themselves. And ever since, she'd had to fight to keep her annoyance in check.

"Joachim, you sound just like my mother. Did it ever occur to you that my learning to read all those 'high-minded pamphlets' that talk about God's Word and its meaning for our lives might actually be something good to share with *you*, my future husband? Or maybe you want me to be just like Mutti and every other common citizen's wife in this city: content to rely on my far-wiser husband to do all my important thinking for me!"

Joachim smiled sheepishly. He edged his stool closer to hers and draped his arm around her shoulders. "Anna, I'm sorry. I didn't mean to offend you. You know how much I adore you."

After a few moments, Anna had calmed down sufficiently to allow Joachim to take her face gently between his hands and look her in the eye. "Anna, you know good and well what's *really* bothering your mother. She's afraid our wedding might not happen before the Catholics decide to attack. But even if they did, she really doesn't need to worry. I swear our defense force is strong enough to kill every Catholic soldier and stick his head on a pike if they dare try to sack this city."

Anna nodded and smiled, trying her best to believe her fiancé's bravado. "I should also have mentioned in all my complaining how proud I am of *you*, Joachim. God couldn't have blessed me with a kinder or braver man to marry."

"Anna, you are so beautiful." Joachim closed his eyes and leaned in to kiss her tenderly on the lips. Anna put her arms around his neck, politely allowing his kiss to linger a bit longer than usual. Inside, she felt what she always did when Joachim tried to express his physical affections toward her: nothing.

Just then, out of nowhere, a crazy, scary, and delicious thought took hold of her mind. She imagined herself not in the arms of Joachim Kappel, but of the man whose attraction she thought she had finally outgrown: Peter Erhart.

It was as if a dam had broken inside of her. Anna pulled Joachim's head harder against hers and allowed her lips to part. Aroused by her newfound passion, he let his hands slide slowly down from her face on their way to encircling her waist.

"*Anna*! What is taking you so long? Will you *please* bring that firewood in?"

Anna and Joachim jumped up at the same time, as if a volcano had suddenly erupted beneath their stools. She looked around the tree trunk and through the low-hanging branches toward the rear door. She breathed a sigh of relief; Mutti hadn't seen them.

"Coming, Mutti."

Anna turned to Joachim. They both burst out laughing.

"Well, maybe your mother *is* a little overcontrolling," Joachim said. "Much to my regret, this time."

Anna smiled and kissed him on the lips. "Enough for now. It's time for me to go help at the orphanage. Get out of here, and go on back to work before Mutti gets more suspicious than she already is."

After Joachim departed, Anna collected three of the drier logs from the woodpile and went inside. She threw the logs onto the cooking fire, then began collecting and stuffing into a bag the small toys and other items that she'd made or purchased herself for the orphans. She knew what joy these little offerings always brought and looked forward to seeing the children's faces once she arrived for work—almost as much as she looked forward to thinking about Peter on her way there.

⌒⌀⌀⌐

Following lunch and during the children's nap time, Ursula's call interrupted Anna in the middle of her cleaning tasks. "Fräulein Anna, would you please join me in the office?"

She went in and sat down.

"Anna, I just got word from Peter that Administrator Wilhelm has finally approved the plan for sheltering our children if the Catholics launch a full-scale attack. Once it's clear that an attack's begun, Pastor Bake will send three of his assistants over here. They'll escort the children to the cathedral, where they can take shelter in the basement. They'll have plenty of adults to watch over them there. As for all of us staff members, it'll be our choice whether to stay here and await our husbands, go home to our families, or go along with the children. Peter wants me to stay here with Josef and Edith until he can arrive. And Katrina told me she also wants to stay with us, since she's unmarried and has no other family in the city. But what about you, dear?"

"Well," Anna said, "since I have no husband to speak for me—at least not yet—I'll plan to go home to my family. But, Frau Erhart, are you sure that three male escorts from the cathedral will be enough to manage fifty frightened children? I hate to think of those men trying to handle them all by themselves. It's nearly a one-mile walk."

Ursula didn't appear concerned. "I'm sure one or more of our other assistants will decide to accompany them. I'll speak to them about it a little later." She paused a moment. "Anna, I just wanted you to know how delighted Peter and I were to see you and your family at church last Sunday. We both hope you and your family found it to your approval."

Anna was deeply touched. Being supervised and mentored by Frau Erhart sometimes made Anna feel as if she were being sheltered by the wings of a beautiful angel.

Ursula had once overheard Anna talking excitedly to one of the other assistants about her determination to improve her reading skills and understand the wide variety of religious tracts and pamphlets spreading with ever-increasing frequency around the city. Ursula had suggested some ideas and had taken an hour each day during the children's nap time to help her read through the materials. Anna was ecstatic at her progress. She especially enjoyed the challenging religious discussions with Ursula that these readings often produced.

Even the subject of relationships hadn't been off-limits for their conversations. Anna had shared her concern about Joachim's obvious lack of interest or encouragement for her reading efforts. For her part, Ursula had confided to Anna about her occasional annoyance with Peter's regular need for two hours of uninterrupted study in the evenings. By any measure, the two women had become good friends.

"Frau Erhart," Anna replied, "to say that we 'approved of' your church is putting it mildly. Compared to Pastor Bake's dry sermons, your husband's message was almost like . . . well, hearing directly from Jesus. He certainly has a special way of preaching. My mother said so as well."

"Will you be back?"

"We're thinking of it. We'll need to convince my father. He has a hard enough time making it to the cathedral each week, even though it's much closer to our house. And I wouldn't want to hurt Pastor Bake's feelings. He's been so kind to us ever since we first started attending his church."

"I'm sure the pastor would understand. My husband sees him often. He can put in a good word to help your transition." Ursula gently changed the subject. "Anna, I've been meaning to ask you—and forgive me for prying—but I was wondering how you're feeling about Joachim's situation, about him being up on the eastern wall ramparts with the defense force. Have you spoken about how he might come to help you in the event of an attack?"

Anna looked down, feeling strangely lost. "No, my lady, we haven't. He's so caught up with Colonel Falkenberg's exhortations that he hardly seems willing to consider the other possibilities. He believes, like so many others in the city, that King Adolphus is only a day away from rescuing us all—and that to plan differently is an offense to God himself."

"But he *does* love you and wants to see you protected, doesn't he?"

"Yes, I believe that."

"And you *do* love him, don't you?"

Anna hesitated. "Yes, I think . . . well, I . . . of course I do."

"Then by all means, dear, make sure you talk to him as soon as possible to make arrangements for your safety. I want to know that you'll be safe and sound with your family, just as I'll be with Peter and my children."

Anna was overwhelmed with a sudden impulse. She walked up to Ursula, hugged her closely, and kissed her on the cheek. Tears flowed down her face.

"Go now, dear," the pastor's wife said softly with tears welling in her own eyes. "Before I lose myself in emotion."

On the way home later that day, Anna struggled to make sense of everything she was feeling. It was all so confusing. But two things she knew for sure.

The first was that Ursula Erhart would be her friend and mentor for life. She was Anna's role model for the perfect young Lutheran wife, mother, and godly servant to others. She hoped with all her heart that she could be that kind of wife for Joachim and that he would love her for it.

The second thing she now knew was that, despite her best attempts to deny it within herself, something had happened last week in the reception line at St. John's. It all seemed so horribly wrong, and yet it was undeniably true. She had once again fallen completely for her mentor's husband, Pastor Peter Erhart.

Waves of guilt began to overwhelm her as she thought of Ursula and Peter together. How could she possibly allow herself the illicit pleasure of imagining herself in Ursula's place, in Peter's loving embrace rather than her own fiancé's? What demon from hell was driving her to such a crazy infatuation?

The answer came quickly, and it wasn't easy to face. Anna craved for herself what she knew Peter provided for Ursula: deep love from the heart. Not the false love of lust or convenience. Rather, a love willing to sacrifice for the well-being of the beloved. She'd sensed Peter's capacity to love fully the first time she'd heard him preach at Grünfeld nearly five years ago. He was calm, gentle, compassionate, good-looking, strong. Highly intelligent in a way that sought not to dominate but to serve. As Ursula herself had confided, Peter was a man who wanted to encourage his wife's interests, passions, and deepest thoughts—not one of those husbands who viewed his wife simply as a personal servant and child-bearer. Peter wanted to love, to teach, and to help his wife, everything that Anna could ever hope for in a husband. Joachim, despite his tender heart and noble intentions, simply couldn't compare.

A sudden, strange rumbling sound interrupted Anna's confused thoughts. As she looked up in unison with the other people on the street, her focus shifted from her own worries to the northern city wall. Just above it, flashes of light accompanied by occasional loud booms illuminated the horizon. An unexpected thunderstorm? Hardly. The rest of the sky was perfectly clear.

The booms increased in frequency, becoming a steady, pounding roar.

"Pappenheim's siege cannons—it's started!" shouted one of several men standing at the street corner and staring with amazement at the sight.

Anna picked up her skirt to keep from tripping and raced down the street toward her family's house.

PART III

TRIAL BY FIRE

CHAPTER 27

Magdeburg
May 19, 1631

"**D**amn it all! I said come to order!" Christian Wilhelm brought down his gavel in a desperate attempt to quell the raucous city hall gathering of councilors, clergy, patricians, merchants, and common citizens.

Peter, seated with Dr. Weber and Otto Gericke at the foot of the long meeting table, tried to control his rising sense of despair. Two days and nights of bombardment by the Catholics had frayed the nerves of every Magdeburg citizen. There was some good news: the northern wall was holding so far, casualties had been minimal, and the damage contained. And, for reasons unknown, the siege guns had tapered off over the past hour. But no one knew how much longer this state of affairs would last. The council was under enormous pressure to decide between accepting Count Tilly's final offer for an honorable surrender or fighting to the death.

The administrator strained once again to make his voice heard above the shouting and commotion. "Gentlemen, if you'd only give me your ear, I have some excellent tidings. According to the report I've just received, the arrival of King Adolphus's main force is imminent!"

"*What?*" Shouts of disbelief and contempt nearly brought down the house.

"Enough of this folly! Wilhelm, do you never stop teasing us with your false optimism?"

"Adolphus will *never* arrive here in time to save us. We must act now to save our women and children!"

"An honorable surrender is far better than a sack. We have no wish to die needlessly!"

"Accept Tilly's final offer. Call the vote, Wilhelm. Now! No more delay!"

Wilhelm's face went stark white. Even his supposed good news had failed to sway the assembly. He glanced wildly around the room, finally focusing on the one face in the radical faction that had never failed him in the past, the face that betrayed no fear. He pointed to his staunchest ally.

"*Silence!*" he cried out. "Pastor Spaignart wishes to speak."

The assembly fell quiet, all eyes turning toward the man seen as the personification of Lutheran resistance to Catholicism at any price.

Spaignart rose slowly and majestically and bowed before taking the floor. "Citizens of Magdeburg, it pains me to say this, but I'm compelled to, nonetheless. Our God in heaven looks down upon this wretched gathering and is grieved. Yes, I say, *deeply* grieved! And why is God grieved? For the simple reason that he sees from their cowardly protests that far too many here tonight prove their faith to be false."

A collective gasp rose from the audience. Council members stared at each other in dismay. Peter gritted his teeth, knowing Spaignart was only getting warmed up.

"Every true Lutheran knows that hope of eternal life in heaven is secured by their baptism followed by a lifetime of continuing faith in Christ, a faith that must be understood and guided by the authority of the Holy Bible alone. But far too many in this room have convinced themselves that their faith need never be *demonstrated* beyond the point with which they're personally comfortable. 'I am baptized,' they say. 'I believe. I confess my sins. I tithe. I do good works. I witness for the gospel. What *more* must I do to assure myself that my faith is true and will lead me to eternal salvation?'

"Well, my dear friends, I'll tell you what you must do—especially if Herr Wilhelm's report proves false and the Swedish king fails to arrive in time to rescue us. You must prepare to *die* for your faith, if it is God himself who calls you to do so. And how can *any* of you possibly claim that God is not calling you to do so now, at a time when Magdeburg's survival as the bastion of German Protestantism is hanging in the balance?"

Reinhart Bake jumped to his feet. "Pastor Spaignart, this is insanity! It is far too premature to even *suggest* that we—"

Wilhelm cut him off. "Sit down and let him finish, Bake! We've heard enough of your weak-willed imperialist protests for one evening."

Spaignart, unperturbed, continued. "I urge each of you, brothers, to remember the words of the Lord Christ as recorded in the Holy Scriptures: 'Whoever is not with me is against me, and whoever does not gather with me scatters.' And then ask yourself: Are you with the Lord, or against him? Do you wish to spend your eternity in heaven with Christ, or in hell with Satan where the fire is not quenched and the worms that eat you will never die? If heaven is your hope, then the time to secure that hope is *now*. Refuse to eat the despicable crumbs of surrender offered by Tilly. He's an antichrist and will stab you in the back. If you accept his ruse, he'll still force your conversion and find some excuse to rape your daughters. No! Do not give in. Instead, join me and follow the example of our noble leaders, Herr Christian Wilhelm and Colonel Falkenberg. Resist Tilly to the end. Prepare your hearts and bodies to boldly embrace the martyrdom that will prove the sincerity of your faith and hence your fitness for eternal life in glory!"

Spaignart sat down as regally as he had stood.

Within seconds, the radical faction began cheering wildly, while the imperialists and the moderates either glowered at Spaignart and Wilhelm or looked confused and cowed by what they'd just heard.

Peter could not let Spaignart have the final word. He raised his hand to speak.

"So," Wilhelm shouted over the din, "one of our moderate voices from St. John's wishes to further illuminate us! You may proceed, Pastor Erhart."

"Herr Wilhelm, there's little time, so I'll be direct. I commend Pastor Spaignart for his zeal, but I humbly submit that he hasn't conveyed the whole truth of the matter at hand."

Konrad Fitcher sprang from his seat, his face contorted with rage. "What? Do you presume, Pastor Erhart, to question the Word of God as expressed in our Holy Bible?"

"No, sir," Peter replied evenly. "I don't question the Word of God. What I question, sir, is Pastor Spaignart's *personal interpretation* of that word, especially his misguided assertion that a faithful Lutheran's eternal destiny is dependent on their willingness to be martyred for the sake of this city."

Spaignart rose slowly from his chair next to Fitcher. He stared at Peter for a long moment. "I speak as the Holy Spirit guides me, Pastor, with the full confidence that God directs what I say. I have prayed diligently for his wisdom and have worked feverishly my entire life to earn it. Who are you to cast doubt on the validity of the counsel I offer?"

"Perhaps, Pastor, it has something to do with your lack of humility that allows you to imagine you could somehow 'earn' exclusive access to God's wisdom. Or perhaps with your lack of consideration for the *entirety* of the Holy Bible when calling this city to martyrdom, not just those verses selected to prove your predetermined points. We should *together* hear and consider *all* scriptural verses that have important bearing on the matter. Some of those might actually point us away from a needless, self-imposed martyrdom and toward a wiser course of action—one that might allow our city to survive and better serve God in the future."

Wilhelm exploded. "Erhart, are you deaf or merely obtuse? What other scriptural verses do we need to consider, other than what Pastor Spaignart has already laid before us?"

Peter smiled. He'd been waiting for this opening. "Herr Wilhelm, did you not once criticize me for taking verses out of context? Please allow me, sir, to suggest just one other passage that certainly has relevance to our situation: Christ's plea in the Garden of Gethsemane. 'Father, if you are willing, please take this cup from me; yet not my will, but yours be done.' Even our Lord didn't seek martyrdom simply for its own sake, especially if other recourse was possible. Pastor Spaignart, on the other hand, uses the threat of eternal punishment as a club to intimidate our citizens into submitting to martyrdom—something that might not be at all what God wills for us."

"Erhart," Wilhelm screamed, "you're wasting this assembly's precious time! We don't need you to further clarify God's will in this matter. Pastor Spaignart has already expressed it!"

"Then if you believe that to be the case," Peter responded, "and if you refuse to consult the rest of us any further on the options before us, then put the issue to a vote. *Now*—before this entire gathering!"

"And what exactly is it, Erhart, that you propose to put to the vote?"

Peter looked straight at Wilhelm. "I move to put forth the following question: Should this city immediately accept Count Tilly's terms for an honorable surrender? Yes or no."

Bedlam ensued as those in attendance shouted and waved their arms.

One thing at least was clear to Peter. Were the vote to be held this moment, the *yes* votes were certain to carry the day. Wilhelm and Spaignart knew it. They retreated to a corner of the hall to consult with each other.

A loud clattering at the hall's front doors announced the arrival of the one man in Magdeburg whose credibility was difficult to dispute: the city defense commander, Colonel Dietrich von Falkenberg. The wide grin on his normally stern face gave an indication of his tidings.

Falkenberg strode with his two junior officers to the corner of the room where Wilhelm, Spaignart, and Fitcher were standing, and spoke with them privately. The brightening smiles on their faces were interrupted only briefly when Wilhelm scowled and pointed in Peter's direction. Whatever he had shared, the colonel indicated his clear disapproval by a vigorous shake of the head.

Together, the four men walked confidently to the podium at the head of the large table. Falkenberg stood in the middle.

"Citizens," he said, stilling the excited chatter in the room, "I bring you great news, just as Herr Wilhelm promised. I've just come back from observing for myself the movement of many Catholic artillery batteries away from the city walls. This is clear evidence that Count Tilly has decided not to risk the assault we'd so feared. Even now, if you listen closely, you'll notice something unusual. The sound of artillery firing has stopped. This can mean only one thing: God has answered our prayers through the intervention of King Adolphus!"

Every face stared at Colonel Falkenberg in openmouthed, wide-eyed shock.

"The Catholics' actions are exactly what we should expect," Falkenberg continued. "It means the Swedes are closing in on the city from the east, and they're now preparing to launch their own assault against the Catholic rear guard. Citizens, this is a great day and a great hour in the history of Magdeburg. I don't claim we're yet free of the threat. But if things proceed through the rest of the night and into tomorrow in the same fashion, we can be assured that this city is safe."

A tremendous cheer broke out, especially among the radical section.

"*Our faith is rewarded!*" Konrad Fitcher shouted. "*Praise be to the true God, who rewards those of us ready to lay down our lives for his cause!*"

Peter was stunned. This wasn't at all the message he'd expected Falkenberg to deliver.

Falkenberg held up his hands for silence, once more quieting the room. "Now I understand from Herr Wilhelm and Pastor Spaignart that a motion has been put forward to vote on the possibility of surrendering this city. Well, in view of the news I've just shared, there can be only one reasonable response. That motion must be denied!"

Peter was overcome with a strange mixture of embarrassment, relief, and hesitation. He was hard-pressed to disagree with Falkenberg's stance. It appeared he himself had been wrong.

Only one man in the assembly stood to ask Falkenberg a question.

"Colonel," Otto Gericke said, "your news is indeed good. But sir, with respect, can we really attribute the enemy's observed movements to King Adolphus's arrival? Isn't it possible the Catholics are merely shifting their positions in support of a new plan of attack? And if so, are we truly ready to throw out our consideration of Tilly's final offer, which still awaits our response?"

"Otto," Falkenberg said, "you know I value your opinion, but you worry too much in this case. I can assure you the Catholic movements reveal their intention to retreat from here. But I'll tell you what. Because of my deep respect for you and other members of this gathering who might not be convinced, I'll honor a request to meet with this same group early tomorrow morning. We can further assess the situation, examine any new reports and, if need be, reconsider our response to Tilly's surrender request."

"Sir," Otto said, "that's a reasonable proposal. My only concern is that the Catholic army representative waits even now at the city gate for our final response. Do we dare keep Tilly waiting throughout the night and into tomorrow morning? Shouldn't we at least inform the representative of our wish for a short delay?"

"I've already made a generous offer to meet with this gathering again early tomorrow. I suggest you and the others accept it as is. Don't attempt to clutter it with further conditions."

Upon hearing no further objections, an ecstatic Christian Wilhelm stepped to the podium. "So there you have it! I move that this assembly gather again tomorrow morning with Colonel Falkenberg beginning at four o'clock to assess the latest situation."

As he walked home with Otto after the meeting, Peter struggled to see the bright side of Falkenberg's report. "Do you think Falkenberg's allowing wishful thinking to cloud his better judgment?"

"Not only that," Otto replied gloomily, "I fear his better judgment no longer exists!"

Peter blew out the candle and lay down next to his sleeping wife. He kissed her gently on the lips.

"*Mmm*. Finally back home, Pastor? So what new tales of terror do you bring back from your meeting tonight? And why have the guns stopped?"

"Actually, darling," Peter said, "the news seems to be fairly good for once."

Ursula heaved a joyful sigh when Peter shared his account of the Catholic retreat. After discussing the happy news together, the two embraced intimately and collapsed afterward in contented mutual exhaustion.

Just before falling asleep, Peter whispered to his wife a final thought. "Dear, should anything unexpected happen tomorrow, just remember to wait for me to arrive at the orphanage for you, Katrina, and the children. I'll get there as soon as I can. We can look at the situation together, make decisions about what to do and where to go next."

"Of course, darling," Ursula whispered back. "Why wouldn't I? But all those worries have now gone away, haven't they?"

Peter held her tenderly. "I think so. We'll know for sure very soon. Now let's get some sleep. Let tomorrow bring what it will. Good night, my love."

CHAPTER 28

Magdeburg
May 20, 1631

5:30 a.m.

Anna awoke with a start. The previous night had been unusually quiet with the relentless cannonading of the previous two days and nights strangely absent. Hopefully, it was a good sign. Maybe the rumor she'd heard late last night from Joachim was true. Maybe King Adolphus's army *truly was* closing in on the city and frightening the Catholics away.

As she groggily rummaged through the clothes in her trunk, she tried to focus. After some hesitation, she selected the dress that she'd deliberately avoided even looking at for more than six months now. It was the same dress she'd worn the day her best friend had departed for Würzburg. Ever since, she hadn't allowed her sweet memories of Barbara to be disturbed with anything that reminded her of their forced parting.

Anna crept toward the loft ladder so as not to awaken Liesa. As she did, she felt something knock lightly against her thigh. She reached into the front pocket and touched a familiar object. Her eyes filled with tears. She'd almost forgotten.

The little carved wooden figurine of Mary didn't reproach her. It merely lay in the palm of her hand smiling tenderly, eyes humbly cast down, arms outstretched. Barbara had given her precious possession to Anna as a keepsake—as if Anna might need something more than the loving memories she would always have of her best friend.

Anna recalled her conversation with Barbara that day by the brookside at the fair. She'd questioned the need for Mary to intervene for her with God. For herself, Anna had learned something else from her experience in facing that devil Dietrich Ackar. She could petition God directly, and he would *always* answer her prayers. Why did she need the intervening help of Mary or the other saints?

Despite her reservations, there *was* one thing about that little figurine that Anna could never deny: it represented something extremely important to Barbara. And if her dearest friend had offered something that valuable to her as a final parting gift, she would always treasure it in her heart.

She returned the figurine to her pocket and climbed down the ladder. She knew that Mutti, still asleep with Vati in the far corner of the room, would appreciate the extra time for a little more rest. After fetching a new log from the pile in the backyard, she put the kettle on the grill and started a fire in the hearth. Once the fire had taken, she went to the kitchen to get some black bread loaves and cheese. Liesa would be down any time now, begging for a little something to tide her over until the family breakfast was ready.

Anna returned to the table and began cutting the bread and cheese into the small slices that Liesa preferred.

Just as predicted, Liesa soon crept down the ladder and joined her older sister at the table. Now ten and a half years old, Liesa had grown over a foot during the past two years. Tall and thin for her age, her figure reminded Anna of her own during those emotionally painful times of early youth. The "beautiful beanpole" her friends had teasingly dubbed her. The one saving grace during that period, Anna recalled, was the exceptional attractiveness of her facial features. It seemed that Liesa was beginning to follow suit.

"Anni, why have the cannons stopped?" Liesa asked, keeping her voice low so as not to wake their parents. "Have the Catholics left?"

"I'm not sure, princess. We can only hope so. Joachim said that was a possibility, but we won't know for sure until the end of today or maybe tomorrow. Here you go. Eat these for now."

"Anni, do we have any pears?"

The elder sister clenched her teeth, annoyed with Liesa's never-ending requests for things that not even the wealthiest of Magdeburg citizens had access to right now. The siege conditions of the past four months had cut off the import of certain delicacies.

"How about thanking me for what I just put under your nose, you little ingrate," Anna said.

Liesa rolled her eyes. Then a coy smile lit her face. "I saw you last night!"

"You saw me . . . what?"

"I saw you and Joachim." Liesa's smile turned into a grin.

"You saw us . . . what?" Anna pressed, her face burning with embarrassment.

Liesa stole a glance at their parents, who were still sleeping. Turning back, she put her hand to her mouth, clearly struggling not to giggle. "I . . . saw . . . you."

"You saw us . . . *what*? You little brat! Tell me before I beat it out of you!"

"I saw you two . . . *smooooooching*!"

So that was it! *Liesa must have peeked around the back door while Joachim and I were saying goodbye in the backyard last night*, Anna thought. Of course, they had been doing more than just *saying* goodbye—even their goodnight "kiss" alone had *certainly* involved more than what Anna would want her impressionable ten-year-old sister to reveal to their parents.

Aghast at her own lack of discretion, Anna tried to console herself. Wouldn't she still be a virgin on her wedding night?

There was only one problem, she had to admit. Her physical passion last night hadn't been oriented toward the young city defender soon to become her husband. Rather, they'd had another focus, and she knew it. Peter Erhart was now constantly on her mind, and she didn't know how—or even whether she really desired—to resist his impact.

Anna knew she'd have to come to terms with things soon. She could not—*would not*—allow her own false pretense to ruin her marriage and destroy her soul. But for now, she had some explaining to do. *Just keep things on a playful level*, she thought. Liesa always liked sisterly secrets and, if she knew one thing about her little sister, it was that Liesa could be trusted to keep these kinds of secrets from their parents.

Catching her in the middle of chewing a huge mouthful of bread and cheese, she reached out with both hands to grab her cheeks. Squeezing them tight, she pulled Liesa's face toward her own and laid down the terms.

"All right, my little princess-spy! So you caught us in the act. It's not like we haven't talked about this kind of thing before. And if you keep your mouth shut, I just might keep my own shut about you kissing your favorite little choirboy Kristoff on the cheek after church last week. So, do you *promise* not to tell Mutti or Vati?"

Liesa nodded.

Anna squeezed harder, not yet convinced. "*Promise?*"

Liesa nodded vigorously, her eyes bulging, her mouth still full of bread.

Anna released her grip, and both girls burst out laughing, waking their parents.

This day was starting out just like old times—much better than Anna had feared. The absence of cannon fire surely meant this crisis was about to pass, just like the last one had under Wallenstein's blockade. Tomorrow, Anna would return to her job at the orphanage. She and Ursula would have a good laugh over their needless worries. Everything would be as before. And somehow, she was sure, God would soon help her overcome her shameful desire for the intimate embrace of Ursula's husband.

CHAPTER 29

Magdeburg
May 20, 1631

6:30 a.m.

Peter couldn't believe the difference. Compared to the previous evening, the general mood at the early-morning council meeting had improved tremendously. Arguing and fist-shaking had been replaced with friendly smiles and rational discussions. No doubt, the changes were justified, considering how quiet things had remained at the city walls during the night and into the morning so far.

Dr. Weber expressed cautious optimism. "Well, I never thought I'd say this, but perhaps God has seen fit to honor the stalwart stands of Wilhelm and Falkenberg in refusing to yield to Tilly's surrender demands. We've been here over two hours so far, with no sign of the barrage resuming or reports of other threatening movements by the Catholics."

Peter glanced at Otto. If anyone would have a levelheaded view of what was happening, it would be him.

Otto shook his head. "I don't know, Doctor. I certainly hope you're right. But there's something about all this that makes me uneasy."

"So, what *would* put you at ease, Otto?" Peter asked.

"The actual appearance of King Gustavus Adolphus himself," he replied with a rueful smile. "At the head of a massive column of Swedish troops, riding through our city gate!"

"Now *that* would elevate Pastor Spaignart's reputation even further in this city," Dr. Weber said. "Confirm his 'holy prophecy' of the arrival of the king."

Colonel Falkenberg approached the podium without so much as a glance at his usual accomplices, Wilhelm and Spaignart. "Citizens, I bid you the most wondrous of mornings! I'm now fully convinced. Today will be the day of our deliverance. The signs are all there: the end to the enemy's barrage, the withdrawal of his batteries, and the lack of any other movements overnight. They all point toward the same thing. Our rescuer, the Swedish king, has arrived! Yet that antichrist Tilly continues his attempts to deceive us into an unwarranted surrender. Even now, as our respected councilor Otto Gericke reminded us last night, the count's representative still awaits our response to his supposed final offer.

"After thinking things over last night and this morning, I'm now in agreement with Herr Gericke's suggestion. Our final answer needs to be delivered immediately to the Catholic representative. But this will *not* be an answer that begs Tilly to delay his attack a little longer. Rather, it will be an answer that will forever be etched into the pages of history. Magdeburg will *never* surrender; we would rather die than surrender!"

A spontaneous burst of jubilant cheers reached to the ceiling—this time not just from the radical faction but from many imperialists and moderates as well.

Even Peter found himself caught up in Falkenberg's intoxicating words. *Smart ploy*, he thought. *Since it seems like the city's going to be rescued, why not be celebrated forever as having delivered a heroically defiant answer to the Catholics' deceptive offer?*

"With your permission," Falkenberg continued, "I'll take my leave to deliver this answer personally to the Catholic representative, who's now sitting under guard in the adjoining room."

More roars of approval.

Falkenberg was already headed out when Otto shouted a last-second question. "Colonel! Are you sure that your men are now back on full alert at the walls?"

Peter knew that one of his friend's main concerns was the defenders' habitual practice of leaving their posts for a short period of refreshment and prayer in the early-morning darkness.

Falkenberg flashed a patronizing smile. "Of course, Otto. They're executing their duties today the same as always. Their prayers should be concluded, and I expect them all to be back at their positions by now. We need not worry, my friend."

Otto turned to Peter as Falkenberg left. "Peter, you asked me earlier what would make me feel more at ease. Falkenberg's overconfidence definitely does not. I pray my concerns are merely the products of my overtired imagination."

7:00 a.m.

"What's that?" Something had caught Otto's attention.

Peter looked at him quizzically. He could barely hear the strange, sporadic popping noises, much less discern their source. "Maybe a flock of woodpeckers come to—"

Otto held up his hand to silence Peter's attempt at a joke. His face went pale. "That can only be one thing. *My God!*"

The noise quickly intensified in volume and regularity. Within moments, the unmistakable sounds of a full-scale musketry clash could be heard coming from the direction of the northern city wall.

The confused looks on the faces of the gathered councilors and citizens soon gave way to panic.

"What is this? What's happening?"

"Where's that coming from?"

One of Colonel Falkenberg's aides burst through the door. The soldier's right shoulder was stained red. Without saying a word, he stalked into the adjoining room, where Falkenberg was meeting with the Catholic army representative. The assembly held their collective breath.

Falkenberg himself soon emerged in a terrible rage and marched to the podium. "Treachery! Even while I personally speak terms with their appointed stooge, the Catholic sons of Satan launch their attack! But I promise you, by God, this city will prevail. I'm ordering all reserve soldiers and citizens-at-arms to the northern wall, where I'm going now to lead them. May the Lord protect each of you and your families." Falkenberg determinedly walked out with his aide in tow.

Pandemonium erupted. Cries of outrage expressed a volatile mixture of fear and bewilderment.

"The imperialists in our own midst have betrayed us!"

"No, the radicals' cursed insistence on stalling is what now seals our city's doom!"

"Where's your savior-king now, you self-deceiving fools!"

"To our families and children!"

A mad stampede toward the door began.

Peter looked with dismay at Dr. Weber and Otto. He knew that if ever there was a critical moment in history for the voice of authoritative calm and reason to prevail, this was it.

"Citizens!" Christian Wilhelm cried. "I implore you: stop and come to your senses!"

The rush to the door ceased as all stood in their tracks, barely willing for one last time to give ear to the man who, more than any other over the last fifteen years, had personally led Magdeburg's Lutheran resistance against the encroachments of the Holy Roman emperor.

"Gentlemen, calm yourselves. We have no indication from Colonel Falkenberg or his aide that our defenses on the northern wall have collapsed—merely that an attack of some sort has begun. I urge you all in the strongest terms: return to your seats. Let's discuss rationally what our next steps should be, not as panicked individuals but as responsible overseers of our beloved city."

Shouts of protest answered his plea.

"It's fine for you to remind us of our sacred duties to this city, Herr Wilhelm, but many of us have crippled or ill family members who'll need our assistance getting to places of safety—if any are to be found."

"Then, go!" Wilhelm bellowed. "You who feel you must, leave now! The rest of us will remain here at our posts, directing others as needed to secure our city treasury and secure other key locations. I, for one, will remain here. I would rather die working and fighting in the flames of my beloved Magdeburg than cower and run when confronted by Tilly's Catholic hordes."

Despite continued grumbling and many angry or fearful looks, most of the assembly chose not to leave and instead returned to their seats. Meanwhile, the sounds of the unseen musketry battle ebbed and flowed. There was no way to tell which way the battle was going.

Peter stared with concern at Dr. Weber, who'd collapsed from exhaustion and stress in his chair. His face had broken out in a sweat and his eyes were closed. His pallor was worrisome. As he knelt down beside his mentor and gently wiped his brow with his handkerchief, Pastor Bake approached.

"Peter, may I have a word with you?"

Peter reluctantly pulled himself away.

"Peter," Bake said quietly, "I've been watching Dr. Weber from my side of the room, and he's clearly not well. I'm concerned he'll have difficulty making it to a safe location, if indeed he can make it anywhere at all from here. Do you or he have any plans for his personal safety?"

Peter shook his head. "I've tried many times to talk with him about this. But he's always told me that since he no longer has any family, his only concern will be to follow the direction that God provides in the moment."

Bake waved his hand impatiently. "Allow me to suggest, then, that you consider having him escorted to the cathedral. We all agreed that it offers the best chance of survival for our unprotected women, orphans, and other helpless citizens. And our dear friend appears to be rapidly falling into that latter category."

Peter nodded. "I'll do my best to arrange that, Pastor. That's very kind of you to suggest."

Weber, now somewhat revived, would have none of it. "Brothers, I know you mean well, but I'm not ready for you to consign me to my coffin quite yet. Too much to do and not enough time. Peter, would you kindly escort me back to St. John's so we can secure the valuables and lock the premises? We can't afford to wait for Wilhelm and the others to provide us with directions on how to do that."

"But, Doctor," Bake protested, "I beg you to consider—"

"My dear Reinhard, I know you love me, and I deeply appreciate your concern. I promise to have myself escorted to the cathedral as soon as I possibly can. But only *after* I look to the needs of my own church. Now, Peter, would you assist me? Maybe if we can leave discreetly, we just might avoid attracting unwanted attention."

Peter looked at Bake and shrugged. "It seems I now have no choice."

He helped his senior pastor from his chair and managed to lead him by the arm to the door and escape any notice—until the moment he put his hand on the handle.

"*Dr. Weber!*"

All eyes focused on them as the two turned to the strident voice at the podium.

"Leaving so soon?" Wilhelm asked with a mocking grin.

Dr. Weber jerked his arm away from Peter and drew himself up. "Don't worry, Herr Wilhelm. I assure you we shall both return shortly after taking care of our own church's security concerns. We would *certainly* not want to miss out on the opportunity to join you and Pastor Spaignart in submitting to voluntary martyrdom!"

"No one's yet saying it has come to that, Weber, and you know it! Leave if you feel compelled. Return only if you wish. The rest of us shall continue on with the work the Lord has given us in this time of extreme trial."

With a sigh of repressed fury, Peter closed the door behind them.

CHAPTER 30

Magdeburg
May 20, 1631

7:05 a.m.

Anna could tell that something unusual was going on. The barely audible popping noises from the northern part of the city had started a few moments ago and were now rising in intensity. Her family, having just completed their breakfast, were still sitting at the table. They all looked at each other with startled expressions.

Anna's father cocked his ear toward the sounds. "Musket shots! Frieda, it may have started. I'm going to the shop to see if anyone knows what's happening. Don't you or the girls go outside until I get back."

"Adam, are you out of your mind? Would you leave your own wife and daughters to the mercies of the Catholic wolves?"

"Dear," her father said gently, "I'll be back in twenty minutes. You'll be safe. There's no way anything bad could happen in so short a time. Colonel Falkenberg assured us the walls can hold out for at least two full days—even if there's a full-scale attack. Besides, we don't even know whether—"

"Herr Ritter, that's nonsense," Frieda screamed, "and you know it! If it's really a Catholic attack, the city walls could fall quickly. Our streets and homes will be overwhelmed. And here you are, ready to tromp off gallantly in the very direction of those same walls that could crumble at any moment. Your soldiering days are *over*. Your responsibility now is to stay close to your family!"

Anna cringed to see her father throw up his hands in exasperation. She knew Vati would feel a relentless urge to do *something* rather than just sit passively in the house like a helpless sheep.

"Mutti," Anna ventured, "I know there's some risk, but maybe it'd be good for Vati to go. Joachim will still be at the shop with his father. He wasn't scheduled to report back to the eastern wall until nine o'clock. He'll know what's happening. And once Vati gets a clearer picture from Joachim about what's going on, he'll know what to do and how to take care of us. Maybe he can even talk with Joachim and his parents about coming to join us here if things get really bad in that area."

Anna recoiled under her mother's withering gaze, but she knew she'd said the right thing. If Frieda Ritter was known for anything, it was the gracious concern she always showed to others in times of distress. And now, reminded of the dangers faced by her future son-in-law and his family, she could no longer focus only on her own family's terrors.

"Well, I suppose you just *had* to put it like that, didn't you, daughter?" she muttered, biting her lip but finally managing a resigned sigh. "All right, Adam, go. But if you're not back in a half hour, I'm personally coming after you—and with your two daughters in tow!"

Adam hugged his wife closely. "I promise I'll be back by then, lovely lady," he whispered. "Don't fret now."

Frieda was unable to hold back her tears. "You'll be back only if the Lord is willing. Come here, girls. Help us pray for your father's protection and safe return."

Following a short family prayer, Adam was out the door and running down the street.

"Hurry back, Adam Ritter!" Frieda shouted. "You know we love and need you!" She burst into sobs.

Adam turned to wave and then disappeared around the corner.

Anna gently pulled her mother back inside, closed and bolted the door, and shuttered the lone first-floor window. Struggling to control her own rising panic, she did her best to console her mother as Liesa whimpered in the far corner of the room. She had to come up with something fast before hysteria consumed them all.

"Liesi, come over here with us. If we're all going to have a good cry, we might as well do it together. Let's all sit down by the hearth and tell each other some stories."

The ploy worked. Before long, Frieda and Liesa were engrossed in Anna's animated telling of the biblical story of Joseph and his eleven brothers. The long passage from the Book of Genesis had been the last scripture that Anna had learned to read with the help of Ursula, and she now knew it by heart. It helped that the musket fire had tapered off over the past few minutes. Maybe a major attack had not started, after all, Anna hoped.

By the time she finished the story, Liesa was asleep, her head in her mother's lap. Lulled into a trance, Frieda stared into the fire's dying embers as the sporadic shooting continued in the distance. A few people milled around out in the street, occasionally shouting things that Anna had no desire to hear. She did her best to shut her ears and mind to them.

Taking her mother's cue, she gazed into the dying fire and thought of Joachim. Would Vati be able to see him before he left to help defend the eastern wall? Would *she* ever see him again? And Ursula—had anyone else besides Heidi and Aloisia shown up to help with the orphans? Anna felt a crushing pang of regret. She knew Ursula would crave her help if the children needed to be transferred to the cathedral. Yet Ursula had insisted that she stay at home with her family after the bombardment had started three days ago.

And then there was Peter. Anna couldn't deny it. Her sin of coveting Ursula's husband had led to the sin of committing adultery in her heart. Sin on top of sin, with only one way out of the mess. Hadn't Pastors Tiedeman and Bake repeatedly drilled the remedy into her? Christ had died for *all* her sins, whether they were sins of deed or sins of thought. She must think now only of him and his grace. Confess to God, pray for his forgiveness. Put an end to the obsessive thoughts she'd allowed her mind to harbor about Peter from the first day she met him. Honor Peter, Ursula, and her own parents by making her marriage to Joachim one that all would be pleased to witness and commend as an example to others. Yes, if only God would rescue her family, her loved ones, and the city from the nightmare unfolding outside, then she would immediately show her gratitude by—

The loud blast of a cannon snapped her out of her trance. She rushed to the window, opened the shutters, and looked out into the street. Two drunken civilians staggered by, supporting each other with one arm and flailing a bottle with the other as they sang some profane tune at the top of their lungs. Spotting Anna, the men stopped and gawked, barely able to stand. "How about some brew, Fräulein? We'll trade you some for your favors! Might as well—the end's coming soon!" The men began to stumble together toward the door.

Anna slammed the shutters closed and locked them. "Mutti, Liesa . . . we need to get into the back room. *Now!*"

⌐⌐

7:30 a.m.

Things could be worse, Peter thought as he and Dr. Weber approached the entrance to St. John's Church. Weber had struggled with his lame hip, but with Peter's help had managed to traverse the hundred-and-fifty-yard distance from the city hall. Unfortunately, the church was that much closer to the eastern wall and to increased danger. As if on cue, booms from musketry and blasts from the Catholic siege mortars rose rapidly in volume. Undoubtedly, the Catholics were now concentrating their superior numbers and armaments at the points they considered the most vulnerable.

Peter had a clear plan in mind upon entering the front doors held open by Samuel Scheidt: secure the church as quickly as possible, return with Dr. Weber to the city hall, and find him an escort to the cathedral. Then proceed immediately to gather Ursula and the children at the orphanage. There still seemed to be adequate time. The city's alarm bells hadn't yet rung, which could only mean that the defense forces at the walls were still managing to hold out, just as Falkenberg had predicted.

Peter worked quickly with Samuel and two junior assistants under Weber's direction. Together they transferred monies, paintings, books, documents, and other valuable artifacts into several hidden vaults in the church basement.

Within twenty minutes, the job was complete. After bolting and locking all the entrances from the inside, Peter and the other men exited the building through a secret passageway in the basement. Emerging into the bright sunlight and the acrid-smelling, gunsmoke-filled air, the five embraced and wished each other well. Samuel and the two assistants rushed off to join their families as Peter and his mentor began their return to the city hall.

A tremendous crescendo of gunfire sounded from the direction of the northern wall.

Dr. Weber looked fearfully at Peter. "Are they yielding? Already?"

Peter said nothing, fighting to maintain his composure. He grabbed tightly onto Weber's arm, trying to speed up their progress.

Suddenly, the elder man drew up short, obviously in severe pain. "Peter, it's my hip. I . . . I have to stop!"

"Here, sir. Put your arm over my shoulders."

With the senior pastor's left arm draped over his shoulders and his right arm around the man's waist, Peter managed to keep the pair going, albeit slowly, toward the city hall, which he now saw just ahead. The gunfire around the northern wall had subsided—hopefully an indication that Falkenberg's men had successfully beaten back whatever the Catholics had hurled against them. *Almost there*, Peter thought. *Get inside, rest a little, and then help Dr. Weber find an escort to the cathedral.*

Peter froze mid-step. Nothing could have prepared him for the spectacle he now saw unfold before him. The city hall doors flew open. Over a hundred and fifty men burst through, stampeding onto the street in a state of panic. The men trampled over each other in their mad rush to escape.

Peter called out to someone he recognized. "Herr Volker, what's happening?"

The terrified man slowed just long enough to shout over his shoulder. "Falkenberg has been shot dead! The Catholics have taken the northern gate. They're trying to scale the wall nearby! Nobody knows how long our defenses can hold out. Hurry and take shelter!"

"Where is Wilhelm?" Peter called.

"Wilhelm and Spaignart were the first to bolt—out the back door!" the man shouted back before fleeing with the rest of the crowd.

Peter could not believe his ears. Wilhelm and Spaignart—the champions of the radical cause, the bold purveyors of martyrdom as the only alternative to eternity in hell—had been the first to show their backs to the enemy?

Still supporting Weber, Peter felt a wave of dizziness. Only the firm grip of a familiar hand on his arm restored his focus. It was Otto. Peter stared in confusion at his friend.

"Peter, are you all right? Listen to me. It was just as I feared. Our soldiers were caught off guard due to the artillery lull. Pappenheim's troops surged forward from the suburbs. They're throwing everything they have against the northern wall. There's only one piece of good news: even with Falkenberg dead, his Swedish soldiers and some of our armed citizens are forming a new line of resistance. It seems to be holding so far. Hopefully, they'll counterattack soon and restore our positions around the gate. But we shouldn't take any chances. I'm going now to reach my wife before things get out of hand!" After a quick embrace, he turned and rushed away.

Peter looked around desperately. There was little time to lose. He had to get to the orphanage where Ursula and his children awaited him. But who was going to escort Dr. Weber to the cathedral? Without help, he clearly had no hope of making it to safety. The thought of abandoning his beloved mentor and friend tore at his heart.

Suddenly it dawned on him—the path to the cathedral also led to the orphanage. Either destination would require taking the same street southward from his current location and away from the nearby fighting.

Peter checked his timepiece. Now nearly eight o'clock. It should take at most a half hour to drop off Dr. Weber at the cathedral and traverse the short remaining distance to the orphanage. Time enough, he was confident, to reach Ursula and the children well before the city wall defenses collapsed.

He made his decision. "Doctor, you're coming with me."

"Peter, I'll just be a hindrance. You need to get to your wife and children."

Peter ignored Weber's protest. Supporting his mentor by the waist and arm, Peter led the way down the street.

They hadn't traveled more than a few yards before the city's alarm bells tolled loudly, announcing the unthinkable.

Peter struggled to smother his rising panic. The prearranged signal could mean only one thing: the northern city wall defenses had just been breached. Collapse could be imminent.

Looking over Weber's shoulder, Peter spotted a familiar figure about to run past them. "Pastor Fitcher!"

Konrad Fitcher at first kept on running but then stopped to face them.

"Please, Konrad, will you help me with Dr. Weber here?"

Fitcher hesitated. "I'm sorry, Pastor, but I have my own wife and children to think about." With that, he turned and fled.

CHAPTER 31

Magdeburg
May 20, 1631

Keeping Dr. Weber hobbling along the street toward the cathedral was an exercise in frustration and perseverance. After much painful effort, they were still only halfway there. Progress was hindered by the dozens of terrified civilians running around in confusion. To make matters worse, a large contingent of defending soldiers had been pulled from the eastern wall to meet the more urgent northern threat. They'd just raced through in the opposite direction, bowling over anyone in their way.

Peter was amazed that despite his mentor's agony, he was still making an effort to keep both their spirits up.

"Pastor Peter," he panted, "my only solace is knowing the tremendous reward you'll one day reap in heaven. Who else would try to salvage this hopeless shipwreck of a body?"

"Doctor," Peter replied, struggling to keep the weight off Weber's right hip, "my solace right now is knowing the tremendous reward my own poor body will reap right here on earth—once I deliver you safely to the cathedral, that is. Keep at it, my friend!"

The defending troops passed by them. *Not a good sign*, Peter thought.

"They've broken through the northeastern gate!" someone screamed. *"Look! Here they come . . . Catholic cavalry!"*

Fifteen mounted imperial cuirassiers at the street intersection sent the civilians into a blind panic. All rushed toward the Magdeburg Cathedral.

Caught in the wild mob, Peter looked over his shoulder. The armored cavalry had formed a single line across the width of the street. Helmet visors closed, sabers and long pistols drawn—they looked poised to charge. But why were they still sitting there as if frozen in their saddles, horses anxiously pawing the ground and champing at the bit? What were they waiting for?

"Clear the street!" someone bellowed in a commanding voice. "Make way! Clear the street, you ragamuffins!"

A squad of twenty city defenders—led by a massive man with a full beard and shoulder-length hair—was attempting to force its way through the fleeing civilians. They dragged along with them a single light cannon. Within seconds, a solid defensive line was established across the full width of the street. *Not exactly well-disciplined Swedish troops*, Peter thought ruefully. They were no more than a motley collection of the now-dead Falkenberg's German mercenaries and armed civilian volunteers. But they were better than nothing. There was only one problem: Peter and Dr. Weber were now the only civilians left standing on the street between the opposing forces.

"I said get out of the way, you blundering fools!" the riled defense force commander shouted. "Are you trying to get yourselves killed?"

Peter looked around in wild despair. Dr. Weber's face paled and his knees buckled.

"Pastor, over here!" called someone from the ground-floor window of a nearby house.

Peter half-dragged, half-carried Weber to the door. Holding it open was a grizzled old man with a strange, nearly toothless grin.

"Two true preachers of the word, woman!" the old man cried out to someone in the back room, presumably his wife. "Saw their clerical garb and pulled 'em right off the street. We'll certainly make it to heaven now!"

"Well, bring 'em in so they can sit down, you old fool!"

"One's old and hurting. For heaven's sake, woman, will you hurry out here and do something to soften up one of the pallets?"

"I'm coming. And make sure the door's locked. Can't have those Catholic devils barging in here before we hightail it out back!"

A rotund, equally toothless, and surprisingly cheerful old lady came bustling into the room. She began arranging some cushions on the pallet so that Dr. Weber could recline without having to fully lie down.

"Here you go, Pastor. Right over here. We'll look after you real well. Don't have pastors stopping by every day!" The old man took Weber's arm and helped him into the room and over onto the pallet.

Peter turned for one last look down the street. The city defense line had their weapons aimed but were holding their fire. What was going on? Peter closed the door and locked it behind him before going over to check on his old friend.

"He doesn't look too good, Pastor," the woman said. "I'll go get some water and cloths to soothe his forehead."

He actually looked a bit better now than a few minutes earlier, Peter thought. Though he was not ready to speak, his color was returning. He gave Peter a weak smile and nod.

The old man resumed his place at the window, peeking around the shutters and staring down the street. Something caused him to start. "Ho! Look at that! Can't believe what I'm seeing. It's *him*—the Black Knight! Pastor, come take a look at this!"

Peter rushed to the window. Now taking his position at the center front of the cavalry line was a knight clad in black three-quarter body armor. A brightly colored, thick red plume rose from behind the knight's close-visored helmet. Peter knew immediately. It was him—Major Schuttman: the man who Peter and Ursula had encountered last month on their countryside walk. *A Black Knight with a flair for blood scarlet*, Peter thought.

"How do you know of him?" Peter asked.

"You've never served in the army, have you, Pastor?"

"No, friend, I can't say that I have."

The old man laughed. "That explains it. Anyone who's ever fought against Count Tilly or talked to any of our own soldiers would know about the Black Knight. Absolutely the best cavalryman that Tilly has in the field. Maybe the best in all of Europe. I heard about him just by listening to one of Falkenberg's Swedes drone on and on at the tavern about a year ago. Guess he's our enemy, but I sure would like to see him in action. Especially if everything they say about him's true!"

"I suppose we're about to find out, aren't we?" Peter said.

"Look!" the old man cried. "The final salute. He's getting ready to go at 'em!"

The Black Knight paced his horse back and forth in front of his troops. He lifted his sword and twirled it ever so slowly above his head, as if defying the defenders to shoot him. None attempted to do so. After reining in his horse, the major lowered his outstretched arm and pointed his sword at the city defense line. His shouted command was immediately followed by a tremendous roar of approval from his men. The Catholic line surged forward.

"Hold your fire, men!" the defense commander shouted. "Don't waste your ammunition. Cannoneers, at the ready?"

"Ready, sir. Chain shot loaded!"

"On my command. Hold . . . hold . . ."

The cavalrymen spurred their horses into a gallop, some with swords poised, others with large wheel-lock pistols drawn. The final charge began. Peter and the old man were in near-perfect position to observe the clash point, right in front of the window, below which they huddled and cautiously peeked over the sill.

"Hold . . ." the defense commander urged yet again. "*Fire!*"

A thundering volley of flame and smoke erupted from the city defenders' muskets and cannon. The loud booms rattled the room. *What could possibly survive such a barrage?* Peter raised his head cautiously and looked out the window.

Only three of the Catholic horsemen had been blasted off their mounts by the cannon shot, including one who'd been completely decapitated. Two others had their mounts shot from under them and were now struggling to reengage the charge on foot. The remaining eleven cavalrymen hurtled forward virtually unaffected. Within seconds, they smashed into the defense line and began wreaking havoc.

It was nowhere near an even match. The defenders lost their leader, cut down by a pistol shot to his head. Several of them broke ranks and ran. One of the cannoneers was grabbed by his hair by one of the dismounted cavalrymen, who repeatedly smashed the man's head against the still-smoking barrel of his own weapon. Other defenders were quickly and brutally dispatched by pistol or the ferocious swing or thrust of a sword. Soon, only five defenders were still alive and engaged. Surprisingly, these five were engaged together against a single common foe: the now-dismounted Black Knight. All of the other imperial cavalrymen were simply standing by and watching the odd spectacle.

This is no time for sport or games, Peter thought in amazement. Why weren't Schuttmann's men rushing to their leader's aid?

The old man could hardly contain himself. "Ha! Look at 'em, Pastor! Spittin' mad, those Falkenbergers are. They won't let the knight go! But mark me: he'll take 'em all. Just watch!"

Surrounded at a distance of about five paces, Schuttmann circled slowly. He grasped the hilt of his saber in both hands, daring any of the enemy to take him on. All lunged at once. Sword tips converged toward the upper body of the single most hated and feared cavalryman in Tilly's army. A certain death trap—one that even the Black Knight could not possibly escape.

Schuttmann didn't wait for the trap to close. He chose one of the men as his target and lunged. Ducking to avoid the defender's sword, he crashed full force into the man and knocked him off his feet. A slight opening was now punched in the circle of death. The major took advantage and broke free. The defenders were forced to fight the Black Knight more or less one-on-one—on *his* terms.

It was an unfair fight. The Black Knight's armor, dexterity, and skill proved too much for any single defender to overcome. Three were quickly stabbed or cut to death. Another ran. The last man threw down his sword and held up his hands. The victor pulled his pistol from its holster and pointed it at the surrendering man's face. He hesitated, appearing to glance at his own men for some kind of approval to proceed. Strangely, they still showed no reaction to his predicament or question, whatever it was. They simply waited for Schuttmann to make his own decision.

Before he could make it, another defender rushed up from behind. Somehow, he had slipped away unnoticed during the earlier melee but now was within striking distance. Schuttmann whirled and leveled his pistol. He fired point-blank, dropping the man in his tracks.

The surrendering defender now saw his opportunity. He reached down to snatch up his dropped sword and swung it with all his might. Schuttmann's armor and quick jump to the side saved him from being cut through, but the heavy blow knocked him off his feet. His opponent straddled him, preparing to jab his sword through the narrow opening of the visor.

As he watched, Peter couldn't help himself. For some reason he couldn't explain, he *wanted* the Black Knight to escape this terrible, final fate. Though a sworn and dangerous enemy, this man had once treated Peter and his wife mercifully.

Please Lord, Peter prayed despite himself, *let Major Schuttmann live.*

Before delivering the death blow, the city defender looked up and shouted one last defiant utterance to Schuttmann's comrades. He must have known it would be his last. "My own death at the hands of you antichrists will mean nothing. For the privilege to rid the earth of Lucifer's best cavalryman right here and now, I say: to God be the glory!"

The Black Knight deflected the distracted defender's sword with his armor-protected left arm. The lightning-fast maneuver created just enough time and space to grab both of the man's ankles and push hard, causing him to fall. The knight scrambled to gain the advantage.

With a movement almost too quick for Peter to follow, he plucked a dagger from a sheath at his waist. He thrust it into the man's throat, extinguishing his cry for mercy.

The tremendous cheer exploding from Schuttmann's comrades was no less shocking to Peter than the violent act itself had been. They rushed over to him and pounded their leader on the back, hugging him or clasping his forearms to the extent their armor would allow. Why hadn't they offered their aid earlier?

The imperial cavalrymen remounted and stormed off together down a side street, Schuttmann in the lead. Toward what end only God knew. One thing at least was clear to Peter: in the heat of battle, the Black Knight's mercy had its limits.

"Ho! What did I tell you, Pastor?" the old man cackled gleefully. "Glad *I'm* not having to face *that* man down!"

Peter cautiously opened the front door and looked up and down the street. Bodies of the dead defenders littered the street, and an eerie quiet had taken hold.

A quarter hour had already been lost to this unexpected episode, and there was no telling what else might await him. He couldn't spare another second. Dr. Weber needed to reach the cathedral, and Peter needed to reach his family.

CHAPTER 32

Magdeburg
May 20, 1631

8:45 a.m.

Peter had caught his second wind. The general alarm signaling complete collapse of the city wall defenses had still not yet sounded. The cathedral entrance was now in sight only two streets ahead. Dr. Weber, though panting heavily, was alert and even able to contribute to their forward movement.

We'll make it now, God willing, Peter thought as he took one last look at the intersection behind him.

Just then, yet another horrifying sight rounded the corner.

"God save us all!" someone yelled. "It's the Croats!"

A good thirty mounted men—all wearing the distinctive long red cloaks, fur hats, and and brightly colored scarves of Count Tilly's most feared mercenary cavalry brigade—surged toward Peter and Weber in a wild charge, shrieking like banshees.

A musket ball hit Weber in the back. It knocked him out of Peter's grasp, pitching him to his knees. Peter fell, exhausted. The horses reached him, dragged him for what seemed like an eternity. His head and body were pounded against the cobblestones.

Awaking in a daze, he could barely move. His left ankle was twisted and throbbing. His hands were cut, and blood dripped from somewhere else. He checked his scalp. Yes, that was the source. *Thank God. Some cuts, but nothing life-threatening. Where am I? What just...?* He looked around slowly. An eerie silence prevailed on the street. No sign of any soldiers or ... Finally, he spotted him. "Dr. Weber!"

Peter struggled to his feet and limped back toward his supine mentor. His heart nearly stopped. The musket round had passed through his body. The hole over his heart oozed, and blood dripped from the side of his mouth. He was still breathing—but barely.

Peter knelt beside his mentor and cradled his head in his arms.

Dr. Weber managed a smile. With a shaky hand, he reached up and grabbed the front of Peter's tunic, drawing his face close to his own. His gray-green eyes appeared glassy. "Peter..." He whispered something Peter couldn't make out.

"What's that, sir?" Peter brought his ear close to Weber's mouth.

"Remember ... even in ... your ... darkest ... hour ..." He drew a final breath before passing into eternity.

Peter knew he'd never forget those last words. But for now, shock and grief overwhelmed any possibility of savoring them. Even his grief had no time to linger.

After wiping away his own tears, Peter carefully moved Dr. Weber's body to the side of the street and closed his eyelids. He said a prayer of thanks for his beloved mentor's life and for his reception into the eternal kingdom. Then he stood. Peter shuddered at the thought of not giving a proper burial for the kindly man to whom he owed so much, but he could have but one thought now: *Get to the orphanage!* It was still almost a mile down the main street leading west, away from the cathedral.

He arrived minutes later at the cathedral's front gate, the pain in his ankle forcing him to pause. He noticed a number of women and small children being led up the steps to the entrance. A good sign. Hopefully, the children from the orphanage had already been escorted there and were already sheltered safely in the basement.

A loud burst of musket fire erupted from the street leading from the rear of the cathedral toward the southeastern section of the city wall. Panicked city defenders, many having thrown down their weapons, streamed into the large open area in front of the church.

"The Kröcken Gate has been taken!" one of the defenders shouted. "Tilly's men are pouring through! Find shelter immediately!"

Livid commanders raised their swords and shouted curses at the fleeing soldiers. They tried to rally them but to no avail. A large group of defenders—including some Swedes dragging cannons—surged in from the west against the fleeing tide. Quickly, they began forming new defensive lines on both sides of the cathedral and facing the city wall. It looked like the last stand for this part of the city.

Peter's heart sank as the general alarm bell signal finally sounded.

Frantically, he considered his options. Limping on his bad ankle all the way to the orphanage at this point? Out of the question. Once Tilly's horsemen broke through, they'd once again easily outrun him on the broad street and cut him off—if not cut him to pieces. Limp back the way he'd come and try another, more circuitous route to the orphanage? That would take far too long and probably result in dangerous encounters with more roving bands of Catholic cavalry.

Which way, Lord?

9:00 a.m.

Even the Swedes and their cannons loaded with lethal chain shot hadn't been nearly enough. The final defense gave way to Tilly's onslaught like a broken dam. Hordes of Catholic cavalry swarmed around both sides of the cathedral and pursued the defenders.

Peter had no more time to think. The Catholics were already

beginning to flood the area all around him, shooting, slashing, and stabbing anyone in their way. He had to find some form of shelter, no matter how crude.

Out of the corner of his eye, he spotted it. Half a block down the broad street leading toward the orphanage was the long, narrow, empty wooden storage shed that he and Otto had joked about on their way to the council meeting last night. It was the same shed that Christian Wilhelm had recently ordered built and stocked with barrels of reserve gunpowder and ammunition to shorten the supply line to the city walls. Thankfully, the shed had never been stocked. Someone must have finally warned Wilhelm that it was too close for comfort to the highly flammable neighboring buildings and houses.

Just make it there, Peter thought, *and pray that no imperial troops will take the time and energy to enter and search.* At this point, it was his only hope.

Peter limped to the shed. By the grace of God, the padlock on the door had been removed and the door itself was open a crack. Peter slipped inside and closed it.

"You friend or foe?" someone asked from the shadows. "Damn you! Tell me quick, or I'll blow your head off!"

"Friend, sir!" Peter gasped. "Certainly *your* friend."

"Then help Fritz and me grab some of these food bags and stack 'em against the door. Don't have no lock. No other way we'll keep 'em out."

Peter hobbled halfway down the shed until the two men, both defense force soldiers, came into shadowy view.

Unable to put any more weight on his ankle, Peter collapsed into a sitting position with his back against the rear wall. "My regrets, friends, but my twisted ankle won't permit me to stand on it."

The soldier grunted. "A fine help you are. Well, just sit there and shut up. Don't make any trouble. Come on, Fritz. Looks like it's up to us again."

Together the soldiers lifted two heavy sacks, carried them to the other end, and stacked them against the now fully closed door.

"That oughta do awhile," Fritz said. "At least until those bastards decide to put a torch to this silly little shed, in which case we'll have to take these away again and surrender or else get cooked to a crisp—blacker than tar!"

Fritz retrieved their muskets and started back across the shed, stopping as he passed Peter. "You don't say." He pointed to Peter's collar. "Hey, Frank, this man's a cleric." He grinned and beckoned for his comrade. "Pastor, why didn't you say so in the first place?"

"I didn't want to presume on your hospitality," Peter said wearily.

Peter froze as something outside captured his attention.

What's that strange sound? Coming from—where? Sounds like . . . children? Children singing? My God, it's that little Lutheran children's song!

The children sounded as if they were passing directly in front of the shed. Peter stood and hobbled over to a small grilled opening at eye level in the opposite wall. The last of the defenders were racing down the street, yelling wildly, firing their weapons over their shoulders. They plunged into the midst of some fifty young children, trampling some in their haste to get away. A line of imperial cavalry formed at the head of the street and charged directly into the mix of runaway defenders and now-hysterical children, who could find nowhere to hide. Hand-to-hand duels with swords and pistols quickly ensued. The cavalry horses reared and bucked, one accidentally stomping on a prone child.

Wait! I know those children!

As if a veil had been yanked away, Peter suddenly understood the debacle unfolding before him. The children were from Ursula's orphanage! Peter could no longer contain his horror. He shook the grille's iron bars, realizing he was now in a prison of his own making. He watched helplessly as the children were overrun by the fighting.

"What are they doing here?" he yelled to nobody and everybody. "Why aren't they already inside the cathedral? And where are their escorts?"

Smoke from gunfire and burning debris obscured the melee. It was hard to make out individual faces. Some of the children clumped together, stooping with hands over their ears or curling up on the ground to protect themselves. Peter noticed that three of these little groups were each partially covered with a brightly colored blanket. Someone—an escort?—was attempting to hover over and shelter each group. It was the barest of protections.

As the smoke cleared, an imperial cavalryman was knocked off his horse. He now lay helplessly on his back. Peter, mesmerized, watched as a city defender approached and plunged his pike first into the horseman's groin and then the narrow eye slit of his helmet. The defender raised his bloody weapon in defiant celebration, shouting some epithet that Peter couldn't make out.

Seemingly out of nowhere, a large horse with a familiar rider galloped up. It reared menacingly on its hind legs within ten feet of the defender. The Black Knight dismounted and drew his long sword. He walked straight toward the defender and began swinging his weapon with arm fully extended in 360-degree arcs. The defender held his pike horizontally in both hands above his face to absorb the impact of the heavy sword.

The Black Knight kept furiously hacking away. Slowly, he backed the defender into the center of the chaos. One last fiendish swing of Schuttmann's sword snapped the defender's wooden pike in half. The defender raised his hands and begged for mercy.

The knight paused only long enough to tighten his grip with both hands on the sword hilt. Peter held his breath. He, too, knew what was coming. There would be no mercy given—the helpless defender was about to receive his payback.

The long, circular arc traced by the Black Knight's sword began. The defender, trying to back away, stumbled over something and fell away to the side.

Simultaneously, someone arose from the cluster of three small children they'd been trying to protect with a blanket. It was a young woman with long blonde hair. The woman turned and stood in surprise to face the commotion behind her. She opened her arms wide, as if proclaiming her innocence. Peter could now see her face clearly.

The Black Knight's sword continued its deadly path downward, slashing diagonally and deeply through the woman's shoulder, chest, and abdomen.

"*Ursula!*" Peter screamed. He felt his own flesh being ripped from his very body, a million knives piercing the center of his heart.

The beautiful, beloved wife of Pastor Peter Erhart pitched forward dead on the bloodstained street.

Peter screamed and shook the bars of the window as he watched the Black Knight rip off his helmet and stare down at Ursula's prone figure. Slowly, the knight lifted his head and looked in Peter's direction.

Peter froze, his scream stuck in his throat. The face that he clearly saw was *not* the one he had expected to see—that of Helmut Schuttman, the legendary Black Knight. The face that he saw belonged to Hans Mannheim.

No more than a few minutes had passed. Faint from emotional trauma and physical pain, Peter lay back against the back wall of the shed. He tried desperately to keep his mind blank, but it was a lost cause. The thought of her standing there with arms outstretched, the swinging sword, the agonizing question of *why* she'd been out there in the street and not safely back at the orphanage like they had planned with . . . *their children! Oh, God, what—*

"Look at 'em!" someone outside shouted in a taunting voice. "Luther-boys, for sure. Hey, Alfons. Get over here!" The leering face of a Catholic soldier appeared on the other side of the grille.

"How many are in there?" yelled someone else just beyond, presumably Alfons.

"Three, from what I can count. Let's show 'em what we mean by purgatory!"

Peter and his two shed-mates looked at each other in dismay.

Fritz lifted his musket, aimed at the Catholic soldier's grinning face, and fired through the ironwork. The man's head was nearly blown off, but it was a Pyrrhic victory. Whoever Alfons was apparently decided that brutal revenge was needed. Peter heard several thumps on the roof of the shed. Within moments, flames had erupted overhead and creeped down the sides. The heat rose to an unbearable level. It was all over, and Peter knew it. He and his comrades had no choice now but to surrender.

Fritz and his partner hurried to remove the sacks blocking the door as smoke filled the shed and the men outside shouted their taunts.

"Come on out now, Luther-boys! Got a nice little surprise waiting for you out here. That's it! Here you come!"

Five Catholic soldiers grabbed Peter and his comrades as they exited and dragged them to a secluded, narrow street. Each was made to kneel.

"Alfons, let's do it. We've been wanting to send these Protestant scum a hard message for too long now."

Alfons, a non-officer but obviously the leader of this group, peered down the street, striving, Peter surmised, to make sure there'd be no troublesome witnesses. "All right," he said, "but get it over with fast."

All three men were forced to stand, one immediately in front of the other. Peter, last in line, was backed up against the wooden wall of a storefront. His stomach churned. He'd heard of this execution "game" before. One of the Catholic soldiers grasped a thirteen-foot-long pike with a large hooked blade.

"I'll wager you can't run 'em all through, Kistler," Alfons said with a laugh.

"Just watch me. I'll skewer all of 'em!"

The defenders in front of Peter wailed for mercy. Peter knew there would be none granted. Nor would there be any time allowed for confession, remembrance, or even regret. Time only for one last pastoral act, driven as much by total despair over his lost family as his desire to protect the others.

Peter pushed the others aside and moved to the front of the line, calmly facing his executioner. "Take me first, soldier."

Kistler looked at his comrades, then shrugged. "Stand in whatever order you'd like, preacher. Really doesn't matter. You'll all be sent to hell in a second with *this* weapon. Say your prayers, Lutheran heretics!" he shouted as he started his charge from fifteen feet away. He drew his pike back, poised to thrust it through all three men.

Peter closed his eyes and braced himself. *Please, Lord*, he prayed, *take us quickly*. His last thought was of Ursula.

"*Halt! What do you blithering idiots think you're doing?*"

Kistler froze at the strident roar of the mounted infantry officer, his pike's tip only three feet from Peter. He tossed the weapon to the ground, stepped back, and saluted.

Peter and the other two collapsed with relief.

"Captain LaFrenze, my apologies," Kistler said. "We were only having some fun with these men. Only bluffing. Never intended to actually spear 'em. Just give 'em a scare. After what Falkenberg's raiding party did to that Catholic priest out in the countryside, we thought it the least we should do to return the favor."

The officer dismounted and drew his pistol. He pointed it at Kistler's head as Alfons and the other soldiers cowered against the wall. "Your superior officers will decide when and how to deal punishment to captured prisoners, soldier. You were told in no uncertain terms about Count Tilly's orders in this regard. Consider yourself lucky I don't blow your fool head off right here and now—along with the heads of your fool friends here. Now pick up your weapon and return to the fight. All of you, get out of my sight!"

A scowling Kistler, Alfons, and the other three imperial soldiers returned to the street, leaving the officer alone with Peter and his comrades. All three were in no state to offer resistance. The officer, keeping his pistol loosely aimed at them with one hand, reached into his tunic and produced a small canteen of water. He handed it to Peter, who refused and motioned for the others to receive their shares first.

While the other men took turns gulping, the officer squatted down next to Peter. "Well, Pastor, it seems that God's providence extends on rare occasions even to Lutheran heretics. How else can you explain my passing by the opening to this little street at just the right moment to save you?"

Peter looked into Captain LaFrenze's surprisingly kind eyes underneath the brim of his large, black felt hat. The officer wore no chest armor but only a scarlet wool shirt underneath his sleeveless tunic. The tunic was tan in color, with none of the usual embroidered symbols of Catholicism or other imperial army insignia marring its appearance. Something about the man cut through all of Peter's inner defenses and hostility. He finally broke down.

"Sir," he sobbed, "God's providence has an entirely different meaning for me today than it did yesterday. My dear wife is now dead, murdered in cold blood not fifteen minutes ago by one of your men. Her body still lies in the main street and grows cold there. My children . . . I don't know their fate. I beg you, sir, let me tend to my wife's body and try to find my children."

LaFrenze nodded and closed his eyes for a few seconds, as if praying. "You must trust me, Pastor. It's best that you not return to the street—not only for your safety, but for your sanity as well. Things that shouldn't be witnessed by anyone are taking place out there now. Lutheran clergy are especially at risk. And regardless, it's against my orders to allow civilians back into the battle area. As for your children, given what I saw out there, it's best that you simply pray for their souls."

Peter lashed out in an agonized fit of fury. "You heathen devil from the pit of hell! Has your heart—if you even have one—frozen in your chest? It would have been far more merciful to let your men kill me as well!"

The captain heaved a deep sigh and slowly stood. "I'm afraid it's not as easy as that. You see, Pastor, God obviously has other plans for you."

"Other plans?" Peter faltered, confused.

"Yes. Plans for you to serve him in a brand-new way."

"How do you mean?"

LaFrenze lifted his chin, staring down at Peter coldly. "Plans to serve him as a special-category civilian prisoner—of the Catholic League Army!"

CHAPTER 33

Magdeburg
May 20, 1631

12:30 p.m.

Hidden beneath blankets, Anna huddled with her mother and sister in the corner of the small utility room.

It had been nearly five hours since her father had left for the blacksmith's shop—four and a half since the city's alarm bells had first sounded. Just before nine o'clock, a huge barrage of musket and cannon fire had erupted much louder and closer to the Ritters' house than anything preceding it. It had come from the east, the same direction her father had headed in to reach his shop. Since then, her mother had vomited twice, sick from fear and worry over her husband's fate. At one point, she had jumped up screaming and dashed out of the utility room toward the front door, determined to go find him. Anna had restrained her by the waist and only with great effort had managed to wrestle her back into the hiding space.

Frieda had since returned to her trance-like state, holding Liesa and sitting quietly with glazed eyes as Anna recited some psalms she'd been taught by Ursula. Anna knew her mother believed that Vati was dead.

The sounds of battle drew ever closer. Shouting and gunfire could be heard in the street just outside, the smell of smoke unmistakable. There was no latch on the inside of the utility room door—not that a latch would have done much good anyway if blasted by the musket of an intruding imperial soldier. Only one source of protection lay on the floor next to Anna: the same pistol she'd used to kill Dietrich Ackar. Once again charged and ready to fire, it was the only weapon that Adam had retained during the family's move from the countryside. Anna prayed she wouldn't have to use it again.

Someone pounded on the front door. Liesa screamed. The women drew as close as possible to each other, with Liesa in the middle. Anna reached out to grab the pistol and hide it under the blanket next to her thigh. She tightened her grip on the handle.

"Frieda! Anna! It's me! Open the door! Hurry!" The voice sounded familiar but hoarse.

Frieda stared at Anna in wide-eyed disbelief.

Anna threw the blanket aside. "Wait here," she ordered. She stood and crept toward the front door with the gun in hand. "Vati?" she whispered through the crack in the door.

"Yes! It's me, daughter! Let me in!"

Anna unlocked the latch and threw open the door. Her relief at the sight of her father quickly turned to dismay. Adam's left shoulder was covered with blood. His clothes were in tatters, his face smeared with grime and smoke.

Adam stumbled into the room, slammed the door shut, and relatched it with his uninjured arm. He wasted no time on explanations. "Where are your mother and Liesa?"

"In the back room. Vati, what happened to your arm? It's—"

"Forget it, daughter. No time. It's all over. The city's defenses have been crushed. They're upon us. And they must've broken into the city's beer and wine stocks, because they're mad, raving drunk. They're going house to house, demanding money and worse."

"Who, Vati? Who's drunk?"

"The Catholics, girl! Who else? They've annihilated the defense force, and now they're after the spoils. No sign of any responsible officers trying to control their men. Now put that gun away. There're too many of them. It's sheer suicide to resist." Adam took the pistol from Anna, laid it on the table, and then embraced her with his good arm.

"Vati . . . Joachim . . . is he . . . ?"

Adam drew back, looked at his daughter sadly, and shook his head.

Hot tears welled up in Anna's eyes. Her whole body shook violently. The thought of Joachim's gallant young face flashed before her. His simple innocence, his ardor for her, his plans and hopes for their wedding, their future life together—all now gone in an instant. She felt a depth of overwhelming compassion for Joachim that she'd never come close to feeling when he'd been alive. And now she didn't even have time to properly grieve for him.

An overjoyed Frieda and Liesa ran into the front room and embraced Adam.

After patiently listening to Frieda's remonstrances over his tardiness and physical state, Adam turned to his elder daughter and took her aside. "Anna," he said quietly, "I've changed my mind. Go ahead and take the pistol. You have to be strong for your mother and sister. Stay with them just where you were in the utility room. Do whatever you have to do to keep them quiet. If the soldiers come here, the money we have on hand in the house won't be enough. I'm going into the yard to dig up our strongbox. If we have to give up everything to secure our safety, then that's what we'll do. Bless you, daughter. Remember, keep Liesa and your mother calm and quiet. I'll handle things out here."

Anna nodded, trying her best to fight back the tears.

∽✺∽

12:45 p.m.

It was the most piercing, agonized human wailing that Anna had ever heard. It came from the Beckermanns' house across the alleyway. The voice belonged to Clara, the fifteen-year-old daughter of Ernst and Gertrude.

The girl's wails were soon accompanied by the sound of harsh male laughter and loud, rhythmic grunts, as if a wild animal had been unleashed to ravage and feed on its prey. Anna nearly bit through her lower lip, knowing exactly what the sounds portended. She clamped her hands over Liesa's ears and buried the little girl's head in her lap. Frieda curled into a fetal position at Anna's side, covering her head with her arms.

Finally, the wailing and grunting ceased. Silence ensued, followed by the slamming of a door.

Seconds later, Anna heard a horrified shriek.

"Clara! My darling Clara! No! Oh, Ernst, they've killed her!"

The mournful cries of Ernst and Gertrude Beckermann for their murdered daughter carried across the narrow passage, penetrating Anna to her core.

Liesa's eyes were wide with terror as she stared up at Anna. "Anni," she murmured, "they won't hurt me, will they?"

Anna nearly broke at the sight of her little sister's terror but remembered her father's last request. Somehow, it gave her strength to say to Liesa what she well knew could prove to be beyond her capability. "No, princess. I swear by our living God: I won't let them hurt you."

1:00 p.m.

Anna knew they would come. It was just a matter of when. Still, she couldn't prevent her own terrified shriek upon hearing the loud thuds on the front door, followed immediately by a tremendous boom and the sound of wood splintering.

A few seconds of silence ensued.

"In the name of the Holy Roman Emperor Ferdinand II," someone shouted from outside, "I command you to open this door immediately, Lutheran swine!"

Anna's mother and sister clung to each other.

Anna held the pistol with both hands. She stood with bated breath against the room's front wall, her eye glued to the small spyhole next to the door. She had a clear view of most of the front living area, where her father was struggling to unlatch the door to the street using only his uninjured arm.

"Sirs," Adam pleaded, "please, give me but one moment. The door latch has been splintered and jammed by your musket blast."

"Hurry up, dolt," bellowed a menacing, deep-throated voice, "or we'll shoot two more round balls through your damned eye sockets!"

Adam finally succeeded in lifting the latch and stepped back.

Anna watched in horror as four imperial soldiers stormed in and pushed her father to the floor. The soldiers swept through the room, grabbing every loose item in sight and putting it in a large sack. Candle holders, plates, spoons, mugs, bedcovers, every stitch of clothing— even her mother's spinning wheel was snatched up. Only the bare bed, table, and chairs were spared.

Anna glanced over her shoulder at her mother and Liesa in the corner. Mutti had pulled the blanket completely over their heads, obviously trying to block out the dreadful sounds. Anna returned her gaze to the spyhole just in time to see the burly leader of the group grab her father by his tunic and throw him against the side wall.

"Where is it?" the soldier hissed.

"Sir, where is what?" Adam asked.

The soldier smashed Adam's jaw with his fist, knocking him to the floor once again. He knelt beside Adam and put the blade of a dagger to his throat. "Don't play with me, scum. Where's the money? Answer me now!"

"I-I'll get it for you, sir. Please!"

The soldier yanked Adam to his feet yet again.

With the soldier's dagger pointed against his back, Adam walked to the opposite wall. He kicked away a loose panel of wood just above the floor, reached outside, and retrieved the small strongbox he'd dug up earlier. Her mother had once told her that it contained several jewels, necklaces, coins, and monetary notes. Together, the items constituted the Ritter family's total assets.

"Sir, please, take it," Adam said. "It's all I have."

The soldier opened the box and examined the contents. "You claim this is everything?" he said with a sneer. "How about we put a match to this nice little house of yours, just to find out for sure? If you and whoever else you're hiding burn up, we'll know you had nothing else to offer."

"Sir, I swear to you by our living God that—"

"*Shut up*, you miserable pile of cow dung! Don't ever try to compare your heretical religion to the true Catholic faith of our Holy Fathers. I've had my fill of—" The soldier cocked his head toward the utility room at the sound of Frieda's brief but loud sob. "What was *that*? Who's behind that door back there?"

Anna tightened her grip on the pistol, her throat so constricted with fear that she was unable to swallow. She was tempted to join her mother and Liesa under the blanket but kept forcing herself to peer through the hole.

"It's nothing, sir," Adam said. "We only keep piles of old, discarded tools and grain sacks back there. It's jammed so tight you'd have trouble getting in."

This much at least was true. At her father's direction, Anna and Liesa had earlier stacked five large grain sacks and wedged several iron gardening tools against the door on their side.

"*Liar!*" The soldier slapped Adam across the cheek. "I know I heard something. Trying to dupe me, are you? I'll wager you've got your women stowed away back there." He motioned for one of his comrades to force open the door, and the man began to kick away at it.

Anna backed away from the wall and pointed her pistol toward the doorway. She knew there'd be no escape if the man succeeded. One shot wouldn't be enough. To her great relief, the door didn't budge.

The sound of trumpets and drums from somewhere outside interrupted the man's efforts.

"Sounds like Tilly's calling us all back to the main street for his victory parade," the lead soldier growled. "Come on, men. We've got enough. Let's get out of here before the count decides to tour this area himself. Knowing him, he won't like what he sees."

Anna, shaking with relief, crouched by the wall and listened as the men filed out of the house.

Before closing the door behind him, the leader paused to deliver one final piece of advice to her father. "I don't know why I should tell you this, but you were lucky, Lutheran worm. I know *exactly* who you're trying to hide behind that back door. Better to get yourselves out of this neighborhood fast if any of you want to live. Your next guests aren't likely to be as tolerant and kind as we've been! *Adieu*, my friend."

Seconds later, her father knocked on the utility room door. "Anna, take the sacks away and open up."

Anna worked quickly to clear the obstacles.

Her father shoved open the door and hurried over to her mother, who was lying on the floor in a dazed state with Liesa crying next to her. Adam sat down next to his wife and held her head in his lap. He spoke to her softly while Anna held Liesa.

Shortly, Frieda was sitting up with her head on Adam's good shoulder, smiling peacefully, and holding Liesa in her arms.

"Listen to me, all of you," Adam said. "This house has become a death trap, and there's no more time to lose. We've got to get out of here—now!"

"Husband, where on earth will we go? And how will we—"

"Frieda, please just hush for once and listen," Adam said. "You've heard me talk before about that small hidden door in the southwestern part of the wall. It's where they wheel out garbage from the local houses and shops to the dump next to the moat. It's hard to see, protected by a thick grove of trees. That's where we're going. And we're taking nothing with us except the clothes on our back."

"Adam, we can't—"

"Frieda, we most certainly can! And if we want to live, we will. There's nothing left for us here. Nothing we can take with us. *Nothing!* Those bastards took it all. It was the ransom required for our lives—and we paid it."

"But, Vati, what'll we do once we're outside the wall?" Anna asked.

Her father glared at her. He was clearly angry at himself for not having prepared a more careful plan. "We take one step at a time, depending on what's revealed to us. But to start, we'll go carefully from house to house down the back streets and alleys toward the wall. Once we get there, we'll wait in the grove until dark and then go through the hidden door and make our way along the moat toward the river. We should be able to join up with someone else trying to escape south. Try to make it to some nearby village or town—maybe even to Leipzig, though it's about eighty miles away. But in any case, we'll have to live off the land for a few days. Luckily, I've had plenty of experience in that arena. If my army life taught me one useful thing, it was how to do *that.*"

Anna was horrified by the idea of leaving the house, but she knew there was no other choice. She said nothing and did her best to hide her dismay.

Her mother, now at last with some sense of direction, returned to her more familiar role of snapping orders at her children. "Anna, fill the four smaller jars over there with fresh water and make sure you cork them tight. Liesa, take two large loaves of bread from the barrel and break them into smaller pieces. Split them up and put them in those four little bags. Each of us will have one water jar and one bread bag to carry in our pockets. It's all we'll have until we get outside the city gate."

Anna was relieved to see her mother alert and purposeful once again. She hugged and kissed her. "Thank you, Mutti!"

CHAPTER 34

Magdeburg
May 20, 1631

2:00 p.m.

Anna, Frieda, and Liesa screamed in unison at the loud pounding on the front door and shuttered window. The sound of wood splintering could mean only one thing: the imperial soldiers were back.

Adam shoved his way past the women, who had gathered in the small hallway leading to the back door of the house. "Let's go. *Now!* Stay close to me. Don't look back!" He threw open the door—the door that Anna hoped would lead to escape and eventual safety.

The blood-covered blade of a long saber pointing directly at Adam's face caused him to draw up short.

"*Ide negdje?* You . . . try . . . go somewhere?"

Anna knew immediately from her father's old war stories who they were now facing. Croats. The strange language, red cloaks, feathered fur turbans and scarves combined to give it away. There were three of them, all roaring drunk. Anna had once overheard her father tell a friend that he'd had to deal with this flamboyant brand of the devil's minions several times before in his former army life. Of all the countries and peoples from which the imperial army recruited its mercenaries, her father said the Croats had the worst reputation for committing inhuman acts against their defeated enemies.

The soldiers prodded the family back into the front room. Four more Croats had just succeeded in crashing through the front door. Seven drunken soldiers now surrounded the family with weapons poised.

A red-turbaned soldier, who was apparently the de facto leader, pointed his finger at Adam. "Money."

Adam took a small bag of coins from his tunic pocket and handed it over.

Red Turban opened it, frowned, and emptied the contents onto the floor. "*Money!*" he screamed, obviously unimpressed with Adam's offering.

"Sir." Adam's voice trembled. "That's truly all we have left. We've already been forced by other soldiers to turn over everything else we had. Please, sir, I beg you—"

Red Turban pulled his pistol from his belt. Holding it by the barrel, he struck a vicious blow to Adam's left jaw, knocking him to the floor. Adam spit out bits of teeth. He was bleeding badly but still conscious.

"*Vati!*" Anna shrieked. She tried to rush to her father but was restrained by two of the soldiers, who then forced her to kneel on the floor next to her sobbing mother and sister.

Red Turban stooped down next to Adam. "Now. Money?"

He could do nothing but shake his head. Red Turban slapped him across the left cheek at the point of the wound, causing him to shriek in pain.

Seeing he was getting nowhere, Red Turban stood and kicked him in the side before turning to discuss with his comrades what to do next. The men spoke to each other in their native tongue, all the while casting leering, ravenous looks at the women. Finally, a decision was reached.

Pointing at Liesa, Red Turban spoke something to one of his comrades.

The man smiled and nodded. He walked out the front door, returning a few seconds later with a coiled rope in his hands.

Red Turban grabbed the rope and once again stooped to confront Anna's father. "Now, Luther-man, where money?"

Adam could only shake his head.

One side of Red Turban's mouth curved upward in a sadistic smile. He leaned over and spoke softly into Adam's ear, "You want see little one hang and wiggle?"

"*No!* Please, sir. I tell you the truth before God. We have nothing left to offer. I beg you, sir. I'll do anything. I'll be your slave. You can rape me, torture me, kill me—anything. But please, in the name of Christ, don't hurt my little girl. Please!"

Red Turban shook his head in mock sadness and quickly fashioned a noose at the end of the rope. He seemed quite skilled at the task. Dangling the noose in front of Adam's eyes, the soldier made one final attempt at persuasion. "Money or little girl?"

Adam sobbed in desperation. "Take *me*, sir. Please, take *me!*"

Red Turban threw the rope to one of the other men, then pulled Adam to his feet and shouted a command.

One of the soldiers placed a chair in the center of the room, just beneath the noose end of the rope that had been tossed over a beam. Two soldiers tore Liesa away from her mother, lifted the screaming girl, and stood her on the chair. A third soldier tied her hands behind her back with a cord and then placed the noose around her neck and tightened it before stepping back. The soldier holding the other end of the rope looked at the leader, awaiting his command.

"Money or little girl, Luther-man?" Red Turban screamed.

Anna's father let go a mournful wail.

Red Turban looked at his comrade holding the rope and nodded.

The man yanked with all his might, lifting Liesa by the neck two feet into the air. Her body began twitching violently. Frieda shrieked in abject horror.

Anna threw herself at the feet of Red Turban. *"Please, sir, in the name of our Blessed Mother Mary! Please don't hang my sister! We're not*

Lutheran. We're Catholic, sir! You make a terrible mistake. Please!" She clutched in her hands the little wooden figurine of Mary, the parting gift from Barbara.

Red Turban stared with suspicion at the little figurine, as if he were having second thoughts.

He drew back suddenly, fear and confusion contorting his face. He raised his arm. *"Zaustaviti!"*

His comrade lowered the rope. Liesa collapsed to the floor, still alive but gasping for air. Frieda ran over to her. She removed the noose and cord and took Liesa into her arms.

An awkward silence followed, broken only by Frieda's soft cries and words of comfort for her youngest child.

Red Turban drew his dagger and began lightly stroking the knife's edge with his fingertips. He appeared disoriented, as if torn between two strong inner forces in violent opposition to each other.

He looked down at Anna and pointed the dagger at her. "You say Catholic, pretty girl?" His eyes narrowed. "How prove?"

Anna knew that God hated apostasy. But if denying her Lutheran faith would now save her little sister from hanging, then she would throw herself into the task.

"Sir, you may test me," Anna offered, continuing to hold up the figurine in her left hand and crossing herself with her right.

"Test?" Red Turban hesitated, apparently unsure of the German word. He turned to his subordinates for help.

"Ispitivati," one said.

"Ah, ispitivati, da, da!" Red Turban laughed, shaking his dagger at Anna before walking over to confer with his comrades.

One of them reached into his tunic and handed something to his leader.

Red Turban smiled, nodded, and returned to where Anna still knelt. "Here, pretty girl. What you think this?" He handed Anna a small, faded, scratched woodcut panel of Martin Luther with the words *"sola Scriptura"* imprinted at the bottom.

Anna stole a glance at her bewildered father. She knew that what she was about to do and say would deny the faith tradition in which her parents had so diligently raised her. But how else could Liesa's life be saved?

Shouting an obscene curse against Luther and the "devil's religion" he'd spawned, she spat on the portrait and hurled it to the floor. She stood and ground the portrait beneath her heel, stomping on it for good measure. "*To hell with Luther!*" she screamed. "I hate Luther! My whole family hates Luther! God's eternal damnation on Luther! And on us if we ever profess that devil's religion!"

The soldiers laughed and clapped their hands in approval.

Emotionally drained, Anna sank to her knees in front of Red Turban. She crossed herself once more and stared up at him with the most tearful, pleading, innocent look she could muster. "Please, sir, in the name of the Blessed Virgin Mary, let my family leave this place now."

Red Turban grinned, thought for a moment, and then said something to his comrades, who indicated their agreement. "All right, Catholic family. You leave. Man first. You last." He smiled at Anna with a mischievous twinkle in his eye.

Anna was unsettled by the man's tone but grateful for his permission to escape.

The Ritter family walked out the back door into the yard. Adam went first, followed by Frieda supporting Liesa, and finally Anna.

As Anna stepped over the threshold, Red Turban called out from behind, "Hey, pretty girl! You not fool me!"

Anna felt her knees start to give way but didn't stop to turn around. She kept right on walking toward the alley, where the rest of her family were now gathering. Her lie hadn't worked. Red Turban wasn't as gullible as she'd allowed herself to believe. But for some reason, the Croats were letting her family escape—and she didn't care to ask them why.

She looked down at the little wooden figurine of Mary, which she was still clutching tightly in her hand. In her mind's eye, the tender, lovely face of Barbara Saller stared back. Fighting back tears, she carefully slipped the figurine back in her dress pocket.

CHAPTER 35

Magdeburg
May 20, 1631

3:30 p.m.

A raging inferno engulfed the city, obstructing the path to the hidden door in the city wall. Anna had noticed the pungent burning smell building up over the past hour, but she'd been too consumed by her family's ordeal with the imperial soldier-gangs to give it any heed. There was no way to avoid it now.

A stiff wind had picked up, fanning huge flames that were consuming the wooden houses and other buildings on both sides of the street. Several buildings had collapsed, spewing flaming rubble into the middle of the street and blocking the way. Residents emerged screaming and disoriented. Some tried to go back inside their homes to pull trapped family members to safety or to retrieve valuable items, only to be repelled by the flames and unbearable heat.

The smoke made it difficult to breathe. Anna choked on the burning ash, and she could barely keep her eyes open. But the streets offered the best chance for survival. Some residents, Anna noticed, had chosen to take shelter in the cellars of their houses. Their cries for help were coming from the vent holes just above ground level—and for good reason. Windblown smoke was beginning to pour into the vents, turning cellars into inescapable death traps.

Her own family's progress was slow but steady. Her father, in the lead, had a knack for finding a way through or around the burning rubble. He was taking less dangerous side streets when necessary but always moving in the general direction of the southwestern wall. Liesa had recovered enough to walk on her own without her mother's help. Anna held her hand in an effort to further comfort her.

Frieda's horrified scream brought everyone to a standstill.

Anna covered Liesa's eyes. On the other side of the street, the double doors of a storefront had been ripped off their hinges and set against the wall. A middle-aged man and woman, probably the store owners, had been stripped naked and crucified side by side, nailed to the doors with stakes.

It was only her father's strong arm that kept Anna from fainting. "Daughter, don't look. Don't even think. Just keep moving. Stay with me."

Anna fought unsuccessfully to fight back the tears welling up from deep within. But still sheltering Liesa's vision, she grabbed her father's hand and pressed on.

Finally, after more stumbling through the licking flames and thickening smoke that was becoming more intolerable with every breath, the wall appeared just ahead.

Before proceeding further, Adam gathered the family to take a drink of water from their jars. "The door stands hidden behind a grove. We'll see it once we turn left up ahead and go down the cross street just a little ways. I'd hoped we could hide among the trees until nightfall to lessen our chances of being seen once we leave the city. But with this fire and smoke getting worse, we can't wait any longer on this side. We have to go right on through and take our chances. But God will protect us. Family, we're almost there!"

Anna studied her father. His bleeding and battered face, tattered clothes, and still-bleeding shoulder wound spoke volumes. The loving smile and encouragement that he directed at his family said the rest. Adam Ritter had overcome so much in his life: his war injury, his own private demons and struggle with drinking, the abuse and tortures of devilish men. Yet never once had Anna feared that her father would ever quit trying or desert his family as so many men in these times were prone to do. She felt a surge of love and respect for the man that she knew she could never express in words.

She threw her arms around his neck and kissed him on his uninjured cheek. "I love you, Vati. Thank you for leading us here." As she began to pull away, she looked down. "Vati, will God ever forgive me for what I said to the soldiers?"

Adam drew her in close, lifted her chin, and returned her kiss. He held her face between his hands for a long moment, tears clouding his eyes. "God bless you, my brave, beautiful daughter," he whispered. "God knows you said what you did in order to save Liesa. You had no choice. Never fret about it again. No man could be prouder to be your father than I." Adam took Frieda by the hand. "Now let's get out of this damned city once and for all, shall we?"

The family finally reached the last cross street and began walking down it toward the grove and the point of exit in the wall immediately behind it.

Anna glanced hesitantly over her shoulder. Thankfully, no Catholic version of Pharaoh's army was bearing down on them, though the smoke had become almost unbearable.

Liesa, no doubt seeking reassurance, looked up at Anna. Anna smiled back, certain of something for the first time since the awful bombardment had begun three days ago: the city might fall, but the Ritter family would make it. God had protected them before, and he was seeing to it again.

Adam's warning shout brought the family to a halt. The grove just ahead had caught fire and was burning out of control. It was unclear whether the wall behind it had been engulfed as well.

"Everybody, follow me!" Adam yelled. "Run as fast as you can!"

After three steps, Frieda stumbled, twisting her ankle.

Anna saw that her mother couldn't continue without her father's help. She feared what the delay might mean. But she also knew her mother wouldn't allow her father to leave her alone again.

"Anna," Adam said, "run behind the trees. See if the door is still accessible. If it is, come back partway where we can see you and signal us. If not, come rejoin us—we'll have to figure out something else. I'll stay here with your mother and sister."

Anna nodded to her father and raced ahead. The wall was still untouched by the flames, and there indeed was the hidden door that Vati had promised—wide open! Anna walked through the small, narrow opening behind the door that had been cut out of the wall itself. She peered out the other side to see if any imperial soldiers were lurking to snatch unsuspecting escapees. Fortunately, no one seemed to be guarding the secluded area. There was still plenty of daylight left. That meant there'd be few places to hide along the moat leading to the river. But that difficulty could be faced later.

Just get the family to this point, she told herself, *and we can hide out safely in the shrubs until dark.*

Anna's heart pounded with excitement. When she could clearly see her family huddled against the wall about fifty yards from the end of the street, she waved wildly.

Her father saw her. He stood, waved back, and then turned to help his wife stand up. The threesome set off toward her, their pace obviously hindered by Frieda's ankle injury. Adam and Liesa did their best to support her from either side. Still, nothing stood in their way but an unobstructed twenty yards of street and thirty more after that to where Anna was standing.

Her parents and sister came abreast of the last house at the end of the street. Large tongues of fire suddenly shot out from the upper-story windows.

Anna's scream was too late. They never saw it coming.

The house erupted in a massive ball of flame and smoke. The front wall, over thirty feet high, collapsed outward onto the street with a frightful crash. With no time or place to run, Adam, Frieda, and Liesa Ritter stood no chance. Anna could only stare in horrified disbelief as she watched her family disappear under the weight of the heavy burning timbers.

"*God in heaven!* No, God! No! Not this!"

Anna raced to the edge of the flaming rubble. She tried to spot her parents and sister in the blaze, but the smoke had become too thick. Frantically, she tried to lift one of the timbers with her bare hands but had to let it go; it was far too heavy and hot. She screamed out for her father. No response. The fire was growing hotter, forcing her back.

"Anni! Anni, help!" It was hardly audible. But the voice was unmistakable.

Startled, she rushed back once more toward the fire. "*Liesa!* Where are you? I'm here!"

Nothing. Her repeated calls brought the same result. She looked around, but there was no one in sight to help. Finally, the smoke and heat overwhelmed her. She turned away from the frightful scene and retreated toward the wall.

Once back at the edge of the grove, Anna turned for one last look at the flaming rubble. The reality hit. Her dear family had been lost forever—and in the worst possible manner. Hot tears streamed down her cheeks, tears that were different than any she'd experienced before. More than grief, more than despair, they reflected an anger in her soul, anger that wanted to lash out at God—the only one who could have prevented this gruesome tragedy but hadn't.

There was nowhere else to go but out of the city. She walked in a daze toward the hidden door. She passed through the opening in the wall and emerged on the other side. A freedom of sorts had been achieved—but at a terrible price. And from the sight that now greeted her, it was apparent she hadn't yet paid that price in full.

Two burly men stepped out from behind one of the thick shrubs. Anna recognized them immediately.

"So, pretty 'Catholic' girl," Red Turban, the leader of the Croat house raiders, said with a sadistic grin. "Where you go now?"

His comrade, the soldier who'd pulled on the rope in the aborted attempt to hang Liesa, joined in the taunting. "You lie, so you pay now, *Luther-kuja!*"

Anna attempted to bolt, but the two moved quickly to block her path on either side. Swords drawn, they backed her up against the wall.

She was hopelessly cornered. There was nothing more to live for. Her life was now at an end, and she had lost all sense of fear. A cold fury began to possess her, a desire to be done with this world and all the devils it was filled with. If God still wanted her, then he could just take her up with him. *Now!*

She glared at the soldiers. "Get it over with and then kill me, you heathen pigs. Just do it fast."

The soldiers didn't kill her. But they had their way with her, and it wasn't fast. There was only one thing that enabled Anna Ritter to endure the pinnacle of her trial: the blackness that finally overtook her consciousness after Red Turban viciously smashed the side of her face with his fist.

CHAPTER 36

Countryside southwest of Magdeburg
May 21, 1631

3:00 a.m.

Peter was awakened by a light tap on the shoulder. At first, he thought it was the imperial guard who had thrown him into a large tent that was reserved for "special-category prisoners"—whatever that meant. Shackled by his injured foot, Peter had been provided only water and a tiny ration of food. Hunger, combined with the horrific memories of the previous day, had made sleep difficult to come by.

By the time he was able to collect his senses and open his eyes, the unseen intruder was no longer present. It was pitch dark. He reached down to massage his sore ankle. To his astonishment, it had somehow been freed from the shackle. The mystery deepened as he discovered next to the chain a small pouch containing what felt like coins and some kind of packet.

Peter quietly arose, crept to the tent entrance, and opened the flap. The only visible guards were situated some way down the path, asleep by their tents. He trod carefully toward a small lantern attached to a vertical stake and glanced around before opening the pouch. Inside, he found twenty thaler and an envelope containing a small, roughly sketched map with a brief message scribbled at the bottom:

Barge north, tonight, nine o'clock. Don't delay.
Blessings and Godspeed from the one who sent you here.

Who had unlocked his shackle? And *why* had that Catholic infantry officer—Captain LaFrenze, who'd saved Peter's life only hours ago but then had so resolutely sent him to this prison camp—now decided to free one of his "special-category prisoners"?

On the map was an *X* that Peter guessed indicated the barge's location along the Elbe River's west bank just south of Magdeburg. A circuitous route off the main road connected his current location with the target. It would involve a ten-mile hike back in the general direction of the city, of all places. Would his sore ankle sustain him for that distance? And once he got there, exactly how was he supposed to gain access to the barge without raising suspicion? Besides that, what was the barge's destination? But little matter. Escape from the prison camp had been mysteriously offered by someone with every earthly reason not to do so. He should accept the gift and not question the details.

Flabbergasted, Peter stuffed the map and money back into the pouch. He took one more look around to see if the open pathway was clear. Just beyond, a wooded glen marked the starting point for the journey—to where and what, only God knew. He began hobbling as fast as his ankle would allow. Ten miles by nine o'clock would be no easy task.

⌇⌇⌇

11:00 p.m.

The Elbe River just east of Magdeburg was unusually calm, in sharp contrast to Peter's disturbed state of mind. Sitting dejectedly in the stern of the fifty-foot-long supply barge, he struggled to count his blessings.

He'd made a successful rendezvous with the barge two hours earlier—but only barely, as his throbbing ankle and the blisters on his feet attested. Ten thaler had been just enough to bribe the barge operator into allowing him on board at the dock. The boat had finally gotten underway and had safely navigated the mid-river islets. It was just now leaving the still-burning city behind.

More than thirty-six hours had passed since Peter's world had fallen apart. Thirty-six hours since Dr. Weber had been mowed down by the Croatian cavalry and Ursula murdered by Hans Mannheim clad in the armor of the Black Knight. Over and over, he replayed the horrific scene in his mind, agonizing over why Ursula had been out on the street in the first place. Why in the name of God hadn't she simply waited for him?

What, Peter asked himself bitterly, *is God's purpose in this continuing nightmare?* True, God had allowed Peter himself a vague hope—the hope of freedom and a fresh start. But a fresh start at what? What did it matter now? What did anything matter without Ursula and the children to share it with?

Wait a minute! Am I crazy? The children! Why was I assuming they're dead just because LaFrenze said to "pray for their souls"? I never saw them . . . Who knows if they were even there on that street? What am I doing here? I need to get back into the city and look for them. Maybe, just maybe . . . Oh, God, please!

Peter struggled to his feet and limped forward toward the bow, where the barge operator was leaning over the side, testing for depth with a long pole. "Operator, you've got to pull over to the bank and let me off this barge . . . now! I've got to get back into the city to see if I can find my lost children!"

"Are you crazy?" the man asked, laughing incredulously. "No way the Catholics will let me land on either side of this river until we get much farther north. You best wait until we reach Hamburg. Then come back down here in a couple days after the fires have died down and sneak back in."

"How long to Hamburg?" Peter asked, already considering how to revamp his original plan. Whatever it took, he would make it back to Magdeburg. He couldn't give up on Josef and Edith.

"Nine, maybe ten hours," the operator replied.

It sounded like an eternity. Peter looked down, shook his head, and said nothing.

A muted explosion in the western section of the city startled both men. Flames arced skyward.

"What was that?" Peter asked, hardly caring at this point.

"Probably an ammunition storage shed. Heard Falkenberg kept several of 'em at different places in the city. Lot of good they're doin' him now!"

Peter suppressed an angry laugh. He was all too familiar with useless ammunition storage sheds.

The barge operator pressed his case. "Seems to me Falkenberg would have done a lot better giving up the city. Doubt he knew what those imperials were capable of doing, especially to innocent children."

Peter stared intently at the man. "How do you mean?"

"Heard it from one of those dockworkers when we were off-loadin' just before you came aboard. Could be only a rumor. But the man sure sounded like it happened."

"What? Tell me. What happened?"

The operator grimaced and spat over the barge's side. "Bunch of children, supposedly from some orphanage or someplace, all singing and walking together down some street trying to get to a safer place, I guess. The imperial cavalry was in a blind rage over Falkenberg's defenders, who'd fallen back and gotten all mixed in with the children. Cavalry went crazy and killed 'em all, defenders and children together. Trampled, shot, or stabbed every last one of 'em. At least forty young ones dead—or so the man said."

So now LaFrenze's strong hint was confirmed. The faint hope that Peter had dared to entertain—that somehow Josef and Edith had survived the carnage inflicted by Mannheim's cavalry unit—had been dashed. The sick feeling in the pit of his stomach rushed to his throat. He struggled to suppress a scream of helpless fury. For several long moments, he could do nothing but gape with horror at the bargeman.

"Pastor, you look like you've seen a ghost! Didn't mean to offend your sensibilities with that little story. But *you* were the one who asked."

Peter blinked and nodded. He walked back to the stern, not wanting the man to see the tears forming. It would be too much to explain.

As he sat back down and tried to pray, he struggled to keep an unfamiliar and frightening force from taking over his conscious mind. It was a losing battle. Grief was giving way to something far more destructive and dangerous: hatred and desire for personal revenge against the one most responsible for his loss.

Hans Mannheim was a son of the Father of Lies. When they had last met, Mannheim had told Peter he was a "Catholic businessman," had expressed such admiration for Peter's beautiful family. He had planted the idea of offering a ransom that had ended up saving the city from Wallenstein's initial threat. But it was clear now that Mannheim's true business had been all about plotting a better time and method to strike down the innocent.

"Hey, Pastor, some funny-lookin' objects seem to be blockin' our way up here."

Peter wearily lifted his head. *What now?* He noticed a rancid smell like rotting meat. It was getting stronger by the moment. He hobbled forward toward the bow.

The barge operator leaned over the gunwale and peered down at something. "My God! What *is* that?"

Just then, something jolted the barge, grinding it to a halt. Had they hit a sandbar? *Couldn't be,* Peter thought. They were already safely past the islets. Peter joined the operator, looked over the side, and gagged.

The barge hadn't been halted by a sandbar. The Elbe River was completely blocked off, choked by what appeared to be thousands of corpses. Men, women, and children—many burned, bloodied, hacked, even dismembered. Many with eyes and mouths still wide open. Human remains, now nothing more than garbage that the city of Magdeburg and the Catholic League Army no longer had the capability or desire to properly dispose of.

Peter rushed to the port gunwale and looked back toward the flaming city. The stench of blood and decaying flesh was overpowering. Corpses flowed around both sides of the barge. Their macabre appearance was made even more ghastly by the light from the flames and the crimson-red sky reflecting off the water. If hell had a counterpart on earth, Peter was staring straight into it.

Yes, he thought as the bile rose in his throat, he had survived this ordeal—for now, at least. But along with Peter's own dear family, Magdeburg, the proud and beautiful Virgin City, had died. They could not have suffered a more horrible, cruel, unjust death. And Peter knew exactly who was to blame.

He turned away from the grisly scene, sank to his knees, and retched.

CHAPTER 37

Countryside south of Magdeburg
May 21, 1631

11:30 p.m.

Countless pinpricks of light dotted the pitch-black sky. Millions of twinkling stars, each shining one moment and vanishing the next. As Anna regained consciousness, she wondered why the beautiful stars didn't stay put. Where did they keep disappearing to?

The wobbling sensation in her head spread to the rest of her body. More questions formed in her mind: Why was she lying down and being jostled from side to side? Was she still alive? Where was she?

The squeaking, crunching sound of wooden wheels treading on a rough dirt path strewn with rocks and pebbles gave her the first clue. The raucous, cranky voice of an old woman complaining to someone gave her the second. Anna was definitely not in heaven—at least not yet.

"Gunther, watch how you drive this thing. Must you keep picking out the largest boulders in the road to steer us over?"

A man responded in a raspy, high-pitched voice. "Enough, old bat. Not exactly like it's daylight out here. And what'd you expect, anyway, having to stay off the main road and all? I'll whip the horse to pull this wagon where he sees fit. He don't need any instructions from someone who can't see more than two feet in front of her own nose. How's the kids and the pretty Fräulein back there?"

"Kids are behaving," the old woman grunted. "Fräulein's still breathing, looks like. A wonder I'd say, considering what they did to her. *Ach!* Gunther, she's opened her eyes. She's coming to. Sure has taken her long enough... *Ouch!* Curse you, old man. *I said* watch where you're steering us!"

Anna tried to raise herself on her elbows, a blanket falling down to her waist. The sharp pain in her lower abdomen and groin caused her to cry out. She collapsed back onto the straw. She noted a dull ache in her jaw and around her left eye. She shakily lifted her hand to the side of her face and winced at her own touch. Her face felt badly swollen. At least her eye was still there, she thought, and she couldn't feel any cuts in her skin.

"There, there, Liebchen. No use trying to pretend you're ready to up and start dancing around the Maypole. You're still bleeding some down here, though much less than before. A good sign, for sure. Looks like you'll still be good for babies."

Anna looked down over her chest and stomach. She flinched at the sight of the old woman peering under the sheepskin blanket at her private parts. Even more disconcerting was the presence of a little boy, no more than five years old, gawking over the old woman's shoulder at the strange view.

"Told you to sit down, Ralf!" the old woman exclaimed. She lowered the sheepskin and grabbed the little boy's arm. "Not nice to invade a lady's privacy. Plenty of chances for that when you're older. Now go sit in the back of the wagon with your sisters."

Aided by the moonlight, Anna was finally able to focus her sight on the woman. Heavyset, wearing a white bonnet topping a wide, round head, with prominent nose and dark features, she reminded Anna of the grandmother bear in a story her mother had told her long ago.

The thought of Mutti brought it all back. The house, the soldiers, the journey, the fire, her parents running, Liesa's last cry, the—

"*No!*" Anna cried out. She tried to sit up, but the effort and pain nearly caused her to pass out once again. She lay back, helpless as an infant.

"Liebchen, Liebchen," the old woman said soothingly. She placed a cool cloth on Anna's forehead and gently stroked her uninjured right cheek. "I know it was rough, but it's all right now."

"What *else* did they do to me? Those men . . ."

"Best you not think about that now. Plenty of time to talk later when you're stronger."

"Right about that, Bekka," Gunther said from the driver's board. "Dare say she got off lighter than them other two we saw near where we picked her up. Them Croats don't leave anything to the imagination. Did you see that one girl they—"

"Stuff it, you dirty old man! This poor thing's had enough to face without you dredging up even more horrible things to picture. Don't you worry, Liebchen. You're going to be just fine in a week or two. No major cuts. Just a few bruises and sore insides for a while. Could've been a lot worse, considering some of the things we've seen along the way. They must've decided to go easier on the Catholic girls. Surprised they even found any in our city."

"Catholic?" Anna murmured.

The old woman named Bekka smiled. She put something in Anna's palm and closed her fingers around it.

Anna looked down at the little wooden figurine of Mary.

"We were hiding in the bushes. Saw those two Croats running away and knew they were up to no good. We didn't want to take any chances on being spotted, so we stayed hidden all night and most of today. Finally sneaked out of our hiding hole. That's when we saw you lying on the ground and your dress hanging in a bush. I found this next to you—just you and little Mary, all alone. So now you can have her back!"

"Old woman," Gunther said, "you have the brains of a cow. How come you never showed that thing to *me*? And how do you know it belongs to the pretty Fräulein? How do you know those Croats didn't just leave their own little Mary there as a sign—a warning to simple Lutheran folk like us never to resist their will, or *this* is what'll happen to us?"

"Somehow I just know, Gunther," the old woman replied softly. "Am I right, Liebchen? This belong to you?"

Anna nodded and clutched the figurine close under her chin.

The old woman smiled. "Being Lutheran ourselves, can't say I approve of Catholics or the idols they like to keep. But if that thing still means something to you even after what your own did to you, then at least I admire you for being a *faithful* Catholic."

Anna closed her eyes as waves of remorse overwhelmed her. She knew exactly why the figurine had ended up next to her—and it had absolutely nothing to do with her being a true Catholic. The Croats had obviously found it in the pocket of her dress. They'd then placed it beside her as a taunting reminder of how she'd earlier cursed her own Lutheran faith. Even now, she knew in her heart that she would have publicly denied the name of Christ himself had that been required to save her little sister from hanging. Vati had tried to console her with the idea that her pretense had saved Liesa, that God would understand. But now? Her parents and sister were all dead—crushed and burned like worthless insects.

The reason for it all now seemed perfectly clear. God had not abandoned her. *She* had abandoned God, bringing all this tragedy on her family and herself. She'd sinned gravely by denying her faith and before that by coveting relations with a married pastor. And God had punished her by allowing her dear family to be taken away, her fiancé to be killed, and Anna herself to be despoiled, beaten, and discarded like someone's trash.

Hot tears burst forth, flooding Anna's cheeks and nearly choking her with quiet sobs. Why had God even allowed her to live? To torture her for the rest of her life with the burden of her own guilt and shame? How could she live with herself, knowing *she* should have been the one to die for her sins, not her innocent loved ones. Never again would she be able to love and care for her family—or receive their love and affection in return. Nor would she ever be able to present herself and the temple of her body as a pure, undefiled gift to the husband of her dreams. What was there left to live *for*?

"Bekka, that smoke is still making my eyes burn. And we're already a good fifteen miles beyond the wall! *Ach!* Look back there! Whole horizon's lit up like the sun's about to rise!"

Gunther's observation answered Anna's earlier question. The stars were appearing and disappearing because of the smoke rising from the still-burning city. It had been blown southward by the strong wind and was now swirling everywhere.

"That's a sight I hope we never live to see again," Bekka said. "Now quit yakking and get us on out of these parts." She patted Anna's arm. "Don't you worry, Liebchen. We'll get you out of here. Find you a nice, safe place and someone who'll take good care of you."

"Where are we going?" Anna asked.

"The good city of Leipzig. Only a couple of days away."

Leipzig. As good as anyplace else. Anna settled back and looked down once again at the little figurine of Mary that she was still clutching. Once again, the gentle face of Barbara smiled back. At least God hadn't taken *that* pleasant memory from her. She would never forget the love they'd shared, nor her friend's love for Mary and her Catholic faith. Barbara believed that Mary had always been there to listen to her prayers and intercede on her behalf with God as only another woman could. Right now, Anna was ready to welcome the presence of *any* saintly woman in her life who could help her return to God's graces. A woman like . . . Ursula Erhart. *Ursula!* What had happened to her? And to the orphans? And to Peter? Had they survived? Had they escaped?

For the first time since emerging from her unconsciousness, Anna permitted herself a slight smile.

"What're you so happy about, Liebchen?" Bekka asked.

"Oh, it's nothing. I just realized there's something I have to do."

"Well, better wait until you can at least stand up straight before you get started!" Bekka said with a hearty laugh.

Ursula and Peter. Surely God has saved *them* through all this. Who better to listen to her confession and console her with reminders of the Lord's forgiveness and mercy? Who better to restart life together with? Anna would search for them, starting in Leipzig and ending wherever she found them. They, of all people, must still be alive!

CHAPTER 38

Countryside southeast of Magdeburg
May 27, 1631

T he pelting rain awakened Peter from his semiconscious stupor. It was early evening. The rain only added to the misery he had experienced since being let off the corpse-blocked barge on the east bank of the Elbe River five days earlier. Nothing had come easy.

With little sense of purpose other than to avoid roving Catholic army patrols, he had been meandering southeast in the general direction of Leipzig, limping along, his throbbing ankle getting worse by the day. Hunger and exhaustion had combined with lack of adequate shelter to deplete his strength and ability to concentrate.

But physical hardships weren't the worst of it. Thoughts of the loss of Ursula and his children continued to harass his mind, eroding his will to live. He wasn't sure he even wanted to survive the coming night, especially if the last few days were any indication of what lay ahead.

He'd long since spent the last of his money, and three days ago he'd finally run out of the small amount of food and beer he'd been able to purchase from isolated cottages along the way. He'd been reduced to desperate measures ever since: taking shelter at night in heavily wooded glades, drinking water from small streams, and digging up edible roots still buried in fallow fields.

Peter had once again encountered the winding Elbe, this time well southeast of Magdeburg. Fighting against the current, he'd managed to cross the river in a small skiff that he'd found abandoned on the north bank. After wearily stumbling into a thicket, he'd collapsed in exhaustion and lain there ever since.

Darkness was now descending rapidly, making it difficult to see beyond the thicket. He knew he had to keep going. Find real shelter. With a supreme effort, he managed to force his aching body to rise and limp to the thicket's far edge. There he was greeted by an unexpected but welcome sight.

Off to the right, a dirt path extended about two hundred yards straight south from the river embankment into a grove of tall, thin trees. A small building stood in a clearing in the center of the grove. From somewhere within, a small but bright light shone boldly. The distance almost seemed too great to traverse in his condition, but he had no choice.

Peter stumbled along the path that was pockmarked with mud puddles and deep ruts left by a heavy wagon. Finally, he arrived at the double doors of the building's front entrance. Thanks to a lantern hanging on the front wall, he was able to make out the rough, hand-painted sign above the doors:

St. Matthew's Chapel
"Come to Me, All Ye Who Are Heavy Laden"

Weariness overtook him. Five feet from shelter, Peter Erhart passed out, his body slumping into the mud at the foot of the Catholic chapel doors.

PART IV

KING'S BLESSING

CHAPTER 39

Countryside southeast of Magdeburg
May 28, 1631

"At last! After nearly twenty-four hours, my ruff-collared comrade has awoken. I knew if I prayed long enough, God would answer me!" The merry, high-pitched voice came from somewhere nearby.

Peter blinked, trying to clear the fog from his brain. He was reclining on something soft. Gradually, a face came into focus.

It was a small, round, full face with prominent features. The bulging brown eyes with bushy brows, the long, upturned nose wrenched slightly to one side, the pointy ears and dimpled double chin all served to remind Peter of the elf his mother had once shown him in a storybook illustration. But it was the man's high forehead and bald crown—separated neatly by a halo of short, thick brown hair—that revealed his true identity. This was not an elf but a monk of some Catholic religious order. It occurred to Peter that he would have greatly preferred an elf.

"Here now, Pastor. It's time to try some of my world-renowned porridge," the monk said with a cheerful laugh as he extended a spoon toward Peter's lips. "I've labored over it for all of three hours, and I don't intend it to go to waste!"

Peter leaned forward and eagerly slurped the delicious, hot broth. He reached out to grab the bowl from the monk.

The monk was quicker. He pulled the bowl back just beyond Peter's grasp. "There, there. Easy now, my friend. Too much too soon won't do you well. Take my advice. I've been through this before with other unfortunate souls. One spoonful at a time is what you need."

Peter, still trying to orient himself, complied with the suggestion.

"Much better," the monk said. "Here. That's it. One spoonful at a time. It's the best way to profit from Friar Rusche's medicine for the weary and downtrodden."

"I . . . I suppose . . . I take you to be Friar Rusche?" Peter managed to croak between swallows.

"None other!" the monk replied with a broad smile. "The most famous representative of the Order of St. Francis within twenty whole miles. Actually, the *only* representative, which naturally makes me the most famous!"

Unamused, Peter stared at the bowl in anticipation of the next spoonful.

Friar Rusche dipped the spoon into the bowl for a refill. Again, he brought it to Peter's lips.

"Though God slay me," the friar murmured as Peter opened his mouth to receive the offering, "yet shall I hope in him."

Peter swallowed. The broth tingled on the way down his gullet.

The friar repeated the sequence. "Though he slay me, yet shall I hope in him."

In a flash, Peter remembered the circumstances and cause of his grief. He glared at Friar Rusche.

"Though he slay me . . ." the friar began once again.

This time, Peter refused to open his mouth. He turned his head aside. How dare this odd-looking, self-righteous little runt of a Catholic friar presume to quote that key verse from the Book of Job to someone of Peter's deep Lutheran faith, theological knowledge, and life experience? What could this man, protected in his secluded rural parish, possibly know what it meant to be slain by the hand of God—to have his whole family wiped out, his mentor gunned down, life as he'd known it destroyed? Wasn't it little men like these who inspired villains like Hans Mannheim to perform their murderous deeds in the name of the Church? Augustinians, Jesuits, Franciscans, Dominicans . . . it didn't matter which order of Catholicism these men belonged to. They were all branches of the same withered vine that elevated its own decrees and judgments above the authority of the Holy Bible alone, and their bad fruits showed.

"Yet . . . shall I hope in him?" Friar Rusche still held the spoon near Peter's face.

It was all Peter could take. He struck the spoon, knocking it from the friar's hand and onto the floor. He'd rather starve than accept this barely disguised, patronizing attempt at humiliation and subjugation.

Friar Rusche sighed. "Ah, would the dog bite the hand that kindly attempts to feed it?"

"If that hand represents the Catholic Church—the power that has robbed my life of happiness, purpose, and hope—then yes, this dog will bite it. And if given the chance, this dog would tear that hand to shreds."

The friar put the spoon back in the bowl. He placed the bowl on the floor just beside the pallet on which Peter was reclining. "Magdeburg?" he asked, looking directly into Peter's eyes.

Peter simply stared back with a cold, impersonal hatred.

The friar looked down at the floor and nodded sadly. "I knew it. Two survivors passed this way earlier yesterday. They told me what happened. Horrors beyond imagining. And this coming from a pair who looked to be in somewhat better condition than you. As soon as I found you lying there in the mud last night, I had no doubts where you'd come from." Friar Rusche paused, as if deliberating whether to reveal his private reflections. "And as soon as I noticed your tattered Lutheran clerical garb, I had no doubts why it was you *in particular* who had mysteriously appeared on my doorstep nearly twenty-four hours ago."

"And why was that, Friar?" Peter growled. "Did I appear in order to provide another opportunity for you to *earn* your way into heaven? To prove to God that, by playing the Good Samaritan, you have met his final requirements for entering his eternal kingdom? For what mortal sin are you still attempting to pay penance, Friar?"

"Oh, Pastor," Friar Rusche replied evenly, "you've no idea the mountain of sins that I've already confessed and paid penance for. And no doubt there's another mountain of which I'm even now unaware. But in any case, praise be to the risen Christ for forgiving me and to the Catholic Church and its holy sacraments for preserving me. No, my own need for penance has nothing to do with the reason you are here."

"And will you allow me the deep privilege of knowing that reason?" Peter asked.

The friar looked at him intently. "God desires to humble me, of course. To teach me what it means to love and forgive my enemy. Even an enemy who callously shows no mercy to innocents."

Peter was incredulous. "How, Friar, can you look me in the eye and speak as if *I* am the enemy that somehow needs *your* forgiveness? Especially after what *your* Church did to *my* city and *my* innocent family?"

"God is often teaching me things that don't make logical sense, Pastor. But just the fact that you've arrived at my little chapel—and that under normal circumstances I should consider you my enemy—leads me to hazard a guess. God *must* be trying to teach me *something* about loving and forgiving my enemies. And who knows?" Friar Rusche arched an eyebrow. "Perhaps, Pastor, God has a similar lesson for you in this encounter as well."

Peter scowled. "If he has, he's certainly chosen a strange and self-deceived little Franciscan friar to help me learn."

"Just the thing one should expect from the God I know," Friar Rusche said with a disarming laugh. "Well, Pastor, I can see this is not going to be the best time to carry on a long conversation with you. But where are my manners? I need to allow you some time to rest and improve your frame of mind. And no doubt, you'll soon want something more to eat. So please, let me prepare something and leave it with you here next to your pallet."

Friar Rusche stood with the soup bowl and walked spryly toward a small table in the back. On the table rested a kettle and some items that Peter couldn't make out. For the next few minutes, the friar labored to put together what Peter hoped would be a mountainous plate of food and drink. Watching him work, he noticed that the friar's squat body was a perfect match for his head. *Definitely an elf disguised as a Franciscan monk*, he thought.

The friar returned with a plate and small jug. He placed the items on a nearby stool and pulled it over next to Peter. To Peter's dismay, the plate contained no more than a few small pieces of black bread, three figs, and some strange-looking vegetables. Thankfully, the friar went back to refill the bowl with more porridge. He returned and placed it on the stool next to the plate. It was not exactly the feast that Peter craved.

"There, my friend. Enjoy the fruits of my small garden, and wash them down with the excellent beer that I brewed myself. After some nourishment and a good night's sleep, you should be ready for more pleasant conversation tomorrow. In fact, I hope you'll consider joining us for a light breakfast in the morning after you awake."

"*Us?*" Peter asked, surprised.

"Please forgive me. By 'us' I'm referring to myself and my faithful little congregation. I'd love for you to meet them."

Peter's eyes widened in alarm.

"Oh, Pastor," the friar said, "there's nothing to be concerned about. I know you'll find my congregation to be unintimidating, unassuming, and unpretentious. And there's no requirement that you join us. It's just an offering of human companionship. Get some sleep. Consider it in the morning. I'll be sleeping in the small room next to this. Should you need anything, please call. And if you'd like to join us tomorrow morning, just walk through the door behind you whenever you wish. I assure you we'll all be there waiting to greet you and enjoy a humble meal with you. Good night, Pastor." Friar Rusche touched Peter's arm, turned, and walked toward the side door with his head bowed. "Though he slay me," he muttered once again as if chanting to himself, "yet shall I hope in him."

Peter sighed. The little elf wouldn't stop. But Peter was too hungry to care. He tore into the plate of food, such as it was. It all tasted surprisingly delicious. Together with the porridge, it fully satisfied him. After his last long swig from the jug of beer, Peter lay back and drifted off into sound sleep for the first time in days.

CHAPTER 40

Countryside southeast of Magdeburg
May 29, 1631

B
right sunlight streamed through a small window. Peter guessed it was midmorning. Strangely, there were no telltale voices or even sounds to indicate that any of Friar Rusche's "little congregation" had yet arrived. Out of curiosity, Peter opened the door behind his pallet. To his great surprise, the door opened directly to a small, dimly lit room that appeared to constitute the main part of the chapel.

"Well, good morning, Pastor," Friar Rusche said. "We were hoping you'd join us!"

The friar stood behind a rectangular table facing the chapel altar at the far end of the room. A white cloth and four place settings covered the table. A silver chalice and plate containing a loaf of bread occupied the center. Two statuettes about three feet tall—one of the Holy Mother and Infant Son, the other presumably of St. Matthew—were positioned behind the table on either side of the altar. The altar itself consisted of a raised platform supporting an elaborately detailed silver cross about two feet tall. The altar was flanked by a small candelabrum and a bowl of holy water with a sprinkler. An oil painting of the crucified Lord graced the wall above and behind.

Peter limped down the narrow center aisle of the tiny nave. Only three wooden benches faced the altar on each side of the aisle. At most, he thought, thirty people could be crammed into the room. And where *were* all the congregants?

"Ah, I know what you're thinking, Pastor," Friar Rusche said with a chuckle. "Where on earth are they? Well, I must confess that my little flock is not of the usual sort that you're probably used to shepherding."

"How do you mean?" Peter asked.

"You see, Pastor, my flock is no longer of this world. They're among the dearly departed. All three of them: Benedikt, Leona, and Markus. My little congregation. They're all I have left after ten years of dedicated service at this beautiful location."

"I don't understand."

Friar Rusche smiled and walked around the table to welcome Peter and help him take a seat on one of the front benches. "Oh, I used to entertain a full house. Each week the local peasants, few though they were, would attend Holy Mass and receive Communion. Some would come on additional days for private prayer or confession. But that was before the war found its way into these parts. It caused my flock to scatter—all except for three who have faithfully remained with me."

Peter eyed the friar warily. Something was not connecting. "But you said they were dead, didn't you?"

"Sadly, yes. But we keep in close contact. Not directly, of course. But through my happy memories of them and through the prayers that I offer daily for their souls in purgatory. Every morning I do so, and afterward I imagine them joining me for breakfast at this table, just as I remember them doing when they were alive. That's the reason for the four place settings that you see."

"Why four and not three?" Peter asked.

"I always like to keep one place open for a special guest who might someday show up when I least expect it," the friar replied with a mischievous glint in his eye.

Peter cocked his head back. "Friar, I hope you're not deceiving yourself into thinking that *I* am to serve as the special guest at your table today. My conscience wouldn't permit me to take Holy Communion with those who believe and minister in the name and decrees of the Church that murdered my family in cold blood. And besides, how could your own conscience allow a Lutheran 'heretic' like me to receive your Eucharist? Have you lost all sense of propriety?"

"Pastor," Friar Rusche responded mildly, "who said anything about receiving the blessed Eucharist? Today, I'm merely offering a small, informal friendship meal of bread and water. Don't you think it's possible—for once at least—to get beyond the hostilities and formalities of the doctrines that separate us? Can't we simply partake together of the gracious nourishment provided to all by the One whom we both worship in our own way?"

"You speak of hostilities of doctrine as if these were minor differences that can be easily cast aside!" Peter said, his voice rising in indignation. "You insult me, you degrade yourself, and you dishonor God by ignoring the sins of that false religion you profess."

The friar bowed his head and closed his eyes. "Though he slay me, yet shall I hope in him."

Peter shook with rage as he glared at the man who reminded him of every evil he'd been forced to witness and endure over the past nine days. "Don't presume to quote that verse to me ever again, Friar. And don't forget: it is *I* who am the victim here, not *you* and your ridiculous little band of imaginary, dead saints."

The friar's fist landed squarely on Peter's jaw, stunning him and knocking him on his back. The friar grabbed Peter by his collar and dragged him down the aisle, through the chapel doors, and along the muddy ground to the rear of the building. There, next to a vegetable plot, three small, plain wooden crosses stood atop an earthen mound. Friar Rusche continued dragging Peter to the top of the mound. He grabbed him by the hair and forced him to kneel and face each cross in turn.

"Markus Rusche, my nephew. Twelve years old. Hung by the neck on a makeshift scaffold in his own front yard a month ago by drunken Protestant army deserters. The price for his parents being Catholic and not offering anything to ransom him with—or so those ex-soldiers told them before they dealt with them as well.

"Leona Rusche, my sister-in-law. Thirty-seven years old. Forced to watch her son's murder, then raped repeatedly and strangled to death by the same villains.

"Benedikt Rusche, my dear brother. Thirty-nine years old. Forced to observe the murder and torture of his son and wife. Then, after refusing to spit on an image of the Blessed Holy Mother, tied to a spoked wheel and beaten with an iron cudgel. Every major bone in his body was broken in multiple places before they finally put him out of his misery with a blow to his head.

"I came across them a day after the event when I arrived at their cottage for our usual dinner together on a Friday evening. Their stableboy, who'd seen everything and was still hiding in the barn when I arrived, explained what had happened. It took me a full day to recover my senses, another to clean and prepare their bodies for burial, a third to cart them here and dig their graves. Finally, on the fourth day, I laid them in the ground."

Friar Rusche, still holding Peter by a fistful of his hair, wrenched his head around and forced him to meet his gaze. "And for what, Pastor? For what divine reason did these innocent souls—the only family and friends I had left in life—have to suffer such monstrous acts of evil? I'll tell you what I believe the reason to be, Pastor. The reason was *not* that my brother's family was divinely punished for their own sins. The reason was *not* that my brother's family was known to be Catholic and targeted in advance for torture and death by agents of the Protestant cause. The cold truth, Pastor, I believe to be simply this: Satan was roaming the area one day looking for someone to devour, and he happened to pass by my brother's cottage at just the right time to recruit some available, willing human agents in his service. And the hardest part for me to accept? The hardest part is accepting the scriptural truth that God knew this specific atrocity could happen, and yet he sovereignly chose *not* to prevent it . . . just as he chose not to prevent Satan's attacks on the prophet Job or even on his own son at the cross.

"Now, Pastor, maybe you can see why I reacted so strongly to your unkind reference to my dear departed family. You're not the only victim of senseless evil that God—for reasons known only to himself—will at times permit Satan to carry out, using perverse men claiming to operate under the banner of their religious authority. And that's also why, Pastor, I know I have the moral grounds to continue proclaiming boldly in your presence: *though God slay me, yet shall I hope in him!*"

Friar Rusche released Peter from his grip. He hunched over with his hands on his knees, his breathing labored.

Peter stared at the ground in silence as he tried to absorb everything. "Friar," he said finally, "as God is my witness, from my very soul, I ask your forgiveness. For disdaining your kind treatment and the love that you've shown me ever since I arrived. For degrading your beloved family and falsely prejudging your circumstances. Most of all, for counting you personally as my mortal enemy simply on the basis of your religion."

The friar's face slowly relaxed. He smiled wearily. "That's quite a list! But rest assured, Pastor, you have my forgiveness. Just as my risen Lord has forgiven me. And now, Pastor, it's my turn to beg *your* forgiveness."

"For what, Friar?"

"For allowing my rage over your insults to boil over into physical reprisal, even in the confines of my own chapel. And worse, for not bothering to first ask about the story that lies behind your own anger. I pray that you would even now allow me to hear it."

Peter sighed. Sooner or later, he knew, a personal accounting of the horror of Magdeburg would be required. *It might as well be now*, he thought.

⁂

Later that evening, Peter and Friar Rusche sat facing each other over supper in the friar's tiny living quarters.

"Friar, may I ask you a question?"

"Of course, Pastor."

"How is it that, after what you've experienced, you still maintain a confident hope in a God who seems so arbitrary in his decisions to allow or not to allow the torture and slaying of the innocent? Especially when you think of how your brother's family was so brutally murdered!"

Friar Rusche bowed his head and closed his eyes for a long moment. Peter feared that his question had been insensitive.

"For me," the friar replied finally, "it comes down to a choice. I can allow my understandable anger toward God to rule my life. *Or* I can choose to live by the scriptural principle that *every* decision God makes ultimately has a good and beneficial purpose. I've chosen the second option. More precisely, I continue *striving to choose* it, even when the evidence or my emotions tell me otherwise! In truth, there are many moments when my anger overwhelms my best efforts—as you've seen today. But I resolve to pick myself up each time and return to what I have chosen to believe: that, despite the presence of evil, God is *always* good—and worthy of my deepest trust and unfailing hope."

Peter nodded. "So you've chosen not to blame God for allowing the horrible evil that befell your family? Not even to hold him accountable to explain to you *why* he allowed it?"

"Yes! That's my choice, and I'm glad that it is. I would drive myself insane otherwise. As the apostle Paul challenged, who am I, a mere man, to question the will of God?"

"And what of the men who committed those heinous acts against your brother's family?" Peter asked cautiously. "Do you wish for revenge?"

Rusche grimaced. "Another interesting question. Of course, Christ *does* command us to love and pray for our enemies, to let God be the one to avenge us. Though I must confess, Pastor, that should God ever appoint me as his human agent for taking *his* revenge on those miserable bastards, I would not at all object!"

"Exactly the way I feel about Hans Mannheim, Friar," Peter said and smiled sadly.

The friar nodded. "Yes, I'm sure that's true. But we must both be careful not to allow our natural sentiments to override what God commands and expects us to do, wouldn't you agree?"

Peter stared down at his empty plate. After a few moments, he pushed back his chair and struggled to stand. "Well, this has certainly been an enlightening conversation. I should return to my room and allow you some time for evening devotions before you retire. I can't thank you enough, Friar, for what you've done to illuminate me. Strange that I would find such relief in talking with a man whom I used to consider one of the hated enemy."

"Oh, make no mistake, Pastor. I'm still your enemy in the broader sense with my devotion to the Catholic Church and its belief system, just as your confusing and heretical Protestant doctrines are still *my* enemy. We have quite different beliefs about the way we should live out our Christian faith and become saved to eternity. And we'll continue to have conflict over these as we strive to win others to our way of thinking. But do remember this: though our religious doctrines and rites may differ, we are both united by our mutual confession of at least one indisputable and cherished principle—that Jesus Christ, crucified and raised from the dead, is Lord over all. And today, God has blessed us both with a special reprieve, a day to realize that we *both* aspire to love and to be loved by him for all eternity."

Peter smiled and reached for the doorknob.

"Oh, and Pastor?"

"Yes?" Peter asked.

"Though he slay me . . . ?"

Peter turned and grinned. "Yet shall I hope in him!"

The next morning, Peter glanced over at the stool near the left side of his pallet and discovered a brown envelope leaning against his mug. What was this? Peter unfolded the paper and pulled out a note that had apparently been scrawled out while he had slept.

My Dear Pastor Peter Erhart:

My deepest regrets, but I've been unexpectedly called away on important business. In the shed behind the chapel, you'll find ample stores of food and beer to sustain you here for the next few days. You're welcome to the meager store of clothes such as I own in my trunk, though I doubt they'll have a chance of fitting you! Better perhaps to wash your own attire in the creek behind the chapel.

I can't express adequately the good that your visit has done for me. It came at a time when I most needed it. And I truly hope that you've benefited as well. For some reason, God has put it on my heart, Pastor Peter, to leave you with an important reminder from scripture. Always remember:

"God is faithful; He will not let you be tempted beyond what you can bear. But when you are tempted, he will also provide a way out so that you can endure it."

May God—the hope of ages past and our abiding hope for the future—bless and keep you always. And may he protect you in your journey to Leipzig.

"Though he slay me . . ."

Friar Rusche

Peter dashed out of his room and through the chapel nave. He opened the doors and looked down the dirt path leading to the Elbe, the path that had led him to this strange place.

He now had his answer to the question that had troubled him that day in the countryside when he'd attempted to explain to Ursula why God sometimes allowed evil to have its way. He'd resorted then to the Book of Job—to the very verse that Friar Rusche was so fond of quoting—to make his case to her. But he'd come away feeling that something was wrong, that *he* was not the right man to be offering such grand counsel to his wife—or to anybody else, for that matter. And now he knew why.

Before the sack of Magdeburg, he had known little about true suffering. And before meeting Friar Rusche, he'd known even less about how to see his own suffering in the light of that endured by his fellow human beings. There was nothing like *experiencing* true suffering, he now realized, to forge the perspective needed for comforting and counseling others.

Peter stopped to read the note from Friar Rusche once again before looking up at the sign above the entrance.

St. Matthew's Chapel
"Come To Me, All Ye Who Are Heavy Laden"

His burden eased for now, he pocketed the note and walked back through the chapel doors. He would give himself at most two more days to rest up and prepare for the next phase in his journey. God—the "hope of ages past," as Friar Rusche had put it—was calling. And Leipzig beckoned.

CHAPTER 41

City of Leipzig
July 22, 1631

"It hurts, Fräulein Anna. Please make it stop hurting."

Anna Ritter huddled in a corner of the large abandoned house that the Leipzig city council had designated for Magdeburg survivors. She held the trembling little girl in her arms and glanced at the stump of the girl's leg. The barber-surgeon had amputated it a week ago, just below the knee. Blood seeped through the bandages that Anna had applied earlier. Not a good sign. Infection had obviously set in, and despite the medical aide's efforts, Anna wasn't sure if the girl would survive more than two or three days. She looked desperately around the crowded room, searching for something—anything—to help ease the girl's pain. The other three caretakers, all males, were occupied with their groaning adult patients. Anna would be the only source of comfort for this dying child.

"It's all right, Liebling, I've got you. I won't let you go," Anna whispered, clutching the girl tighter and leaning over to kiss the single tear that rolled down her cheek. Something in the five-year-old's face reminded her of when Mutti had asked her to hold Liesa after she'd fallen from a tree. While Mutti had run to fetch Vati, Anna had comforted her sister with the same lullaby that her mother had sung to Anna as a young child. She no longer remembered the words, but the tune was still fresh in her mind. Softly, she began to hum it over and over. Before long, the little girl's eyes began to glaze, and the tension in her face ebbed. Within minutes, she was asleep.

"You certainly have a way with the young ones, Fräulein."

Anna looked up at the smiling face of Herr Kiefer, the shelter's superintendent. It was hard to tell whether his compliment was sincere. The short, heavily mustached man seemed to laud Anna's performance on just about every task she'd undertaken. Still, she much preferred his positive responses to the suspicious, glaring expressions often cast her way by his even shorter wife, the only other female working in the shelter.

"Thank you, sir," Anna said.

"No doubt it's a skill you picked up working at that Magdeburg orphanage before the siege, am I right?"

"Yes, I suppose so, sir."

"Well, I must say, all of the caretakers here are impressed with your talent. Not to mention your diligence and self-sacrifice in volunteering to work here so soon after the sack."

Anna looked down at the child, wishing that Herr Kiefer would simply leave them alone. "They've all been very kind to me, sir, as have you." Out of the corner of her eye, she saw his wife staring her way. Squat, never-smiling, bird-faced Frau Kiefer had been assigned the monotonous task of sitting by the door, monitoring the comings and goings of visitors and patients. Staring at people suspiciously seemed to be the most important part of her job.

"I can't imagine what it must have been like . . . I mean . . . all that killing, especially the torture and raping of those poor, innocent women and girls," he went on, an odd gleam in his eye.

"It's not something I wish to think about anymore, sir. I'm just so thankful that you find my help here to be useful. It has meant the world to me to be able to come here for a few hours each day and comfort those suffering far more than me. It's helped to take my mind off memories I can barely stand to recall."

Herr Kiefer straightened to his full, unimpressive height. "We're all blessed by your presence here, Fräulein," he said coolly. "Please let me know if there's anything I can do to help your marvelous efforts with the patients." With a curt nod, he walked away. Anna breathed a sigh of relief.

Rocking the sleeping child, Anna counted her blessings. Caring for the child and the other patients today had again been a good thing for her gradually healing body and spirit. And in fewer than ten minutes, the productive afternoon at the shelter would be over, her volunteer duties transferred to one of the paid overnight caretakers. Her new gentleman-acquaintance, Eduard Janz, had promised to meet her at quitting time. He would be escorting her to the tavern where she now worked nightly as a barmaid. If everything went as planned, Eduard would pay the tavern owner to let her off a little early tonight. That would allow her to join Eduard and some of his friends at their table for grub, ale, and general merriment. Anna had initially resisted her new friend's offer—carousing had never been one of her preferred activities. But he'd persisted, and she'd finally relented. She needed a break from self-sacrificing labor and female-only companionship. Besides, she thought contentedly, an evening with Eduard Janz was not the most unpleasant way to be passing the time. Especially after all she'd been through over the past seven weeks.

Things had not gone as Anna had hoped ever since the old woman Bekka and her husband Gunther had dropped her off in Leipzig and left her in the care of Bekka's older sister Birgette. Desperate for money, she'd leaped at the tavern job that had opened up a month ago. It seemed like the perfect solution, but reality had soon set in. The small income from tips barely outweighed the constant annoyance of dealing with the demanding owner as well as the drunken, rowdy customers— every one of whom seemed bent on ogling, groping, and patting Anna's behind or slipping a quick hand up her dress as she passed by.

More encouraging had been the easy friendships that she had developed with Johanna and the other two barmaids. All three were peasants born and raised near Leipzig, and Anna had felt an immediate connection with them. They'd included her in their after-hours conversations spiced with lively chatter, town gossip, and sexual innuendo.

Anna had tried to laugh off the other girls' teasing and crude talk. They obviously didn't understand what it had been like to endure the kind of abuse she had suffered—or what it was like to revisit the terrible memories that plagued her nightly. But the bawdy after-hours banter had gradually worn her down. They had reduced her resistance to a possibility she thought had died in Magdeburg along with her virginal purity—the possibility of ever desiring to be with a man again.

Events had taken a turn two weeks ago when Eduard and his friend Clemens had shown up late one night at the tavern. The two young men had said they were university students from well-to-do families in another city. At Johanna's invitation, the two had joined the girls for one of their after-work chats. Eduard, a tall, dark-haired man whom Anna found physically appealing and fun to talk to, had seemed immediately attracted to her as well. The two men had continued to show up and join the girls almost every evening since then.

Earlier this week, Anna had permitted Eduard to walk her home. He'd been the perfect gentleman and companion, listening to her tales of woe concerning her work at the survivors' shelter and the tavern. She'd been tempted to invite him inside but had refrained, as Birgette would not have been available to chaperone at such a late hour. In parting, Eduard had kissed her hand and suggested the idea of accompanying her walk to the tavern tonight.

The light knock at the shelter's entrance caused Anna's heart to leap. Eduard was here. The child still in her arms, she stood and walked over to greet him.

"Fräulein Anna," he said, bowing. "Am I too early?"

Anna looked at Frau Kiefer, who seemed to be taking close measure of this new, unfamiliar presence at her doorstep. "Go on, girl," she said crossly. "Guess we'll have to make do without your exalted presence around here until tomorrow. Give the child to Hermann, and go enjoy yourself."

"Wait here," Anna told Eduard. She walked to the medical aide Hermann, who was freshening up one of the pallets. Before handing her over, she whispered into the sleeping girl's ear, "I'll be back soon, Liebling—before you know it."

⁂

Much later that night, Anna lay on her pallet, unable to fall asleep. The evening with Eduard and his friends had gone very well. The taverner had gladly accepted Eduard's minor bribe, freeing Anna to join the party. She hadn't laughed so hard in months. There had been only one small, strange incident to slightly mar the otherwise delightful evening. While walking home after the party, they'd encountered a trio of escorted, well-dressed young women walking in the opposite direction. One of the women had appeared to recognize Eduard and had glared angrily at him. When Anna asked about her, Eduard had laughed and said he'd never seen her before. Other than that, the evening was pure bliss. Afterward, she'd even permitted Eduard to kiss her goodbye at her doorstep, after accepting his request to escort her again the following week.

At long last, she'd experienced a night devoid of loneliness and terrible memories. Not only that, the possibility now loomed for a budding relationship with a charming and handsome young gentleman of means.

CHAPTER 42

Leipzig
July 27, 1631

T he bells of St. Nicholas Lutheran Church extended their joyful call to the faithful of Leipzig. In fifteen minutes, the worship service would begin.

Devout parishioners, status seekers, and the simply curious from all strata of the city's diverse population rode or strolled toward their morning rendezvous with the divine. Anna was more eager today to participate in a church service than she could ever remember. She'd stayed away far too long. Today would mark a new beginning.

After the tavern party, Anna had made some drastic changes. At Eduard's urging, she'd quit her barmaid job two days ago after being approached by a friend of Birgette's who wanted to take her on as a seamstress. The new job offered about the same weekly pay but required fewer hours. The only drawback was that the work wouldn't begin for another month. Money and even food would be hard to come by in the meantime. But Eduard, expressing delight over the prospect of a full month of free evening time with Anna, had promised to tide her over with some of the allowance received from his wealthy father.

Reassured by Eduard's support and equally eager to spend more time together, Anna had refused the tavern owner's final offer to stay on a little longer. The fact was, she was happy to leave the debauchery of tavern life behind. It was time to concentrate on the things she believed God would bless her for doing: devoting herself to the shelter work; reading the Bible that Birgette had lent her; praying diligently for God's direction and support; and, most of all, reengaging the habit of worship with fellow believers. And where better than Leipzig's highly regarded St. Nicholas Church to find support for this new, more respectable life?

As she entered the spacious nave, Anna felt as if she were returning home from a long and hard journey. The beautiful sound of the pipe organ, the impressive pulpit from which the word would be preached, the magnificent altar over which hung a large and elegantly carved wooden cross—all reminded her of the Magdeburg cathedral.

Anna took a seat on the end of an unreserved pew, next to what appeared to be a friendly elderly couple. Each extended a gracious smile and trembling handshake of welcome. Anna settled back and closed her eyes, then took a deep breath and exhaled slowly. She tried to ignore the odd feeling that other congregants were staring at her, that she was being watched, evaluated, even judged.

The organ prelude soon shifted into the processional hymn, casting out her resurgent doubts and bringing her to a flood of tears. *Everything will be all right now*, she thought. She had faithfully returned to God's house, and he would surely reward her with his long-awaited peace.

"May the words of my mouth and the meditations of our hearts be pleasing to you, O Lord, our Rock and our Redeemer!" the pastor intoned prior to launching into his sermon. Something about his voice and manner transported Anna back to that unforgettable day more than five years ago. It was the day that Pastor Peter Erhart had first stood to address the little Grünfeld congregation, igniting a fire in her heart that had never quite died.

It was a wonderful sermon, Anna thought afterward. It was based on the story from the Gospel of John about Jesus's defense of the woman caught in the act of adultery. The Messiah had written strange words in the sand, daring anyone without sin to be the first to cast a stone against the woman. Of course, no one had. Then he'd told the woman that her sin was forgiven but to go and sin no more. Undeserved love and grace with a stern warning—Anna understood the message. For some reason, she knew it had been meant just for her, and she intended to obey it.

At the end of the service, the strange feeling of being watched came over Anna again. It was probably just a passing fancy. Or was it? She looked back toward the front of the chancel, and her eyes widened in disbelief.

It was him!

Anna nearly leaped with joy at the sight. Peter Erhart was walking up to the dais to shake hands with the assistant pastor. He limped slightly. Presumably Ursula and the children were also up front somewhere. She could hardly wait to embrace them all again. Unfortunately, there were far too many congregants crowding the aisle for Anna to fight against the flow. It would be better to just go with the crowd and exit through the front doors. Surely the Erharts would gather with the others to go through the pastoral reception lines.

Once outside, Anna had only one goal in mind: locate Peter and Ursula. As she strained to look over the heads in front of her, she finally spotted Peter talking with the pastor at the end of the reception line about thirty yards away. She was hardly able to contain her excitement as she edged forward.

"Excuse me, sir . . . Oh, I'm sorry . . . Please excuse . . . Thank you . . ."

Only twenty yards away now.

"Oh, I'm sorry . . . I'm so clumsy . . . Forgive me, Frau . . ."

Ten yards.

Peter completed his conversation and turned in her direction. She was about to raise her hand to get his attention when, out of nowhere, four well-dressed young women converged to block her path. Anna immediately recognized three of them as the trio that she and Eduard had come across during their late-night walk home from the tavern last week. The fourth woman didn't look familiar.

"How dare you!" hissed one of them. Taking a closer look, Anna realized it was the woman who had glared at Eduard the other night—the one he'd simply laughed off.

Anna stood her ground. She was in no mood to be deterred from greeting Peter. "How dare I *what*, Fräulein?"

"Do you have no sense of shame?" the woman retorted, her voice rising. "Didn't you hear the pastor's sermon?"

People nearby were beginning to notice.

Anna glanced beyond the women to see if Peter was still there. He'd moved on to another group even farther away and out of earshot.

"Of course I heard it. What of it, Fräulein? And of what am I to be ashamed?"

The woman flew into a rage. "You brazen minx!" she said in a voice now loud enough to cause those nearby to stop their conversations and turn toward the disturbance. "How dare you have the gall to seduce my sister's husband and then show up unrepentant at this house of worship, strutting around in the courtyard to attract the attention of your future male conquests! Especially after hearing that our Lord has commanded us to sin no more!"

Anna broke into a cold sweat. "Your . . . sister's husband? Do you mean—"

"Oh, stop pretending you don't know who Eduard is. And look at what you've done to his poor wife—my sister!" The woman pointed to the one young woman in the group that Anna hadn't recognized. She was teary-eyed and glaring with hatred at Anna. She was also quite obviously with child.

"My ladies," Anna protested. "I . . . I don't understand. Eduard never told me—"

"Will you add lies to your wickedness? Haven't you degraded yourself enough already? And to think that Eduard would become so smitten with your devilish charms that he's run off and left my sister all alone to fend for herself and her child! We can only assume you're secretly visiting with him somewhere!"

Anna flushed scarlet. She could feel the accusing stare of every St. Nicholas congregant within earshot. Her throat constricted as hot tears formed in her eyes. "Please, my ladies, I'm so sorry for what's happened. But I *swear* to you that I didn't know anything about Eduard being married. And I also swear to you that nothing happened beyond—"

"*Enough!* Don't disgrace yourself further with your false claims of innocence. You should leave and never return to this place. Find another church that'll tolerate your foul presence."

White-hot with fury, Anna stalked through the crowd toward the entrance gate. She turned onto the street and began walking aimlessly in the direction of Birgette's house, trying desperately to make sense of it all.

One thing at least was clear: Eduard had betrayed her, to say nothing of his own wife. How could she have been so naïve to believe his claim that he didn't know this woman who had glared so openly at him? Whether or not Eduard's feelings for Anna had been genuine, he couldn't have put her in a more vulnerable position. She had quit her tavern job based on his assurances of support, and there was no chance now that the owner would take her back. There would be no income for a month until her new job started. Worse, she had now been publicly labeled as an accused adulteress—something that would be difficult if not impossible to disprove. And knowing how malicious church gossip had a way of spreading like wildfire throughout the city, there was no telling who might be accusing her next.

On an impulse, Anna began walking in the opposite direction. The shelter was only a half mile away. Even though this was her day off, she needed above all to reconnect with something solid, something supportive and familiar. Herr Kiefer would be pleased to see her. He would ask her to check up on the little girl with the amputated leg who, amazingly, had taken a turn for the better in the last couple of days. Gradually, Anna's anger and confusion began to fade. She'd been through so much worse. Somehow, God would see her through this trial as well.

Ten minutes later, Anna knocked on the door. Frau Kiefer would usually have flung it open within seconds, greeting whatever poor soul happened to be standing on the step with her worst scowl. Today, it was taking her a very long time.

Anna knocked again, harder. She heard low voices on the other side of the door. They sounded like they were arguing. Finally, the door opened. Herr Kiefer stood with his short, wide frame blocking the entire entrance.

"Hello, Fräulein Anna." His voice had a strange, surly tone.

"Good evening, Herr Kiefer. I hope you don't mind, but little Karin was on my mind at church today, and I thought I might drop by to see how she was doing."

Kiefer cleared his throat. "Fräulein Anna, you can't come back to work here anymore."

"B-but sir, why? Why can't I—"

"Certain allegations have been made, Anna. And it does not look proper for an unmarried, single woman to be tending to our male patients."

"But Herr Kiefer, you know I've never attended the men, but only the females and the children."

Kiefer shifted uncomfortably. "*I* know that, Fräulein, but there are good, God-fearing Christian people in this city who don't seem to have as much trust in your good intentions and behavior here as I do. Especially after . . ."

"After . . . what, sir?" Anna could feel the bile rising in her throat. She followed Kiefer's gaze as he turned his head in response to someone prompting him from behind. Frau Kiefer stood behind her husband, her pinched scowl reflecting utter contempt and disdain.

Frau Kiefer stepped forward and clasped her husband's arm with both hands. "It might serve you well, girl, to remember your place. Your beauty is not meant to be used as a weapon to corrupt happily married Christian gentlemen. Why don't you just—"

Anna did not need to hear the rest. She turned and ran as fast as she could back to her small room in the back of Birgette's house. Her head spun with hurt, indignation, and confusion, but mostly with hatred—hatred for Eduard, hatred for her four accusers, hatred for the Kiefers and all those other supposedly Christian men and women who had stood in the churchyard shaking their heads at Anna's supposed guilt, hatred for the church that tolerated them and, yes, she had to admit, even hatred for God. Had the loss of her entire family and fiancé not been enough for him? What *else* was he demanding of her?

Maybe, despite all that God had put her through in Magdeburg, despite her best efforts to recover and seek his presence, he was still punishing her former sins. Or maybe he still didn't trust her to control her unholy attraction to Peter, a holy man after God's own heart. Yes, that made more sense. God was using these false, public accusations of adultery to discourage any lingering thoughts of pursuing Peter for her own selfish purposes.

Well, she thought bitterly, *if that's what God is worried about, then I will put his mind at ease.* She would stay away from Peter Erhart—permanently. She would *gladly* stay away from his church. If God had a better idea in mind, he would just have to reveal it. She had done all she could.

Reaching for the unopened bottle of brandy in Birgette's tiny cabinet, Anna pulled out the stop and poured herself a cup.

CHAPTER 43

Leipzig
August 1, 1631

S t. Nicholas's assistant pastor, Gabriel Carver, couldn't stop expressing his amazement. "Imagine! My old friend Peter Erhart, survivor of Magdeburg. Of all the ways that our Lord could have brought us together again, I do believe this to be the strangest. They never taught us at the university that war can restore as well as destroy relationships, did they?"

For more than an hour, Peter and Gabriel had been sitting on the small patio bench in the church courtyard, catching up with each other. The two had studied together at the University of Strasbourg more than seven years ago. Their rebonding had been immediate when Peter had surprised Gabriel with his appearance at the church service last Sunday.

Peter sighed. "As much as I love seeing you again, Gabriel, I have to admit I'd trade it along with everything else to have my family back again."

Gabriel blushed and looked down. "Of course. Forgive me, Peter. I can't imagine the pain you've been through. Tell me, have you found a comfortable place to live in the city yet?"

"Yes, thank God. After staggering through the city gates one after-

noon nearly two months ago, I was approached by a kind old gentleman and his wife. They'd heard about Magdeburg and from my ragged
appearance, they guessed I was one of the victims. They took pity on
me, and they insisted I stay in the back room of their house until I was
able to get back on my feet. Ever since, they've fed me and given me
odd jobs to do for them. It's the Lord's provision. But I must admit I'm
anxious to move out and start earning my own keep."

"Well," Gabriel said with a laugh, "you won't have to look far for a
new place of employment, my friend."

"How do you mean?"

"After talking with you after yesterday's service, Pastor Wagner and
I retired to his study for a chat. We agreed that in you the Lord has
provided the perfect answer to our prayer for another experienced
assistant pastor. One with a heart not just for preaching but also for
actively ministering to the poor, especially those beyond the city
walls. Not only that, but an ordained Lutheran cleric with an excellent
reputation and personally known to at least one of us! We should have
no trouble gaining city approval. The only question is whether you'd be
interested in joining our little crusade."

"I don't understand," Peter said. "Aren't *you* the assistant pastor for
St. Nicholas?"

"Ah, that I am," Gabriel replied. "But if you'll remember, Peter, my
forte has always been theological research, debate, and preaching. To
my eternal shame, I've never been especially excited about getting my
hands dirty with the actual pastoral care that many in the countryside
so desperately need. Both Pastor Wagner and I recognize this short-
coming. But he's been very patient with me. We've talked about the
possibility of bringing on another assistant pastor to lead this aspect
of our ministry with passion and energy—as long as we could find the
right person, that is. And here you show up at our doorstep!"

"But do you have the finances to support another assistant pastor?"
Peter asked.

"That's another strange piece of good news that the war has
surprisingly produced. You've no doubt heard the rumors that Leipzig

could be Count Tilly's next target?"

"Yes, but what does that have to do with your church's finances?"

"Peter, have you already forgotten the effect of mortal fear on churchgoing citizens? The closer an enemy army draws to a city, the more tithes and offerings tend to start rolling in to the city's churches. Didn't that happen in Magdeburg?"

"Of course, Gabriel. But that was when the situation had gone far past the point of rumor. Is there any substance to what we're hearing of Tilly's next move?"

"More than what you might think, I'm afraid. Tilly's force is now only twenty miles west of here. He wants to consolidate his gains after Magdeburg. He knows King Adolphus and his Swedes have recently allied with the prince-elector of Saxony's German army about fifty miles north of us. They're all hungering for bloody revenge against the Catholics, and Tilly wants to strike them before they become too potent through their local recruiting efforts. Leipzig stands between the two armies, and Tilly doesn't want Adolphus to take the city first and use it to his advantage. So the strong word is that Tilly will try to forcibly occupy it himself before very long."

"What good fortune I get to experience," Peter moaned. "To survive the massacre of the walled city of Magdeburg, only to suffer that very same fate in the walled city of Leipzig! Is this city preparing to defend itself, or will it yield to Tilly's demands? I have to tell you, Gabriel, I refuse to remain here if the answer is the former. I can't relive the horrors of Magdeburg yet again."

"I doubt very much that our city leaders will dare resist Tilly after what they've seen him do," Gabriel said. "But in any case, it's likely that several weeks at least will pass before Tilly commits to action. He needs time to replenish his forces. And so . . . I return to my original proposal. How does the position sound to you, at least on a trial basis? You wouldn't have to worry anymore about room or board. And if at some point you should decide it's in your best interest to flee the city, that would certainly be understood. You'd no doubt have a lot of company, probably including myself and Pastor Wagner!"

Peter hesitated. "And will I serve alone in this ministry of pastoral care?"

"Definitely not. You'll have the able assistance of two of the most cheerful, hospitable, and capable ladies I've ever had the privilege of serving with. For years they've served this church faithfully—visiting the sick, disabled, and poor both in the city and the nearby countryside. I tell you, Peter, whether the needy be Protestant or Catholic or anything else, these ladies don't withhold their Christian love and care."

Peter didn't have to think long. "How can I refuse such a great offer, Gabriel? I'll pray on it tonight and let you know tomorrow morning. But please give my sincere thanks to Pastor Wagner for even considering the possibility. And thank *you* for making it happen."

"Peter, you know it's God we should thank. Most of all, I thank him for the privilege of seeing you still alive after what you've suffered."

Peter and Gabriel shook hands and embraced.

Peter started to rise, eager to return to his temporary lodging and start conceiving plans for the exciting new countryside ministry that Gabriel had described. An unpleasant memory gave him pause.

"Gabriel, I'm curious. What *was* all that shouting about here in the courtyard after last Sunday's service? Something about a woman who was accused of adultery?"

Gabriel frowned. "Yes, I'm afraid so. It was a terrible charge to bring out in public like that, and very possibly it was a false one. But, any way you look at it, the poor woman was treated worse than a dog. And to think—by longtime members of our own church! It was as if they'd deliberately clapped their hands over their ears during Pastor Wagner's sermon. I've had some unpleasant dealings with those women and their gossip in the past, but this takes things to a whole new level."

Peter shook his head. "From where I stood, I couldn't see or hear much, but I definitely sensed the commotion. You say the accused woman ran out. Did anyone get her name?"

Gabriel closed his eyes for a moment. "I seem to recall from two elderly congregants who'd spoken earlier with her inside the church that her name was Anna . . . Anna Ritten or Ritter or something of the sort. She told them she was originally from Magdeburg."

Peter's eyes widened. *"Anna Ritter?* From *Magdeburg?* Gabriel, I *know* this woman! She worked with my wife at the city orphanage. They'd become close friends, and my wife convinced her to visit my church, where I met her. She was engaged to be married and . . ."

Painful memories overwhelmed Peter's mind before he cut them off. "Gabriel, do you or anyone else have any idea where this woman lives or works?"

"I gather from what I overheard that she works as a barmaid at the tavern on Nettelbeck Strasse. That's supposedly where the accuser's husband Eduard met her and started to cavort with her and her friends every night after-hours. It's not the first time Eduard's been rumored to be running out late at night to a place of questionable repute. It seems to be a bad habit that finally got the best of him."

"Thank you, Gabriel," Peter said, grinning ear to ear. "You've just reaffirmed my full faith in God's wisdom and goodness!"

Before Gabriel could respond, Peter turned and began running down the path to the church gate.

"Peter, where are you going?" Gabriel called after him.

"To catch up with another dear friend," Peter called back, "before the tavern closes!"

⚬⚬⚬

The next morning, Peter set the food basket that he'd purchased for Anna in front of her door, took a deep breath, and knocked. She was his one link to a much happier past. And given what he'd learned last night from Johanna and the other barmaids concerning her tragic circumstances, Peter would doubtless be the one link for her.

Receiving no response, Peter knocked again, this time louder. A slight scraping sound from inside was followed by a loud thud, as if someone had fallen against the door. Then came a woman's laugh—drunken, resigned.

"Fräulein Ritter!" Peter called through the door. "Anna, are you all right?"

No response.

"Anna, are you there? Are you all right? It's me, Pastor Peter Erhart."

"What? Who? Pascal? Are you back again this morning?" Again, the mirthless laugh. "Was last night's goodbye kiss not enough to quench your appetite? Surely you don't expect a good little girl like me to offer you more than that!"

"*Anna!* Did you hear me? This is Peter Erhart, from St. John's Church in Magdeburg. The husband of Ursula, your supervisor at the orphanage!"

A long pause followed.

"*God in heaven!* Pastor Erhart, is it . . . is it really . . . ?"

Peter smiled in relief. "Yes, Anna, it's really me. Can you open the door?"

Another long pause. This was taking too long.

"Anna, is something wrong? Are you all right?"

"Pastor, I . . . I can't let you in. It's not right. Please go."

Stunned and worried, Peter tried to gently force open the door, but it was locked from the inside. "Anna, please. Just let me—"

"I said go away. Leave me alone! Did you not understand me?" Her voice betrayed exasperation and tears.

"Anna, I beg you to let me see you again. We have so much to talk about. And I've brought something for you."

Another pause. Finally, he heard the sound of a latch being lifted. The door swung open.

"There, Pastor. Are you satisfied to see the depths to which this peasant girl has sunk?"

It was hard to look at her. She was not the simply adorned yet alluring young lady he'd met at St. John's. She was still beautiful, of course. In fact, if anything, she was even more ravishing than he'd remembered— but in an entirely different and far more disturbing way. Hair askew, shoulders and bosom amply revealed by her low-cut dress, eyes heavily painted with seductive makeup—she showed all the telltale signs of a committed tavern wench.

But it wasn't just her physical appearance. The empty wine bottles on the table behind her confirmed the obvious: Anna was drunk out of her mind, barely able to stand straight.

"So, Pastor," she said with a coy smile, "are you here to join my parade of gentlemen-callers?"

As shocked as he was, Peter tried to remain calm and respectful. He didn't want to risk alienating her. "Anna, I come only as your friend who's so happy to see you alive after what we . . . after what you . . ."

"After what, Pastor?"

Peter looked down. "I heard from your friend Johanna about what happened to you and your family in Magdeburg."

"Oh, and I suppose Johanna also told you every other piece of gossip about me in *this* city as well. Don't even talk to me about it, Pastor. I've sickened myself thinking about it all, over and over again. Worn my knees out in prayer. Read my landlady's Bible every single day for the past week—as much as a stupid peasant girl like me's able to understand, anyway. I just want to forget it all—*everything* that's happened. But God won't let me. He keeps sending them back to haunt my mind. One night it's my accusers. The next it's my parents and sister. I wake up in the middle of the night screaming for them to run, to run faster, to . . . oh, God help me!" Anna sank to her knees, her face buried in her hands as she sobbed.

Peter stooped and tenderly grasped her wrists. "Anna, dear friend, please don't despair. You don't have to bear this alone anymore."

Anna looked up, head wavering and eyes still glazed from the wine's effect. "Oh? And who do I have the privilege of bearing this wonderful burden with, Pastor? *You?* Why would someone of your noble character and devotion to God want to have anything to do with a known adulteress, a city tramp?"

"Because I know who you are, Anna. I know from Johanna those charges against you are untrue. I know you're not an adulteress, a tramp, or anything else you may have been accused of. You're still every bit the woman my wife was so fond of talking about—her love and admiration for you, your love of the children. And besides, it's not just me who wants to help you."

Anna eyed Peter suspiciously. "W-who do you mean?"

Peter smiled. "I know this may sound strange, but there are people—good people—at St. Nicholas Church who I—"

Anna yanked her hands away from Peter's and stood up. Her face was beet-red with anger. "I assure you, Pastor," she hissed, "I don't want *their* help. Ever. The whole judgmental lot of them. So quick to cast their stones. So eager to look down their noses. I *hate* every last one of them!"

"*Now* who's being judgmental? I assure you, Anna, if you would just let me introduce you to some—"

"Get out!" Anna screamed. "Get out now!"

"Please, Anna, you don't know what you're saying. You're—"

"I said get out now! And don't come back! Just go on home to your perfect wife and your perfect children, and on Sunday you can all attend your perfect little church together. You don't need a naughty peasant girl like me to drag you down, *Herr Pastor Perfect*!"

Peter's father had taught him never to strike a woman under any circumstances. If he hadn't, Anna would have been lying flat on the floor now. Hadn't Friar Rusche leveled Peter for spouting similar nonsense? How dare this self-absorbed, self-pitying girl insult the memory of Peter's dear family? There was no excuse. She'd never even troubled herself to ask about them.

Peter turned to leave. He nearly stumbled over the food basket as he did so. Turning back one last time to face Anna in the doorway, he smiled grimly. "It's a good thing we sometimes get additional chances in life, isn't it, Anna? Please, at least accept the gift. I'd hate to see it wasted."

With that, he walked down the alley. He hadn't gone ten steps before he was struck in the back of the head with something hard. He whirled around, noticed a small object still rolling at his feet, and picked it up. It was a brown pear—the same one he'd selected at the market and placed in the basket for Anna. He looked up just in time to see her slam her door shut, leaving the food basket outside.

It was too much. Peter took aim and hurled the pear with all his might. The fruit splattered dead-center against the door. He spun around and stalked away, hot with anger but knowing he could never let things end this way.

Peter Erhart was not about to give up on Anna Ritter—not by a long shot. There was something about her, a magnetic pull that he couldn't now escape, even if he wanted to.

CHAPTER 44

Leipzig
August 8, 1631

Anna awoke just before nine o'clock in the morning in a cold sweat. She surveyed her small room that barely managed to accommodate a pallet, table, chair, and cabinet. She tried to say a prayer of thanks for the private space, but as usual, the prayer degenerated into an eddy of depressed thoughts. It had been this way each morning since Peter's surprise visit last week, and each day was bringing her closer to the point of utter despair.

The city clock tower signaled the new hour's arrival. She sat up and put her hands over her ears to block the painful reminder that another day lay before her. After the chimes mercifully ended, she reached for the bottle of brandy that had been left last night as a gift by Pascal, her latest tavern companion. Two long swigs burned all the way down, but she hardly cared. The liquor would help brace her to face the day.

She stood slowly and stumbled the short distance to the table, where she splashed water from the washbowl to wipe off last night's makeup. She held up the looking glass and cursed silently at what she saw: herself or, rather, what had become of her. She ran a brush through her tangled hair. Disgusted with the result, she gave up trying to fix herself this early in the day. Clearly, she was a lost cause.

She fought the urge to lie back down and cry. Instead, she walked toward the front door and opened it a crack. Something inside her desperately wanted to see Peter Erhart standing there, but at the same time, she didn't want to face him again. At least not in this condition.

Peter had not given up on her. Another food basket packed with a full day's ration of bread, cheese, fruit, and hard-boiled eggs stared up at her from the stoop, just as one had for the past six mornings. Well, Anna thought, she knew exactly what to do with this one, just like all the others. She dressed, then picked up the basket, and marched down the street to the poor Engler family. Hadn't Peter said he didn't want his gifts to go to waste? Certainly Frau Engler, mother of five young children, had a far greater need of such a bounty than she did.

Around ten o'clock, Anna sat down to another one of the meager breakfasts that Birgette always managed to scrape together and share. It came at a price. Aware that Anna had recently quit her job at the tavern, Birgette had put her to more useful employment: serving as the unfortunate listening ear for her incessant chatter and complaints about distant or deceased family members and friends. By noon, Anna was totally spent from the effort. She gratefully retired for a three-hour nap, marred once again by disturbing dreams.

Awaking in another depressed mood, she began the tedious process of freshening up and applying makeup. By four thirty, she was off to the tavern. She arrived in time to engage with one of the lively groups of younger people that met there for supper and brew. It was the one part of her dreary day that kept her going to the next. It also helped that Pascal, the unmarried son of a well-to-do tailor, had fallen for her and was quite eager to court her pleasure by paying the fare for her food and drink.

After the tavern closed, Anna permitted Pascal to walk her home. She knew he wanted to be invited inside, but given her experience with Eduard, she had no desire to encourage Pascal past the bare minimum needed to maintain his interest and support. She returned his rather awkward goodnight kiss, then politely dismissed him and closed the door. Not even bothering to undress or take another swig from the brandy bottle, she threw herself down on the pallet. Familiar terrible memories and fears for the future began to take hold. The result was total misery, compounded by her recent rejection of Peter Erhart and his family, the only friends from her past life still living and accessible.

Some time after finally falling asleep, Anna awoke with a start. A new resolve had taken hold—and she was sure it could only have come from God. No longer could she go on living isolated and alone, in danger of going insane or even taking her own life. Her days and nights of mindless behavior, drinking, and despairing self-pity had to end. Things would be different, starting tomorrow. She would make an honest effort to rehabilitate herself—starting with a proper confession and apology to Peter, difficult though that might be. As a godly Lutheran pastor, he would surely understand and accept it. Maybe he would invite her to visit his family and play with his beautiful children again. And maybe, by coming to love Peter and Ursula together like her new brother and sister, it would help her own life to be restored.

Yes, tomorrow would be different. She would make sure of it.

Early the next morning, Peter set the food basket down on Anna's door stoop. This time, he wasn't going to simply drop it off as usual. He knocked on the door, steeling himself for yet another rejection. He was ready. He had a message to deliver to Fräulein Anna Ritter today.

Peter was surprised to hear quick and steady footsteps on the other side of the door. He was even more astonished at the figure that appeared in the doorway a second later. Anna had prepared herself to receive *somebody*, if not him. Her hair, face, and dress were a far cry from her dingy appearance of last week. At least he wouldn't have to contend with a drunken, self-degrading tavern wench this morning.

"Uh . . . good morning, Pastor," Anna said awkwardly.

Good, Peter thought. After last week's reception, she deserved to feel ill at ease—hopefully even a touch guilty.

"Fräulein Ritter," he asked, "may I?"

"Oh, certainly." Anna eyed him warily as she let him in then closed the door behind him. "Pastor, I wanted to tell you that I'm—"

"Anna," Peter interrupted, "do you disdain me so much that you pretend to accept my gifts and then give them away to someone else?" A parishioner had told Peter that she was giving away the food baskets to the Englers.

"Oh, I do so beg your pardon, Pastor," Anna said, clearly trying to regain her composure. "I was only doing what I've learned from the Bible about giving to those in far greater need than myself. Certainly your wonderful, kindhearted congregation at St. Nicholas would approve."

"Anna, I bought, prepared, and delivered those baskets especially for *you*. For *your* enjoyment and benefit. Maybe to share with your landlord. But *not* to just give them away to your neighbors out of some misplaced sense of charity. How long were you planning to keep this charade going?"

Anna stiffened. "I assure you, Pastor, this was no charade. I can take care of myself. I don't *need* your charitable gifts. I don't *want* your charitable gifts. And so, as long as you keep on bringing them, I'll gladly use my right to give them away to others!"

"Anna, what have I done to offend you so? I—"

"You just can't understand, can you, Pastor?"

"What is it that I don't understand, Anna?"

"That maybe what I've been through—the wretched trials I've been *privileged* by God to suffer—just might have a little something to do with my actions lately. That maybe my coldness toward you last week was partly because of . . . well . . . jealousy."

"Jealousy?"

"*Yes, Pastor, jealousy!*" Anna shouted.

"Jealousy?" Peter was bewildered. "Over what?"

Tears streamed down Anna's face. "Over the way God has so obviously blessed and protected you and your family through all these past terrible months. Why didn't he hear *my* prayers and do the same for me? Over the fact that my dear friend Ursula has found her perfect husband and borne him two of the loveliest children I've ever known. I'll likely never enjoy such good fortune. Over the fact that I—"

Before Anna could finish her sentence, Peter seized her by the arms. She offered only weak resistance. "What, Pastor?" she protested. "Would you now behave like the men at the tavern and try to take advantage of me?"

"Anna, Ursula and my children are dead! Murdered by the Catholic army in Magdeburg. You're not the only one in this world that's had to bear the loss of all you held dearest!" Peter turned away, not wanting Anna to see his tears or the pain on his face.

A silence took over, broken only by the soft weeping of both.

He felt her hand on his shoulder. It was the lightest of touches—yet more tender than any he'd ever experienced. She nestled the side of her head between his shoulders, her hair caressing the back of his neck.

"Peter, I am so sorry," Anna whispered through her tears. It was the first time she'd used his given name.

Peter turned slowly and took her hand in both of his. He lifted it to his lips and kissed it. He looked at her, his eyes still moist. "Maybe we should start again?"

An hour passed as Peter sat with Anna at her small table. They shared the contents of the food basket, relating their experiences in Magdeburg and afterward. Any sadness or lingering sense of shame was eased by the tremendous relief he felt in unburdening himself to someone who understood the emotions of losing one's family in an instant. Like Anna, Peter held back nothing—with one exception. He mentioned nothing of his encounters with the Black Knight or Hans Mannheim, and he was determined never to do so in the future. Those terrible memories were meant to die with Peter alone.

Peter stood and helped Anna from her seat. He held her at arm's length and smiled. "Now, Fräulein Ritter, I know you and I have many more stories to share. Unfortunately, I have to return to work. But tomorrow morning, I'd be delighted—with your permission—to return and escort you to a proper place for a meeting."

Anna offered a hesitant smile in return. "Where did you have in mind, Pastor?"

"Why, tomorrow being Sunday, I thought the library of St. Nicholas would be the perfect spot—right after we attend the service together."

Anna glared indignantly. "Pastor, how on earth do you expect me to return to the very place that is so ready to condemn me to the stake for something I never did?"

"Because, Anna," Peter said, "this time you won't be alone. You'll be escorted up the aisle by someone who's ready to take on the entire church—no, the entire world—to defend your honor. I guarantee they'll have to slay me before they slay you. Will you trust me?"

Anna looked at him suspiciously. "Exactly *why* should I trust *you* to defend me?"

Peter hesitated, then broke out in an embarrassed grin. "Because, Fräulein Ritter, I simply . . . uh . . . well, because . . . *I insist!*"

Anna stared at him in shock for a long moment. Then she fell back in her seat, laughing hysterically. "Well, in that case, Pastor Erhart, how can I possibly refuse?"

It had been a long time since Peter had seen someone laugh so hard at one of his own silly utterings. In the past, he might have taken offense. Today with Anna, it was different. He wished the sweet sound of her laughter would never stop.

⚬⚬⚬

Even with Peter escorting her, Anna's walk up the aisle of St. Nicholas was turning out far worse than she'd feared. The leering glances, the cold stares, the hand-shielded whispers—even after the incident two

Sundays ago, nothing could have prepared Anna for this reception. Peter had made a bad mistake in bringing her to the morning worship service today.

Not yet halfway up the aisle, she latched onto his arm with both hands. "Pastor," she whispered out of the side of her mouth, trying to look as unfazed as possible, "I'm not meant to be here. Please turn around and get me out of here."

Peter placed his hand over both of hers, which were now ice-cold. He leaned over to accommodate her shorter height and whispered back, "Just trust me, Anna. Things will get better. I promise."

Anna closed her eyes and clenched her teeth. She would see this horrid trial through.

The St. Nicholas nave was configured much like that of St. John's in Magdeburg: three sections separated by two transverse aisles, with the front center section reserved exclusively for unmarried women, widows, and married women with young children. At the third pew from the front of the women's section, Peter drew up. He gestured for Anna to seat herself on the end.

"What, Pastor?" Anna muttered before sitting down. "Are you going to dump me off and leave me here alone?"

Peter smiled back. "Anna, I do need to sit in the chancel with the other pastors—but look: it's not that far away. And by the way, there are some wonderful ladies right here who I know are very eager to meet you."

Anna looked at the women who would be sitting next to her in the pew. Smiling back at her were two of the kindest, friendliest, and most welcoming faces she'd ever seen. Both rose to greet her.

Peter made the introductions. "Adele and Kirsten, I'd like you to meet someone who is very dear to me, Fräulein Anna Ritter of Magdeburg."

Each of the elderly women gave Anna a warm hug and kiss on the cheek.

"Welcome, Liebchen," Adele said. "It's so good to see you. We were hoping you'd come back. Please come sit here between us. I promise the two of us will take good care of you. Pastor Peter would expect nothing less. And after the service, we have some things we'd like to talk to you about. Don't we, Kirsten?"

Anna smiled politely, cast one last suspicious glance at Peter, and then took a seat between Adele and Kirsten. It was a strange sensation: the feeling of unconditional love and support on each side of her, with arrows of suspicion and hatred being shot at the back of her head from the pews behind her.

Following the liturgical preliminaries, Pastor Wagner stepped up to deliver the sermon. There was something different about him today. Something firm and uncompromising—almost angry.

"Brothers and sisters, it has recently become apparent that some of the messages delivered from this pulpit are not always taken seriously. In particular, it seems that some in this congregation have taken it upon themselves to play God. They somehow feel it's their duty to cast stones against those to whom they've taken a personal dislike. They consider it their right to make severe judgments about the actions or character of others based on their own unfounded jealousy or fears.

"But as we all know, this is *not* the way of our Lord. And so, my brothers and sisters, after much prayer and consultation, I thought it necessary to devote my entire message today to one simple but powerful instruction: *Do not judge, or you too will be judged!*"

Anna felt her heart leap. She barely suppressed a self-satisfied smirk. Hadn't she once used those very words to scold herself for wrongfully gossiping against poor old Pastor Tiedeman? Now others must face the uncomfortable truth.

After the service, Anna stood outside in the courtyard sheltered by Peter and the two ladies. At least ten married couples of all ages, as well as a number of widows and young single women, came up and greeted her warmly. They all acted as if nothing had happened two weeks ago.

Anna did her best to maintain a friendly demeanor and to respond politely. Her effort wasn't made any easier by what she saw from the corner of her eye. The four women who'd accused her of adultery were gathered together with several other ladies under a nearby small tree. All were staring with obvious hostility in her direction. Pastor Wagner's sermon apparently hadn't moved the hearts of *everyone* in attendance today. Still, Anna had quite a different feeling about St. Nicholas Church than the one she'd had after her first visit. Maybe with a little more time and getting to know the right people—

"Come along now, Anna," Kirsten said. "We want to treat you to a proper welcoming lunch—with just the two of us. Pastor Peter is certainly capable of entertaining himself for an hour or so. We have you all to ourselves for now!"

Anna had been hoping that Peter would escort her directly home. She could see now that her wishes would be overruled. She shrugged and smiled helplessly at him.

Peter laughed. "Well, I see that my exceptional talents are no longer needed for a while. I'll be back for you in an hour, Anna. In the meantime, allow these good ladies of the Lord to take care of you. I boldly predict you'll never be the same after spending time with them."

As she turned to walk with the ladies toward Kirsten's home, Anna hoped with all her heart that Peter's prediction would prove true.

CHAPTER 45

Leipzig
September 3, 1631

"Here. Wear this, Liebchen." Adele held up the silver necklace. "It'll look beautiful on you."

Peter would be arriving any minute now to escort her to the church library. He'd said he wanted to read her something from one of his favorite books that he thought she'd like. Anna had no idea which book Peter might have in mind, nor did she really care. She was thrilled just to have another opportunity to talk with and be close to him.

Anna looked up from her chair. Her eyes filled with tears as Adele attached the clasp of the necklace behind her neck. "Adele, how can I thank you enough for all you and Kirsten have done for me? It was so sweet of you to invite me to join your countryside ministry. And you— taking me into your own home! Honestly, I just don't deserve so much kindness."

Adele smiled. "Nonsense, Anna. After all, Kirsten and I *do* have an interest in your well-being. We knew from the first day we met you that the Lord had sent you to us for a very special purpose."

Anna took Adele's hand in both of hers and held it to her cheek.

Adele leaned over and kissed the top of her head. "Now, call me if you need anything else. I'll wait for Pastor Peter in the front room. I can't wait to see his expression when he sees you today!"

"Oh, Adele!" Anna protested with a modest laugh, though in truth she was basking in the compliment. "You make far too much of my appearance!"

Anna had been ecstatic about her first meeting with the ladies and hearing them describe their roles and experiences in the ministry. She'd accepted without hesitation their invitation to join them, subject to the approval by Peter as their supervisor, which of course he'd quickly granted. At the meeting, Adele, a widow, had suggested that Anna come live in the back portion of her own small house and keep her company. Within two days, Anna had found a replacement tenant for Birgette and moved in with Adele.

The very next day, Anna had accompanied Kirsten on her daily ministry rounds. And starting last week, she'd actually begun taking on her own assigned visits to the Hofmanns, a sweet elderly couple who lived in the countryside. Never had she felt so fulfilled in her daily work. For the first time, she sensed that God was revealing the true purpose for her life.

Anna sat in her chair and applied the finishing brush strokes to her hair. Her spirit unburdened, she allowed herself to imagine what it would be like if Peter asked her to marry him.

All the signs had been there over the past three weeks: the way he looked at her, the little things he would do or say to make her smile or laugh, his prayers for her full recovery from Magdeburg, his offer of his arm whenever they took their walks together. Today would mark the fifth time this past week that he had found some reason to see her. Supposedly, his visits to Adele's house were for the purpose of talking with the ladies about their upcoming ministry rounds. But they'd always ended up with Peter escorting Anna for short walks along nearby streets.

No longer guilt-ridden by the notion that she was stealing him away from Ursula, Anna finally felt free to fan the flames that his close presence had rekindled. She sensed, or at least hoped, that he was feeling the same way toward her.

"Anna, he's here!" Adele called.

Anna's heart skipped a beat at the thought of Peter standing there, politely waiting for her with his pastor's hat in hand and that gorgeous smile on his face. She opened her door and went out to greet him.

⸙

The church basement library was small, with room enough for only three tables and a few wooden chairs and stools. But its walls were lined with thick volumes of handwritten and printed manuscripts that represented one of the best collections of religious writings in Germany.

Anna lifted a small lamp as she stared up at Peter, who was standing on a rickety ladder and attempting to pull one of the volumes from the top shelf. "My, Pastor," she teased, "must you always ascend the mountain to find the words to enlighten others with?"

Peter pulled a book off the shelf. He turned carefully on the ladder's top step and looked down at Anna with a stern frown. He stretched his arms wide with the thick book in one hand. "Prepare, thou mere mortal, to receive the words that will calm your spirit, inform your mind, and make your heart grow fonder toward your fellow man—or at least toward the one standing up here preaching to you!"

Anna tried to stifle her giggle upon seeing Peter nearly lose his balance and grab the edge of the shelf just in time. "Maybe, Pastor, you should stop pretending you're Moses and come down off that ladder before you hurt yourself."

Peter grinned sheepishly and climbed down the ladder.

Putting the lamp on a nearby table, Anna reached out to grasp his elbow with both hands and help him off the last step. She didn't let go but instead pressed in close beside him, allowing her head to rest ever so lightly against his shoulder as he opened the book. Her heart was pounding. She was about to turn her head and look directly into his eyes but thought better of it; she was already stretching the limits of modesty and self-control.

Peter flipped through the pages. It seemed to take forever for him to find what he was looking for, but Anna savored every delicious moment as she quietly held on to his arm.

"Ah, here it is," he said. "This is the passage I was telling you about, Anna. In the words of the great Lutheran theologian Johann Arndt himself, from his book *True Christianity*. May I read it to you?"

Anna smiled and gripped his arm a little tighter, her head still nestled against his shoulder. "Of course, Pastor." She prayed she wasn't being too forward, that Peter wouldn't suddenly jerk his arm away in disgust.

He didn't.

Anna closed her eyes. She heard the words, but the passage was difficult, and she quickly lost track of its meaning. She didn't care. The beautiful sound of Peter's voice was more than enough to satisfy her. Her mind drifted to the first day she'd heard him preach in Grünfeld. That very night she'd dreamed that she'd one day be married to him, that he'd read to her and share his heart with her every night by the light of the blazing fire. And here she was, on the verge of her dream being realized.

Peter reached the end of the passage. He closed the book and cocked his head to look at her. "Well, Fräulein Anna, what did you think?"

Anna pretended to have heard and understood everything. "It's beautiful, Pastor. I can see why you like it so much."

Peter grinned, obviously pleased. "Well, if you thought *that* was good, I know you'll like the other writing I wanted to share with you, if I can find it. Why don't you sit at the table with this book, while I search the shelf again."

She reluctantly released his arm and took her seat. She was relieved he hadn't asked for a more educated reaction to the passage that she hadn't really understood.

"Anna," he called down from the top of the ladder after a few moments of searching, "now that I think about it, I believe the second passage is in the same book that you're holding. The beginning of the twelfth chapter, as I recall. Could you please turn there and read the first few sentences to me? Then I'll know for sure."

Anna felt her body tense. A lump formed in her throat. She tried to ignore her silly fears and turned to the twelfth chapter. She stared at the words of the first paragraph. With few exceptions, they stared back at her like so many tiny demons, daring her to correctly pronounce them, much less understand their meaning. She found it hard to breathe and felt beads of sweat forming on her brow. Hadn't she read passages from a book before? What was so different about this one?

In a flash, she knew. Ursula was not here to help her. Anna had never successfully attempted a first-time reading of *anything* this complex without her patient coaching.

"Anna," Peter called again, "did you find it?"

Anna froze, too terrified to let Peter know of her difficulty and especially the reasons behind it. "Uh, yes, Pastor, but . . . the ink on the page seems to be marred," she lied, "and I'm having trouble making out the words." She closed the book and smiled up at him with as much innocence as she could feign.

"Well, that's strange," Peter said. "I thought it—"

"Pastor Erhart!" Assistant Pastor Gabriel Carver stood in the doorway, an amused look on his face. "Somehow I knew I'd find you here, though I'd hoped it would be with your feet planted solidly on the ground. Fräulein Anna, it's good to see you again."

"Thank you, Pastor Gabriel." Anna breathed a huge sigh of relief.

"Peter," Gabriel asked, "can you come down from the clouds for a moment? I've something to tell you."

Peter climbed down the ladder and sat next to Anna. "Do we need to speak in private?"

Gabriel, who had taken a seat across from them, shook his head. "No need to hide this. Pastor Wagner and I just received word. It seems that Tilly's army is on the move again, and they're definitely heading toward Leipzig—probably with the intent to invade."

Anna gasped and clutched Peter's arm. She trembled at the thought of having to endure yet another siege and possible sack. Peter placed his hand over hers.

"What's the city's position on this, Gabriel?" Peter inquired.

Gabriel grimaced and waved his hand in a gesture of clear disgust. "Incredibly, we're hearing that our city defense commander will try to resist. Just like Magdeburg, he's relying on the idea that the Swedish king's army is nearby and will come to our rescue. I hear he's already ordered the razing of the outlying suburbs beyond the city wall to slow the Catholics' approach."

"And what about the common citizens?" Peter asked, the anger in his voice unmistakable. "Is the commander prepared to see them slaughtered, just like they were in Magdeburg, should his grand scheme for defense fail?"

"Hard to say," Gabriel said. "I know he's calling for citizen volunteers from all trades and professions to man the city walls. He's even challenging clerics like you and me to step forward!"

Anna's hands turned cold. Out of the corner of her eye, she saw Peter's jaw tighten. He said nothing for a long moment. She prayed he wouldn't feel obligated by some false sense of duty to accept this crazy challenge. She'd already lost Joachim and her entire family to the Catholic army's savagery. The thought of losing Peter—her only connection to the past and her greatest hope for the future—was too much to bear.

"So, Gabriel, how will you respond?" Peter asked.

Gabriel smiled uncertainly. "As the Lord leads me in the moment of crisis, I suppose. I don't wish to get ahead of his plans by prematurely accepting such a radical call to arms. And you?"

Anna held her breath, bracing herself for Peter's response.

He shrugged. "As you suggest, Gabriel, I'll let the Lord show me when the time comes."

After refilling a cup with sweet Riesling wine, Peter stood at the single window of his one-room flat and stared out at the setting sun. He loved the wine's taste and was now in the habit of indulging himself with one or two cupfuls each evening after supper. Surprisingly, it never failed to help him think more clearly. And after today's conversation with Gabriel in the library, there was plenty to think about.

The situation was evolving fast—much faster than Peter had anticipated. The approaching Catholic tide was a grave threat, but the more he thought about it, the less inclined he was to fret. The Leipzig commander, knowing the outcome of Magdeburg, would surely come to his senses sooner or later. His recent bold speech and actions were, in all likelihood, an attempt to bluff his way into a favorable negotiated truce with Count Tilly. Regardless, Peter knew exactly what *he* would do, should an invasion look imminent. The strategy was clear: he would leave this city behind. He would insist that Anna join him and offer to escort the ministry ladies and anyone else willing to leave along with them. There was no way that Peter would once again entrust his life to the foolish bravado of some half-witted city defense commander.

The other rapid development had a far more pleasant prospect. In little more than a month, Anna Ritter had gone from trying to split his head open with a piece of fruit to clearly enjoying his lighthearted conversation and his affectionate, yet gentlemanly, touch. The evidence that she cared for him showed in the way she'd held his arm and rested her head against his shoulder in the library. And on the way home this afternoon, she'd turned and looked at him so expectantly when they'd said goodbye at her doorstep. He would certainly have kissed her had not Adele appeared in the doorway to welcome them back.

Peter thought about Anna constantly. He wanted her with him *all* the time—not just while in church, praying with the ministry ladies at Adele's, or taking short walks to the church library. Peter wanted her to accompany him as he was performing his ministry rounds. He wanted her to sit next to him and offer her thoughts as he was preparing his reports. He was excited by the prospect of one day sharing his favorite pastime of reading and discussing classical literature with her. There was a sparkle, a freshness about her that Peter found intoxicating.

There was also the other obvious reason for his attraction. Peter had tried his best to keep those thoughts at bay. But what man would have been able to remain in Anna's presence for long without becoming aroused by the exceptional allure of her face and figure? Memories of Ursula and their times together were still strong and sweet. But late at night and upon awakening, his thoughts were increasingly focused on Anna. They were the kind of thoughts he knew he should be avoiding but had little willpower to fight—perhaps not the best position for a widowed Lutheran pastor to be in, he thought wryly.

Yes, things were progressing quickly with Anna—*far* quicker, probably, than most people would have considered appropriate. But knowing how quickly life could change in these perilous, war-torn times, he had no desire to slow things down.

Dr. Weber had always counseled Peter that, if he were smart, he would seek God's approval before every major decision. Well, as far as he could tell, God was making it perfectly clear that Anna was indeed the one.

Peter drank the last of his wine and closed the curtain. He would read and then pray before turning in for the night. He might even ponder the words he would use to propose to her.

Anna lay awake on her pallet later that night, unable to sleep. Her feelings for Peter were a tangle of confusion. They'd hardly spoken on the way back from the church library. Though they'd walked arm in arm, Peter had seemed lost in thought, no doubt thinking about what Pastor Gabriel had just revealed. She'd been at a loss over what to say to help bring him out of his shell, to get him to unburden his thoughts. Ursula, on the other hand, would have known exactly what to do.

Maybe, she worried, she wasn't the right woman for him. Peter was a highly educated, deep thinker—a man who might never be satisfied with Anna's naïve thinking on important matters. Ursula had been born and raised in a university setting. She had reveled in supporting her husband's intellectual gifts. But for someone of Anna's background, these gifts could be downright intimidating. Would she always feel the need to hide her ignorance from him as she had in the library today? Or, worse yet, would she end up driving him away if she proved unable to fully engage his learned mind in addition to his heart, as Ursula had done?

Then there was that other fear lurking in the back of her mind. Would Peter *really* accept her in her defiled state? Would he eventually become disgusted by thoughts of her bridal impurity, maybe even allow himself to believe she'd engaged in sexual relations with Eduard or one of those other men from the tavern?

Anna knew she was hopelessly in love. She had been from the moment she'd first laid eyes on him five years ago. Each morning, she awoke with eager anticipation, knowing it would be only a few hours before she would see him. Every night, she dreamed of his close embrace and intimate touch. With all her heart, she wished that he would ask for her hand, that she could then look him in his gentle, kind eyes and say, "Yes, Peter, *yes!*" But how could she say that if she couldn't meet the standard he would certainly expect of a wife, the standard that Ursula had set?

She didn't yet know the way out of the dilemma. Hopefully, she would find it soon, before it was too late. Once again, it seemed, the Catholics were coming.

CHAPTER 46

Leipzig
September 6, 1631

"Ladies, we're so fortunate to have Fräulein Anna join our sewing circle today," Kirsten announced to the fifteen women gathered in the church library. "If you could see the beautiful quilt she's just finished for Frau Hofmann, I guarantee you'd wonder why she hasn't already set up shop as a seamstress!"

"Yes, yes," some said in unison. "Welcome, Anna!"

A few, seated together, refused to even look up from their projects to acknowledge Anna's presence.

She blushed, smiled shyly, and then took the open seat next to Kirsten. She recognized at least two of the women sitting across from her as her public accusers from that awful first day on the church patio. Her throat tightened. Even though Eduard's philandering ways had been exposed and Anna had been absolved of blame by most of the congregation, Eduard's wife and her sister and close friends still harbored hard feelings.

According to Kirsten, these meetings were the best way for a new young lady to make friends and become more engaged in church life. Especially, Kirsten had said, someone with Anna's unique background and talents. Anna was not so sure the other women would be as taken with her as Kirsten, but she'd gamely agreed to attend.

As soon as the meeting was over, she could go back to preparing for her ministry visit to the countryside tomorrow. Peter had requested to accompany her—the first time he'd done so. *I wonder if he'll propose,* Anna thought.

"Well, ladies," Kirsten said, interrupting Anna's daydream, "it's time to offer up our weekly praise reports and prayer requests. Frau Bette, would you like to begin?"

Before long, the group was engaged in an animated discussion about family issues, sick relatives, and the growing rumors concerning the Catholic army's intent to invade Leipzig. A few of the women seemed on the verge of panic and were urging the others to leave the city. Anna remained silent, but she was grateful to observe how well Kirsten was able to steer the talk away from the rumors and harmful gossip. The ladies seemed to be on friendly terms with each other, and Anna was beginning to warm up to them. At one point, one of the women graciously asked Anna about her experience with the country ministry.

Anna's eyes lit up as she described her last visit to the Hofmanns. Watching them remain kind and loving toward each other despite their chronic aches and pains, she said, had taught her more about the true meaning of Christ's love than she could have ever taught them.

Kirsten couldn't contain her admiration. "And this coming from a young lady who has taught *me* a thing or two about Christ's love. Honestly, to have suffered so much in Magdeburg and still be willing to sacrifice like she does for others—it's simply astonishing!"

"Oh, Kirsten," Anna said with a modest laugh, "you build me up far too much. My 'teaching' amounts to nothing more than occasionally talking about my experiences and trying to quote the few relevant scripture verses I know."

"Well, Liebchen, you could have fooled *me,*" Kirsten said.

"Me too," agreed one of the other elderly ladies. "If I still had one smidgen of Fräulein Anna's looks and obvious ability to minister to others in the Lord's service, I'd probably be bragging about it all from the highest mountaintop—trying to charm everyone with the special gifts that God had given me."

Anna cringed at the comment. Though innocent on the surface, something about it seemed inappropriate. Her discomfort grew as she noticed the raised eyebrows and irritated glances exchanged between some of the women.

"Yes, just as she seems to have charmed our new assistant pastor," one of Anna's original accusers said with a smirk. "I've never seen a clergyman so obviously smitten over the Christlike qualities of one of his faithful female parishioners!"

"Oh, Fräulein Christel, there's no call for teasing the poor girl," another woman said.

Anna could feel her face turning red.

"Tell us, Fräulein Anna," asked a third lady, who looked quite well-to-do based on her clothing and hairstyle, "did we hear that you were originally from the countryside outside Magdeburg?"

"Y-yes, that's right, my lady," Anna replied, trying to remain as calm as possible. "A little village just west of the city called Grünfeld."

"*Grünfeld?* I have a sister who used to live there. Why, isn't that the town where that silly old pastor—Tiedebach or Tiedeman?—constantly attempts to stumble and bumble and shout his way through sermons about God's wrath every Sunday? Is he still there, or did the Catholic army finally bring God's wrath down on *him*?"

"Frau Jund, really," Kirsten said, "I . . . I don't think we should—"

"Oh, yes, Kirsten, I think we definitely *should*. We should all be getting to know Fräulein Anna just a little better. You *did* invite her to our circle, didn't you? And she *does* seem to be demonstrating qualities that our new assistant pastor finds attractive. Shouldn't we try to learn what it is that makes her so special? Maybe we can all come to follow her model."

The room fell silent. All of the ladies had put down their sewing projects and were staring at Anna. Some exhibited horrified expressions; others seemed to be gloating.

Anna could hardly control her fury. She narrowed her gaze at Frau

Jund. "To answer your question, my lady, yes, Pastor Tiedeman was the pastor of the Grünfeld church. He was *my* pastor, and I'm proud to say that he was. At heart, he was a very good and kind man who meant well for all. He once protected me and my best friends from harm. And I'm terribly ashamed to confess that, before he came to our aid, I myself had badly misjudged and gossiped about him for far too long."

"Well said, Fräulein," Frau Jund said, unperturbed. "I'm sure you've just earned yourself a higher place in heaven with that stirring defense of your former pastor."

"I didn't say it to earn myself a higher place in heaven, Frau," Anna retorted, her voice shaking with anger. "I said it because the Lord commands me to defend those unfairly accused of things they didn't do or things about themselves that they can't help. I know I've sinned greatly by accusing others in these ways over the years, and I ask the Lord's forgiveness."

Frau Jund offered a patronizing nod. "You speak very eloquently, Fräulein—far better than anyone would predict from your country upbringing. My congratulations. And is it possible you could refer me to any specific verses in scripture that support your point that we need to defend others from slander? Surely you know at least one."

Anna could no longer think straight. Boiling with rage, she struggled to choke back her tears and maintain a semblance of manners. "Well, my lady, of course. I ... I believe you might try ... uh ... Leviticus 10:18." The moment she suggested it, she wished she could take it back. She knew she had made a mistake but couldn't quite pinpoint where she had erred.

"Let me see," Frau Jund said with a condescending smile. "I just happen to have my husband's Bible here with me. I'll just look up that verse." Upon finding it, Frau Jund read it aloud to the group. "'Since its blood was not taken into the Holy Place, you should have eaten the goat in the sanctuary area, as I commanded.'"

Several of the women snickered.

Frau Jund's smile disappeared, replaced by a ruthless gaze. "Allow me to help you, Fräulein Anna. Perhaps you meant to say *Proverbs* 10:18, which I already know will say: 'Whoever conceals hatred with lying lips and spreads slander is a fool.' That's indeed a good message for us all to take to heart. We're each guilty of that sin at some point in our lives. But, Fräulein, I must say I'm astounded. I should have thought that *you*, of all people, would be able to quote the right verse to back up a principle you consider so important. How on earth can you expect to win Pastor Erhart's affections if you can't even properly quote a verse that is supposedly near and dear to your own heart? Or do you think your looks alone will suffice?"

"Frau Jund!" Kirsten exclaimed. "That is quite enough!"

It was too late. Anna stood up, hot tears filling her eyes. "You're right, Frau Jund. Pastor Erhart would certainly not be attracted to someone who blindly misquotes the Holy Word. But I assure you, I'm not out to 'win' his affections with my looks or anything else. Peter is a wonderful man, but I'm not *that* desperate as to fling myself upon him—despite what you all might think!"

With that, Anna spun around and stalked out. As she hurried toward the bench by the little brook beyond the church wall, her thoughts ran wild. She swore to herself that she would never return to the sewing circle. She even briefly entertained a delicious vision of Frau Jund stretched out on a torture rack, with herself poised to turn the crank. But then, the familiar self-critical thoughts returned. She sat on the bench with her head buried in her hands, crying uncontrollably.

A few minutes later, Kirsten and five other ladies from the circle approached. They offered a sincere apology for Frau Jund's behavior and their heartfelt wishes that Anna would not give up on the church.

Anna was appreciative. At least she'd found *some* people whom she could count on for support at St. Nicholas. But it did nothing to change a decision she'd just made. She would not turn her back on St. Nicholas or the path God had chosen for her. She would continue with the countryside ministry. She would continue to be the best friend and support to Peter that she could possibly be. But she could *never* marry Peter. Frau Jund, in her own cruel way, had been right. She was just a pretty country peasant girl, reliant on her physical appeal to cover for her disgraceful ignorance and incompetence concerning the things that would really matter to Peter. Without a doubt, he needed and deserved much more than that in a wife.

Anna made Kirsten swear to never tell Peter about the incident. She didn't want to complicate things for him. But should he ask her tomorrow to marry him, she knew what her answer would have to be.

CHAPTER 47

Leipzig
September 14, 1631

"Maybe, Peter, God has a better plan in mind—for both of you." Gabriel Carver sat back, looking resigned. Peter gripped his mug with both hands. He didn't mean to seem ungrateful, but so far Gabriel's efforts to cheer him up by inviting him out for supper weren't having the intended effect. Anna's kind but firm rejection of his marriage proposal last week had been a crushing blow.

"Gabriel," Peter said glumly, "I'll never fathom God's plan until the day I die."

Peter's depressed spirit contrasted sharply with the jovial antics of most in the tavern—and for good reason. While Anna had turned down *his* proposal, the city of Leipzig, on the other hand, had accepted Count Tilly's.

Leipzig's military defense commander, facing overwhelming odds, had wisely decided just hours earlier to accept Tilly's demand to open the city gates and allow entry of an imperial army garrison of more than a thousand soldiers. There would be no siege of Leipzig. No merciless sack. No massacre of innocent civilians. Contrary to everyone's expectations, the garrison soldiers were, so far, behaving like perfect gentlemen—in some cases even offering to pay partial compensation for the residences they'd requisitioned. Churches and businesses were being allowed to function as usual, and citizens were being permitted to carry on with their normal activities without harassment.

Peter suspected the real reason behind the Catholic army's present display of good manners was fear of retribution. Word had it that the German Protestant armies now operating under King Gustavus Adolphus's supreme command were out for every last ounce of Catholic army blood in revenge for Magdeburg. The ironic new rallying cry "Magdeburg Mercy!" was being unofficially promoted by some of the lower-level army commanders. It was meant to be interpreted only one way: German Protestant troops were now expected to show the same mercy to surrendering Catholic soldiers as the Catholics had shown to the citizens of Magdeburg—none. Count Tilly would therefore have no desire to aggravate the Protestants further by tolerating any imperial army misbehavior in Leipzig.

With fears now diminished, taverns everywhere were filling up with relieved citizens as well as imperial soldiers seeking rest from their recent march to the city. It seemed the perfect time to eat and drink up together, since it wasn't clear how long the fragile peace would last.

Too bad, Peter thought, that he was in no mood to enjoy it. With Anna's rejection, his zest for everything else had departed.

Gabriel tried another approach. "Isn't it possible that Anna's emotions from Magdeburg are still too raw for her to even think about marriage right now? After all, she *did* lose her fiancé there as well as her family."

Peter shrugged. "That could be, but I think it's something beyond that. She seems very attracted to me but at the same time wants to keep a safe distance. When I asked her to help me understand, she said that, while she has affections for me, she needs to remain focused on what God is calling her to do right now. She said she'd brought enough trouble on herself by trying to run ahead of him, doing things her own way. She *did* tell me how grateful she was for the countryside ministry and how thankful she was to God and to me for allowing her to participate. But for now, she said, it was her obligation to concentrate on that. And ever since she said it, that's exactly how she's been acting the last couple of days—as if she now desires no other role for me besides speaking to her as her friendly ministry supervisor."

Gabriel chuckled. "How ironic. The godly activity that could have been the shared focus of a great marriage is now the main problem."

"So it seems. But I still think there's something more that she's not telling me. All along, she's been fine when we're talking about lighthearted things or practical matters about the ministry. But she'll get very quiet and look down at the ground after I've said something deeper about God or theology or civic affairs. It's like she wants to say something, but she's afraid or embarrassed. I don't know if it's that she just disagrees with me and doesn't want to hurt my feelings or that she feels ... well ... not versed enough to converse with me on certain subjects."

"What a surprise!" Gabriel said with a laugh. "Who would *not* feel humbled by the grand musings of that great sage of Lutheran wisdom and thought, Pastor Peter Erhart?"

Peter managed a slight grin. "Speak for yourself, Carver. *You're* the one who causes men and women alike to grovel at the feet of your mad theological ravings."

"Yes, well, I suppose you're right, my lovestruck friend. At any rate, it looks like our mugs need refilling, and the barmaid's avoiding us. Even without our clerical garb, we must be easily detectable as God's agents, sent here to spy on hell-bound sinners. Allow me to do the honor of fetching us each one more mug. Unless, that is, you'd rather go home and sulk alone in your sorrows."

Peter shrugged in resignation, and Gabriel left for the other end of the room, where the ale was being dispensed.

Anna's rejection had come as a shock, and her purported reason had somehow sounded hollow. Only a few days earlier, she'd seemed so eager for his constant companionship and close affections. What had happened? Was she really responding to a new direction from God, or was she trying to run from something? Was it some kind of false guilt concerning the assault she'd suffered? If so, she was torturing herself needlessly. It made no difference to Peter what evil men might have done to her. He would always love and accept her as his pure bride.

He glanced across the room. What was keeping Gabriel so long at the counter?

A loud crash of bottles against the wall brought the entire tavern to a standstill.

"Shut up, Protestant dog! How dare you insult the name of the supreme commander of the Catholic League Army? Didn't you learn the lesson of Magdeburg?" An inebriated Catholic soldier yanked his equally drunken civilian offender out of his seat by the collar. He pointed a pistol at the young man's mouth and spit out his terms. "Kneel down, you bastard, or I swear I'll shove this gun through your teeth and blow your head off!"

The civilian staggered but remained standing, apparently too drunk to be cowed by the threat. "Your pardon is begged, most noble sir. I had no evil intent in calling Count Tilly a—"

The hard slap against the civilian's face had the intended effect. Kneeling now, the civilian silently awaited his fate.

Peter noticed the hands of many customers—soldiers and civilians alike—moving subtly toward whatever weapons they had available.

"Now, swine," the soldier said, "you will lick the entire seven-inch length of my pistol barrel ten times with that foul serpent's tongue of yours. Then you will beg the mercy of the pope, the Holy Roman emperor, and the supreme commander of the Catholic League Army: Count Tilly, the *liberator* of Magdeburg. After that, I just *might* consider letting you live."

The alehouse clientele gasped in horror. Angry grumblings began to rise. Peter could feel the hot rage stirring in the pit of his stomach. He was at once gratified and terrified to see that the civilian was making no attempt to comply with the soldier's order.

"I will count to three. You'll do it, or your life is over, you miserable slug! *One!*"

The nightmarish vision returned to Peter in an instant. Ursula. Her lovely face and flowing blonde hair. Arms outstretched in a posture of helpless innocence. The sword of the Black Knight beginning its terrible, merciless, downward arc.

"*Two!*"

No mercy. Mannheim's sword continuing downward, ripping the very life from Peter's beautiful wife, the mother of his precious children.

Peter could stand it no longer. Ursula would be avenged. Hans Mannheim would pay. Personally. He jumped up from his seat, pulled the dagger from his pocket, and rushed forward.

Two Catholic army officers, racing toward the soldier from behind, were a second quicker.

"Private Brunner, put it down!" one of them cried as he grabbed the soldier's waist.

The other seized Brunner's arm and deflected his aim downward toward the floor. The gun went off with a loud blast. Amazingly, no one was hurt. The officers wasted no time wrestling their subordinate out of the tavern. The other Catholic soldiers present followed suit, clearly not wanting to provoke things further.

Peter, like everyone else left in the tavern, collapsed with relief into his seat while two men helped the distraught and still blind-drunk civilian back to his table. One more second, Peter thought, and his own life might well have been over, sacrificed on the altar of the memory that continued to haunt him day and night.

A few moments later, Gabriel reappeared, approaching the table with two filled mugs in his hand. An unknown man followed close behind.

After the two had taken their seats, Gabriel patted Peter on the shoulder. "Survive the fracas?" he asked with a grin.

"Seems I did. Where in heaven's name have you been all this time?"

"Catching up with another old friend. Pastor Peter Erhart, please meet my brother-in-law, Herr Herbert Martz. He has a proposal for you."

Peter shook hands. "A pleasure, Herr Martz, though obviously under some trying circumstances."

Martz leaned forward. "Pastor," he said with a grim smile, "it's my pleasure as well. But as there are no doubt Catholic spies all around us, allow me to come quickly to the point."

"Of course, sir," Peter said, taken aback.

Martz continued to speak quietly while Gabriel and Peter nursed their mugs of ale. "Pastor, you're no doubt aware of what's happening in the vicinity of this city."

Peter nodded hesitantly. "I've heard certain things, but please refresh my memory."

"The main body of Tilly's troops have stationed themselves just to the northeast, where they're awaiting reinforcements from Austria for what promises to be a decisive battle against the Protestants. But, I tell you, Tilly's efforts are in vain. Leipzig will very soon be returned to its rightful status as a Protestant city, freed from the chains of this Catholic occupation and no longer forced to bow at the emperor's whim."

"What gives you the notion that will be possible?" Peter asked skeptically.

Martz stared at him fiercely, a gleam in his eyes. "Because the king is here, or very soon will be! Gustavus Adolphus is on the march. The Swedes have now been joined by the German Protestant forces of John George, prince-elector of Saxony. They'll defeat Tilly's army and be here within three days at the latest."

Peter sat back in his chair with a cynical smile. "Herr Martz, I'm sorry to say this, but I am sick and tired of hearing that the Swedish king will soon be coming to the rescue. That line of thinking was one of the main reasons for the slaughter at Magdeburg. The city's leaders believed such a false fable and convinced others to go along with their ridiculous plans for holding out."

Martz shook his head emphatically. "This time will be different, Pastor. I know you don't know me and have no reason to trust me, but I tell you the truth. It's yours to accept or reject."

Something in Martz's expression and voice caused Peter to sit up and listen intently.

"I'm in the service of one of John George's infantry units," Martz continued. "They recruited me several months ago to perform certain, shall we say, *clandestine functions* to provide intelligence on enemy positions and plans in this area. Also to locate and recruit other citizens in the region who might have one or more of the special skills now in short supply in the king's own Swedish units. These skills are going to be sorely needed when the inevitable clash with Tilly comes in the next few days."

"And what does this have to do with me?" Peter asked.

"Pastor, is it true what Gabriel tells me—that your university experience included two years of anatomy and medical training?"

"Yes, but that was—"

"There's no need to downplay it, Pastor. That's a year and a half more than the usual preparation for barber-surgeons now serving with the Protestant armies. The main question is this: do you have any desire in your heart to employ these abilities, together with your pastoral gifts, in the service of the great Protestant cause?"

Peter now understood the reason Martz was grilling him. "I'd be hard-pressed to deny my sense of duty. But really, Herr Martz, I have no actual experience serving like that in a combat situation. Wouldn't you want—"

"Previous experience isn't required, Pastor. Many of those serving will be tasting combat for the first time. The only thing that's required beyond your special skills are trust in God and courage. Bolstered, of course, by a passion to see our own soldiers saved and our enemies crushed."

Unsure how to respond, Peter continued to stare at Gabriel's brother-in-law. It was a crazy request, but somehow it made perfect sense.

"Pastor Erhart, I can't afford to wait here any longer. I know you'll need a little time to make your decision. Should you decide yes, meet me at eleven thirty tomorrow night, just outside the northeast gate. Bring nothing but the clothes on your back. Everything else will be provided. If you don't appear, I'll of course understand and respect your decision."

Martz stood, shook hands with Peter, and embraced Gabriel. Just as quickly as he had arrived at their table, he left the tavern.

After a few moments of stunned silence, Gabriel looked at Peter with an odd smile. "Well, Peter, what's it going to be?"

⚮

Later that night, after much sweat and prayer, Peter made his decision.

His mind was surprisingly clear on the matter. It had been God, not mere chance, who had led him to the tavern that day to witness the Catholic soldier's brutality and immediately afterward to hear Martz's offer. And why else had God led him to obtain his earlier medical training for which there was now such a critical need? Besides, Anna had rejected his proposal. Maybe she cared and even had strong affections for him, but it wasn't enough. Just as Anna had recognized her new calling, so now had he. He would join the fight.

The next day, he walked toward Adele's house to say his goodbyes to Anna and the ministry ladies. He knew it wasn't going to be easy.

It had been hard enough saying goodbye to Gabriel and Pastor Wagner earlier that morning. Pastor Wagner had been supportive but had cautioned him to make sure he wasn't acting primarily out of revenge-seeking anger toward the Catholics. The only rationale pleasing to God would be a sincere desire to help preserve the wounded bodies and souls of whomever he encountered. When Peter asked whether that meant he was obligated in the Lord's eyes to provide equal care to Protestant *and* Catholic wounded, Pastor Wagner had merely smiled grimly and said, "God bless and protect you, Peter. You'll be doing a magnificent and glorious service for everyone in this city." Peter had embraced the two pastors and then left the grounds of St. Nicholas, not knowing if he would ever see them again.

As he approached the front door of the house, Peter could see Anna through the window. She was sitting with the other women as they prepared for their usual ministry visits tomorrow. When he spotted her smiling, his heart sank. He'd felt so empowered after talking with

Pastor Wagner, especially after receiving his blessing for his decision. But now, as he listened to Anna's warm laughter, Peter's resolve waned at the thought of possibly never seeing her again.

He drew a deep breath and knocked—a confident knock, he hoped, the knock of a newly recruited soldier in the Swedish king's army.

The door opened to reveal a smiling Adele. "Pastor, to what do we owe this pleasure?"

"I have some news I'd like to share, if you ladies don't mind the interruption."

Adele pulled the door wide. "Of course not. Please, come in."

Peter followed Adele into the sitting room. The ladies smiled at him with expectant eyes—all except Anna, whose expression betrayed concern.

Peter's throat turned suddenly dry, and he coughed. "Well, I'd better just come out and say it. Ladies, for too long I've sat idly by and watched others fight to preserve our faith and our freedom." He paused, swallowing hard. "I've decided to join the fight."

Adele shrieked. Kirsten stood and then swayed, as though she might faint.

Peter's gaze fell on Anna, who held her hand to her mouth. Was it hurt, or anger, that seemed to burn in her eyes? When he opened his mouth to offer further explanation, she turned away with arms crossed and shoulders shaking.

Peter crossed the room to the other two and embraced each in turn. "Now don't worry about the ministry. Pastor Carver has everything well in hand and will look after you."

Adele drew a handkerchief from her apron pocket and dabbed at her eyes. "Pastor Peter, with all due respect, the ministry is the furthest thing from our minds right now."

"Yes, Pastor," Kirsten said, "are you sure this is something you really want to do?"

"I believe it's something I *have* to do, Kirsten. And don't worry about me. I know I'm following God's plan."

Anna still avoided his gaze. He approached her cautiously and placed his hand on her shoulder, but she jerked it away. Clearly, something more was troubling her than mere sadness at having to say farewell.

Peter decided not to press. He leaned over, his mouth inches from her ear. "Goodbye, Anna."

He hadn't walked ten steps down the path to the street before he heard someone's footsteps behind him. He turned just in time to receive Anna's full embrace, her tear-stained face lifted toward his for perhaps the last time.

"May the Lord bless you and keep you, Peter. Please come back to us. We ... I ... need you!"

Peter cupped Anna's face with his hands and then gently turned her head to rest against his chest. One thing he knew, if God were to graciously preserve and deliver him from the hell on earth that no doubt loomed ahead, he would do whatever it took to make sure that Anna Ritter never said no to him again.

⚬⚬⚬

Just before retiring that night, Anna completed her second glass of brandy. It had helped, but only a little. The terrible thought kept preying on Anna's mind: Peter could be killed, and she would be partly responsible. By rejecting Peter's proposal, she'd provided him an excuse to cast aside worldly concerns and sacrifice himself to the coming fray. She tried to console herself with the thought that it was for *his* sake that she'd rejected him. She'd only wanted to spare him from the mistake of marrying someone who could never be the wife he surely deserved. Couldn't she take comfort in knowing that she'd only tried to do what was best—not for herself but for Peter?

Anna said a prayer for Peter's protection, lay down on her pallet, and cried herself to sleep. True comfort would have to await the safe return of the man she loved but could never marry.

CHAPTER 48

Plain of Breitenfeld, five miles north of Leipzig
September 17, 1631

11:00 a.m.

Nothing had ever stirred Peter's awe of the Lord's mighty power more than the incredible sight he was now witnessing. Only a short distance away, King Gustavus Adolphus fearlessly rode his majestic chestnut steed to the head of the massive Swedish strike force. Thousands of pikemen, musketeers, artillerymen, and cavalry stood as one and cheered. It was enough to send exhilaration coursing through the blood of every Protestant soldier within sight and facing south across the battlefield plain that extended east to west between the small villages of Seehausen and Breitenfeld, just north of Leipzig.

"It's him, the Lion of the North. He's here!" shouted Sergeant Anders Christerson. "And look, Pastor Erhart! He's going to lead the charge himself! Just look at him. I wager you'll never see anything like this in your life again!"

Peter could only stand transfixed, a wide grin on his face. Christerson could not have put things any better. No regal trappings or jewel-studded crown for this man, Peter marveled. This was a true warrior king who had chosen to disdain armor and finery in favor of a simple buff leather coat and green feather in his soft hat.

"*Ja!*" Corporal Lars Almstedt shouted at the staging area for Second Company, Commanded Musketeer Reserve. "Our Golden King has merely to appear, and Pappenheim breaks at the sight! Over there, Pastor! See the Catholic cavalry pulling back? And look! Their infantry lines look confused as well! They know what's coming. *Prisa Gud!* It's turning for us now. About time."

From everything he could see and hear from his vantage point, Peter had to agree. The Swedes had a right to be proud. The Catholics had already had their opportunity earlier in the day. Now it was the Protestants' turn. They were well poised to turn this battle into a rout, and King Adolphus's brigades would be taking the lead.

Corporal Almstedt left his musket on the ground and walked back to where Peter was crouched. "A little swig, Pastor. That's what I need to get me ready."

Peter dipped a mug in the bucket of lukewarm water and handed it to him. "What are you hearing, Lars?"

Lars drained the mug in three huge gulps before handing it back to Peter for a refill. "I just overheard the lieutenant's battlefield report a few minutes ago. Seems we barely avoided disaster earlier this morning. Catholic cavalry overran our left wing. George's troops turned tail and ran like rabbits."

Peter nodded. Many in the Swedish camp doubted the toughness of John George's German forces, the left wing of King Adolphus's Protestant army. This morning, the doubters had obviously been proven correct.

"Anyway," Lars continued, "Tilly got overconfident. He overcommitted his troops to chasing down the Germans on that side of the battlefield. Left his infantry weakened and his artillery vulnerable on our side."

Peter handed him the refill. "So, what's the plan now?"

Lars drained the mug and shot him a wide-eyed stare. "You serious, Pastor? Can't you see for yourself? What d'you think we've been building up to for the past two hours?"

"I'm a religious man by profession, Corporal," Peter retorted with an embarrassed laugh. "Please educate me on the fine points of Swedish battlefield strategy."

Lars grinned and spat to the side. He pointed out across the plain. "We're getting ready to execute a powerful charge against the Catholics with our right wing cavalry and reserve musketry forces. If we're successful, we'll sweep all the way down the Catholic left flank, capture their weakly protected artillery positions. Just think, Pastor! That artillery can then be turned against the main body of the Catholics. They'll be caught in a vice grip between the left and right wings of our force. Whatever's left of Tilly's army at that point—well, we'll squeeze and pound 'em to pieces with their own captured siege guns. And after that, it's only a five-mile trek south to liberate Leipzig from the Catholic garrison."

"Are you saying we're going to win this thing, Lars?" Peter could feel his own sense of jubilation building.

"What I'm saying, Pastor," Lars replied with a confident grin, "is that all that separates Adolphus's Protestant army from certain victory is one final all-out charge. Blast through Pappenheim's weakening cavalry units, capture the Catholic artillery on those small hills over there, and the day is ours. Won't be long now before the king gives the signal."

A bold stroke, Peter thought admiringly. *And who better than the Lion of the North himself to lead it?*

Peter lay on the exposed ground just behind the forward lines. He tried to cover his head with his arms, but it seemed like a futile effort. Cannonballs ripped through the Swedish advance ranks, leaving a trail of carnage in their wake.

"Hey, Pastor!" Sergeant Christerson cried. "Time to pull your head out of the ground. We've got the devil pinned. Sure to have a few of our men needing your services before long, though."

Peter couldn't stop shaking. Up until now, he'd been held in reserve along with the rest of the Commanded Musketeers—out of range of infantry and cavalry clashes, though vulnerable like everyone else to the fire of the Catholic siege guns. From here on, there'd be no shelter available on the open plain. The mortal danger would cease only if and when the artillery batteries on the other side were captured.

It was turning out to be a much tougher job than he'd bargained for. Assigned as chaplain and medical aide to Second Company and given only one day of basic training and preparation, Peter had tried to introduce himself to as many of the soldiers as possible. It helped that he was conversant in Swedish, as Ursula had insisted on teaching him her native tongue. Still, only about half of those he'd met had displayed any interest in talking or praying. The rest had denied they'd ever have need of his special services. Christerson and Almstedt had taken Peter under their wing. He had even accepted their private confessions last night at their request. Now the two battle-hardened veterans' joking was calming his nerves.

"Well, Pastor, any last thoughts you'd like to admit to us before we all scurry like frightened rats across this wretched plain?" Almstedt asked with a laugh.

"*Ja, ja.* It's all right to say it," Christerson added. "We know exactly what's happening inside your breeches right now. Don't worry. General Baner said it even happened to him his first time. Of course, it's *never* happened to either of us!"

Peter made a lame attempt to present a calm, unfazed front—something he thought soldiers would expect to see in a cleric with constant, direct access to the peace of God. "Don't trouble yourselves over my backside, brothers," he said with a weak grin. "The Lord's seen fit to keep my bowels from exploding so far. Just concentrate on maintaining your own perfect records in that regard."

Lord Jesus, help me, he prayed with all his might.

A signal must have been given from somewhere. Christerson and Almstedt scrambled to their feet along with the other musketeers. Peter followed suit, unsure what was happening.

"Men, prepare your weapons!" the company commander shouted from his mount. "We follow immediately behind the king's cavalry charge in five minutes. And I don't want to see a single one of you scurvy bastards lagging behind!"

"We'll outrun our own cavalry, sir!" one enthusiastic but naïve-looking lad cried. "Don't worry!"

"Don't want you to outrun them, soldier," the commander growled. "Just keep up with them. Let them play the heroes. Our job is to mop up whatever Catholic scum they leave behind in their trail."

"*Magdeburg Mercy for the Catholics*—right, sir?" someone yelled.

Peter felt the color drain from his face. He understood the sentiment but had no wish to see it acted upon.

The commander wheeled his horse around and scowled. "What d'you think, soldier? You think the king will tolerate that kind of vile nonsense from his prize units? Let George's troops do the dirty work after us. Now quit your jabbering. Prepare your weapons and muster up into formation."

While the soldiers primed and loaded their musket barrels and checked the firing mechanisms, Peter reached down to confirm the contents of his medical bag. Along with items useful for battlefield first aid, it included a small Bible and a loaded flintlock pistol. If all else failed, a round through the brain would put an irreparably wounded soldier out of his misery.

"Two minutes, men! Form your battle lines! God with us!"

"God with us!" every man in the unit cried.

Christerson and Almstedt embraced Peter and said their goodbyes. They'd be moving up to take their positions in the second line of musketeers, now forming behind the Finnish light-cavalry brigade. Peter would lag behind the rear ranks with the other medical aides and support personnel. As the charge developed, and if it showed clear signs of success, he would receive orders to move forward and seek out soldiers with treatable wounds. Priority, of course, was to be given to wounded officers—the higher the rank, the higher the priority.

"Pray for us, Pastor," Almstedt said, suddenly sounding nervous. "And keep your eyes peeled for us, just in case we need to dip into your little bag of magic potions."

"God's eyes will be on you as well, my brothers," Peter said. "Trust him to carry you through this."

Christerson laughed. "He'll either carry us through it, or he'll carry us home to heaven, Pastor. Either way, we'll be seeing you again sooner or later."

The two men left for their positions. Peter's shakes returned.

A tumultuous shout arose, seemingly from everywhere. "*This is it!*"

The Finnish horsemen screamed like tormented demons. "*Hakaa Pääle! Hakaa Pääle!* Cut them down! Hack them to pieces!"

Adolphus stood up in his saddle and faced the front ranks of his cavalry units, sword raised above his head. Peter could barely hear or see him from where he stood. But he could sense the king's tremendous impact on the troops. Their doubts had suddenly fled, their backs had stiffened, and their minds were focused now on only one thing: capturing the Catholic artillery. No one wanted to disappoint the Lion of the North.

The command was given. The decisive charge began.

"*God with us!*"

11:30 a.m.

Whether it was from exhaustion, panic, or both, Peter could hardly breathe. The swirling, acrid smoke was bad enough. Worse was the hand-to-hand fighting taking place fewer than fifteen yards from where he knelt over a wounded musketeer. But worst of all was the sight of the soldier's severe abdominal wound—the very same wound Peter had accidentally stepped on while stumbling forward through the thick haze. The poor man was screaming in agony from the terrible gash, inflicted by a pike or battle-ax, and no doubt widened by the sole of Peter's boot.

He forced himself to concentrate. He knew this soldier wouldn't make it. No use wasting time on bandages. No time even for prayer. The man's howls of pain were severely fraying his nerves. His hands trembling, Peter reached into his bag and removed the pistol. Just as he was preparing the firing mechanism, the man fell silent and he saw that he wouldn't have to complete his terrible task. The soldier's eyes had already rolled back into his head. After muttering a quick prayer for the salvation of the deceased's soul, Peter squinted through the dense smoke. Nowhere to go now but forward, he told himself. *Keep moving forward.*

With pistol in one hand and medical bag in the other, Peter stood and resumed his charge in the direction of the Catholic artillery. Everywhere he looked, the Swedish infantry was killing or scattering their enemies. They were especially skilled at shooting the heavily armored cavalrymen in the face with their muskets or toppling them from their horses with their long pikes. Racing across the field behind the king's cavalry charge, they had now turned the left flank of Pappenheim's force in on itself, creating panic and confusion. It seemed that Adolphus and the Swedes were on the verge of carrying the day, if not turning the tide of the entire war.

Looking ahead, Peter spotted it in the near distance through the murky haze. Like a mirage, the mounted soldier's form seemed to materialize and freeze in place.

Peter came to an abrupt stop, mesmerized by the image. Disoriented as he was by the noise, smoke, and stress of his first combat experience, was he imagining things? And yet, there was no mistaking the black armor, the scarlet-red plume. The Black Knight sat peacefully astride his horse, sword in hand at his side, calmly observing the ghastly proceedings taking place all around him.

The knight turned his helmeted head. He seemed to look through his visor directly at Peter. He slowly bowed his head as if in respectful acknowledgment. Or was it mocking contempt? Was it really Hans Mannheim—and did he really recognize Peter?

Peter's throat tightened as he gripped the pistol in his hand. He lowered his medical bag to the ground, his body shaking with anticipation. He started to walk toward the murderer of his wife and children. It didn't matter that his small pistol stood little chance against the knight's armor and sword. All he wanted was one close-up shot. Even if he were to die in the effort, he had a score to settle. And if God so willed, he would settle that score once and for all.

It took but a second. Just as mysteriously as it had appeared, the image dissipated in the swirling smoke. A mirage.

Peter shook his head, returned the pistol to his medical bag, and kept on moving. His direction was clear. He would follow the bloody trail to victory being carved out ahead by the king's cavalry charge. Leave the Black Knight free to pursue his own dark fate. There were plenty of other, more deserving men who now required Peter's attention.

CHAPTER 49

Plain of Breitenfeld
September 17, 1631

12:30 p.m.

The elated cheers of the Swedish artillerymen grew louder with each thundering blast from the captured Catholic siege cannons. Twenty-four-pound balls tore great bloody swaths through Count Tilly's enveloped troops. The Swedes' own considerable artillery had also just been turned and wheeled closer to join the slaughter. Now closing in from all sides, their cavalry and musketeers decimated the imperial ranks.

Not long now, Peter thought. From where he stood with other support personnel on a knoll behind one of the captured cannons, he had a commanding view of the plain. The young Swedish artillery commander was doing a brilliant job directing the fire. Peter couldn't help joining in the jubilation, not only over the imminent Protestant victory but also over his own personal performance. Within thirty minutes after encountering the mirage of the Black Knight, Peter had treated three wounded Swedes. One had suffered a shattered arm.

The other two had sustained leg wounds of moderate severity. He had worked efficiently, calming the soldiers with gentle words, reciting psalms and prayers while applying the lotions, oils, and bandages contained in his medical bag. In each case, he'd managed to stabilize the wounded man's situation and turn care over to follow-up medical aides. Peter knew he'd done his job well. As a result, his self-confidence had soared.

"General Baner, Captain Ekstrand's been hit. He's hurt bad!"

The shot had come from behind somewhere. The young artillery commander lay on the ground, writhing in pain.

The general bolted into action. "Must be imperial stragglers. Fosburg, take a detachment, find 'em, and wipe 'em out! Captain Ingerson, take over for Ekstrand."

"*Ja*, sir!"

"Lieutenant Landeen, find a medical man—*quick*. Don't know if Ekstrand's going to make it. You know the king won't be happy."

Two men hurried up to Landeen, the general's junior staff officer, to offer their services.

Probably inexperienced barber-surgeons wanting the glory of taking on a high-profile case, Peter thought. They could have it. He had done quite enough for one day. Still, he continued to watch as the two men struggled to restrain the captain's movements and examine his wound. The men were concentrating on his upper left arm.

After a few minutes, one of the men called for a crude table to be set up under the shade of a nearby tree. With the help of three others, Ekstrand was carefully placed on a flat board and transferred to the table.

Peter's curiosity got the best of him. What treatment was being planned here? Maybe he could watch and learn a thing or two that would prove useful. He moved cautiously toward the little group gathered around the wounded officer.

"Damn you, man! You won't take it! I'd rather die! I swear I'll have your head removed if you—"

"Please, sir, you're losing blood rapidly. We can't find the round. It's lodged too deep. We need to do this now. The king will have my head if I fail to save your life. Sergeant, hand me the saw!"

"No, you son of a whore!" Captain Ekstrand screamed. "I won't give it up, I tell you!" He kicked at his restrainers and managed to sit up before once again being forced to lie down with his wounded arm extended.

Something about the young man's pitiable cries and determination to fight against the inevitable spurred Peter to speak up. "Sirs, before you cut, may I take a look?"

The surgeon, already poised to begin the terrible procedure despite Ekstrand's protests, looked up and glared. "And who are you, Pastor, to question my diagnosis?" he snarled.

"With respect, sir, I'm looking at the wound, and I'm not convinced it's a hopeless case—at least from what I can see. May I examine things more closely?"

"We have no time to fool around testing your amateur medical knowledge of major surgical—"

"Surgeon!" the wounded man interrupted. "Let him look. It's *my* arm, and I command you to let him observe it. Don't disobey me if you want to keep your career."

The surgeon reluctantly stepped aside, allowing Peter to get his first close look at the patient and his wound.

Peter placed his hand on Captain Ekstrand's forehead and smiled. He was surprised at his own sense of peace. "Captain," he said, "do you know the Twenty-Third Psalm?"

Ekstrand nodded and smiled back hesitantly. His eyes fluttered. He was sweating profusely and on the verge of losing consciousness.

Peter had to act quickly. "I want you to keep saying it silently to yourself while I probe your wound. Can you do that?"

Ekstrand nodded again and began mouthing the words.

Peter turned to concentrate on the young commander's blood-soaked arm. He wiped away the blood oozing from the musket-ball entry hole. Probing gently but persistently around the entire upper arm with his fingers, he was able to actually feel the ball. He was right. Things weren't as bad as the surgeon had assumed.

"Sirs, this is treatable."

"What?" the surgeon yelled. "How dare you try to usurp my—"

"Put your damned saw away and let him speak, surgeon!" Ekstrand gasped.

"The ball is lodged deep, but it's in the fleshy part of his triceps and not in the bone. If you can extract it quickly and stanch the blood flow, you can save his arm."

The surgeon looked dubiously at Peter, then at Ekstrand. "Sir, he may be right. But I have to warn you . . . in trying to save your arm, we may lose your life."

"I'll take my chances," Ekstrand said. "Just get on with it."

"As you wish, sir. Hand me the forceps."

It took longer and required the surgeon to push the instrument deeper into the wound than Peter had hoped. The captain screamed in pain before nearly passing out. Finally, the surgeon succeeded in locating and extracting the blood-soaked ball.

While the other men worked feverishly to apply a clean bandage, Peter took the captain's left hand and held it tightly in both of his. "Praise be to our Lord of Hosts, Captain," Peter said. "He not only brought us victory on the battlefield today, he saved your arm for future service in his name."

Ekstrand smiled back weakly. "God bless you, Pastor. I'll never forget this. I swear it. What's your name, Pastor?"

"Peter Erhart, sir."

The officer managed another weak grin. "Well, Pastor Peter Erhart, I'll expect you to come visit me in the field hospital soon. Don't . . . disappoint me."

Peter laughed. "As you command, sir, but—"

Ekstrand's eyes closed before Peter could finish. The captain would need his rest, especially since the wound would need to be cauterized and rebandaged shortly in order to prevent infection.

Peter shook hands with and offered a kind word to the humbled though greatly relieved surgeon who'd been so ready to challenge his credentials. He turned to leave.

"Pastor, you *do* realize whose arm it was that you just saved, don't you?" someone behind him called in a deep-throated voice.

Peter whirled. He couldn't believe it. It was General Baner himself.

"Why . . . no, sir. Please forgive me. Who was it?"

The general smiled. "The nephew of the king."

"Which king is that, sir?" Peter asked, so nervous he couldn't even think straight.

"King Adolphus, of course. Captain Ekstrand is his nephew."

CHAPTER 50

Woods near Breitenfeld, five miles north of Leipzig
September 17, 1631

5:00 p.m.

Peter lay exhausted on the ground, wiping the sweat from his eyes with fingers caked with dirt.

Though victory was now assured, it was not complete. And it wouldn't be, Peter knew, until the last remnant of Count Tilly's once-proud army had been hunted down and captured or killed. Most of his fleeing troops were from General Pappenheim's cavalry units. After somehow breaking through the tightening Protestant cordon, they'd made a dash for the temporary safety of the wooded area just south of the main battlefield. King Adolphus had ordered General Baner to send a force of musketeers and light cavalry in pursuit. Peter and several other medical aides had followed in their wake. Once the defeated Catholic soldiers were rounded up and prevented from fighting another day for the emperor, the true celebration for Adolphus and his men could begin in earnest.

The day was waning, though, and from what Peter could observe, the pursuing Swedish troops were exhausted. On top of that, the woods were offering far too many hiding places for the Catholics. The air still crackled with musketry and pistol fire.

Peter took a deep breath, rose to his feet, and peered around the trunk of the large tree. While hiding there for the past five minutes, he'd been listening to the soft moans of someone who had fallen up ahead. Peter had tried a few minutes earlier to check on the soldier when three imperial cavalrymen had nearly run him down in their haste to escape their pursuers. The way appeared clear now.

His pistol drawn, he crept toward the moaning sounds. He pushed aside a cluster of tall reeds and stared down.

An imperial soldier with black upper-body armor lay on his side, bleeding profusely from a deep gash on the side of his leg. The man looked up at him. Peter stepped back in shock.

Hans Mannheim, the slayer of Peter's beloved wife, stared back at him as if beholding a ghost.

Neither man spoke for a long moment. Finally, Hans managed a weak smile. "Greetings, Pastor. It seems our paths have crossed yet again. Fortunately for me, God be praised. Do you have anything to relieve this pour soul's misery?"

Peter placed his medicine bag on the ground and leveled the pistol at Hans. "The answer depends entirely on you, Mannheim," he said quietly.

"*What?* Peter, why are you . . ." Hans's voice trailed off as confusion and fear spread over his face.

"I saw what you did in Magdeburg," Peter said.

"You . . . saw what, Peter?"

"The woman on the street outside the cathedral—the woman who was protecting the children. You killed her. Slashed her through like a side of beef."

Hans shut his eyes and looked away.

"It's true, isn't it, Hans?"

Hans nodded his head slowly.

"Do you know who that woman was?"

"No, Peter, I don't."

Peter bent down, pressed the tip of the pistol hard against Hans's temple.

"That woman you butchered was my wife, Hans! My precious wife Ursula, for whom you expressed such beautiful, tender sentiments when we last met."

Hans's lips quivered as tears formed in the corners of his eyes.

Peter cocked the pistol's hammer back. "Please, Hans, tell me it was an accident," he hissed. "Allow me to entertain one shred of hope, before I pull this trigger, that what you did was not meant to be."

Hans said nothing.

"Just tell me it was an accident, Hans, you miserable Catholic son of hell!" Peter screamed in his ear. "Tell me you didn't mean to strike my wife but rather the defender who'd fallen in front of her! Give me some excuse not to pull this trigger. "

"Peter, I swear to you I had no idea it was your wife. But it was no accident. I saw her in time. I could have stopped."

Peter blinked, trying to absorb what he'd just heard. This was not at all the lying, deceitful excuse he had expected. The pressure of his finger on the trigger lessened slightly. "Why didn't you stop, Hans?" he asked, his eyes brimming with tears.

"Because in that split second, I didn't see the innocent face of a defenseless woman."

"Then if not her, what *did* you see?" said Peter, his voice tightening.

"The f-face . . . the face of my father," Hans faltered, "screaming at me not to be a coward, a disgrace to the family, a disappointment to him and to the Catholic faith. *'Do it! Get it done, boy! No more hesitation! No more mercy for Protestants! Remember Prague. Never let our family's name down again!'* I swung my sword, and the memory has tormented me ever since."

A wave of nausea swept through Peter. He lowered his gun and placed it on the ground, struggling to accept what he had just heard.

"Peter, you have every right to kill me. I deserve to die. I ask you to spare me only for the sake of my wife Marie."

Peter stared at him incredulously, rage once again boiling inside his chest. "Hans, how can you ask me to spare *you* for *your* wife's sake? Especially after I learned that not only was my own wife slain by you, but also my dear children were murdered by men under your command in the same incident! My heart has been rent in two, Hans. I see them all in my dreams every night. I long to take them in my arms, to hug and kiss them for hours, to tell them I'll never let them out of my sight and care again. And now you expect me to—"

The sound of movement in the thicket behind them announced the arrival of unexpected visitors.

"*Vad är det där?* Would you look at this?"

Peter, still kneeling, whirled around to face the gruff voice.

Three Swedish infantrymen had crept up unnoticed. They stared down at Peter and Hans, halberds resting jauntily against their shoulders. Covered with blood and dirt, these men had obviously experienced the worst of the fighting, yet seemed in no mood to stop.

"Do you see what I see, Private?"

"*Ja*, I see exactly what you see, Sergeant. Looks like one of our chaplains is a bit confused as to who it is he's ministering to!"

"Seems you've mistaken one of Tilly's cowardly eunuchs here for one of our own brave soldiers, Pastor. Now why don't you step aside and let us finish off this antichrist in the manner he deserves."

The familiar voice inside Peter's head struggled for control. *Here's your opportunity, Pastor! This lying Catholic devil deserves to die. Let these Swedes do it for you with no blood on your own hands. Avenge Ursula, Josef, and Edith!*

Like an angry hornet, the tempting idea buzzed around his brain. It would be so very easy to yield to its powerful, bittersweet sting. And yet, he knew, there was only one choice that would allow him afterward to live with himself—the choice that Grandfather Nikolaus, Dr. Weber, and Friar Rusche would all have made.

Sheltering Hans with his body, Peter stretched out his hand to the Swedes. "Brothers, I beg you in the name of Christ our Lord. Spare this man. I don't know why God has sent me to help him, but I know that's what he wishes. Please have mercy on him."

The sergeant laughed mirthlessly. "Mercy? Mercy on a Catholic League Army soldier? Pastor, do you not live in this world? Haven't you heard of the *mercy* extended recently by Catholic soldiers to the poor, innocent citizens of Magdeburg? That vile slime you're trying to protect was no doubt one of those murderers. Maybe, Pastor, you've lived the easy life just a bit too long, preaching at your nice little church with your nice little family and all. Maybe you haven't lost good friends or loved ones like we have to these sons of hell. Mercy? There's only one kind of mercy that we should deliver to this Catholic scum: *Magdeburg Mercy*—no mercy at all! Even if King Adolphus doesn't approve of it, *I* certainly do. Now move over before I get angry." The man went to move his halberd off his shoulder.

Peter was quicker. In one smooth motion, he grabbed his pistol, stood, and pointed the barrel at the sergeant's face less than a foot away.

The other two Swedes froze in place.

"*Put your weapons down and move away, or I'll blow your sergeant's head off!*"

The two subordinates hesitated but then complied with the command.

Peter gazed with burning anger at the shocked man standing in front of him. "Who are *you* to lecture *me* about Magdeburg, Sergeant? My wife, children, and dearest friend were slaughtered there by men like the one I now seek to protect. If I choose to follow God's command to show mercy to a man such as this, through my suffering and sorrow I've certainly earned the privilege to do so. Now take your men and get out of here before *I* get angry."

The officer stared in disbelief before finally smiling gamely. "*Ja*. As you command, Pastor. Who are we to interfere with the redeeming work of God?" Backing up, he turned to his cowed subordinates. "Come on, men. We've wasted enough time here."

Peter didn't lower his pistol until the Swedes were out of sight and earshot. With his knees shaking, he knelt once again beside Hans.

"Peter, you could have been killed," Hans said. "Why did you do it . . . and for the man who killed your wife, no less?"

Peter stared at the ground. He finally lifted his head and locked eyes with the enemy officer who, strangely, no longer seemed to be an enemy. "I can't say. All I know is it seemed to be the right thing to do. And if I delay any longer in treating your wound, all my efforts up to now to keep from putting a lead ball in your head will have been in vain."

CHAPTER 51

Woods near Breitenfeld
September 17, 1631

6:00 p.m.

Except for an occasional muffled shout or musket shot coming from elsewhere in the thick woods, the sounds of battle had diminished. Peter assumed the victorious Swedes had successfully flushed the fleeing Catholics from their hiding places. Those they'd caught alive had either been killed outright, left to die of their wounds, or taken prisoner. The rest would no doubt retreat toward Leipzig.

The frightening thought struck Peter like a lightning bolt: would the Catholics attempt to take bloody revenge on the Leipzig citizens before yielding the city to the pursuing Protestant army? He had to get back there—soon. He had to make sure Anna and the ministry ladies were safe. If nothing else, just to let them know he'd survived the fight and would soon be able to return to them permanently.

But first, he had a seriously wounded enemy officer to consider, and he knew God was not about to let him cast this burden aside.

"Major, I think it'd be best to move you a little distance from here. This place is too near the path. I have no idea who'll be tromping through here next. We were fortunate those men were Swedes. Had they been George's Saxons, neither of us would have gotten off so easily."

Hans nodded. "The German boys would have had even more motivation to insist on Magdeburg Mercy, though between the two of us, I know I would have received by far the worst of it. Especially if they'd been able to recognize me as the Black Knight without my helmet and leg armor."

"And why *aren't* you wearing those?" Peter asked.

"I discarded 'em somewhere back there along the path—just before that squirrel of a Swedish infantryman popped out of his hiding hole and gashed my leg with his battle-ax. I dispatched him to hell with my pistol, but my horse bucked. He threw me and ran off. I had to drag myself at least a hundred yards to this spot. Lost my pistol along the way. Now, where and how do you propose to move me? I don't think I can be much help."

"Stay here while I do a little scouting. I'll be back soon. Just try to rest."

Walking back along the path, Peter found a well-hidden copse of trees with soft ground cover. A small brook trickled nearby. It would provide adequate shelter at least for the rest of the night. He also found something else. Returning to Hans, he knelt down and placed the Black Knight's plumed helmet on the ground. "Still want this?" he asked with a grim smile.

Hans stared at the helmet as if beholding his own head lying unattached on the ground. "So you've found the one item by which I'll be unmistakably identified."

"Do you want me to take it back?"

Hans hesitated, then let out a long sigh. "I suppose I can't just take the coward's way out, throwing away forever the main evidence of whom I'm supposed to be. Let's move, Pastor. I'll find a way to discretely drag this thing along with me somehow. And if I ever get out of this mess alive, I swear to you I'll put it to more noble use than I have up to now."

Peter rewrapped the temporary bandage around Hans's wound, then helped him to stand up and begin the arduous trek together through the brush to the new location.

Twenty minutes later, they were sitting exhausted on the soft forest floor, with their backs reclining against a tree trunk. Hans, with his wounded leg propped up on a small log, drank gratefully from the canteen that Peter had just refilled with cold water from the brook.

"Pastor, speak the truth. Is there any possibility with this wound that I'll be able to avoid turning myself over to the Swedes—make it back to visit my wife in Munich?"

Peter didn't mince words. "From what I can tell, the cut's fairly deep. Some of the ligaments are severed. Luckily, it looks like the blade only nicked the bone. But it's going to take several weeks of rest to heal. In your condition and without a horse, reaching Munich soon is out of the question. It's hard enough to imagine you making it beyond these woods without help. You'll need food and additional medical attention soon. I'd stay here with you, but my own responsibilities to God and my army supervisor will soon require me elsewhere, starting tomorrow morning."

"So," Hans said with a grimace, "it seems I have no choice. Before I starve to death, I drag myself out of these woods and grovel before the first Swede I come across. Show him my helmet and humbly introduce myself as the Black Knight of the Catholic League Army. Beg him to spare me from Magdeburg Mercy and instead assist me to the nearest prison warden, then thank him profusely for his kindness and help. I have to say, my chances don't appear too good, Pastor."

"God has kept you alive so far, Hans. I trust he had a good reason for doing so and will show you the way to take. Why else would he have involved someone like *me* to intervene on your behalf? Try to get some rest now. Sleep and pray on it. And if it's your desire tomorrow morning, I'll help you out of these woods to offer your surrender."

Hans gripped Peter's arm, overcome with emotion.

10:00 p.m.

The crescent moon and stars peeked through the branches over the men's heads. Thankfully, the day had been warm, and the night so far appeared ready to follow suit. The two men were exhausted from their earlier exertions and concerns about what lay ahead. They had been conversing around their fitful attempts at sleep.

Hans, whose leg pain appeared to have eased somewhat, took a long drink from his canteen as Peter eyed him warily.

"Hans, I'm still baffled about one thing."

"What's that?"

"How was it that you shifted so quickly from the life of a humble Catholic businessman to suddenly appear as the Black Knight at Magdeburg? What happened to Helmut Schuttman?"

Hans closed his eyes and sighed. "The businessman story was a ruse. I've been serving under my father's cavalry command in the Catholic League Army for the past thirteen years. As fate would have it, I rose quickly in rank and reputation. The last time you and I met in Magdeburg, I was on special assignment to Count von Wallenstein to spy on the city council and plant the idea of a ransom offer. And the reason you saw me in the full battle armor of the Black Knight on the day of the sack is quite simple. The night before, I *had become* the Black Knight—the newest incarnation, that is. Helmut Schuttmann is dead."

Dumbfounded, Peter stared at him.

"A few days before the sack, I was imprisoned and stripped of rank for failure to carry out Tilly's order to execute a young Protestant prisoner accused of torturing civilians. But then a very unexpected thing happened. The day before the sack, Schuttmann was leading a small patrol of cavalry when one of Falkenberg's Swedes pierced him with a pike. He escaped from the ambush, but he bled to death two hours later back at the base camp.

"Tilly knew he couldn't afford to have the Magdeburg defenders' spirits raised and his own men's broken by the news of Schuttman's death. So, after consulting with my father, he came up with a grand scheme: a new Black Knight would immediately arise to replace the fallen one. And the man appointed to fill this daunting role would be none other than the second-most skilled cavalryman in Tilly's ranks . . . *me!* Despite Tilly's anger over my failure to execute the prisoner, I was granted a special dispensation for the offense. And instead of languishing in prison, I was now commanded to lead Schuttman's heavy cavalry unit at the very point of the attack!

"On the eve of the battle, my father visited my tent. He threw Schuttman's black chest plate and helmet down on the ground. Told me I had to keep the Black Knight's legend alive, that the Catholic League Army's morale and reputation depended on it."

Peter looked away, his brain struggling to make sense of the incredible turn of events that Hans had just described.

"I'll never forget Father's last message to me that night." Hans paused for a moment, as if bringing back to mind the exact words. "'One more chance, Mannheim. Don't *ever* let your family name down again. Your behavior in Prague was perhaps excusable. You were still young. But that's no longer the case. Weakness and softheartedness are unacceptable for an officer in the Catholic League Army. You have one last chance to prove yourself, though you don't deserve it. And remember—your new subordinates will be watching you closely tomorrow. They'll want to see that you have what it takes. *Do not fail them, and do not fail me!*'

"And from there, Peter, you already know the story of what happened. Including the killing of your wife . . ."

Peter looked up as Mannheim's voice had suddenly trailed off. Hans's eyes were closed and his body totally still, except for the slow rise and fall of his chest. Exhaustion and sleep had obviously overtaken him.

Now it all made sense, Peter thought, including the initial hesitation of Hans's own men to rush to his aid when he'd been cornered in that first street fight. He had to prove his toughness to them if he expected to earn their passionate loyalty.

Within minutes, Peter fell asleep himself.

4:30 a.m.

The sound of snapping twigs awoke Peter from his deep slumber. An odd snorting noise followed. A wild boar? Once again, it was silent.

Peter reached over to alert Hans before snatching his pistol from the medical bag. He crept toward where he thought the sound had originated. Tightening his grip on the gun, he pushed the thick brush aside with his free hand. A small clearing loomed just ahead.

Peter couldn't believe it. Standing serenely in the middle of the clearing was a fully saddled cavalry horse. The stallion tossed his mane and neighed, then turned his head and stared at Peter.

Peter approached carefully and took the reins in his hands. He stroked the horse's muzzle. The beast didn't seem to object.

Peter led the horse through the brush to Hans, who was sitting up now and wearing a stoic expression. One look was all it took. Hans buried his face in his hands.

"What is it, Hans? Whose horse is this?"

"He's mine, Peter. That's *my* horse—unhurt and sent back by God's grace to deliver me from my enemies!" Judging from its constant pawing and whinnying, the horse seemed anxious to begin the journey—nearly as anxious as Hans.

It took nearly a half hour for Peter to clean and rebandage Hans's wound as the two discussed the best way to proceed.

"I have no idea where I'm going from here," Hans said, "other than to get out of these woods, while avoiding Protestant soldiers along the way."

"Once you leave the woods, try to find some local residents willing to help you or at least give you some food. If you're lucky, maybe someone will put you up for a few nights' rest. That'd give you some time to figure where to go next."

"If they don't kill me first," Hans muttered sadly. "But what other choice do I have?"

"None, really." Peter applied the final wrap to the bandage. "Or so it would seem for now."

Hans lifted his head. "Peter, you've graciously spared my life, and I'm forever grateful to you for that. But can you ever truly find it in your heart to forgive me for what I've done? Will God himself ever forgive me?"

As he gazed into Hans's devastated, pleading eyes, Peter realized why God had placed Major Hans Mannheim in his life—the first time as an abused and terrified fourteen-year-old boy at the castle in Prague, and now as a wounded cavalry officer in the Breitenfeld woods. "Major Mannheim, do you sincerely believe that Christ died and rose again to pay for all your sins?"

Hans nodded.

"Are you sorry for your sins, and do you freely acknowledge and confess Jesus Christ as the one and only Lord and Savior of your life?"

"Peter, there's no question but that I do."

"Then, Hans, based on everything I know and personally believe as a Lutheran pastor, you can rest assured that God has already forgiven you, just as he has forgiven me. And as God forgives us both, so—from the bottom of my heart—do I forgive you as well."

Tears flooded Hans's eyes as he grasped Peter's hands. "May the God and Savior of us all bless you richly, Pastor. And if I may be so bold, may the Blessed Mother of the Risen Christ always protect you and advocate for you. I'll never forget the mercy and kindness that you've shown to me despite what I have done to you. You will always be in my prayers."

"Maybe, Hans," said Peter, "God will allow us to meet yet again under happier circumstances. Maybe one day you'll find the means to visit me at St. Nicholas, my new church in Leipzig."

Hans smiled. "That would indeed be my honor and delight to visit you there, Pastor, and to hear you speak once again of God's mercy and grace on undeserving fools like me."

Peter helped Hans onto the horse and gave him his pistol. "I won't be needing this anymore, Major. It's not the size or caliber you're used to, but it might come in handy."

"No doubt more handy than my helmet that's now stuffed at the bottom of my saddle bag. I'll probably decide to toss it aside yet again if any Swedes get hot on my trail." He saluted and walked his horse out of the copse as Peter followed along close behind.

At the path, Hans turned in his saddle, smiled, and shrugged. "Which way, Pastor Peter? Left or right? Each way seems equally perilous. Protestants—Protestants everywhere! Just tell me: which is the way God would choose for me?"

Peter looked into the eye of the man he had nearly slain in revenge just hours earlier. "I think God wants you to take responsibility and choose for yourself, Hans. Just ask God to help you consider wisely."

"Goodbye, my Lutheran friend. I'll never forget you!"

As he lifted his hand in salutation, a glint of reflected sunlight caused Peter's eye to focus on something that, amazingly, he hadn't noticed until now. Strapped tightly to the side of Hans's saddle was a scabbard from which the hilt of a heavy sword protruded—the very weapon Hans had no doubt used to slay Ursula.

Peter abruptly dropped his hand. He turned his head and stared at the ground, not wanting Hans to see the tears forming in his eyes.

"Pastor, are you all right?" Hans asked.

"Yes, Hans, I'm fine. Just a momentary sadness. God be with you."

Hans smiled hesitantly, as if he wanted to say something more but couldn't. He turned his horse and rode off slowly down the path.

Walking back to the clearing to retrieve his medical bag and refill his canteen, Peter noticed the first rays of dawn illuminating the tree branches above. His spirit began to lift. With God's help, he had done his Christian duty, and had done it extremely well. He had set a guilty man free in body and spirit and, as a result, his consuming hatred for Hans Mannheim—the Black Knight of Magdeburg—no longer burdened his heart. Never had he imagined that the ministry of forgiveness could be so powerful.

Yes, a beautiful display of godliness, Pastor, said the familiar, taunting voice in his head. *Grandfather Nikolaus would be proud. And now that you've demonstrated your deep compassion and willingness to forgive your enemy—even to the point of risking your life for him—maybe God will soon see fit to reward you. Who knows? Maybe he'll even convince Anna to marry you! God loves to shower his faithful children with good gifts, doesn't he, Pastor?*

It was an enticing thought and another good reason to postpone his return to his medical unit and instead try to make it back to Leipzig, where the Catholic garrison would still be present. Ensuring Anna's safety was the only thing that mattered now.

CHAPTER 52

Leipzig
September 18, 1631

P eter peered through the front window of Adele's house and breathed a sigh of relief. As usual, Anna and the ladies were huddled around the table for their morning prayers and devotions—exactly what he'd hoped to see.

He knocked on the door.

Adele opened it and screamed with delight. Kirsten jumped up at once, praising God for his mercies and nearly swamping Peter with hugs, kisses, and tears.

Anna waited for the others before throwing her arms around Peter's neck, kissing him on the cheek and then resting her head against his chest. Although she clasped him tightly and was weeping with obvious gladness, Peter sensed she was content to enjoy his close, friendly embrace. He was disappointed by her platonic reaction—a stark contrast to the wild passions that he felt stirring in his own heart.

Peter sat with the women at the table for more than an hour and recounted his experiences of the previous day and night, though he avoided revealing details of his encounter with Hans Mannheim. He noticed Anna staring intently at him, but she didn't ask any questions or express much reaction like the others. At the end of his account, Anna stood abruptly and insisted on preparing a light meal for everyone.

After the meal, Peter urged the women to stay in the house together for the next few days. The Protestant army would no doubt be retaking the city soon. And, while it didn't appear that the Catholic garrison was planning revenge against Leipzig's citizens, it seemed wise to stay out of harm's way until the situation cleared up. Later that morning, Peter told them, he planned to check on Gabriel Carver before returning to his duties at the Breitenfeld field hospital. Once he was released from *that* responsibility a few days hence, he'd return, and life would hopefully resume as before.

Peter bid Adele and Kirsten goodbye and then asked Anna to walk out with him to the deserted street. She politely accepted the offer and even took his proffered arm with both hands, just as she had in times past. But as they approached the edge of the street, she tensed.

"Anna, is something wrong?" Peter asked.

She stepped back with arms crossed. "Wrong? Of course not, Pastor. How could anything possibly be wrong? You've returned safely to us! What more could I possibly ask?"

"Anna, I don't wish to make you uncomfortable in my presence. You know my feelings toward you, but I understand and respect your response. And the last thing I want to do is make a nuisance of myself. If it would be easier for you to have me stay away from—"

"Oh, don't be silly, Pastor. You'll never be a nuisance to me. After all, you *are* my supervisor—and the very best one that God could have blessed me with! I . . . I'm just a bit overwhelmed with all the work that lies ahead for our ministry. I'm so concerned for the Hofmanns, all alone out there beyond the city walls. It's been ten days since I've visited them. God knows how they've been faring through all this turmoil. I pray they're not injured or their house raided. I . . . I . . ."

Peter could stand it no longer. He grasped the woman he loved by the shoulders, bent down, and kissed her passionately on the lips.

Anna yielded for a deliciously long moment, her lips melting into his, before she finally broke away.

Deeply embarrassed by his own lack of propriety and self-control, Peter attempted an apology. "Anna, please forgive me. I promise I'll never do that again—without your permission."

Anna was silent for a long moment, seemingly unsure what to do or say. At last, she found the words. They were the ones, Peter thought sadly, that would keep her safely in whatever place it was that she wished to hide. "Of course I forgive you, Pastor. And in fact, I wasn't at all offended. Why should I be? Especially when I *know* full well there are dozens of other young women in this city who would *crave* your affections and the chance for marriage you've offered me. Ladies far more deserving of your love than I. It's just that, as I've said before, I don't yet feel myself ready for marriage. I believe God calls me *now* to concentrate on the ministry of caring for those less fortunate."

Peter was about to dispute Anna's self-deprecating comments but then thought better of it. He'd made enough of a fool of himself for one day. Anna obviously had no intention of changing her mind.

"Well, my lady," he said, "I'm the last person who should be hindering your work for the Lord, especially since I'm the one supervising it. I can only commend and admire your commitment to his purposes. And you know I look forward to rejoining you and the other ladies in just a few days. May God bless and protect you, Anna." Peter bowed and turned to leave.

"Peter! Please don't give up on . . ."

Peter froze in his tracks. He turned to face her. "Don't give up on . . . what, Anna?"

"On . . . on . . . the power of God to . . . to . . . bless and protect us!"

Peter struggled to suppress his irritation. Was she serious? "You don't need to worry about *me* on that account, Anna," he said with a harsh laugh. "Good day, my lady."

CHAPTER 53

Swedish army field hospital, village of Breitenfeld
September 24, 1631

It was one thing, Peter thought, to tend to a solitary wounded or dead soldier on the battlefield. It was quite another to enter the large hospital tent on the edge of the village and witness dozens of mangled bodies exhibiting a grisly assortment of saber cuts, bullet holes, punctured organs, and severed limbs.

Peter was relieved that today he'd been assigned to assist in the partitioned-off officers' recuperation section. There he'd be less exposed to the overpowering stench and ghastly sounds from the operating tables. He would also have a chance to check on Captain Ekstrand, who had been moved there only two days earlier after receiving additional treatment for his arm wound. He would likely be in much better shape today than when Peter had first tended to him in the field.

Things were looking up, Peter knew, not only for Ekstrand but also for the overall Protestant cause. A full week had passed since the great battle. Adolphus's combined forces had lost around three thousand men, the Catholics nearly twelve thousand. Tilly's army, including Pappenheim's cavalry units, were routed, though not quite extinguished. The survivors had fled in every direction and, with the coming of winter, it would be quite a while before they'd be able to regroup. For the time being, they posed no serious threat.

Adolphus had been content to leave the recapture of Leipzig to John George and his Saxons despite their poor performance on the day of the battle. Only yesterday morning, the Catholic imperial garrison had surrendered to George, once again returning the city to Protestant control. To thank the victors for rescuing their city, the mayor and other Leipzig luminaries had invited the king and prince-elector along with their retinues and honored guests to a celebratory dinner at the city hall the following night.

But Peter had more important things on his mind this morning as he entered the officers' section. He had much work to attend to over the next day or two, and the Swedish surgeon's assistant would be expecting him to do it well. It wouldn't be easy, especially with Anna's latest rejection to ponder.

Peter felt his spirits lift when he spied Captain Ekstrand waving to him from his pallet.

"Pastor Erhart! I knew you wouldn't forget me. Welcome, sir! Come and meet my comrades. They've been teasing me mercilessly ever since they got here."

Peter approached the tent and bowed to the reclining Ekstrand and the three infantry officers seated beside his pallet. "Good morning, Captain. I'm glad to see you recovering so well. Sirs, it's my honor."

"And theirs also, Pastor." Ekstrand smiled mischievously. "Without you and your timely services, these kind gentlemen wouldn't have me here today to kick around for the sole purpose of inflating their own proud egos."

"We just don't want you to cave to the luxuries of this comfortable hospital, Ekstrand," one of the officers joked. "Stop faking it. Arise—we command you—and join the rest of us noble knights in pursuing our enemies to their rightful places in hell!"

Ekstrand groaned. "God in heaven, save me from these insane—"

A noisy commotion at the side entrance to the officer's area interrupted his mock plea for divine intervention. Two soldiers burst through the tent flap and took up position on either side of the entrance.

A third soldier then appeared. "God with us!" he announced. "The king is here! The king is here and enters now! All who are able, display the honor he deserves!"

The loud gasps and astonished cries of joy from every person within earshot gave way to breathless silence. All those not confined to pallets kneeled in unison, hats held over their hearts and beaming faces uplifted to behold their hero.

The Lion of the North stood in the entryway.

Everything that Peter had heard about the thirty-six-year-old king's physical appearance proved accurate. He was a huge man: tall, blond, and broad-shouldered, though somewhat stout around the waist, elongated face with large eyes and a pointed reddish beard.

"Rise and relax, men. *You* are the ones before whom *I* should be kneeling. You have sacrificed your bodies and dedicated your souls to a rightful and just cause. To you be my never-ending gratitude, and to our great God be the thanks and glory for our tremendous victory!"

A huge cheer erupted as the king entered the officers' section, backslapping and hugging those soldiers able to stand and greet him. It was easy, Peter thought, to see why Adolphus was so well loved by his men and so greatly respected by his enemies.

"Don't get too comfortable, men," Ekstrand muttered to his fellow officers and Peter. "Before long, he'll be insisting that all you unwounded sluggards—and you, too, Pastor—accompany him out to the field for the regular morning worship service."

"*Ja*," one of the officers quietly replied. "And God help anyone he catches in here joking about the faith, Ekstrand. I'm surprised he's never caught *you* in the act, given your constant vulgar utterings to us."

"Quiet! He's coming our way."

Peter stood at attention with the three officers as the king walked to the head of the pallet, knelt down, and kissed Captain Ekstrand on the forehead.

"Thank you, Your Majesty!"

Adolphus smiled tenderly at his nephew. He grasped the hand

of his healthy arm. "Well, nephew, it appears that God has spared you for his glorious purposes. I've already sent word to your mother, who'll no doubt have me assassinated if I don't allow you some time to return home for rest and recuperation. You performed wonderfully on the battlefield last week. I've already authorized your promotion to colonel of artillery. But don't think I'm going to let you off too easily. I'll expect you to return to lead your new unit once we begin our spring campaign."

Captain—now Colonel—Ekstrand didn't try to hide his gratitude. "Uncle, you're too kind. I . . . I don't know what to say except *thank you*. Thank you, sire. I will not disappoint you." Ekstrand embraced the king, then leaned back on his pallet and gestured to Peter. "Uncle, I am fully intact in body today because of this man. Without his bold intervention, the surgeon would have cut off my arm and cast it to the circling buzzards. This is Pastor Peter Erhart, sire."

Adolphus looked up at Peter, who instantly felt reduced to a quivering mass of jelly. "Ah, yes. So this is the Pastor Erhart of whom I've heard so many good things!" the king said with a warm smile. "Thank you, sir, for your service to our cause—and most especially for your invaluable aid to my beloved nephew."

"Oh, it was . . . my honor, sire." Peter struggled for the appropriate words. "Wh-what I did was only what God enabled me to do."

The king stood and grinned. "Now that's what I like to hear: a man crediting the glory to the One to whom we're all accountable."

"Even God would object to this man's modesty, Uncle," Ekstrand protested. "He not only saved my arm but also the lives of at least three other soldiers in bad shape on the field. And to think, he served with us despite having suffered the horrors of Magdeburg."

The king stared at Peter for a few seconds and then looked down. "So you were at Magdeburg?" he asked gruffly.

"Yes, my lord."

"Hmm. I see. *Ja*, well, it's time I go pay tribute to some of the other patients. Congratulations and take care, nephew. Get some rest and call for me if anyone gives you any trouble. And thank you once again,

Pastor, for everything you've done in the service of the Swedish army."

As the king visited other pallets beyond earshot, Peter quietly voiced his concern. "Was the king displeased to learn of my presence at Magdeburg?"

Ekstrand took hold of Peter's arm. "It's nothing to worry about. Magdeburg is a sore subject with him, but he knows there's no way we can avoid mentioning it from time to time. It's now a fact of life, and the king is not one to run from the truth, even if he might prefer to do so."

After personally greeting every single wounded officer and even some of the enlisted men, the king retired to his private quarters to prepare himself for morning worship. Peter decided it was a good time to take his own leave to attend to the other wounded.

As Peter was saying goodbye to Colonel Ekstrand and his comrades, a soldier appeared at the side entrance of the tent and approached the group. He handed Peter a folded message, saluted, and left.

Peter opened the handwritten note, which read simply:

Your presence is requested in the king's tent quarters
this morning immediately following the worship service.

CHAPTER 54

Swedish army field hospital
September 24, 1631

J udging by the reception area of his tent quarters, Gustavus
Adolphus was not a king concerned with royal luxuries in war
zones: two straight-backed chairs faced each other in the center of
the small, otherwise-empty room.

The king entered through the rear and strode toward his chair. Peter
sprang to attention. He bowed deeply and then knelt on one knee
with his hat over his heart, just as he'd seen the soldiers do earlier that
morning.

"Oh, Pastor Erhart, please!" the king said with an impatient laugh
as he took his seat. "There's no need for such antics in these rustic
surroundings. Really, my friend, just take your seat, and join me for a
little conversation."

"Thank you, sire. I'm most pleased to accommodate your desires."

The king stared at Peter for a long moment, his face darkening. "You
survived Magdeburg, did you? If I may be so bold, I want to hear of
your experience there. All of it. Leave nothing out."

For the first time since his encounter with Friar Rusche, Peter
described in full detail his personal account of the Magdeburg siege

and its aftermath.

King Adolphus said not a word during Peter's narrative. He merely sat with his elbow resting on the arm of his chair and his hand on his chin. But his eyes betrayed strong emotion, especially when Peter described Ursula's death by the sword of the Black Knight, Anna's loss of her family and abuse by the Croatian soldiers, and Peter's own observation of the corpses choking the Elbe River. When Peter recalled the false hope entertained by many Magdeburg citizens that King Adolphus would certainly come to the rescue, the monarch's eyes flashed with the indignant anger of someone falsely accused of a major crime.

At the conclusion of Peter's account, the king sighed deeply, folded his hands over his ample belly, and looked down at his lap. He seemed to be saying a silent prayer.

Peter waited politely for him to finish.

The king looked up, his eyes moist. "Pastor Peter—if I may refer to you so informally—words can't express the sorrow I feel for your personal losses and for those of the woman you now befriend. If it had been within my power to prevent such a tragedy, I would obviously have done so. And should God grant me the power at some time in the future to find and punish those responsible for such unspeakable crimes of war—well, I promise to do so with alacrity. But, Pastor, I must ask you a question."

"Of course, sire," Peter replied eagerly, wishing to alleviate the king's obvious discomfort.

"What do they say about me now?"

"Excuse me, but . . . who do you mean, sire?"

"Those citizens and clergy who you know in Leipzig," the king replied. "Especially any Magdeburg survivors."

Peter smiled tentatively. "Well, sire, I can tell you for certain there is no intelligent citizen in Leipzig who hasn't heard stories of the magnificent accomplishments of King Gustavus Adolphus. And not just your military exploits and technical innovations, sire, which are impressive enough, but also your masterful international diplomacy, your efforts to improve your countrymen's lives through your support of education and the arts, your—"

The king cleared his throat impatiently. "That's not what I'm talking about, Pastor." He leaned forward, his eyes boring into Peter's. "Twenty thousand innocents were massacred in Magdeburg! What I want to know is: what are people saying about my supposed *failure* to rescue those poor souls?"

Peter squirmed. "Sire, there are many different opinions. Some, I'm sorry to say, believe that it demonstrated your lack of true compassion for the German people, that it exposed your real purpose of expanding power and territory for your own country. Others—and I count myself among them—believe that your overriding purpose in coming to Germany was to save European Protestantism from the Holy Roman Empire's encroachments. And we also believe, sire, that your best efforts to reach Magdeburg were thwarted for reasons largely beyond your control."

"Insightful, Pastor. Very insightful." The king smiled sadly. "I can't tell you how many nights I've lain awake tossing and turning since receiving the news of Magdeburg's destruction. Despite our tremendous victories over the past few days, I can't divorce myself from the uneasy sense of being unfairly blamed for what happened. I have but one defense and source of consolation, Pastor, and that's knowing that *nothing* could have overcome the petty rivalries of those wretched local German princes and dukes, who conspired to block my army's efforts to rescue their own people. I tried repeatedly to convince them to let us through their provinces to reach Magdeburg in time, but they kept finding reasons to fear my supposed ulterior motives and to threaten our advance. As a result, my army was blocked and Magdeburg was destroyed."

Peter could see that the king was still haunted by what had happened. "Maybe it would also be helpful, sire, to recognize that the massacre was not just due to your inability to arrive in time."

"And how exactly was *that*, Pastor?"

"In my view, sire, the leaders of Magdeburg bear direct responsibility. Christian Wilhelm, Pastor Spaignart, and the other radical Lutheran pastors would not face the truth. They kept trying to convince the city council that your arrival was imminent, and that failure to hold out amounted to rejecting faith in Christ himself. They believed their own propaganda and pridefully rejected Tilly's final terms for an honorable surrender, blinding themselves and others to the terrible consequences of doing so. I can't hold *you* responsible for *their* irresponsible speech and actions, sire, and neither should you!"

The king, obviously touched, was unable to respond as he struggled to control his emotions.

At length, he spoke. "Well, Pastor Peter, you've given the king a helpful new perspective. It seems that Sweden has yet one more thing to thank you for.

"And now," he continued grandly, "let it be Sweden's turn to provide a service to Pastor Erhart. Is there *anything*, my dear man, that I might be able to help you with? Don't be shy!"

Peter laughed. "Actually, my lord, the one thing I'm in most need of is almost certainly the one thing beyond Sweden's control."

"Oh?" Adophus replied, a sparkle in his eye. "And what might that be, Pastor? Don't underestimate the king's power to overcome at least *some* of the difficult obstacles he's faced with!"

"Well, sire," Peter said, grinning in embarrassment, "if I knew that it was within your power to bend the stubborn will of my beloved Anna to accept my offer of marriage, I'd be tempted to contract as your personal vassal for the remainder of my life."

The king roared with laughter. "Oh, you needn't sell your entire life for such a small favor. Tell me more about this woman, Peter."

Peter related Anna's story and how they'd met. How Ursula and Anna had come to love and admire each other through their work together at the orphanage. How Peter's interest in Anna had grown after meeting up with her again in Leipzig and helping her struggle against false accusations. And how Anna seemed attracted to him yet was now so determined to defer marriage in favor of ministering to the poor and needy.

The king listened patiently. He appeared to take great pleasure in the story. At its conclusion, he had but one question. "Tell me, Pastor. Do you really think this matter is something beyond the power of the king?"

"Uh . . . no, sire," Peter said haltingly. "Well, maybe so, but . . . I'm not sure."

Adolphus grinned mischievously. "You might not believe it, but this king has had more than his share of experience in cajoling willful women into making the proper decisions for their lives. I won't trouble you with tales of my courtship and marriage to Maria Eleonora, but suffice it to say, this king knows a thing or two about what motivates young women. Or at least I think I do, which no doubt makes me extremely dangerous! But I'll tell you what, Pastor Erhart. If you would grant your trust to me, I'd like to attempt something bold on your behalf."

"And what is that, sire?"

"Tomorrow night, as you might have heard, John George and I have been invited to a formal dinner in Leipzig that's being held in honor of our victory. It would be my honor to invite both you *and* the object of your love, Fräulein Ritter, to sit at the main table with myself and my retinue—in thanks for your services to Sweden, of course."

"Oh, sire, that would be a great honor, but I don't know if Anna would feel—"

"Do not refuse me on that score, Pastor," Adolphus said, his face taking on a stern expression. "The king expects you *both* to be there tomorrow night. And one other thing."

"Yes, sire?"

"It would also be my honor at some point in the evening to hold a brief, private conversation with Fräulein Ritter to discuss certain matters of mutual interest to the both of you. I believe there are some things I might share with her that could have a positive bearing on the outcome you desire. Of course, it would be best if you don't alert her ahead of time to all this. What say you, Pastor? Are you willing to give this king a chance to at least partially redeem himself for past failures?"

Peter was stunned by the proposal but believed it just might be God's answer to his prayers. He grinned from ear to ear. "I am indeed, sire."

CHAPTER 55

Leipzig
September 25, 1631

When they'd arrived an hour ago, Peter and Anna had been escorted into the banquet area where most of the other guests were already seated in honor of King Adolphus's great Breitenfeld victory. Heads turned, eyes seemingly fixated on Anna. Noticing the stares, she had wondered in typical self-accusatory fashion whether she was walking the wrong way or maybe her gown had somehow betrayed its borrowed status.

"Your natural elegance is lighting up the room," Peter had whispered reassuringly when she'd questioned him. "Just try to relax."

It was no easy task. She was a nervous wreck. It wasn't every day that a young woman of common stock had a chance to sit at the table with a monarch, especially one like Gustavus Adolphus, who was being hailed throughout the city and increasingly throughout Europe as the glorious Savior of Protestantism.

Once seated, she had let Peter carry the conversation for both of them, doing her best to smile and nod and pretend that she was enjoying herself. She at least needed to do that to show Peter her appreciation for being invited. If she could just hold up a couple of hours longer, it would all be over. Starting tomorrow, she could return to her familiar role as countryside lay minister under his kind supervision. Their safe relationship could continue as before. *God, please let this banquet end quickly so Peter can take me home!*

Fortunately, the lavish dinner proceeded smoothly. Feeling an impulse to reach out with friendliness and Christian goodwill, Anna leaned over and politely inquired about the daily work of Herr Brand, a recently elected city councilor and member of St. Nicholas. The pompous gentleman's eyes lit up with delight. For the next several minutes, he regaled her with proud tales of his accomplishments as Frau Brand shot icy glances her way.

When Herr Brand finally ran out of breath, his wife could contain herself no longer. "Well, Fräulein Ritter, congratulations! You've succeeded in drawing more out of my husband over the past five minutes than he's shared with me over the past five months. Tell me, Fräulein, are you *always* so good at gaining the admiring gazes and confidences of gentlemen—enough for them to open themselves up to you like that?"

Herr Brand, clearly embarrassed by his wife's reaction, stared down at his plate.

Anna tried to maintain her composure. "Oh, of course not, my lady," she said with a hesitant laugh. "I was just curious, since I heard your husband mention earlier that he had a difficult job."

"Yes, it *is* a difficult job, Fräulein. And he earns every pfennig. And what about *you*? May we inquire as to the nature of *your* work? Are you still performing your nightly shifts at that awful tavern?"

It was all Anna could do not to lunge across the table and slap the woman across her fat, puffy cheek. She sensed the others at the table staring at her. "Frau Brand," she hissed, not bothering to disguise the anger in her eyes, "I hope you're not suggesting that I'm—"

Only Peter's firm hand on hers under the table prevented Anna from lashing out with all the vexation that she felt. "Frau Brand," he interjected sharply. "I know Fräulein Ritter has no wish other than to have a friendly conversation with both of you. But we'd both be happy to take our leave if one of us is upsetting you in any way."

Herr Brand tried to rescue the situation. "Oh, Pastor, Fräulein Ritter, there's absolutely no need for you to leave. We're all here tonight for a wonderful cause. The last thing I'd wish is to spoil the joy of this occasion by small misunderstandings."

Frau Brand, making no attempt to hide her smug smile, settled back in her chair as the other guests returned to their conversations. Anna smiled good-naturedly but continued to simmer inside. This evening couldn't end soon enough as far as she was concerned.

After the meal, the king offered a gracious speech thanking all the guests, after which he excused himself and turned the entertainment over to a group of string players. Anna tried to relax and enjoy the music, but she couldn't stop thinking about earlier. If Peter had delayed one more second in restraining her, she would have made a complete fool of herself and created great embarrassment and hardship for him. It was just another indication that she wasn't the right woman for him. It wasn't enough that—though she had tried for his sake to hide it from him—she now loved and desired him more than ever. As a pastor, Peter needed someone for a wife who could handle situations like tonight more graciously. Someone who wouldn't let her own history and insecurity overwhelm her good sense and concern for the welfare of others. No, she could never measure up to the high standards of a pastor's wife.

A few minutes into their performance, Anna noticed a uniformed attendant approach Peter and discretely hand him a folded note. He read and refolded it, then handed it to her with raised eyebrows. She opened it, then read it through twice.

Pastor Erhart:

The king wishes to hold a brief, private conversation with Fräulein Ritter in the greeting room on the second floor. It concerns a delicate matter on which he desires her opinion. The king thanks you both graciously in advance and will have Fräulein Ritter escorted safely back to you by the conclusion of the musical entertainment.

Anna stared at Peter with a mixture of excitement and stark terror. "Pastor," she whispered, "why on earth would the king ask for *my* opinion on something rather than yours? You *did* tell him you were my supervisor, didn't you?"

Peter shrugged and offered a bewildered smile. "I'm at a loss, Anna," he whispered back. "But it doesn't sound like a request that either of us should refuse."

Trembling all over, she stood and took the attendant's arm.

CHAPTER 56

Leipzig
September 25, 1631

T he greeting room was beautifully decorated—fitting for the reception of important dignitaries and their entourages. Richly upholstered couches lined the walls, which displayed framed portraits of aristocrats and royalty. In front of a large fireplace built into the rear wall were two comfortable-looking armchairs facing the room's center and arranged for easy conversation. King Gustavus Adolphus occupied one of the chairs.

He looked up, smiled, and placed a leather-bound book he'd been reading onto a small side table. He rose and extended his hand in welcome.

Anna struggled to keep her whole body from shaking.

The king sought to put her at ease. "Ah, Fräulein Ritter, thank you for coming to see me. Please, Fräulein, come sit next to me."

"Thank you, sire."

Anna was amazed by his gracious greeting. She could feel herself begin to relax.

"So, Fräulein Ritter—may I call you Anna?—I'm sure you're curious why the king of Sweden should wish to speak with you privately."

"The question had crossed my mind, sire," Anna said with a shy smile.

Adolphus looked at the floor for a moment, as if deliberating how best to explain.

"Are you aware, Fräulein, that I have a family who will soon be joining me in Germany for the extent of my campaign here?"

"I've heard from Pastor Peter, my lord, that you have a beautiful wife—the queen consort—and a five-year-old daughter. But I'm sad to say that's all I know."

"*Ja*, that's true. And as you might suspect, once they arrive here, they'll no doubt face some major adjustments. In particular, my daughter Christina will sorely be missing her friends and daily routine in Sweden. I fear she'll become even more painfully withdrawn than she already is." The king leaned forward in his chair, eyes twinkling. "Which brings me, Fräulein Anna, to the reason I requested this meeting."

"Excuse me, but I don't understand, sire."

"The queen and I have decided that we need to find a young lady whom we can trust to befriend Christina, to help her adapt to her new surroundings and learn the language and customs of another land. We seek someone native to Germany, who greatly enjoys children and has much experience working with them. Someone of the true faith who can teach our daughter what it means to serve others less fortunate in a ministering capacity. In short, someone like . . . you, Fräulein Anna."

Anna tried to suppress her panic. Was the king actually asking her to become the German nanny for the Swedish princess? And did she really *desire* such a position? "Oh, sire! I thank you for your kind consideration for such a noble task. But, sire, why me?"

"I have your escort Pastor Peter to thank for the answer to that, Fräulein."

"Sire, did *Pastor Peter* recommend my services to you?" Anna asked suspiciously.

"No, Fräulein," the king responded with an indignant frown. "Pastor Peter is quite unaware of the things I've just shared with you. What he *did* provide me, as part of a discussion I had with him yesterday, was a glowing description of your work in support of his beloved wife

Ursula at the Magdeburg orphanage. He raved over your effectiveness in teaching and leading the children and their obvious love for you. He couldn't say enough about the wonderful work you're doing now under his supervision for your church's countryside ministry. And, if I may say so, your appearance, conduct, and speech in my presence here do nothing but amplify my good opinion of your capabilities for this role."

Anna could already feel her feet and hands turning cold at the prospect. It wasn't just the idea of leaving her ministry behind. Far more terrifying for her was the prospect of leaving Peter behind in order to follow the king's family on the campaign trail.

"My lord, forgive me, but I've sensed for some time that the work I'm doing here in Leipzig is a calling from God, and that Pastor Peter needs and wants me to help him with it."

"Certainly, Fräulein," the king acknowledged. "But how do you know that God is not now offering you a new calling, one that will have a direct impact on the life of a young child who is destined to one day become the queen of Sweden? Just think, your service over the next year or so will likely benefit the lives of millions in the future! Isn't that prospect worthy of consideration as a calling from God?"

"W-well, of course, sire. I suppose it would be worthy. But I'd have to pray deeply about whether it's indeed *my* calling or someone else's. And, sire, there's still the issue of Pastor Peter needing my help."

"But, Anna, isn't it possible that Peter could eventually find someone else to perform your ministry function here? Perhaps not as ably as you, but certainly sufficient for the purposes. And, as I understand from Peter that you've expressed no desire to marry him, is there any reason for you to remain behind in Leipzig for *his* sake?"

Anna felt her face burn with embarrassment. What else had Peter revealed about their relationship? "It's *not* that I have no desire to marry Peter, my lord," she confessed.

"Oh?" the king asked, seemingly surprised. "That certainly seems to be *his* impression."

Anna hesitated, unsure whether she should reveal to the king of Sweden, of all people, what she'd hidden from Peter and everyone else—the *real* reason for her rejection of Peter's proposal. In a flash, she made her decision. She could no longer hold this inside.

"I *do* desire to marry Peter, sire, with all my heart. It's just that I also know in my heart that I couldn't be the wife I know he needs."

"My dear girl!" the king exclaimed. "How could you possibly think such a thing? Are you not aware of the esteem and affection in which Pastor Peter holds you? Don't you know he's so enthralled with the prospect of a life with you that he despairs of that possibility with anyone else?"

Anna looked down. "That's just it, Your Majesty. Pastor Peter blinds himself to my faults. He refuses to see that I'll *never* be accepted as his wife by those above my station in life. He overlooks my lowly background. He ignores the accusations against me here in Leipzig despite the grief this has already caused him on my account. I ask you, sire, how can a pastor of such great education and talent as Peter—a man who will one day become the senior pastor of a large city church—possibly benefit from an ignorant wife who can't even control her angry emotions for the good of the entire flock!"

"*Cannot* control?" Adolphus asked, his voice hardening. "Or *will* not control?"

"How do you mean, sire?" Anna asked.

"It's one thing," the king observed, "to say that a person has a certain fault but is struggling to overcome it. It's quite another to have that fault yet knowingly give up and stubbornly resist any help from others in trying to correct it. The latter choice essentially amounts to *pride*, Fräulein. And I wonder if somehow a bit of *that* little vice might not have crept into your thinking about all this."

Anna's memories of the last eleven months all combined to create a sudden rush of pent-up venom. The words rose from the pit of her stomach to her throat.

"*Pride*, sire?" she exploded, eyes flashing with anger and hot tears. "Is *my pride* the reason that dozens of proper women—and God knows how many men—at St. Nicholas still consider me an undeserving country bumpkin turned husband-stealer? A seductive adulteress now out to lure away their beloved and innocent assistant pastor? Is it *my pride* that must be somehow overcome or theirs? I cannot and will not deny it, my lord. I despise every last one of those rich, arrogant snobs who continue to insist on falsely accusing me of despicable sins. I've made mistakes, but I am better than *that . . .* and I am better than *them*! I—"

Anna suddenly remembered where she was and who she was addressing. She froze in mid-sentence and then broke down in a fit of sobs.

After several moments, she managed to collect herself. "God forgive me, and may you forgive me as well, sire. I've just proved that I'm the child of my mother—given to hysterical outbursts over the least things."

Adolphus handed her a handkerchief and touched her arm. "You *are* better than them, Anna," he said softly. "But you can't allow your bitterness toward them to persist, or it will eat you alive. Nor can you run away from it. Sooner or later, God will find ways to confront you with those feelings again. You have to learn to forgive these women— for your own sake, if not for theirs."

Anna nodded tearfully. *"Forgive others, as I have forgiven you,"* the Lord had commanded. Somehow she had to find the strength to forgive her accusers.

The king pressed his case. "But there's one other thing you need to accept, isn't there, Anna?"

"What is that, sire?"

"The memory of the one person who continues to come between you and the man I know you love."

As soon as he spoke the words, Anna knew what he was suggesting. She'd known it all along but until now had avoided confronting it directly. Ursula. The model pastor's wife, the perfect mother. The beautiful, intelligent, all-gracious, and compassionate friend of both rich and poor. The dear friend and mentor even of the likes of Anna Ritter, who had yearned secretly in every way to steal her husband. Ursula. Born to the upper class, educated and well-read, raised in holiness and preserved in purity for her wedding night. Ursula had possessed all the qualities that Anna jealously craved for herself in order to be the wife that Peter deserved, the kind of wife he could truly love.

The memory of Ursula had been distorting her feelings about marrying Peter. She'd covered over the memory with pious talk about following God's will instead of accepting his proposal. When really, all along, it was her fear of measuring up to Ursula that had determined her decision.

"Yes, sire. As good and loving and wonderful as she was, and as much as I loved and admired her, I can *never be her*. I can never be Ursula." Tears flooded Anna's eyes and cascaded down her cheeks. The devastation she'd experienced over all these months had now run its full course.

The king leaned forward and took her hands in his. "Fräulein Anna . . . listen to me. *Stop trying to be Ursula*. With all my heart, based on everything I have seen in you and have learned from that wonderful young pastor you so love, I can tell you with absolute certainty it's not Ursula who he wants or needs now. It's *you*, just as you are, Anna."

Anna looked into his eyes. The realization finally hit. No longer did she need to hold Peter at arm's length to save him from herself. She didn't need to *be* Ursula in order to be the perfect wife for the man she desired so badly. Peter would love her for exactly who she was.

Anna took several moments to compose herself. Finally, the king stood and offered his hand. Anna arose to accept it.

"My lord," she said with a shy smile, "may I be so bold as to ask how you became so skilled at speaking to the heart of a woman?"

King Adolphus chuckled. "Did you already forget, Fräulein? I've had years of practice with a beautiful though complex lady—my dear wife, the queen—who in so many ways reminds me of you. But I must be improving. The conversation I just had with you took but a few minutes. The last one with the queen took over three hours and achieved not half as much good."

Anna, acting on bold impulse, took the king's hand in both of hers and kissed it. "Thank you, my lord, for what you've done . . . and for permitting me that little pleasure."

The king's eyes glistened. "The pleasure was mine, Fräulein. Now, hurry back to my good friend Pastor Peter and waste no more time on silly excuses. That man is worth his weight in gold—I promise you!"

The attendant opened the doors and stepped forward to offer his arm to Anna.

As they were leaving, the king had one last question. "Oh, Fräulein Anna," he said, grinning impishly, "I suppose this means you'll be turning down my offer to leave Leipzig for the sake of helping to raise the next queen of Sweden?"

Anna giggled. "Regrettably, my lord, that's correct. I'm hoping there's another offer still awaiting me that—thanks to you—I'm now more inclined to accept."

"God be with you, Fräulein!"

The king had spoken. And what a blessing it was. Anna's radiant smile said it all.

⌘

The after-dinner musical performance had already concluded. Peter held the carriage door open as Anna approached. She averted her gaze and said not a word as he helped her in.

Anna, still silent, stared straight ahead as the carriage proceeded on the route back to Adele's house. Peter didn't dare attempt to break through her apparent pique.

As the carriage passed the entrance to a quiet, secluded street halfway to their destination, Anna requested the chauffeur to halt. "Pastor, please help me down from this vehicle immediately."

Peter was petrified. What was wrong with her? Was she angry with him and determined now to walk the rest of the way home on her own? *What* had King Adolphus said to her?

"Pastor, I'd appreciate it if you would accompany me on a short walk down the street a ways while the coachman waits."

"Of course, Anna. As you wish."

As Peter strolled with her down the street, he grew annoyed by her continued silence. If the king had somehow ruined the opportunity to change her mind, it was better to know it now. "Anna, please tell me if something's wrong. We can't continue to—"

Anna stopped and whirled to face him, her eyes blazing. "So, Pastor Peter Erhart, was it *you* who put the king of Sweden up to prying into my deepest thoughts and longings?"

Peter's knees nearly collapsed. Obviously, her talk with the king had *not* gone as planned. "No. Well, yes, but . . . Anna, can't you see—"

Anna reached up with both hands and grabbed the collar of Peter's doublet. "Pastor," she whispered, eyes moist with tears, "stop making weak excuses and ask me the question again."

"The question? Which question are you—" Peter froze. He couldn't believe it. "Anna, are you asking me to—"

"Yes, Peter!" Anna smiled.

"Fräulein Ritter . . . Anna . . . will you—"

"*Peter, Yes! Yes! Just say it!*"

"Anna, will you marry me?"

"Peter, my darling Pastor Perfect. Just let *this* be my long-overdue answer." She gently lowered Peter's head toward hers and, for the second time in seven days, opened her lips to receive his. This time, she didn't pull away.

Ten minutes later, the driver called in a hesitant voice from the coach. "Pastor Erhart . . . Fräulein Ritter . . . is everything all right?"

"Of course, Heinz, we're fine, and we'll be right there. Just a few more minutes!"

⌒⌒

At the church service the following Sunday, Peter and Anna beamed at each other across the aisle as an exuberant Senior Pastor Kurt Wagner made a special announcement from the pulpit.

"It pleases me greatly to inform the congregation of St. Nicholas Church that on Christmas Day, Thursday, December 25, 1631, it is the intention of Assistant Pastor Peter Erhart and Fräulein Anna Ritter to partake of the sacrament of holy matrimony. It will be my distinct privilege to officiate the proceedings, which will take place immediately following the conclusion of our Christmas worship service. The entire congregation is invited and encouraged to attend."

Gasps of astonishment were followed by shouts of approval, expressions of joy, and applause from many in the congregation. Some, however, sat with stony expressions, refusing to join in.

On his way out of the narthex with Anna, Peter was pulled aside by Pastor Gabriel who had a distressed look on his face.

"Peter, I hate to trouble you at a time like this, but the bailiff is requesting Pastor Wagner, you, and me to meet him down by the riverbank. There's been a development—something he wants us all to see."

PART V

GENTLE WHISPER

CHAPTER 57

Countryside northwest of Leipzig
December 22, 1631

(Three months later)

P eter mulled over the early-morning news from the Leipzig bailiff while leading the horse on which Anna was perched along the narrow country path.

Yet another mutilated corpse had been discovered on the White Elster riverbank just outside the city. It was the fifth to wash up in the aftermath of the great Breitenfeld battle. Each had displayed two things in common with the first one: the insignia of a Catholic soldier on its shredded clothing and seven deep grooves in the torso extending from just below the groin through the top of the head. It was as if seven sharp knives had been simultaneously ripped through the flesh by some hellish instrument designed by the prince of demons himself. It seemed, according to the bailiff, that "vigilante justice" was being executed against renegade Catholic soldiers still roaming the area for food and plunder following their defeat.

As to the perpetrators of the gruesome murders, a new rumor had just come to light that a mysterious "ex-clergyman" was somehow behind all of them. As a precaution, the bailiff was now requesting the clergy at all Leipzig churches to be on special alert for any further clues from their congregations.

Determined to enjoy his rare morning time alone with Anna, Peter forced the sickening thoughts and images from his mind. He looked across the open field. The first substantial snow of the season had fallen overnight, depositing a five-inch blanket of bright-white powder over the landscape. The sun had peeked through the clouds a short time ago, and the wind had died down to a faint breeze. The muffled clomping of the horse's feet on the snow was the only sound to be heard.

Peter paused to adjust the horse's bridle. He looked up at Anna and marveled that only three days separated him from the joyous union with her that he'd dreamed of for months now. Today, they would conclude their last round of countryside ministry visits before the wedding.

"So, my dear, will it really take three whole days to perfect your already goddess-like appearance for the wedding?"

Anna put one hand on her hip, cocked her shoulder, and patted the back of her head with the other hand while giggling and batting her eyes. "*Yes*, Pastor, it really *will* take that long for me to arrange my beautiful long hair and everything else to meet your high expectations!"

Peter dropped the reins and slowly walked around to face his fiancée. "Fräulein, it's simply not fair for so ravishing a damsel to tempt a poor man of the cloth like myself. You know I'm required to maintain the strictest propriety with members of the opposite sex. But that won't stop me from . . . *teaching that ravishing damsel a lesson in godliness!*"

He grabbed Anna's waist with both hands, lifted her light frame with ease off the saddle, and swung her round and round as she squealed in feigned protest.

"Pastor, put me down—*now*! Peter . . . *please!*" She tossed back her head and laughed with uninhibited delight—an emotion Peter had not so long ago wondered if she'd ever be able to experience again.

"So you want down, Fräulein? Very well. I'd be happy to put you . . . *down!*"

Peter dropped Anna unceremoniously in the soft snowdrift beside the path. He stood over her with hands on hips, waiting for her to stop laughing.

"You get down here with me, Pastor Perfect—*right now!*"

"Oh, no, you don't," Peter said with a grin. "Lead me not into temptation, woman! What would Kirsten say?" Ever since the wedding announcement, Kirsten and Adele had made it their primary task in life to preserve Peter's and Anna's reputations. He couldn't take her anywhere in the city without one or the other of the ladies attending as a chaperone.

"Well," Anna said with a coy smile, "I'll just have to pick myself up and walk alone the rest of the way. Seeing as there are no suitable gentlemen in the area."

"All right, Fräulein. You win."

The ruse worked to perfection. Just as Peter lay down and rolled over to kiss her, Anna reached up with a handful of snow and rubbed it in his face.

"Now you'll *really* have to learn your lesson, Fräulein," Peter said, laughing as he wiped the snow off. He placed his hand gently behind Anna's slender neck and stared into her enchanting green eyes. "Did you know, Fräulein Ritter, that I stood not a sliver of a chance of resisting your charms from the first moment I saw you?"

"Well, it certainly took you long enough to cave in. Prove it to me now, Peter."

Peter drew her face toward his and kissed her passionately. His only frustration was the thick layers of winter clothing that separated their bodies from the full, unencumbered embrace they both desired. Three more days, and the wait would be over.

Anna pulled away, lay back, and closed her eyes while Peter continued stroking the back of her neck. "Hmm . . . was that my lesson in godliness, Pastor? I think I just might benefit from a few more of those."

After a few moments, Peter noticed that Anna's expression had changed. "What's the matter, dear?" he asked. "Do I need to rub some snow in *your* face?"

"Oh, it's nothing, Peter. Really."

"Anna, tell me."

A tiny tear appeared in the corner of her eye. "It's just that when you twirled me around in the air, I remembered doing the same thing one day on a hillside with my little sister."

"You miss Liesa, don't you?"

"Oh, Peter, I still miss *all* of them so terribly. Liesa, Mutti, Vati—I still have dreams about them almost every night. Mutti would've wanted so much to be here for our wedding. I can see her now, running around every which way, trying to make sure every little detail was exactly as she desired. And Vati . . ." The thought of her father was too much. Anna let her tears flow freely as Peter cradled her head against his chest.

"Peter, you *do* think about them, don't you? Your children, I mean."

"Yes, Anna," Peter said with a long sigh. "Hardly a night goes by that I don't remember playing Brave Knight with little Josef or tucking Edith into her crib."

"I miss them too, darling. They were so gentle and sweet. But, Peter, we'll have our own children one day, won't we?" Anna looked at him as if she had her doubts.

"Of course, dear. Why shouldn't we, God willing?"

Anna looked down. "It's strange, isn't it?"

"What's strange?"

"How God has brought us together. It seems that . . . that . . . our families had to die so that we could . . ."

Peter gently cupped her cheek with his palm. He had known this would come up sooner or later. "It's a hard thing to understand," he said softly. "I only know that God wants us together, and he's gone to great lengths to make sure that has happened. Not the way *I* would have chosen, but I've given up questioning his reasons and methods. All I know is . . . in you he's restored my happiness in this life, and in Christ he's secured bliss for both of us in the next. What more can I possibly ask of him?"

"Well," Anna whispered, "I at least will keep asking him one more thing, Pastor."

Peter kissed her. "And what's that, my lady?"

"That you'll never, ever stop loving me."

"I think I already know his answer to that request," he said, planting another kiss on her lips.

"Pastor?" she asked in a cautious tone.

"Yes, Fräulein?" Peter replied with a laugh. He wondered how much longer they could put off their arrival at the Hofmanns. They were already late.

"Does the Bible say that we have guardian angels?"

Peter looked at her quizzically and scratched his jaw. "Well, there are several verses that speak of a great company of holy angels sent forth as ministering spirits for those who believe in the name of Christ. Exactly *how* they go about ministering to us—whether it's in the physical or spiritual sense or both—is another question. Why do you ask?"

"It's hard to explain. It's a strange feeling I get every time I take the Hofmanns' clothes outside to wash in the stream. It's as if something or someone is hovering close by. Watching over my every move. It feels like a comforting and protective presence. I'm not afraid of it. But I look all around, and I see and hear absolutely nothing besides the birds chirping and the wind blowing through the trees."

A tiny alarm sounded in Peter's mind, but he decided not to probe further. Anna had been through so much over the past several months.

"Well then," he said, "let's just assume that it *is* a guardian angel who's watching over you out there, dear. And we'll thank God for sending him."

"As you suggest, Pastor," Anna said and smiled. "I just thought you might like to know."

The alarm in Peter's mind sounded just a bit louder—not nearly enough, though, to question her further.

"Well, Pastor," Anna said as she sat up to brush the snow off her cloak, "we really *should* be going. Don't you think?"

As she stood up, Peter noticed something on the ground. It had apparently fallen out of Anna's pocket. It was the parting gift from Barbara Saller.

"Why are you still carrying *that* around in your pocket?"

Anna picked up the figurine and dusted the snow off of it. "In three days, I'm marrying the Lutheran pastor of my dreams. I know Barbara's memory will forever be close to my heart, so I finally decided it's time I give my little Mary away to the Hofmanns. They're Catholic, and they'll surely benefit more from her than I will."

"You've come a long way, darling," Peter said.

Shortly after, Peter helped Anna off the horse. He kissed her and watched as she walked up the short side path to the Hofmanns' cottage.

She knocked on their door and awaited a response. Before it came, she turned to wave goodbye. "You'll be back soon, won't you? Please don't stay any longer than you have to."

Peter was surprised by the plaintiveness of Anna's tone. He wanted to run up to her and offer a reassuring hug. But he didn't. He would wait until he returned later today to do exactly that.

CHAPTER 58

Countryside northwest of Leipzig
December 22, 1631

"Yes, Anna. Please just come in. The door's unlocked. I'm helping Herr Hofmann back into bed. He's not feeling well this morning."

Krista Hofmann's voice sounded strained, Anna thought as she pushed the door open and entered the living area of the Hofmanns' cottage.

"Make yourself at home, Anna. I'll be out in just a few minutes."

Anna hung her cloak on a hook, then took a seat at the small dining table. Reaching into her ministry-support bag, she pulled out the Bible tracts and other devotional materials that Peter had provided for today. Since the Hofmanns were Catholic, Peter had selected readings that were straightforward and unlikely to cause confusion or stir controversy. The goal was simply to bring Christ's love to the elderly couple, not convert them to Lutheranism. Among Anna's assigned tasks were reading and discussing the materials with them, praying with them, and offering any physical assistance they might request. But her main purpose was to be a sympathetic ear and watchful eye, keeping alert for any new signs of ill health or emotional distress.

The old woman came out from the sleeping area and greeted Anna. Her face was pale.

"Frau Hofmann! Is something wrong? You don't look well."

"Oh, it's nothing, dear. Just another one of my headaches. They come and go—nothing to worry about. I'm much more concerned about Herr Hofmann. He just hasn't seemed himself the last few days."

At seventy-four, Herr Franz Hofmann had already far outlasted just about every peasant Anna had ever known. It seemed almost inevitable that he would be having more frequent bouts of fatigue or confusion.

"Would it help for Pastor Peter to examine him when he returns this afternoon?" Anna asked.

"If he's not up and about by then, maybe it would. But I really don't think it's anything physical so much as . . ."

"Krista, what's troubling him—and you?" Anna asked gently.

"What? Oh, nothing, Liebchen. I'm tired of fretting so much over Herr Hofmann and myself, especially when I know there's a far more joyful story to hear. So tell me, Anna, how are the wedding preparations coming along? I want to know all the details!"

Frau Hofmann was avoiding something, but Anna decided not to press further for now. She laughed. "Oh, Krista, I'm not so sure you want to know all those. But I *will* say they're taking every last ounce of my energy. Even so, Peter and I are both getting very excited! And we've been so grateful for all the goodwill and help that others in the church are providing."

Over the past three months, the tide of church opinion had turned overwhelmingly to approval of Peter and Anna's marriage. Peter had said that a big part of this was due to the favorable impressions that she herself was creating—not only through her ministry work but through her many unselfish acts of kindness and gracious speech toward everyone she interacted with.

Two months ago, Anna had returned to the ladies' weekly sewing circle. It had quickly become clear she was gaining the respect and appreciation of many of the previously unwelcoming women. Even Frau Jund had put in a good word to Kirsten the other day, saying,

"Fräulein Ritter seems to have improved somewhat in her knowledge of scripture. At least now she's able to identify the right chapter and verse numbers with the passage she's quoting." Frau Jund had even admitted that perhaps she'd been a tad harsh on Anna during her first visit to the circle—although she was glad to see Anna had taken her advice.

The biggest breakthrough had come the night that Eduard's young wife Franke had stopped by, holding her one-month-old baby in her arms. Franke had broken down into a torrent of tears. She had apologized for joining in the false accusations against Anna. She had even admitted to her own suspicions at the time that Eduard had been seeing other women in the city for many years. She'd long believed her marriage to Eduard had been doomed to fail. As things had turned out, not only had their marriage dissolved, but Eduard was now rumored to be in prison for conducting fraudulent business in another city. Franke had begged Anna's forgiveness, and the two women had tearfully embraced. Overwhelmed with compassion for Franke, Anna had invited her to come for a visit each afternoon that the ministry ladies met in preparation for their next day's rounds. Franke had gratefully accepted and was now a regular and enthusiastic supporter of the overall ministry effort, occasionally even accompanying Anna on her visits.

"And I suppose all the invitations have long ago been sent out?" Frau Hofmann asked.

"Oh my goodness, yes!" Anna replied. "And we didn't stop with the St. Nicholas congregation. We even sent an invitation to King Adolphus and the queen consort!"

"No! Oh, Anna, that is simply divine! Will he really. . . ?"

"Oh, there's no chance he will be able to attend even if he wanted to. Peter says he has a few 'slightly more pressing concerns,' like completing his military campaign in the Rhineland before winter sets in. We sent the invitation just to inform His Majesty and thank him for all he did to encourage our marriage. Honestly, Krista, you know my story. If he hadn't knocked me off my stubborn pedestal, this wedding would not be happening."

"Well, whether he attends or not, it was very kind of you to—"

"*I'm here!*" A thin, shabbily dressed young man, no older than twenty or twenty-one, had not even bothered to knock. He'd simply opened the front door, walked in, and offered his brash greeting.

"Good morning, Herbert," Frau Hofmann said in a strained voice.

The man sauntered up to the table and acknowledged the women in a surly voice. "Frau Hofmann, Fräulein Anna. So what do you have for me today?"

Anna said nothing. She'd disliked Herbert Sturm from the moment she'd first met him during one of her previous visits, and for good reason. Sturm was a close friend—some said a former lover—of Franke's sister.

Sturm's commissioning by the church to help cut firewood and perform other outside tasks for the Hofmanns had all seemed innocent enough on the surface. After hearing about their need from comments Anna had made at the sewing circle, Franke's sister had suggested her good friend Sturm to Pastor Wagner as the perfect solution. She'd told him that Sturm, who lived in a large, ramshackle cottage shared with four other men only a half mile from the Hofmanns', would be delighted to help out for a nominal fee. Pastor Wagner had had little reason to refuse the generous offer. And ever since, Sturm had been showing up two days a week to perform his tasks.

Anna suspected that Franke's sister had suggested Sturm as a way for her to keep tabs on Anna's activities at the cottage. But it wasn't just Sturm's connection with Franke's sister that bothered her. She didn't like the way he looked at her. He spoke politely enough to her, but underneath the surface, Anna sensed the young man bore her a deep dislike—a dislike tinged with lust, if his lingering glances at her body were any indication. Maybe, she thought, he coveted what he knew he couldn't have.

Most disturbing of all was the arrogant manner in which he spoke to the Hofmanns—as if, being Catholic, they were undeserving of his help.

"So, Frau, where are they?" Sturm asked impatiently.

"Where are what, Herbert?" Frau Hofmann was obviously confused.

"The potatoes you wanted me to peel," Sturm said gruffly. "Have you forgotten already? It's only been two days since you asked me."

"Oh, my. Yes, yes. Of course, Herbert. They're in the three large baskets over there in the far corner. And there are three more baskets just outside. Herr Hofmann didn't have the strength to bring them in yesterday. He's not—"

"Don't trouble me with Herr Hofmann's problems, Frau. It's just as well. I don't have time today to do more than the baskets in the corner."

"But, Herbert, we'd really hoped you would—"

"Excuse *me*, Frau Hofmann. I don't mean to set a bad example for all the other good Lutherans in this area who offer their charity to *Catholics* like you. It's just that I have important business to take care of this afternoon. Surely you can understand, Frau."

"Oh, Herbert, I understand. Please, just peel as many as you have time for today. We're grateful for anything you can do. I'll have my husband finish the rest as soon as he's feeling better."

Sturm gave the elderly woman a sour look before stalking over to the small stool next to the potato baskets. He took his seat, pulled out his knife, and began to peel one of the large spuds.

Frau Hofmann looked as if she were about to cry.

Anna knew the poor woman had a tender heart and hated the thought of offending anyone. She was desperate to do or say something to lighten the mood for Frau Hofmann's sake. "Krista, I brought you something I thought you and Herr Hofmann might like."

Her old eyes brightened with surprise and delight as Anna took the figurine of Mary out of her pocket and placed it on the table.

"Anna! She's beautiful! Where on earth did you find her?"

Anna had the distinct feeling that Sturm was listening in on their conversation from his corner. She tried to keep her voice low, but her hostess was hard of hearing and certainly unable to read lips. "A dear friend gave her to me, Krista. God used this little Mary to help save my young sister's life in Magdeburg. It's a long story. But I don't want to keep her any longer for myself. She's in my heart. I'd much rather give her to you two. I know you'll appreciate her even more than I could."

"Anna, she's so lovely!" Frau Hofmann exclaimed tearfully. "How can we ever thank you? Here! Help me up, and let's go put her in the shrine."

Anna took Frau Hofmann by the hand and led her to a little covered table. On it rested a wooden cross, a candle, a chain of rosary beads, and other devotional articles.

After carefully setting the figurine on the table next to the cross, Frau Hofmann knelt down with some difficulty, crossed herself, and began to pray.

Anna knelt and prayed silently along with her.

As the two women returned to the table, Anna glanced at Sturm. He'd paused his potato peeling and was openly glaring at her.

Before the women could resume their conversation, Sturm decided to make some of his own. "I'm so touched by your kind gesture, Fräulein Anna."

"Thank you, Herr Sturm," Anna replied warily and took her seat facing away from him.

"You know, ladies, I was just thinking how hard it must be for someone to be living a double life."

Anna's back stiffened. Trying her best to remain calm, she stared straight ahead and focused her eyes on the wall behind Frau Hofmann.

"Oh, dear, Herbert!" a flustered Frau Hofmann said. "What in heaven's name would lead you to say such a thing?"

"Nothing, Frau. It's just that when I saw Fräulein Anna so piously kneeling and praying with you over there, it reminded me how hard it is for someone to stay true to their faith. So many times, I've come across hypocrites in the church—even in the church that Fräulein Anna attends. You know: people who say they believe certain things, but then they deliberately do other things that show their words were nothing but a lie. I call that living a double life."

"Well, young man, aren't you glad that you don't have to deal with anyone like *that* in this cottage today? I'm not sure why you're bringing it up."

"I'm not sure, either, Frau," he said with a curt laugh. "Maybe it was sparked by seeing a good, faithful Lutheran woman like Fräulein Anna here pull a little wooden Catholic idol out of her pocket. It's obvious she's been holding onto it for quite a while. I was just kind of surprised, that's all."

Anna felt her face burn with rage. Still, she managed to control her voice. "Herr Sturm, you've no idea the significance that 'little wooden idol' bears for me."

"Oh, but just maybe I *do*, Fräulein. Didn't you tell Frau Hofmann that your little Mary saved your sister's life in Magdeburg? It all leads me to wonder what kind of life *you* were leading in Magdeburg, and exactly how it was that your Mary came to save your sister."

Anna whirled in her seat to face Sturm. "That, sir, is none of your business!"

"Maybe it *is* my business. I know from Franke's sister that you've stirred up a lot of sympathy for yourself at St. Nicholas, based on your story about being a Magdeburg survivor. You've even won the heart of their assistant pastor—despite rumors of your sin with Franke's husband. But I think you should know something, Fräulein. You're not the only survivor to spin a dark tale of horror about the city's sack. Maybe it would help you to know that *my own sister* has an even more believable claim than yours: *she's dead!* When I went to Magdeburg to find her soon after the sack, I found her raped, mutilated, and decaying body. Her husband and child were nowhere to be found. The neighbors told me my sister had begged the Catholic soldiers for mercy. But they laughed in her face and then went on to torture and kill her. So forgive me, Fräulein Anna, for wanting to know the true situation behind your story. At least *you* are still alive and obviously enjoying life enough to talk about it!"

Anna, livid and eyes brimming with tears, got up from the table and marched over to Sturm. "Must I be *dead* for you and your friends at St. Nicholas to believe my testimony, Herr Sturm? I'm sorry for the loss of your sister, but *you* have no right to accuse me of lying about my own experience. You have no idea what I've been through."

Sturm glared back at her with the eyes of a snake coiled to strike. He threw the potato bud into the basket. Standing abruptly, he jammed the knife back into his belt and brushed past Anna. "You won't be needing *my* services again, Frau Hofmann. I'm sure Fräulein Anna and her soon-to-be husband will help you find somebody else."

"Herbert, please!" Frau Hofmann cried. "I'm so sorry you feel you have to—"

The young man waved his hand in disgust and turned to open the door. He paused and looked over his shoulder at both women. "Oh, yes, I almost forgot to check," he said in a strangely casual tone. "Frau Hofmann, I hope you passed my warning from yesterday on to your husband. You know it's the last warning I'll be giving."

"Y-yes, Herbert. I told him. Thank you for alerting us."

Sturm slammed the door behind him.

Anna turned to Frau Hofmann in dismay. "Krista, what was he talking about? What warning?"

Frau Hofmann began to sob.

Anna went around the table to sit next to her and wrap her arms around her.

"Oh, Liebchen, it's the very thing that's made Herr Hofmann so upset that he wasn't able to get up and join us this morning."

"Please tell me, Krista," Anna prodded. "What is it?"

"Herbert told me yesterday that renegade Catholic soldiers from the great battle are still in the area, and some sympathetic Catholic families in the countryside are secretly sheltering them. He said *he* personally trusted us, but he couldn't speak for others, including the other men at his own cottage." She paused to compose herself.

"Go on, Krista."

"Then he talked about how the desire to avenge the Magdeburg massacre has reached a fever pitch in the local area, that posters have been put up in the city promising a reward for the capture or killing of any renegades. So he warned me and Herr Hofmann not to give him or his friends any reason to think we're harboring any. After what he says the Catholics did to his sister, he and his friends would have no problem raiding and even torching *any* house in the area—including ours—if he thought renegades might be hiding there.

"Oh, Anna, I'm so afraid of Herbert. At first, he seemed polite and kind, but he's become so mean and hostile as time has gone on. It feels like he personally blames *us* for what happened to his sister. And that rundown cottage where he lives! Every night now, it seems that some kind of mischief is taking place there. Even though it's a half mile away, we can hear men shouting and cursing. We think they're drinking themselves into a lather. And lately, it sounds like many more people than just the five who've been living there. I can't help but worry about what they might be plotting."

So *that* was it, Anna thought. No wonder she had seemed so shaken earlier. "Krista, we'll speak with Pastor Peter about this when he comes to pick me up later this afternoon. He'll know what to do. I know he'll tell Pastor Wagner about the situation, and they'll find someone to replace Herr Sturm. I'll even insist that Peter tell the Leipzig bailiff about what's happening at Sturm's cottage. Maybe the bailiff will send a deputy out to see what's going on. Anyway, there's no reason for Sturm to think you're hiding anyone around here. So why worry about him?"

"Thank you, Liebchen. You always know how to make me feel better about things."

Anna could tell Frau Hofmann was still troubled, but there was little more she could say or do. "How about we read the devotional I brought for today? Of all things, it's based on Psalm Twenty-Three—your favorite."

Frau Hofmann managed a weak smile. "'The Lord is my shepherd'—just what I need to be reminded of on a day like today."

After nearly a half hour of reading, discussion, and prayer, she retired behind the partition to nap with her husband, who still hadn't yet arisen.

Anna got busy preparing lunch. She wanted to have everything ready and laid out on the table for the Hofmanns once they awoke from their slumber. She tried not to think about Sturm. Peter would be back soon. He would know exactly what to do.

CHAPTER 59

Countryside northwest of Leipzig
December 22, 1631

B y the time lunch was over, Anna felt much calmer.
The elderly couple looked greatly refreshed. Herr Hofmann even seemed cheerful at the prospect of finding a replacement for Herbert Sturm. Like Anna, he urged his wife not to worry about things beyond her control.

Anna left the Hofmanns to tend to their various chores. She collected the laundry in a large basket and walked through the melting snow to the creek about fifty yards from the cottage. The sky was clear blue. Only a few puffy white clouds floated just above the tree line. The air had become mild, and she was thankful she'd left her winter cloak inside. She set the basket of clothes down at the water's edge on a large flat rock that was perfectly situated for the task, then sat down. She drew a deep breath and closed her eyes.

It never seemed to fail. It was the same every time she sat in this place. Just as she had tried to describe to Peter this morning, she had the strange feeling of another presence nearby—the odd sense of someone or something watching over her.

After saying a short prayer for the Hofmanns' safety and Peter's timely return, Anna opened her eyes.

What was *that*? Across the creek and among the trees lining the far embankment about a hundred feet away, she thought she'd detected a slight movement. She squinted but couldn't see anything unusual. *Just a passing shadow*, she thought. A light breeze had kicked up, and the sunlight could play strange tricks with the bare branches this time of day.

Anna returned her attention to the clothes basket and pulled out a pair of Herr Hofmann's breeches. Could the elderly man have picked up any *more* mud while stomping around his garden? She reached down into the cold water and began her familiar routine of scrubbing and rinsing. Hopefully, the rest of the items in the basket wouldn't take as long as this one. She wanted to have plenty of time to wring and hang the clothes on the line in the front yard before Peter arrived.

The sound of footsteps in the crunchy snow behind her caused Anna to jump from her perch on the rock and onto the embankment.

It was Herbert Sturm. He lurched as he walked toward her.

Anna's eyes narrowed. *What does he want now?*

"Hello, Fräulein Anna. I didn't mean to startle you. Can I talk with you?"

Anna quickly took stock of the situation. No one else was around. Sturm stood only a few paces away, blocking her path back to the cottage—if that was what he wished to do. She could scream for the Hofmanns, but there was no chance that, even if they heard her, they'd be able to respond in time. The basketful of clothes was her only defense.

"Yes, Herr Sturm, but only for a few minutes, please. My fiancé Pastor Peter will be returning shortly, and I *must* complete this wash before he arrives."

"Of course, Anna. I just wanted to . . . well, no . . . I wanted to apologize to you for my . . . yes . . . my . . . behavior earlier. You see, things have been a little rough lately."

Sturm had been drinking. He took two unsteady steps toward her.

She backed up, now only a foot from the edge of the creek. "No need to come any closer, Herr Sturm. I can hear you just fine from where you are." Her firm tone of voice seemed to sober him quickly.

"Anna, you've nothing to fear from me. I just wanted to say I'm sorry. Losing my sister at Magdeburg has affected me in ways I'd never have thought. I was wrong to take my anger out on *you*."

Anna was unsure whether it was him or the alcohol talking, but she wanted to be gracious and give the young man a second chance. "I accept your apology, Herr Sturm, if that's what it was."

Sturm grinned. "Oh, an apology it definitely was, Anna! So . . . can we be friends again? Really, we Lutherans need to stick together, don't we? Especially those of us who know what it's like to have family members slaughtered by those Catholic pigs."

That did it. She'd heard this kind of "let's all stick together" talk before—from the lips of Dietrich Ackar. Anna knew immediately where this conversation was heading.

"Herr Sturm, I think I'm done here after all, and I really must be returning to the cottage." Anna moved to pick up the basket.

"Oh, Fräulein Anna, I didn't mean to offend you. Here, let me help you with that."

Just as Sturm reached out, Anna jerked the basket up to protect her torso.

"Anna, please, I just want to help."

"Get away, sir. Just get away. I can do this myself."

Sturm's voice suddenly changed to a threatening growl as he tried to wrestle the basket from Anna's hands. "I said I'd help you, you stubborn girl. Please."

He finally wrenched the basket away. It fell to the ground, spilling the clothes onto the snow and mud.

Anna turned to run, but Sturm lunged and grabbed her arm, spinning her around to face him. He seized her by the shoulders. "Anna, please. Just let me kiss you. Ever since I first saw you, I've wanted to caress every part of you." He lowered his face toward hers as the horrible memory of Dietrich Ackar's piercing black eyes flashed in her mind.

She managed to wrest her arm free. She slapped him hard across the face.

Sturm looked stunned for a moment. Then he laughed and grabbed her arm roughly once again. "I knew all along this was the kind of wench you are, Anna. A beautiful, empty-headed tease. No need to pretend anymore. Let's just stop fighting and enjoy each other for a short time, shall we?"

"Let this 'empty head' tease you some more, Herr Sturm." Anna spit in his face—and instantly paid the price. He slapped her, knocking her back to the edge of the creek. He lunged at her drunkenly once again. Anna raised her forearms in self-defense. Just as he grabbed for them, she stepped to the side. Sturm slipped on the snow and stumbled face-forward into the ice-cold water.

Anna wasted no time trying to retrieve the clothes basket. She ran toward the cottage and didn't look back. It was just as well. What she heard was terrifying enough.

"I knew it! A lying Catholic whore! Spit in my face, would you? You haven't seen the last of me, Fräulein! I swear it!"

CHAPTER 60

Countryside northwest of Leipzig
December 22, 1631

Anna tried to subdue her rising panic. Once she reached the cottage, she gathered the Hofmanns together and told them what had happened. Only the calming arms of her husband kept Krista from fainting.

"I'm going to unlimber my matchlock musket in the rear shed, just in case Sturm decides to return," Herr Hofmann said in a huff.

"Please don't," Anna said, aghast at the thought of the aging man even attempting to load and fire a gun in his condition. "We should wait for Peter to return before we make any decisions. He should be back in less than an hour, and I really don't think Sturm will try to do anything more today."

Within ten minutes, she was proved wrong. The sounds of approaching footsteps and angry male voices were followed by pounding on the cottage's locked front door.

"Let us in, Hofmann! We need to talk!"

Sturm was back—this time with his cohorts.

He pounded louder. "Let us in now! We know what you sympathizers have been up to!"

Herr Hofmann didn't attempt an answer. Quietly, he motioned for Anna and Frau Hofmann to follow him out the back door of the cottage. Thick woods were only a few yards beyond the vegetable garden. If the men remained stymied by the locked door for another half minute or so, there might be a chance for escape.

Anna and the Hofmanns fled half-running and half-stumbling as fast as the elderly couple's legs would allow.

It was a short journey. Sturm had obviously predicted their strategy. Two of the men had rounded one side of the house, three the other side. All five converged on the would-be escapees caught in the middle of the slush-covered garden.

Sturm wasted no time on pleasantries. "So, Herr Hofmann, it's time to come clean. Where are you hiding them?"

"I'm not sure who you're talking about, Herbert," Herr Hofmann said.

"Hofmann, you know I warned you about harboring renegades. We know they're around here someplace. In fact, I just heard from one of my friends back at my cottage that two or three were seen snooping around here only yesterday."

"Herbert," Herr Hofmann pleaded, "I swear, we don't know anything about Catholic soldiers in the area. And we're certainly not harboring any!"

Anna exploded. "Herr Sturm, you know you're only doing this because—"

"*Shut up*! I've run out of patience with you Catholic rats. Schmitz, Lambert, keep watch over the two old buzzards. Maybe take 'em into the toolshed. No need to rough 'em up—at least not yet. Just try to talk some sense into them. Unfortunately, Fräulein Little Mary here will need a slightly different approach."

The two youngest men in the group grasped the Hofmanns and led them off toward the shed.

Sturm turned to face Anna. "Well, Fräulein, it seems your chickens have come home to roost—maybe sooner than you'd thought! Shall we have a little chat together back in the cottage? My two friends and I would love to get to know you better."

Anna tried to bolt but was quickly caught by the waist by one of the two hulking accomplices. Together, the men dragged her back toward the cottage. Once inside, they bound her arms together in front of her chest. After tying her wrists with a small cord he'd obviously brought along for the purpose, Sturm ordered the men to keep restraining her while he searched for something.

It only took a few seconds to discover what he was after. It was stashed in a small barrel in a corner. "Ah! I knew old man Hofmann kept this somewhere!"

Sturm tied one end of a rope around Anna's wrist cord and then hurled the other end over a ceiling beam and handed it to one of his accomplices. He stepped back and ordered the man to pull the rope taut, fully extending her arms above her head.

Sturm stalked over to the little shrine and picked up the figurine of Mary. "Meissner, give me your knife."

After a few seconds of hacking and sawing, he returned to confront Anna. Waving his knife and the decapitated figurine in front of her face, he began to stroke the back of her hair with his free hand.

"S-sir," Anna said nervously, "my fiancé will be here any minute now. How will you get away with this?"

"Once again, Anna, I know you're lying. You know full well your pastor friend won't be here for almost another forty-five minutes. One thing I've noticed about that man: he shows up at exactly the same time to pick you up every day you're out here. Don't think I haven't been watching! And really, Anna, it's actually better that he *does* show up today—after you and I are finished, that is. Meissner, unlock the front door so we can give the pastor a proper welcome once he arrives."

"W-what do you mean? What are you going to do to . . . oh, no! Please, sir! Do what you want with me, but don't hurt Peter or the Hofmanns. Please!"

"But, Anna, can't you see? We can't leave *any* hostile witnesses alive. Especially if we want to make the city authorities believe it was those merciless Catholic renegades on the loose who killed all of you and burned down the house!"

Anna's mind went numb. She could see it in Sturm's eyes. She'd seen it before in Dietrich Ackar's and in Red Turban's—the look of pure evil. And she knew Sturm had every intention of carrying out his satanic plan.

She made one last plea. "Sir, please have mercy."

"Do you see your little Mary here, Anna? Do you know why she's headless?"

Anna shook her head, tears streaming down her face.

"Let me tell you why. Your little Mary here is headless because that's exactly the condition my sister was left in by the Catholic soldier-dogs in Magdeburg. Did they have any mercy on her? No, Anna, they didn't. And you—you lying Catholic whore—have the nerve to spit in my face and then ask for *mercy*?"

Anna knew her life was over. Peter's and the Hofmanns' would likely soon be as well. God had finally abandoned her completely to the devil's hand.

Sturm held the point of the knife at the base of her throat. "Would you like me to take your last confession now, Fräulein?"

Anna shrieked. Sturm whirled. Meissner drew his sword. All stared dumbfounded at the fearsome apparition standing in the doorway.

The black-helmeted knight did not hesitate. He strode toward Anna and Sturm with his sword held casually at his side, stopping only when the point of Meissner's sword touched the lower-center plate of his torso armor. The knight stared down at the sword tip through the eyeslits of his visored helmet, as if considering a pesky fly that had suddenly landed on his belly.

"No further, black devil!" Meissner said with a sneer. "I know who you are!"

The knight stared like a metal-beaked bird of prey into the man's eyes. "I suppose it's my black helmet and breastplate that gave me away. But if you truly know who I am, my friend, you shouldn't have wasted time telling me so."

With one deft, lightning-fast motion, the knight knocked Meissner's weapon aside with his free arm. He thrust his sword straight through the huge man's chest—all the way to the hilt. He withdrew it and stepped aside, letting the man fall face-forward onto the floor.

Sturm and his other accomplice scrambled to opposite sides of the room and drew their swords. Anna, arms released but wrists still tied, took shelter as best she could in the corner.

The knight looked from left to right at his opponents. Both seemed paralyzed with fear. "You must excuse me, gentlemen. I didn't mean to disturb your afternoon. It's just that when I see the honor of a beautiful and noble lady about to be compromised, it raises my ire. To put it another way, gentlemen—here we are. Take me on if you dare, you worthless piles of dung. Just think of your reward if you succeed!"

They charged simultaneously.

The knight took two quick steps backward toward the entrance. Choosing to deal with Sturm first, he easily parried the man's wild thrust and knocked the sword out of his hand. But strangely, instead of dispatching his disarmed opponent before he could flee, the knight allowed his own weapon to drop to the ground. He clutched his left leg just above the knee, obviously in pain and unable to fend off the slash of the other man's blade across his upper right arm.

"You've got him now!" Sturm screamed from the corner to which he'd retreated, too cowed to retrieve his own sword. "Finish the bastard off!"

Sturm's accomplice closed in for the kill.

The knight snatched his sword off the floor with his left hand. With three violent swings, he pinned the other man against the far wall. A straight jab through the abdomen finished him off.

With the knight distracted, Sturm took the opportunity to flee through the other door.

The other two men guarding the Hofmanns in the shed spotted him running away. "Sturm, what's the matter? What's all the ruckus in there? Where are you going?"

"We've been ambushed! Come on! We need to go back and get the others!"

The knight clutched his bleeding right arm as he limped toward Anna, who was still cowering in the corner. "Fräulein, come with me."

Anna recoiled. After all she'd been through, she wasn't about to allow this strange new metallic monster to sweep her away somewhere for his own obscene pleasure. "No. Just . . . just . . . stay away from me!"

"Fräulein, we can't delay. Those men'll be back with help in minutes. Neither of us will survive their next assault. You have to come with me—*now!*"

"I said *no*! I'm waiting for my fiancé. He'll be here any minute now."

The Black Knight stood frozen, breathing heavily, as if debating what to do next. Suddenly, he reached out and grabbed Anna by the shoulder.

She barely saw his fist before everything went dark.

⁂

Peter stroked his horse's mane and patted her neck. What a way to end his last workday before the wedding! The Eilerts had sent him off joyfully, with boundless thanks for everything he'd done and with best wishes for his marriage. They'd even presented him with the only wedding gift that their humble means could afford: a beautifully boxed collection of sweet-smelling dried spices and herbs.

Only a quarter mile now separated him from the Hofmanns' cottage. He couldn't wait to see Anna, to hold and kiss her. By now she'd no doubt be fretting, wondering why he was a few minutes late when she'd specifically asked him to be on time. Hopefully she wouldn't complain much about it. Peter quickened the horse's pace.

As he rounded the bend in the lane, the cottage came into view. His eyes strained at the strange sight several hundred feet distant, far past the cottage. It almost looked like . . . he could barely make it out . . . *men fleeing on horses?*

Peter quickened his horse's pace further. As he drew closer, he saw two people huddled together against the side of the cottage facing him. It was Herr and Frau Hofmann! But what were they doing out there?

And where was Anna? Peter spurred the horse to a full gallop and quickly closed the distance.

Frau Hofmann's husband was holding her by the waist as she leaned over to retch.

"Herr and Frau Hofmann, are you all right? What's going on? Where's Anna?"

Herr Hofmann looked up, his face a mask of worry. "Pastor, he took her."

"*What?* Who took her? What happened?" Peter, frantic, swung down off his horse and raced to the couple.

Frau Hofmann, with her husband's support, finally managed to stand up straight. Herr Hofmann seemed unable to speak further. He simply shook his head.

Peter grabbed his arm. "Herr Hofmann, tell me *now*: where's Anna?"

"She's gone. They took off after her."

Peter's jaw dropped. A sickening mixture of disbelief and terror filled his heart. "*Who* took off after her? Herr Hofmann, *who took off after her?*"

"Herbert Sturm and his pack of friends. Vigilantes out for bounty. Sturm and Anna had a run-in earlier when he tried to take advantage of her. She put him off, but he came back later with his friends and caught us all in the garden. Accused Anna and us of hiding Catholic renegades. They took her inside the cottage, I guess to force her into confessing. Somebody unexpected must have suddenly shown up. Whoever it was, looks like he killed a couple of 'em in there and took off with Anna on his horse. Afterward, Sturm rounded up a bunch more of his friends from the cottage and went after Anna and the intruder. I overheard him as he passed by. He was swearing he'd butcher Anna once he caught up with them."

Peter froze. An intruder abducting Anna? Protestant vigilantes planning to butcher her? Why would they possibly—*oh God!* He pushed the vile, gut-wrenching memory of the Black Knight's sword slashing through Ursula's torso from his mind. There was only one thing to concentrate on now: *get to Anna.*

Jumping onto his horse, he swung the reins to point the horse's head in the only direction that made sense. He would follow the posse—north—toward the Breitenfeld woods.

The mare took off at a quick gallop, spurred on by Peter's hard kick to her sides. Focused on nothing but the path ahead, he barely heard Herr Hofmann's hoarse shout.

"Pastor, be careful! Those men will kill anyone trying to get in their way!"

Peter reached down to feel the bottom of his satchel. The small flintlock pistol was indeed still there. It wasn't much, but it and his dagger were all he had.

"God, don't take the love of my life from me!" he shrieked into the wind. "Not again!"

CHAPTER 61

Woods near Breitenfeld
December 22, 1631

Anna woke to the soothing rhythm of the horse's steady gait. She felt a throbbing on the right side of her head. Within moments, other strange sensations intruded on her consciousness. The left side of her head felt like it was bouncing against a steel pillow. She tried to move her arms but couldn't. Something encircled her body, holding her close.

She groggily opened her eyes. Darkness was closing in, the last rays of the sun barely illuminating the trunks of the trees. *Wait! The trees? What trees?* Where was she?

It all came back in a rush: the scuffle at the creek with Herbert Sturm, his knife against her throat in the cottage, the sudden appearance of the strange knight wearing a black helmet and chest armor, the—

She jerked her head up with a start, the top of her hair brushing the chin guard of whoever it was that was sitting in the saddle behind her. She cocked her head back and peered through the metallic slits of the black visor into the eyes of the man who minutes before had pummeled her into oblivion. *No!*

Struggling to free herself, she nearly fell off the horse. Only the man's firm hand around her shoulders kept her safely in her sidesaddle position. After a few moments, she gave up the effort.

"Easy, Fräulein," he said. "No need to panic."

Something about the man's soft voice surprised her. It wasn't threatening, wasn't impatient. It didn't even sound devious. It sounded like the reassuring voice of a gentleman truly concerned for a young woman's well-being.

Bone-weary and growing dizzy, she let the left side of her head fall to rest against the man's breastplate. "Sir, why can't I move my arms?"

"I had no choice, Fräulein. I had to bind you so we could ride fast without you falling off in your unconscious state. My apologies, of course, for being the one to cause *that*."

Anna looked down. She could only see her winter cloak. The man had apparently wrapped it around her after tying her up. "Where are we, and where are you taking me?"

"First things first, Fräulein," the knight said with a gentle laugh. "We're on a country lane north of Leipzig. I knew this would be the best route for giving the slip to those vigilantes. Seems, so far, I was right. As for where I'm taking you, well, that's for you to decide."

"Uh . . . how do you mean, sir?" Anna asked suspiciously.

"There aren't any cottages in this area where I can safely drop you off with the dwellers. So it seems you have two choices. The first is for me to stop this horse, cut your cords, and turn you loose right here. You'd be taking your chances that the posse won't catch you alone and unprotected as you try to get back to the city."

"And the second?"

"The second, Fräulein, is to trust me to take you to Breitenfeld on the other side of the woods up ahead. I know you'll be able to find some law-abiding citizens there who can give you shelter and escort you safely back to Leipzig soon."

The idea of allowing this fearsome renegade soldier to carry her through thick woods in the dark was terrifying enough. But the thought of giving Herbert Sturm and his thugs another chance to molest or kill her sent shivers down her spine. She had only one real choice.

"Sir, if I choose to go farther with you as you suggest, I must first tell you something."

"What is it, Fräulein?"

"I am betrothed. My wedding is set for Christmas Day, and I have no intention of disappointing my fiancé."

Anna half-expected the man to laugh and ridicule her audacity, but the Black Knight was silent for a moment.

"Well then," he finally said, "it would seem that we need to quicken our pace. We can't have you late for your own wedding now, can we?"

After drawing Anna even closer to him, the knight spurred his horse to a light canter. A few minutes later, they entered the woods. Darkness swallowed the last light of day.

⁂

She must have fallen asleep, her dizziness having overtaken her. The horse's sudden stop jolted her eyes open.

"Fräulein, we're at the end."

Anna lifted her head off the knight's chest. They had stopped in the middle of a small clearing, illuminated by the light of the early, rising full moon. "What? Where are we? How long have we been riding?"

"Only about twenty minutes, Fräulein. We're near the point where the path exits the woods. The village lies just ahead, and I can't take you any farther."

Anna could just make out the twinkling of village lights through the trees on the other side of the clearing.

The knight dismounted, then reached up to lift Anna off the saddle. He gently lowered her bound body to the ground before kneeling beside her.

Anna noticed for the first time the blood flowing from his upper right arm. "Sir, what are you doing?"

"I'm sorry, Fräulein, but I can't take any chances."

Anna's eyes opened wide in terror as the knight clamped his left hand firmly over her mouth. With his other hand, he untied the neck cord of her winter cloak and opened it. The rope wrapped tightly around her arms and chest prevented any possibility of resistance.

The knight pulled his knife from its sheath. He jammed the blade up between her bodice and the bottom loop of the rope that was around her torso.

She shut her eyes tight, tears squeezing from the corners. *This is it. Christ have mercy on me. Peter, I love you.*

"Fräulein, don't fear. I swear to the risen Christ I won't hurt you."

He began sawing away. The bottom loop snapped.

Anna opened her eyes.

He cut the next loop and then the next.

She tried to cry out, but his hand over her mouth prevented it.

He cut the top loop, the last of the seven. Her arms had been freed, though her wrists were still tied.

"Fräulein, can I trust you *now* not to scream?"

Anna nodded, and the knight took his hand off her mouth. She gasped for air, her heart pounding and her body still trembling with fear.

He helped her to her feet, lifted her bound hands, and placed the knife blade in between them on the top of the cord.

"And with this last cut, Fräulein Anna Ritter, I set you free."

Anna stood flabbergasted, unable to move or speak. *How did this metallic monster come to know my name?*

The knight sheathed his knife. He picked up her cloak and hung it around her shoulders. Suddenly, she understood. He truly meant to let her go.

Her shaking slowly subsided as the knight retied the cord on her cloak.

"Sir, who *are* you? And how is it that you could possibly know who I am?"

The knight stepped back and unfastened and removed his helmet. Anna caught her breath. With his shoulder-length, tousled black hair and finely hewn features, he was quite possibly the finest-looking man she'd ever seen.

"It's a long story, Fräulein. Let's just say for now I'm a longtime acquaintance and admirer of that man you're preparing to marry—Pastor Peter Erhart."

Anna stared at him incredulously. "You know Peter? B-but how? And what, may I ask, sir, is *your* name?"

The knight took a long moment. He seemed reluctant to respond.

"Hans Mannheim, Fräulein. I'm a major of cavalry for the Catholic League Army."

"Major . . . Hans . . . *Mannheim*?" Anna mulled the name over and over, to no avail. "Why is it that Peter has never spoken to me about you?"

"I can't say for sure, but I'm sure he had good reasons," said Mannheim in a voice tinged with sadness.

As she looked into his handsome face, Anna noticed a tear flowing down his cheek. "Sir, your arm is bleeding terribly."

The knight looked at his wound as if for the first time and grinned. "So it is, Fräulein."

She should have just bolted. Reunited with Peter. Let this strange, renegade Catholic knight fend for himself. He had put her through enough terror for one day. But she couldn't do it. Something prompted her to say the unimaginable. "Major Mannheim, please. Sit down over there by that tree."

Mannheim looked all around, as if confused by her request. "Fräulein, this isn't a good idea. There's no time to—"

"Please, sir. Do as I say." Anna led the knight by his good arm over to the tree and knelt next to him as he sat down, obviously in pain from the gash left by the vigilante's sword. "Give me your knife."

Mannheim looked at her quizzically for a moment before granting her request.

Anna proceeded to cut several long strips from the bottom of her dress. After cutting away his bloody sleeve, she wrapped the strips around his upper arm and held them in place with both hands to stanch the flow.

Mannheim gazed at her, as if beholding the face of an angel.

"Sir, why did you rescue me?" Anna asked shyly.

"Because, Fräulein, from the very moment I found out who you were, I somehow just knew it was my destiny to do so."

Anna looked at him sharply. "But, sir, you just laid eyes on me for the first time back there in the Hofmanns' cottage. How could you possibly have already known about me and my connection with Peter?"

Mannheim smiled. And as soon as he did so, Anna knew. The comforting presence she'd sensed watching over her every time she'd washed clothes in the creek by the Hofmanns' cottage—it was *him*. Her guardian angel. Now he sat right next to her. But clearly, this was not a divine being. This was a real, flesh-and-blood soldier, only a man.

"So it was you!" Anna exclaimed in a huffy tone. "Spying on me by the creek all those times. But what led you there in the first place?"

Mannheim looked up at the moon, half-covered with clouds. "The fortunes of war, Fräulein. Even supposedly invincible knights like myself are sometimes knocked from their pedestals by a lucky musket shot, the thrust of a long pike, or the swing of a battle-ax. In my case, it was the latter. I took it badly on my leg just above the knee. Ended up getting cut off from my men after the big battle and had to hightail it through these woods. I knew I'd be out of commission for a couple of months to let things heal, so instead of trying to rejoin Count Tilly, I made a bold dash down to Munich to see my wife. That's where I got word that some of my injured comrades had been stranded in the Breitenfeld area, hiding from ruthless local vigilantes out for blood. I couldn't stand the thought of forsaking them for my own comforts, so I came back to see if I could help. I disguised myself, linked up with a few sympathetic Catholic families out in the countryside, and started asking questions. I did odd jobs for them, and they kept me sheltered and fed.

"One day, I started a new daily task—picking weeds in the field next to the Hofmanns'—and I saw you through the trees at the creek. I made some more inquiries, learned about your ministry visits to the Hofmanns, and—shock of my life—your engagement to my old friend

Peter Erhart. I thought about approaching you but decided it would be too risky, given the city's bounty on my head. Until, that is, I witnessed your brief scuffle by the creek with that rat Sturm. I couldn't get there in time, but once I saw you run away, I knew what Sturm and his cohorts were capable of and knew I had to act."

Anna sensed that Major Mannheim wasn't revealing his full story but decided not to pry. "Well, sir, I must say you got yourself into a lot of trouble on my account."

"That may be so, Fräulein, but it was worth every ounce. And I would do it again in a minute for a woman as kind and brave as you."

Anna looked up at Mannheim's winsome face with tears of gratitude. "Thank you, sir. I'll never forget you."

"And may the grace of God and the Blessed Virgin be always with you and Peter, Fräulein, even if you *are* Lutherans."

"Speaking of Peter, Major Mannheim, am I *ever* to learn how you first came to know him, and why—"

"Quiet!"

Mannheim sat up straight and stared at something on the other side of the clearing. Anna followed his gaze. The village lights, previously barely visible through the trees, had been joined by other lights. But there was a difference. The new lights were moving and coming closer, as were the sounds of horses' hooves and gruff voices.

Mannheim jumped up and pulled Anna to her feet. Limping to his horse, he refastened his helmet and pulled his sword out of its scabbard. He returned and whispered in her ear. "Run, Anna! Back into the woods as far as you can get!"

Anna hesitated. She was terrified but didn't want to leave the wounded knight alone. The men were almost upon them. A few more seconds, and they would spot their prey.

"Go—*now*!"

Anna ran to the far edge of the clearing and hid behind a large tree. She peered around it and waited. Twelve men on horseback entered the clearing and surrounded Mannheim. Some were carrying torches. One horseman approached the center of the clearing where Mannheim stood. The torchlight revealed the rider's face, though Anna had already known it would be him—Herbert Sturm.

"Well, Sturm, looks like you guessed right on this one!" one of the men said with a laugh.

Sturm grunted. "So it would seem, though I wonder what he did with the whore."

"Doubt he'll be willing to give up *that* information too easily, Sturm," another man said.

"Maybe not here, but somehow I think he'll be more ready to talk about *everything* once we take him to see the Raker," Sturm said ominously. "All right, let's get on with it. Three of you men, comb the woods for the whore!"

Sturm stared down at his cornered quarry. "And so, brave Black Knight, are you finally ready to meet your just fate at the hands of the Raker? To pay the debt you've incurred at the bloody expense of so many others?"

Mannheim laughed, as if he were facing just one more set of money-loving bounty hunters trying to act tough. "Whoever in the devil's hell 'the Raker' is, I've got better things to do with my time than pay my respects to him."

"The Raker doesn't like his invitations turned down, knight."

"Then I'm afraid you'll have to come and take me, Herr Dung-bag."

"You arrogant slime!" Sturm snarled. He hurled his torch at Mannheim's feet, signaling the assault to begin.

Anna turned and ran.

⁕

Peter took the only path through the Breitenfeld woods that he could navigate in the dim moonlight. It was one of the main paths—and the same one he'd so happily trod in the opposite direction the morning after the great battle. Back then, he'd looked forward to a joyous reunion with Anna back in Leipzig. Now he could only try desperately to avoid thinking the worst for her.

He recognized the near hopelessness of the situation. Finding Anna in these thick, dark, and sprawling woods seemed almost impossible. There was no guarantee that her abductor and his pursuers had chosen this particular path through the woods, if indeed they'd entered them at all. Still, something inside told him *this* was the way. *Take it.* And in his present state of mind, he had no desire to question it.

Not quite halfway through the woods, he drew his horse to an abrupt halt. He squinted to make sure he wasn't imagining things. No, it was definitely there: a soft glow of yellowish light in the distance. A camp-fire? That seemed unlikely. Why would Anna's abductor take a chance on drawing the attention of pursuing vigilantes? Possibly a brush fire deliberately set to divert attention or destroy evidence of—

An agonized howl sounded in the far distance. *God have mercy. Was that Anna?* He couldn't tell whether the scream was that of a man or a woman. It had come from the direction of the yellowish glow. He tried to ignore the vomitous feeling in his stomach as he dismounted and tied his horse to a small tree. Pulling his pistol and dagger from the satchel, he stuffed them into his belt and ran stealthily toward the glow. Minutes later, he reached the edge of the clearing and took shelter behind a large tree. He peered around it, drawing the pistol from his belt.

The clearing was illuminated by several smoldering torches scattered on the ground.

Holding the weapon tightly in his trembling hand, he ventured into the open. On the far side, something on the ground near one of the torches caught his eye. He approached it and looked down at what appeared to be a pool of blood, in which lay two crumpled strips of cloth. Kneeling to pick one of them up, he stretched it out and held it as close as possible to the flickering embers of the torch.

In between the bloodstains, the material's basic color and fabric were unmistakable. Peter knew immediately where these bloodied strips had come from. They had been ripped from the olive-green wool dress that Anna was wearing today.

CHAPTER 62

Leipzig
December 25, 1631

T he early afternoon sky was overcast and light snow fell on Christmas Day. After two days of warming temperatures, the cold weather had returned.

Pulling his cloak tighter, Peter Erhart shuffled along the tree-lined bank of the White Elster River, which ran just beyond the thoroughfare outside the city's western wall. No one else was in sight. Anna would have liked it that way. It was just the way it had been the first of many times he had strolled with her along this bank together. They'd been returning home from one of their ministry rounds, and Anna had commented on how much she loved the peace and quiet here.

If Peter needed anything right now, it was peace and quiet.

Earlier today, Leipzig's citizens had gathered in the city's churches to joyfully celebrate this glorious day of the Savior's birth. Peter didn't care that he hadn't been among them. Let the faithful believers offer their praise and adoration. He couldn't bring himself to even pretend to express joy today.

Things were supposed to have been different. Anna and he should have been raising their glasses to each other and their guests right about now, initiating the first of several feasts to be held in honor of their wedding earlier that morning. But it was not to be. God, Peter thought bitterly, had seen to *that*.

⌒∞⌒

Two days earlier, Peter had stumbled into the Leipzig bailiff's office, exhausted from his fruitless, all-night search for what he feared would be Anna's body. His appearance and story, especially concerning her abduction, had jolted the bailiff into action. That afternoon, he'd taken a deputy with him to visit the Hofmanns. There they'd found everything at the scene and in the Hofmanns' testimonies to be compatible with Peter's story. Upon returning to the city, the bailiff had ordered an extensive search of the woods to be conducted, starting early yesterday, Christmas Eve.

Word of the wedding's cancellation and the reason for it had gone out yesterday afternoon. The St. Nicholas congregation had reacted in shock and horror. Adele had passed out. Kirsten had gone to stay with her and had offered her assistance. The church was besieged by concerned congregants wanting to know how they could help.

Late last night, Peter had been sitting in the rectory with Pastor Wagner and Gabriel, who had been trying to console him. But no amount of heartfelt prayer or comforting scripture had put a dent in his misery. The bailiff's deputy knocked on the door, heralding what he had already feared. The search party had completed its task, and the horrible story was about to get infinitely worse.

In another remote clearing near the western edge of the woods, large pieces of Anna's winter cloak had been found—covered with blood. It was obvious that the cloak had been torn up and gnawed on by wolves known to be rampant in that area. No body or remains had been found, but the evidence and its implications had been clear. The most likely scenario was that the vigilante gang had caught up with Anna and her abductor, raped and murdered her at the original torchlit clearing, then left her body to be dragged off and devoured by the wolves. As to the whereabouts now of the vigilantes or the mysterious abductor who had interfered with Sturm's operation at the cottage and taken off with her, there were no clues.

Peter had collapsed in his chair and retreated into shocked silence. His sole hope—that Anna had somehow made it out of the woods alive—had been shattered. Rising to take its place was the worst nightmare he could imagine.

Since it was getting late, Pastor Wagner had offered his own private quarters next door for Peter to spend the night. He had politely declined, saying he needed some time to be alone in his grief but would plan on attending the Christmas Day service the next morning. After thanking and embracing his comforters, he had left the rectory and disappeared into the night.

The snow fell harder. Peter knew he needed to sit down somewhere soon before his aching head and churning stomach caused him to vomit yet again. Eight mugs of stale beer at the tavern late last night had helped to temporarily dull his heartache, but he had been ill-prepared for the hangover effects.

Twenty yards ahead and about ten feet from the river's edge, he spotted it. It looked exactly as he remembered. The makeshift wooden shelter was rectangular in shape and consisted only of a flat roof supported by two sides. Intended as protection from the sun in the summer months, the structure had no front or back walls. A large, long log placed directly underneath the shelter's roof provided a convenient backrest or seat for casual strollers and river-watchers. He and Anna had sat side by side in this very spot only two months ago, legs outstretched and backs against the heavy log, holding hands, discussing the results of their ministry visits that day, and planning details for their upcoming wedding.

After reaching the shelter and brushing off the light layer of snow on the log, Peter sat down in front of it with legs extended on the wet, pebble-strewn ground. Exhausted, his head still spinning, he tilted his head back onto the top of the log and stared at the roof.

So this is it, he thought. *This is where God has finally taken me.*

It had not been enough of a faith test for Peter to helplessly witness the barbarous murder of his first wife, to see her nearly cut in two by Hans Mannheim's heavy sword. It had not been enough to hear of the helpless orphanage children, his own two among them, having been cut down and mercilessly hacked to death by Mannheim's men.

No, God obviously expected much more from an assistant Lutheran pastor who had the audacity to aspire to his grandfather Nikolaus's bold example. So a new test had been devised by God. Only *this* time, God had not been content to allow Peter's beloved to be killed with one quick, clean slash of a Catholic knight's sword. This time, God had allowed what he *must* have known would break Peter's heart and his faith along with it. God had allowed Anna Ritter—the woman who had restored his zest for life and love, the woman he believed God had given him to marry this very Christmas morning—to be savagely raped and murdered by revenge-seeking Protestant thugs, her body devoured by wolves.

How, Peter wondered, could the God he thought he knew allow such a monstrous story to unfold? Where but from the pit of hell itself could a more demonic plan have been devised?

Though God slay me, yet shall I hope in him!

The voice was back. It had been a while.

Peter laughed bitterly at its reminder of Friar Rusche's last exhortation before their parting.

Yes, Pastor. You're right! How ridiculous that bold profession of blind faith by the prophet Job sounds now! And how arrogant, heartless, and hypocritical you've been to hold it up as the standard for others, when you're obviously unable to hold it up for yourself! Remember reciting that silly verse to your beloved Ursula when she asked you to explain why God allows the innocent to suffer? Pastor, come now. In view of all that's happened to you and your loved ones, isn't there a better way to approach things? Why not follow the advice of Job's wife in despair over the prophet's endless calamities: just curse God and die!

Peter had no desire to curse God. At this point, he simply wanted to die. He wanted the nightmare to end once and for all, the voice inside his head to cease with its torturous taunts.

We couldn't agree more, Peter. And you know it's within your power to make that happen. This is the perfect place. Forget the examples of stronger men like Grandfather Nikolaus, Dr. Weber, and Friar Rusche, who blindly relied on their hope that God is good and will sustain them through any trial. You, Pastor Peter, have seen the cold evidence of what God is really like. He's beyond your own ability to understand him, and you've reached the limit of your endurance. It's time to take your rest. You've earned it!

Peter reached into his pocket. The handle of the flintlock pistol felt ice-cold in his hand as he lifted the gun and stared at the barrel. One shot now and the anguish would be over. Hadn't even Martin Luther allowed that suicide was a forgivable sin? God would forgive him and accept him into the kingdom, wouldn't he? Ursula, Edith, Josef, and Anna . . . wouldn't they all be there to greet him, along with Christ himself?

Peter gazed out at the river and saw them. They were there, just as he'd always remembered them. Their images rippled on the water as they smiled tenderly at him. Ursula held Edith close to her bosom. Little Josef stood by her side, with Anna holding his hand. Ursula beckoned Peter to come join them, as if he'd been delaying far too long.

Yes, Pastor, there they are, all of them, waiting for you. No need to put them off any longer. God expects nothing more from you. He will forgive you. Just do it. Do it now!

A wave of nausea rose to his throat. Peter closed his eyes and lifted the pistol to his head. Friar Rusche's last reminder flashed in his brain: *God is faithful; he won't let you be tempted beyond what you can bear.*

Once again, Peter looked out at the river. Anna's lovely face was all he could see.

Yes, Peter, yes! Do it . . . end it now!

He tightened his finger on the trigger. He hesitated . . . on the brink . . .

At that instant, Peter Erhart remembered to whom his life belonged. A loud cry arose from the core of his soul.

"God, though you slay me, still I will hope in you!"

He reached back and hurled the pistol with all his strength out into the icy water of the White Elster River.

The voice was silent.

Peter trembled, weeping from the terrible realization of what he'd nearly done.

A heavy weariness overtook him. He leaned back against the log, barely noticing the snowfall becoming heavier and the light breeze vanishing. He imagined his dear old friend and mentor Dr. Weber sitting beside him, offering the encouragement he had tried to utter one final time on that bloody street in Magdeburg:

"God will always watch over and care for you, Peter. He will never leave you nor forsake you . . . even in your darkest hour."

As Peter drifted off, a strange dream took hold. Once again, he saw the mirage he'd witnessed three months ago on the Breitenfeld battlefield.

Peter stood with his pistol in one hand and a small Bible in the other, barely able to make out the Black Knight staring at him through the swirling smoke. Appearing to nod in recognition, the knight closed his helmet visor, wheeled his horse around, and began to approach, slowly at first, then picking up speed to a full-out charge. Peter froze, unable to lift his pistol. The Black Knight kept coming, his saber raised. Peter could do nothing but stand and accept whatever the dark, mighty warrior wished to dole out.

Only three feet away, the Black Knight's horse halted and reared. The imposing figure dismounted and dropped his sword at Peter's feet. He unbuckled his helmet and removed it. Peter was dumbstruck. It was the severely beaten face of Hans Mannheim. Mannheim tried to smile and sputter something through his mangled lips. Only blood spurted forth. But as he continued to stare, something marvelous happened. The disfigured face transformed before his very eyes into that of one of the finest-looking men that Peter had ever seen—just as Peter remembered him from the first time they'd reunited as adults in Magdeburg.

Mannheim grinned and touched his brow with his right hand in an informal salute. "Perhaps, Pastor Peter," he said, "things aren't exactly as they seem . . ."

He couldn't tell how long he'd been asleep. It had felt like only a few minutes. Even before fully waking, Peter knew something was different. Mannheim's strange last words in the dream continued to ring in his mind. But what did they mean?

He could feel it now. *Someone is very close by.*

Peter opened his eyes. The snow had stopped. He looked across the river to the west. The clouds had cleared on the horizon, revealing a glorious orange-red sunset. Was he still dreaming?

Peter looked down with a start. Two soft arms encircled his chest from behind, hands resting over his heart. Soft hair caressed the back of his neck.

My God! This is no dream!

"And so, my darling Peter," Anna whispered in his ear, "did you think that God had forsaken you?"

Tears welled up in his eyes. It was just as he remembered from that special day he'd discovered her living alone in Leipzig—the day she had spoken his given name for the first time.

Peter unclasped her hands and turned to face her. Never had she looked so beautiful. He embraced her, unable to stop shaking. Several minutes passed before he reluctantly broke away from her impassioned embrace. Holding her face between his hands, he searched the depths of her jade-green eyes. "Anna, what happened? How did you . . . how did they . . . how did you get away from them?"

She clutched his forearms, a wild look in her eyes. "Peter, who is Hans Mannheim?"

Peter dropped his arms and stared at her in disbelief. "*Hans Mannheim?*"

"Yes Peter, Hans Mannheim—the Catholic cavalry officer. He saved my life!"

CHAPTER 63

Outskirts of Breitenfeld
December 26, 1631

I t had taken nearly all night, but Peter's idea had paid off. A hundred yards ahead through the early-morning mist, he was barely able to discern the outline of the solitary farmhouse next to the White Elster tributary. It was just where the terrified, old Breitenfeld village patrolman had said it would be—extremely well hidden behind a thick grove of trees.

Somewhere in that house, it was highly likely that Hans Mannheim, if he wasn't already dead, was now being subjected to the most hideous punishment imaginable at the hands of Herbert Sturm and the mysterious entity known as "the Raker"—to whom, according to the patrolman, Sturm was reportedly beholden.

Peter, though exhausted to the bone, knew he had to keep going if he had any hope of seeing Hans alive again. Especially if his suspicion that the Raker was behind the recent spate of torture-killings in Leipzig was true.

His search for Hans had started twelve hours ago, after Anna had breathlessly recounted her experience of the last few days.

Hers had been a wild ordeal. While fleeing from the clearing in the woods, her cloak, bloodied by Mannheim's wound during their ride together, had caught on the branches of a thorny bush. She'd been forced to leave it behind, and wolves had obviously gotten to it. She had spent the long, cold night hiding under a thick bush to evade Sturm's search party. The next morning, she'd left the woods and had met a peasant farmer and his wife making repairs to their small cottage. The woman had taken Anna into the cottage and fed her, while the man tried to locate some safe means of transport back to the city. It had taken another full day, but last night the man's brother had happened to stop by with a cart loaded with supplies for one of the city markets. He'd offered to hide Anna in the rear of the cart and drive her back to the city this morning. Upon arriving, Anna had raced to St. Nicholas, where she'd been mobbed by ecstatic congregants as they emerged from the Christmas service. They'd told her that no one had seen Peter since the previous night. Everyone had been worried about him—for obvious reasons. Fortunately, she'd had a hunch where Peter was and set off to look for him there. God be praised, her intuition had proved correct.

At the end of her recounting, Anna had mentioned overhearing Sturm at the clearing saying he planned to subdue and take Mannheim to see someone called "the Raker" in order to collect some kind of "reward." Peter had immediately recognized the bone-chilling implications. Despite Anna's protests of concern for his safety, he knew what he had to do. There was no time to lose.

After instructing Anna to go directly to the Leipzig bailiff's home and tell him what had happened, Peter had ridden to Breitenfeld to see if he could discover any clues from the locals about where the vigilantes might have taken Hans. Anna—hopefully along with the bailiff and his deputies—would join him at the village patrolman's post later this morning. They could all then begin a thorough search together for Hans Mannheim.

So why am I out here now on my own, trying to play the hero before the others arrive? Peter kept asking himself as he crept closer to the ramshackle farmhouse for a better look. Suddenly, he froze, ducking behind a tree at the sight of two shadowy figures emerging from a side doorway no more than twenty yards away. The two carried between them a heavy sack. Stopping beneath a large oak tree, they heaved the sack into a hole in the ground that was bordered by a pile of fresh dirt.

"We forgot the shovels," growled one of the men. "They're back in the house. I'll go get 'em."

"Don't bother," the other man said. "Might as well wait 'til they've finished off the knight. Sturm says it'll be this morning."

"Right. No use wasting our breath digging another hole when we can just as easily fit two in here."

The second man laughed. "Especially with the burial grounds around here starting to get a bit overcrowded!"

The men returned to the house. Peter crept to the hole and peered over the edge. The sack had fallen partially open, revealing the horribly mutilated face of a fresh corpse.

Peter recoiled at the gruesome sight. He returned to the shelter of the trees, his thoughts racing. He had his pistol, but that would certainly not be enough to overcome whoever was guarding Hans. Still, it was clear there was no time to return to Breitenfeld for help. If he truly had any hope of saving Hans, he would have to act alone, with little chance of survival.

His mind swirled, vivid images of Anna, of Ursula, of Hans flashing by in lightning-fast sequence. Why take this crazy risk? Hadn't he already shown the love of Christ to Hans by forgiving him for Ursula's murder? Why now sacrifice himself, completely forsaking the blessing that God had provided by returning Anna safely to him?

A powerful thought emerged, quickly laying all his confusion and hesitation to rest.

He's worth it—go for him and don't doubt.

Peter squinted through the mist that was now beginning to lift. Only a few yards away, the partially open door of a small portico beckoned. *Just get inside, listen for voices, take things from there.*

"Enjoying the view, trespasser?"

Peter whirled around. Two hulking men approached, their swords drawn.

◠◠◠

The rotting stench of death pervaded the pitch-black cell into which Peter had been unceremoniously tossed over an hour ago. He listened with increasing desperation to the voices that filtered through the small ventilation gap above his head.

"How long we going to wait for him, Sturm?"

"Not a second longer. Raker should've been here an hour ago. Can't take any chances. If Erhart found his way here, you know others'll be coming soon."

"But what about the money?"

A pause followed.

"We'll collect it ourselves from the Raker's sponsors in Nuremberg. I know exactly where to find them."

"*What*? Are you out of your mind? We just ride all the way there, say hello, and demand payment?"

"Neumann, you idiot, you *do* realize what a price the Black Knight's helmet and chest plate alone would bring, don't you?"

"Exactly what the Raker would have paid us. It's great money, but—"

"So can you imagine what we'll receive for his *body* as well?"

"Sturm, you can't be serious! You know only the Raker's allowed to work in that trade."

"*To hell with the Raker!* He's cut me out of the full deal one too many times. Besides, I've got a special hankering to play his part and finish off the knight myself, here and now. Especially after what he did to our own people back at the cottage."

"You're going to do it right here?"

"You have a better idea, Neumann? Come on, bring 'im out. Let's get on with it."

"What about the pastor?"

"What about him? Let him rot in the cell. On second thought. Let's bring him out too after we've got all the preparations ready. Let him enjoy the full spectacle."

Several minutes later, Peter cringed at the clanging sound of the cell's heavy bolt being opened. Two men entered, grabbed him by the arms, and dragged him out into a small, dimly lit room enclosed by rough stone walls and a ceiling. In the center of the room, Herbert Sturm stood on the other side of an iron-legged table, a wicked grin on his face. On the table, a white sheet covered what Peter could only guess was a man's body—whether dead or alive, he couldn't tell.

"Greetings, Pastor. My apologies for your discomfort. Come, take a closer look at the object of our ceremony." The men made Peter stand. They forced him toward the head of the table. A wooden plaque on a short post was nailed to the table's edge, rising ominously above the covered man's head. Its chilling message, scrawled in what looked to be dried blood, was clearly illuminated by a single candle on a nearby stand:

MAGDEBURG MERCY!
This Sinner's Debt: Now to Be Paid in Full

Sturm reached out, grabbed a corner of the sheet, and ripped it away from top to bottom. "Behold, our brave Black Knight!"

Peter gasped in horror. Hans Mannheim lay stretched on his back, his ankles and right hand manacled to the side of the table and a metal chain looped tightly around his neck. His face had been beaten to a bloody pulp. Dark-red stripes crisscrossed his bare chest and stomach. His left arm had been cut off above the elbow. A tourniquet applied to the stump was no doubt the sole reason he was still alive, as evidenced only by the shallow rise and fall of his chest.

Breaking away from his restrainers, Peter rushed to kneel by Hans's side. He took his head gently between his hands. "Hans . . . Hans, can you hear me? It's me . . . Peter."

For a long moment, there was no response. Finally, Hans's badly split lips quivered. "Pe . . . Pet . . . ?" was all he could manage.

"Yes, Hans. It's me. I'm here now. You're not alone."

Hans managed a slight nod. A tiny tear appeared in the corner of his swollen right eye.

"Enough tender expressions of love, Pastor," Sturm growled. "He doesn't deserve it."

Peter stood slowly, his cheeks flooded with tears, his chest and throat constricting with helpless rage. He glared at Sturm. "Has your heart turned to stone? Do you not realize what you have done to this man?"

Sturm stared back with a twisted smile. "I know *exactly* what I've done to him, Pastor, just as *you* will see what I'm about to do to him." He turned and walked toward the far corner of the room, which was in shadow. He seemed to be searching for something, then returned to the light. In his right hand was the instrument that Peter knew would be used to subject Hans to the utmost, final agony.

"It has to be done, Pastor. His sins are too great." Sturm held the rake by its three-foot handle, gazing as if enchanted at the seven sharpened knife blades welded to the crosspiece at the end.

"Sturm," Peter cried out, "in the name of Christ, I beg you. No human being deserves this. Please, have mercy on him."

"*Mercy?*" Sturm snarled. "Perhaps that's something the Black Knight and his kind should have shown to my sister and so many others in Magdeburg. Just ask that Catholic-loving whore you were planning to marry, Pastor. I explained it all to her just yesterday, right before this scum burst in and ran off with her. God knows what they were doing with each other in those dark woods before we arrived. If I were you, Pastor, I would *thank* me for doing this."

"*You demon from the pit of hell!*" Peter sprang from his knees and lunged for Sturm's throat. Grabbing it with both hands, he forced the stunned man backward and up against the stone wall. Sturm dropped the rake, trying desperately to free himself from Peter's grip. Peter continued to squeeze with all his might. The young man's face, eyes bulging and lips peeling back from the teeth, began to turn purple.

A heavy blow to the side of Peter's face knocked him to the floor.

Peter awoke to the salty taste of blood in his mouth and a high-pitched ringing in his right ear. Painfully, he opened his eyes—just in time to see the movement of the bucket. The cold water hit his face, shocking him out of his stupor. He tried to focus. Where was he?

The sound of Herbert Sturm's voice quickly reminded him. "You sure clubbed him good, Neumann. Looks like his jaw's broken."

"Lucky for you. Come on, Sturm, we've got him awake now. He won't trouble us this time. Let's get this over with."

Peter looked around dazedly. He was seated in a narrow, high-backed chair, two feet away from the table on which Hans still lay. Peter's arms, chest, and neck were tightly bound with rope to the back of the chair.

Sturm walked over and stooped beside him, a large pistol in his hand. "Your brave attempt to do me in didn't quite work, did it, Pastor? Too bad, because now I'll just have to blow your head off after you've enjoyed the final act of our performance."

Peter—his physical energy sapped, his jaw throbbing, and his mind still a dizzy blur—said nothing. He closed his eyes in abject despair. *God, where are you?*

Sturm laid the pistol on the ground, rose, and took the rake that Neumann handed to him. Positioning himself behind Hans's head, he lowered the crosspiece onto Hans's thighs, just below the groin, pressing the sharp blades against the flesh. Hans cried out, his chest arching in a vain attempt to free himself from the restraining manacles and neck chain.

"Now, brave knight," Sturm hissed, preparing to sink the blades deep into Hans's thighs and rake them up the entire length of his torso, "are you ready to see what it feels like to suffer the ultimate pain like my sister did at the hands of people like you?"

"*Sturm, wait!*" Neumann shouted.

"What—" Sturm looked up, bewildered. He looked behind Peter, his face as white as a sheet.

Slowly, he lifted the rake away from the prisoner's body, clutching it in both hands next to his own chest. "Sir, I . . . I apologize. We didn't know if—"

The explosion rocked the room. The rake fell from Sturm's hands. He stared down at the large hole turning red in the center of his chest, then raised his head toward the origin of the gunshot. Sinking to his knees, Herbert Sturm fell forward, his chest landing on the upturned blades of the rake.

"Get this traitor out of my sight. I will finish what he began." The voice somehow sounded familiar. Sturm's henchmen scurried like rats to obey the order, picking up his body and exiting the room.

Unable to twist his own body against the restraining rope, Peter waited for the intruder approaching from behind to show himself. Out of the corner of his eye, he saw a hand reach down and pick up the gun that Sturm had laid next to the chair. The unknown man walked past him and laid the gun carefully on the table, next to Hans's head. After gazing at Hans for a long moment, he slowly turned around to face Peter, removed his hood, and revealed his face.

Konrad Fitcher bowed. "Pastor Erhart. We meet again."

Peter understood in an instant. Fitcher—faithful assistant to Pastor Spaignart, the spiritual leader of the Magdeburg radicals—had escaped the city's flames, only to sell his soul to the devil by becoming the Raker of Breitenfeld.

Fitcher smiled. "What, Pastor? Nothing to say? No self-righteous condemnation of my actions at Magdeburg or later in this house of God's justice and retribution?"

"Your actions and their results condemn themselves, Fitcher."

"Ah, but you still don't understand, do you, Erhart? I have never acted except as God has spoken to me clearly through his Holy Word. I tried my utmost at Magdeburg to help Spaignart steel the spines of those who would compromise the true faith that Martin Luther taught us. And in the case of our Black Knight here and other Catholic army renegades like him—well, they had it coming. Especially considering how these fiends butchered our innocent Magdeburg citizens. 'An eye for an eye,' as the scriptures say."

"Fitcher, for God's sake, you know good and well the scriptures also say that Christ later *condemned* the Old Testament principle of an eye for an eye. He commands us instead to forgive and love our enemy."

"*To love our enemy?*" Fitcher shouted incredulously. He stepped back, untied his cloak, and let it drop to the floor. He untied his tunic and ripped it open, revealing a horrid mixture of deep scars and burn marks covering his entire torso. "Thousands of our beloved Magdeburg citizens—including my beloved wife—mutilated like this or far worse by the Catholic beasts. Preach to me, Pastor, about loving my enemy!"

Peter, stunned, said nothing. Dizziness overwhelmed him. Once again, he noticed the taste of blood in his mouth and the strange ringing in his ears.

Fitcher retied his tunic and cloak and picked up the gun. He walked to the opposite side of the table from Peter, then pointed the gun at Hans's head. "And so, Black Knight, the moment has arrived. In my mercy, I'll refrain this one time from inflicting the torture that murderers like you deserve. Still, God's justice demands that you should die. There's now only one choice left, if you want to receive pardon and live. Your choice is this: will you now renounce the self-proclaimed divine authority of the pope and his doctrines and accept *sola Scriptura*—the Bible alone—as the only inerrant and infallible rule for the true Christian faith? Just nod yes, and I'll spare your life."

Hans did not respond. It wasn't clear that Fitcher's question had even registered with him.

"You refuse to answer? Then you have made your final choice."

"Konrad," Peter cried out. "Look at him! He's in no state to respond. I beg you—for once at least, leave doctrine and judgment and vengeance to God. Prove your *own* faith in Christ and *his* mercy to be true. *Put down your gun, and let this man live!*"

Fitcher stared at Hans for a long moment. He looked across the table at Peter tears flooding his face. "I'm afraid, Pastor Erhart ... that my faith in Christ is not what I once thought." He grabbed Hans's head by the hair and pressed the barrel deep into his mouth.

Peter turned his head away, unable to bear the sight. He heard the sound of the pistol being cocked.

Please, Jesus, protect Hans's soul.

The loud bang was followed by a heavy thud.

Peter opened his eyes. Konrad Fitcher lay sprawled across Hans's body. Blood gushed from the side of his head.

The gruff voices sounded far away.

"Raker shot himself, sir. But looks like the pastor's coming around."

"Must've passed out from that blow to his face and the stress of it all."

A woman's voice—softer, familiar—seemed much closer. "Peter, can you hear me?"

The fog in his brain slowly began to lift, replaced by a dull throbbing pain on the right side of his face. He realized he was outside, lying on the hard, cold ground. The woman was kneeling next to him, clasping his hand to her cheek. Her face suddenly came into clear view.

"Anna, thank God. What's happened? What am I . . . is Hans. . . ?"

She smiled at him, nodded, tears flowing freely.

He felt a gentle pressure on his other hand. He looked down at his side. A hand was clenching his. It was the hand of someone lying next to him, covered by a blanket. He turned his head farther to behold the bruised, blood-caked face of Hans Mannheim.

"Hans?"

Mannheim's eyes fluttered open for a brief second, his mangled mouth displaying the barest hint of a smile.

CHAPTER 64

Leipzig
February 12, 1632

P eter winked at Anna, who was standing on the other side of the church infirmary bed. "It's time, Major Mannheim. If we delay any longer, Adele will remove our plates and throw our portions to the dogs."

Hans grimaced. "I certainly don't want to be the reason for us all missing out on a wonderful supper. I've caused enough trouble around here already."

"*That* is an understatement!" Anna laughed. "Here, Major, let us help you up. Adele's house isn't far from here, and the walk will do you good."

Peter and Anna helped Hans to stand. Together, the three walked slowly out into the street and began the trek to Adele's.

Hans seemed to be recovering well, Peter thought, considering what he'd been through. Six weeks had passed since the incident with the Raker. It had taken some convincing, but the Leipzig bailiff had finally agreed to Peter's request. In view of the bravery Hans had shown in rescuing Anna and the severe injuries he'd sustained, the bailiff would *not* insist on turning him over immediately to the local Protestant military authorities. Instead, Hans would be allowed to recuperate under Peter and Anna's recognizance in a private room of the small St. Nicholas Church hospital. That would give the bailiff more time to consult with his civilian superiors about the complicated matter.

Anna had visited Hans every day, discussing his medical treatment with the caretaker and writing letters for him to his wife Marie in Munich to let her know he was safe, he loved her, and hoped to return to her soon.

Her visits had also been the occasion for Hans to reveal the full story of his relationship with Peter and his responsibility for Ursula's murder. Anna had been shocked, hardly able to reconcile the two images of the Black Knight as slayer of Peter's wife and rescuer of herself, his fiancée. Still, his story of receiving Peter's forgiveness had warmed her heart and helped her to understand the driving force behind his recent bravery in saving her from Sturm and his thugs.

As the threesome neared their destination, an unfamiliar sight appeared just ahead.

"Peter, what's *that*?" Anna asked, suddenly drawing to a stop.

Peter squinted through the gathering darkness. About fifty yards away, a covered carriage stood on the side of the lane just across from Adele's house. She was standing next to the carriage door and seemed to be engaged in a lively conversation with someone inside the vehicle.

"Adele!" Anna shouted.

Adele's hands flew to her mouth at the sight of Peter, Anna, and Hans. She said something briefly to the coachman and then hurried to greet them.

Peter took her into his arms.

"Oh, Pastor Peter," Adele cried happily, "praise be to God!"

"Praise be to him indeed, Adele. What? What is it, Adele? Why are you looking at me like that?"

Adele stepped back, casting a strange glance at Hans. She reached out to grasp both Peter and Anna by the hand. "Pastor Peter, God has a special blessing for the two of you today."

They all turned to face the carriage.

The driver looked up, nodded, and stepped down from his platform.

"Holy Mother of Christ," Hans said softly, his hand reaching out to grasp Peter's forearm, "can this really be happening?" Peter looked at him. Something on Hans's face said he already knew the answer to his own question.

Carefully, as if following some royal protocol, the man opened the carriage door. He solicitously reached inside, took the hand of one of the occupants, and helped her down. She was a young, thin girl, dressed in a simple, plain dark dress and a white bonnet. The coachman turned her around to face Peter and Anna.

"*Anni!*" the girl cried.

Anna screamed and sank to her knees. Peter shouted with joy.

Liesa Ritter ran toward them with arms outstretched.

Together they caught, embraced, and kissed her and then swung her around wildly, unable to contain their emotions. Anna could not stop kissing her little sister.

Peter could barely speak. "Liesa, what . . . ? How . . . ?"

Adele pulled on Peter's arm, her face beaming. "Later, Pastor. You'll hear it all later. God's not done with you yet!" She pointed back at the carriage.

The driver was helping another occupant out, this one a small child.

"*Josef!*" Peter cried. He ran to greet the elder of his beloved children, now seemingly resurrected from the Magdeburg dead. Peter scooped the little boy up in his arms and kissed him over and over.

Little Josef kept laughing, as if his father were trying to play Brave Knight with him once again after all these months.

Peter finally set Josef down and looked up to see the coachman, who was standing over him and holding yet another child in his arms. Peter stood as the man handed the little girl over to him.

As Peter took her in his arms, he couldn't contain his sobs. "My beautiful, beautiful daughter!"

Edith looked at Peter, smiled shyly, laid her head against his chest, and returned her thumb to her mouth. Obviously, it had been a long day for little Edith.

After several minutes of mutual embraces and tears, Peter handed

Edith and Josef over to Anna and Adele. He turned back toward the carriage. Its last occupant was standing politely by the open carriage door as if uncertain whether to leave or stay. The man was tall, well dressed, and wearing a fashionable tricorn hat. Peter could not make out his face clearly in the fading light. But he knew immediately that *this* was the man responsible for bringing Liesa and his children to him.

Peter walked toward the man to thank him. He stopped and gasped in astonishment. "Are you . . . ? No! It can't be!"

The man removed his hat, revealing his handsome, grinning face.

"*Captain LaFrenze!*" Peter shouted, throwing his arms around the kind-eyed Catholic League Army officer who had rescued him from certain death in the Magdeburg alleyway.

LaFrenze laughed. "You'll have to forgive me, Pastor Peter, for taking so long."

"*Taking so long?* Captain, how in heaven's name did you *ever* manage this? How did you even know to—" Peter stopped short, noticing that LaFrenze was staring at someone over Peter's shoulder. Peter turned.

Hans Mannheim's face was flooded with tears. "Well done, Captain," he said softly.

Peter looked in amazement at LaFrenze, then back at Hans. "Would someone *please* explain what is going on here . . . and how all this could be possible?"

Hans smiled. "As someone in your position might say, Pastor, it seems the Lord himself must have directed our paths."

Peter laughed. "All right. Out with it. What happened?"

Hans took a deep breath before launching into his story. "You'll recall that after we parted the morning after the Breitenfeld battle, I made it home to Munich, where I was able to spend several divine days with my wife."

Peter nodded and then cocked his head. "But Magdeburg—or what's left of it—is a long distance from Munich. So how does that all connect with Captain LaFrenze and the children?"

Hans looked down for a moment. He seemed to be struggling for the right words. "Peter, your forgiveness for what I had done to Ursula meant everything to me. Still, my sin kept weighing on my heart after I left you. And several months ago, before returning to this area, I finally made up my mind to do something about it. By then, my leg had healed enough to ride my horse solo to Magdeburg. I decided to go there and see if I could verify the rumor that had been swirling in Munich—that the Magdeburg cathedral and a nearby monastery building had survived the terrible fires, along with nearly four thousand women, children, and elderly citizens who'd been able to take shelter inside.

"I recalled you saying, Peter, that you hadn't actually *seen* your own children slain. Just maybe, I thought, I could discover some information about what had *really* happened to them. If nothing else, put to rest in my own mind that they were indeed dead. And if good fortune or divine miracle should lead me to find one or both of them still alive, well . . ."

Hans bowed his head, unable to continue. Peter placed his arm on his shoulder. "Go on, my friend," he said after a few moments.

Hans gathered himself and continued. "Once I arrived and started asking questions, I was soon introduced to Captain LaFrenze here. He was part of the small garrison left behind by Count Tilly, and he supposedly had good knowledge of some 'massacre of orphanage children' the day of the sack. We spoke and, when I mentioned your story, he immediately remembered who you were, how he'd saved you that day, and later arranged your escape from the prison. He said he would be glad to look into possible child survivors, but that it could take awhile—longer than I could afford to remain in the city. We parted, with the understanding that he would contact me in Munich if he found out anything."

LaFrenze took up the amazing tale. "I started checking around, but nobody seemed to have any clues. Finally, just two weeks ago, I had a chance encounter with the director of the small monastery that had somehow survived the city fires. He said there were over thirty orphans being cared for there, and he sent me to one of the buildings still standing at the corner of the grounds. I went in and walked through a large room with scattered little groups of children and their caretakers.

I kept calling out your name. I was about to give up and leave the room when suddenly, from the far corner, a young, thin girl cried out, 'Peter Erhart! Yes, sir! We know him! We know him!' It was Liesa."

At the mention of Liesa's name, Peter could hardly keep his chest from exploding with joy. He could almost predict the rest of the wonderful story.

"So I ran over to her," LaFrenze went on, "told her who I was, and asked how she knew you. She pointed to the two small children playing by her feet. She said Josef and Edith were your children—alive and unharmed! When I told her that you and Anna were still alive and well in Leipzig, she broke down and fell into my arms."

Peter was beside himself with emotion. "Captain, how did my children and Liesa ever get there safely?" he finally managed to ask.

"It's a harrowing story, told to me by the monastery director," LaFrenze replied. "It started back at the city orphanage the first day of the sack. With the gunfire growing, your wife was concerned that none of the expected escorts from the cathedral had yet shown up. So she asked her aide Katrina to watch over Josef and Edith, while she and two other helpers left to escort the other children to the cathedral. Ursula had intended to return to the orphanage and wait there with your children for you to arrive, just as you two had originally planned. But things went awry. Ursula never returned, and you never showed up. Katrina panicked. She left the orphanage with the little girl in her arms and the boy in tow. Somehow, by God's grace, she managed to lead the children through the burning city to the basement door of the cathedral. They were let in and escorted to a small room, where other orphaned children were gathered. That's where they stayed for the next three days."

"But how was it," Peter broke in, "that the cathedral wasn't destroyed like everything else in the city?"

"You can thank its senior pastor, Reinhard Bake, for that miracle. On his knees, Bake personally beseeched and finally persuaded Count Tilly to grant his official protection to the building and its occupants taking shelter there. When the sack finally ended several days later, most of the survivors were either escorted out or voluntarily left the city on their own. A few, including many of the orphans, were turned over to the care of the monastery staff, who'd volunteered to take them in for the time being. Edith and Josef had been among those, since Katrina had left earlier to try to find some of her distant relatives in Hanover."

"But what about Liesa?" Peter asked.

LaFrenze smiled. "Maybe we should ask *her*."

All turned to face Liesa. Anna put her hand on her shoulder. "It's all right, Liesi. Go ahead."

The young girl's voice trembled as she spoke. "Somehow, I was able to free myself from that fire that killed my parents."

Anna broke in. *"But I saw the house collapse on all of you!* And I heard your voice calling when I ran to help. I looked and looked, but I couldn't see or even hear you anymore . . ."

"I don't know, Anni. All I can remember is sitting on the ground, coughing and crying, when a couple of young boys ran up and helped me stand. Together, we made it through the street fires and soldiers to the monastery where one of the boys' older sister worked. I spotted Josef and Edith when they were brought in later and remembered them from the times I'd helped Anni out at the orphanage."

Captain LaFrenze picked up the story. "Liesa and the children stayed together there at the monastery until the day I came across them. The next day, I sent a message to Munich to alert Major Mannheim. His wife wrote back, informing me of his situation here in Leipzig and that you were caring for him at the church. She also gave me the name of Adele's street, where the major had told her to send her letters to him. I commissioned the coach, and here we are! We've just arrived after a three-day's ride."

Peter shook his head in bewilderment. He turned to Hans, embraced him, and kissed him on the cheek. "I never dreamed I would see them again," he whispered in his ear.

Turning back to LaFrenze, he took both his hands in his own. "Captain, why—and how—did you have me freed from that prison camp? Wasn't it enough for you to save my life in that cursed narrow street?"

"I felt great sympathy for your situation, after you told me about seeing your wife killed. Knowing the warden of the prison where you'd be taken, and counting on the fact that he owed me a few favors, I sent my instructions to have you freed and provided with the map and some money for your barge journey."

"Captain, I can never thank you enough."

LaFrenze gave him an odd smile. "Actually, Pastor, there *is* a way you can do just that. You see, I'm under strict orders from the dear wife of the major to bring him back home to her in this very coach. I know that releasing him may put you at risk of incurring the wrath of the Leipzig authorities. But maybe you can console them with the fact that Major Mannheim—given the loss of his arm—will never again be in a position to threaten the forces of Gustavus Adolphus or any other Protestant army."

Peter looked at Hans, whose eyes had widened in astonishment and joy at the proposal.

"Captain LaFrenze, I would be more than willing to release Major Mannheim to you—under one condition."

"And what's that?" LaFrenze asked hesitantly.

Peter grinned. "As he well knows, the rescheduled wedding ceremony for Anna and me is only two days away. Since neither of you will be able to attend, the least you can do is stay here for just a few more hours and join us for supper."

LaFrenze, appearing somewhat uncertain, looked at Hans.

Hans broke into a wide grin. "Pastor, seeing as I'm the superior officer in rank here, I will make the decision. It would be our privilege and delight to stay for supper with you and Anna this evening!"

~ ⚜ ~

It could not have been a happier occasion. The meal that Adele and Kirsten had prepared so diligently was superb. Even with the two unfamiliar guests, the conversation was easy and delightful, filled with gratitude, relief, and merriment over the prospect of the upcoming wedding.

Peter noticed in passing that Hans, though clearly relishing the food and smiling along with the others at the antics of little Josef and Edith, had been strangely quiet. More than once, out of the corner of his eye, Peter had spotted him staring wistfully at both Anna and himself.

As the meal concluded, Hans leaned forward toward Peter. "Could I speak with you in private?"

Peter drew back and eyed him with curiosity. Something in the man's expression told him this was not a casual request. "Of course. Is everything all right?"

A tight smile formed on Hans's face. He nodded to Anna and the others. "Everything's fine. I just need a few minutes of Peter's time—a personal matter, if you will."

Anna glanced at Peter, her eyes reflecting concern. Whatever it was with Major Mannheim, she appeared to have noticed it too.

"I'll wait for you outside, Major," Captain LaFrenze said. "I should make sure the coachman has the horses harnessed and everything else ready to go."

Anna stood, cueing the rest to do the same. She skirted around the table toward LaFrenze, tears in her eyes. "Thank you, brave and honorable soldier, for what you've done. I'll never forget what you did to save Peter and restore my sister and the children to us." She embraced him. Choked with emotion, LaFrenze stepped back and bowed before exiting to the street.

Peter and Hans moved into the living area and settled into two comfortable chairs.

"Hans, this is an amazing turn of events. I'm so happy you'll be able to return home. Is there *anything* I can do to help you in some way, to pray for you and your wife, to—"

"Peter," Hans broke in gently, "there's nothing more you'll ever need to do for me. In fact, Pastor, it is I who am still greatly in *your* debt."

"*What?*" Peter asked. "After giving your arm, your career, and nearly your entire life to rescue Anna—and then taking it upon yourself to find our beloved children—you still consider yourself to be in *my* debt? What nonsense is that?"

Hans didn't respond.

Peter knew for certain now that something was bothering him. "Well, whatever it is you think you still owe me, Major Mannheim, I promise that *you* will be the first one I'll think of calling upon the next time I'm in serious trouble! I have your address in Munich, after all."

"I'll have to accept those terms for now," Hans said with a sad smile.

Peter couldn't stand the suspense any longer. "Hans, what's wrong? You seem strangely morose tonight despite all the wonderful things that have happened and your indispensable part in bringing them about. And look, man, you're going home to Marie!"

Hans looked at Peter in a way that made him recall the time he'd stared into the eyes of that terrified, cowering teenager in the Prague castle fourteen years ago.

"Hans, what is it? Please tell me."

"Peter, I know that you've forgiven me for killing Ursula. Still, the thought of her beautiful, innocent face when I swung that cursed sword still haunts me every night. And now, Pastor, here I am—permitted to return to my own wife, when I never permitted you to return to yours. Peter, my sorrow for Ursula overwhelms me. I know she lives on in eternity, but will *she* ever be able to forgive me for robbing her of life and happiness with you and your children?"

Peter arose and went to Hans's chair. Kneeling on one knee, he took his friend's head in his hands, drew him close, and kissed him gently on the forehead.

"Hans, just as God has forgiven you—and so, from the bottom of my heart, have I—I *know* that Ursula forgives you as well. It's true that you're still in debt to her. *That* is what's still troubling your soul. But I know that I speak for her when I tell you there *is* a way you can pay that debt."

"What? How can that be, Peter?"

Peter looked into Hans's eyes. "It all starts, dear friend, with writing me from Munich about what your home there is like. Should Anna and I unexpectedly die while my beloved children, borne by Ursula, are still young, I want to picture what they'll be happily experiencing with you and Marie—when you take Josef and Edith home to raise them as your own."

The heavy burden that had been contorting Hans's face fell away. His expression now reflected what Peter knew could only be complete inner relief and peace. "Peter, I know of no one besides Christ himself who could have said such a thing to me, after what I've done."

Peter smiled tenderly at his friend. "Perhaps, Hans, it was Christ himself who enabled me to say it."

The men spoke quietly to each other for the next few minutes. After a few more parting words of encouragement and a final embrace from both Peter and Anna, Hans went outside. Captain LaFrenze helped him up into the carriage, then gave a crisp command to the driver. With a final salute through the small window, Hans Mannheim settled back into his seat. The carriage soon disappeared around the bend in the lane.

CHAPTER 65

Leipzig
February 14, 1632

T
he day could not have been more perfect for a Saturday in the middle of winter. Bright, crisp, and cold with crystal-clear blue skies and only a slight breeze, the weather had cooperated beautifully. The official wedding ceremony of Assistant Pastor Peter Erhart and his fiancée Fräulein Anna Ritter would begin in thirty minutes. *Nothing* was going to delay their wedding this time.

As Peter walked toward the church with Pastor Gabriel Carver, he marveled at how his personal sense of elation seemed to be reflected on the face of every person he passed. Then again, he realized, why should that be a surprise? There was good reason for renewed joy and confidence throughout the entire city of Leipzig, as well as the entire region.

For those of Protestant persuasion, the news from the warfront was especially encouraging. King Adolphus and his army were now poised for a spring offensive to obliterate once and for all the scattered forces of the Holy Roman emperor. Protestantism in Germany—and indeed throughout central Europe—would be saved. Word had it that, just two days from now, Adolphus would be traveling to Leipzig to discuss these grand new developments with the emissaries of other countries. It would be a great honor for the city to host the event.

But nowhere in Leipzig today was the spirit of joy and thanksgiving greater than at St. Nicholas Church. According to what Pastor Wagner had told Peter yesterday, it seemed that no wedding in the history of St. Nicholas had ever been met with such eager anticipation. The congregation's enthusiasm was perfectly understandable. After all, had not the fiancée of their beloved assistant pastor been saved from the devil's clutches and his own children restored to him?

The traditional Lutheran wedding ceremony would have called for Peter and Anna to meet outside on the church steps. There they would take their vows with the wedding party and gathered guests as witnesses, then all would enter the church together for Holy Communion.

However, because Peter was ordained and considering the seeming "miracles" that God had performed to preserve Peter and Anna through all their trials, Pastor Wagner had decided to do away with protocol for one day. At his direction, the entire ceremony today would be taking place *inside* the church. Congregants would be preseated in the nave pews. Anna would be escorted down the aisle to the altar, where Peter would be eagerly waiting.

The two had discussed several possibilities for her escort. In the end, though, Anna had made a rather unusual decision. She would walk down the aisle unescorted. If she couldn't have her father there to escort her, she'd insisted, she would imagine that he was. Peter had yielded to Anna's desires.

Of course, a few people felt uneasy about Anna's decision. Frau Jund, upon getting wind of the plan, had expressed her humble opinion that it seemed a "perfectly scandalous" idea for an unescorted bride to approach the altar. She had tempered her remarks by observing that "perhaps Fräulein Ritter can be excused in light of her country peasant upbringing—how could she be expected to appreciate the decorum of a large urban wedding?"

"So, Peter," Gabriel said, slapping his friend on the back as they walked to the church rectory, "it appears we're rapidly approaching the point of no return. Do you have any last thoughts you'd like to get off your chest before marital bliss descends upon you and your bride for the rest of your days?"

Peter considered his best man's question and then smiled. "I really can't think of anything, Gabriel." Actually, he could. Peter thought of Ursula looking down from heaven. He knew she'd be happy for him, just as she would be for Anna.

⚬

At precisely eleven o'clock, the wedding ceremony began with the prelude, a beautiful piece that was skillfully played by the organist. Just before it ended, Peter and Gabriel strode from the transept to the front of the nave and stood next to Pastor Wagner, facing the congregation.

The church was packed to capacity. Even the balconies were full. As he looked out at the sea of smiling faces, Peter felt his knees shake in nervous anticipation. He had felt the same while preparing to deliver his test sermon at St. John's Church nearly three years ago in Magdeburg. *Oh, if only Dr. Weber were alive to experience this day with me!* Peter thought.

He glanced over at Pastor Wagner, who was smiling oddly at him. Peter wondered if he'd forgotten to adjust his collar or had a stain somewhere on his tunic.

The prelude concluded. It was as if up until now blankets had been muffling the organ pipes and finally someone had decided to remove them. With a tremendous blast, the opening strains of the processional hymn filled every crevice of the cavernous church.

The congregation rose to their feet and began to sing in unison.

"A mighty fortress is our God, a bulwark never failing . . ."

Behind a curtain, Anna nervously brushed the shoulder of her gown one more time to smooth an imagined wrinkle. She sighed deeply, looked up at her surprise escort one final time, and clutched his proffered arm with her hands. She knew that, besides Vati, there was only one other man she would ever allow to escort her down the aisle, and he was now standing beside her.

"Ready, my lady?" He winked at her, his affectionate gaze expressing everything he felt toward her and her groom.

Anna smiled, leaned in close, and rested her head against his shoulder. "With you here to accompany me, sire, I am *more* than ready!"

She could feel all eyes turn toward the threshold between the narthex and nave as an attendant slowly drew the curtain aside. She strained to see Peter's face at the other end of the aisle. The surprise appeared to have been complete, just as she'd hoped. Peter's hand flew to his mouth in astonishment; others followed suit. At least four of the female congregants, Frau Jund being the first, swooned at the sight.

Anna Ritter, the country girl from the tiny village of Grünfeld, took her first step down the aisle—arm in arm with His Majesty, the crowned potentate of Sweden and the Lion of the North, King Gustavus Adolphus.

⸎

Peter stood at the window of the luxuriously appointed suite that the mayor had provided for the wedding night. *What is taking Anna so long?* he wondered. She'd disappeared around the partition more than ten minutes ago, saying she needed to "properly prepare herself."

As he gazed out the window at the cityscape, Peter reflected on the wedding feast that afternoon. He and Anna had been graced with the presence of King Adolphus at their table. The king had apologized to Peter for his unexpected appearance at the wedding, explaining that after receiving the invitation, he couldn't resist the idea of arriving in Leipzig a few days before his diplomatic meeting to honor the couple he'd helped to bring together.

The king had toasted the bride and groom at the post-wedding feast. With both close by his side, he'd called for their holiness, health, and happiness. Before leaving, he'd drawn them aside for a parting word. He had kissed each of them affectionately and had said with tears in his eyes, "Don't forget, young ones, the goodness of the Lord our God. Maintain your hope in him always. The king might fail you, but God never will." After a final embrace, the king had departed.

Just like King Adolphus to say something humble like that, Peter thought. He could not have agreed more strongly with the message, though he *did* have to confess: God certainly had some strange and disorienting ways of displaying his "goodness." A God who would use a little elf of a Catholic friar to knock humility into the thick skull of an arrogant, self-pitying Lutheran pastor? A God who would use the power of forgiveness to transform a Catholic "Black Knight"—the guilt-driven murderer of that pastor's first wife—into the noble rescuer of his new fiancée and the restorer of his children? Yes, *that* was a God whose ways were strange indeed.

Peter removed his collar and laid it gently next to the newly printed German Bible that someone had put on the nightstand as a wedding gift. He opened the cover. On the inside someone had written:

> *To Peter and Anna Erhart:*
>
> *"May the God of hope bless you and keep you; may he fill you with all joy and peace as you trust in him"—all the days of your life together.*

"Do you plan to keep staring at that Bible all night long, Peter?"

Upon hearing Anna's enticing voice, he closed the cover and let his hand rest on it. Slowly, he turned to face her.

She stood next to the bed. Well-placed candles dimly lit the room, enough to reveal her beautiful face and form, the latter covered only by the sheerest of chemises.

Peter moved toward Anna with a reassuring smile. He touched her bare shoulders and gazed into her eyes, which were radiant with joy.

Tenderly, he swept her up into his arms. The long wait was over.

Hope had won.

AUTHOR'S NOTE

On a brisk, windy day in May 2012, my wife and I crossed the Charles Bridge and ascended the hill rising behind the west bank of Prague's Vltava River. Our Czech tour guide stopped and pointed to the top, where an imposing castle stood. She mysteriously intoned that we would "see something there that you'll never forget." Knowing nothing of this castle's history, but having already trekked through many other castles during the earlier "German Phase" of our Central European vacation, I figured I was hearing just another idle boast of a proud local determined to impress her American visitors.

Finally reaching the top of the hill, we entered the castle grounds and were led to the top room of a tall tower that was supposed to have some kind of special historic significance. At the end of the sparsely furnished and rather unimpressive room, a single window looked out on the Prague cityscape. Just beneath this window, a small, engraved metal plaque announced something totally unexpected: "On May 23, 1618, two Bohemian Catholic provincial governors and their scribe were viciously attacked by a mob of Protestant officials and hurled from this window to the ground far below . . ."

Observing that sign, I was inspired to dig into the real story behind the violent act and the even more terrible tragedy that it unleashed on millions of everyday people throughout the continent over the next three decades, especially in Germany. Soon after arriving home in California, the idea came to me of capturing both the reality and the spirit of that story and its heroes in a dramatic and compelling historical fiction framework. My writing flame—fanned by a long-held desire to share a special message of hope with those desperately longing for one in the face of difficult trials and suffering—was lit. This novel is the result.

Four key events in the long, blood-soaked nightmare known to world history as the Thirty Years War (1618–1648) provided the driving impetus and backdrop for this work:

1. the Prague Castle incident (known later to history as the "Defenestration of Prague"), May 23, 1618
2. the Blockade of Magdeburg (led by Count von Wallenstein), July–August, 1629
3. the Sack of Magdeburg (led by Count Tilly), May 20, 1631
4. the First Battle of Breitenfeld, September 17, 1631

Locales, dates, timelines, and the composition, general positioning, motivations, and actions of opposing combatant forces depicted in chapters/scenes directly dealing with these events are consistent with historical records. The one exception is in Chapter 15 when Count von Wallenstein meets outside the city with two Magdeburg city councilors and accepts their bribe to spare the city. There is no record of any such meeting, although Wallenstein *did* accept a ransom offer from the city and *did* withdraw his besieging forces as a result.

For the purposes of plot, I created two fictional locales as the settings for a number of the countryside scenes in Parts I and II: the small village of Grünfeld and the town of Hohenstadt to the west of Magdeburg.

The specific actions, words, and thoughts of all historical figures (see Main Characters) in the novel are products of my own speculation. However, I have striven to keep all of these generally consistent with the known overall character, demeanor, major decisions, and actions of these figures to the extent they can be gleaned from available biographical descriptions. My main intent was to capture the spirit, if not the letter, of the role these historical characters would likely have played in the various novel scenes in which they are placed. Please note that, for dramatic purposes, Christian Wilhelm, the deposed Lutheran Administrator of Magdeburg, is placed in the city for key scenes of Part I (1629). In fact, during that period, the historical record indicates he was still living in exile in Sweden and elsewhere as a result of his military debacle at Dessau Bridge in 1626. However, his ardent supporters on the Magdeburg city council carried on his legacy during this period and helped to ensure his return-in-force in the fall of 1630 to reassume his former role as depicted in Chapter 16 of Part II.

As for the invented characters (chief among these being Peter Erhart, Hans Mannheim, and Anna Ritter), their actions, words, and thoughts are purely fictional—except when they are referring to true historical events, quoted scripture, or prevailing religious doctrines. Any resemblance to real persons is entirely coincidental.

Some readers may be interested in the life trajectories and ultimate fate of the novel's historical figures, as well as the progress of the war itself after 1631. Brief summaries of these are provided.*

- **Counts William Slavata and Jaroslav Martinic** (Bohemian Catholic provincial governors who were hurled from the Prague castle tower window in the Prologue): Following the miraculous survival of their falls, both men eventually escaped from their Protestant would-be captors and went into exile in Germany. Both returned to Bohemia following the defeat of the Protestant rebellion by the Catholic League Army in 1620. Slavata became a strong proponent for the restoration of Catholicism to the country and was appointed as a colonel-chancellor of Bohemia by the Holy Roman emperor in 1628. Martinic's return was handsomely rewarded with the lands of several beheaded Protestant rebellion leaders. Both men survived the remainder of the Thirty Years War, fathered many children, and lived out their lives peacefully.

- **Count Heinrich von Thurn** (primary leader of the Bohemian Protestant rebellion in the Prologue): Following the defeat of his forces by the Catholic League Army at the Battle of White Mountain (near Prague) in 1620, Thurn was exiled by the Holy Roman emperor and lost all of his Bohemian estates. He soon made quite a comeback, joining the Swedish army of King Gustavus Adolphus and quickly rising in rank. In 1633, he led a force against the rejuvenated Count von Wallenstein but was defeated and captured. Ransomed soon thereafter, he retired to Estonia and eventually died there.

- **Count Albrecht von Wallenstein** (supreme commander of the Catholic Imperial Army in Parts I–II): Wallenstein's outlandish personal ambitions incurred the wrath of friend and foe alike. After being suspected of treason and dismissed from his position by the Holy Roman emperor in late 1630, he retired in comfort to the Duchy of Friedland. It was not long, though, before the emperor recalled him to his former position, following the death of Count Tilly in battle in 1632. Wallenstein achieved mixed success on the battlefield, and he eventually began plotting to desert the emperor's cause. Losing the support of his army, he withdrew to a small castle, where he was assassinated by imperial agents one night in 1634.

- **Christian Wilhelm** (Lutheran administrator for the archbishopric of Magdeburg in Parts I–III): Wilhelm was badly injured during the Sack of Magdeburg and taken prisoner. His Jesuit caretakers in the army prison camp tended his wounds and persuaded him to convert to Catholicism. After signing a public pamphlet promoting the principles of his new religion, he was released and ultimately rewarded with lands and a lifelong pension by the Magdeburg archbishopric. He died in 1665 in a Catholic monastery.

- **Christian Gilbert de Spaignart** (senior pastor of the Lutheran Church of St. Ulrich and leader of the radical faction of the Magdeburg city council in Parts I–III): Spaignart was captured during the Sack of Magdeburg. Count Tilly—determined to sharply punish him for his prominent role in bringing about the Magdeburg debacle—ordered him to be locked hands and feet and thrown into a dark dungeon for several months. Spaignart survived and was freed once the Catholic garrison was forced to withdraw. He then sought the help of a Swedish army general, who ordered him restored to his pastorship in the ruined city. He continued to live, preach, and write there until his death in 1635.

- **Otto Gericke** (mathematician/physicist and Magdeburg city councilman in Parts I–III): Gericke was taken as an imperial prisoner shortly after the sack, but his freedom was soon ransomed by a local aristocrat. He returned to Magdeburg with his family and participated in the rebuilding of the city. In 1646, he became the city's *burgomeister* (mayor), a position he held for the next thirty years. He also continued with his scientific and engineering pursuits, eventually publishing a treatise famous in the field of electrostatic experiments. In 1666, he was ennobled by the Holy Roman emperor and his name was changed to Otto von Guericke. He died in 1686, fifty-five years to the day after surviving the flames of Magdeburg. The Otto von Guericke University of Magdeburg, founded in 1993, is named after him. Guericke's personal account of the Sack of Magdeburg provides one of the most poignant historical descriptions of the horrors experienced by that city on May 20–22, 1631.

- **Reinhard Bake** (senior pastor of the Magdeburg cathedral and leader of the imperialist faction of the Magdeburg city council in Parts I–III): After saving the lives of over four thousand Magdeburg citizens taking shelter at the cathedral by his direct plea to Count Tilly for mercy, Bake was taken captive. However, attempts by Jesuits in Tilly's camp to convert him to Catholicism proved unsuccessful, and he was eventually allowed to leave Magdeburg and take on a position as superintendent in another German city. In 1640, he returned with his family to the rebuilt city of Magdeburg, where he was granted the honored position of First Composer for the Magdeburg cathedral. He died in 1657.

- **Johann Tserclaes, Count of Tilly** ("Count Tilly": lieutenant general and supreme commander of the Catholic League Army in Parts I–V): After his disastrous defeat at Breitenfeld, Tilly managed to regroup his forces and launched a campaign to prevent King Adolphus and his army from crossing the Lech River into Bavaria in south Germany. During the Battle of Rain in April 1632, he was wounded by a cannonball, contracted tetanus, and died several days later at the age of seventy-three. It is reported that, as a sign of compassion and respect, King Adolphus sent his personal physician to help care for Tilly during his final hours, prompting Tilly to tell the man, "Your king is truly a noble knight!"

- **Gustavus Adolphus** (king of Sweden and commander of the combined Protestant armies in northern Germany in Parts II–V): Building upon his huge battlefield victory at Breitenfeld, Adolphus completed the year 1631 with a highly successsful campaign in the Rhineland before turning his sights toward Bavaria. In November 1632 during the Battle of Lutzen, Adolphus was killed when, at a crucial point in the battle, he became separated from his troops while leading a cavalry charge into a heavy cloud of fog and gunpowder smoke. He was succeeded on the throne through the regency of his young daughter, Christina.

The death of Gustavus Adolphus on the battlefield was a terrible blow to the Protestant cause. Without his inspiring leadership, the Protestants suffered a number of devastating defeats over the next three years and the Swedish army was driven entirely out of southern Germany as the emperor's forces rallied to spread the religious tenets of the Catholic Counter-Reformation. After that, however, the war entered a new phase. It became far less about religious purity and far more about other European powers (notably Catholic France) joining with Lutheran Sweden in a desperate effort to prevent the Habsburg family leaders in Catholic Austria, Spain, and the Netherlands from expanding their control over *all* European territories and economic markets.

In the end, the French–Swedish military alliance proved successful: on October 24, 1648, the Peace of Westphalia was signed by the Holy Roman emperor, the German princes, and representatives from France and Sweden. The Peace enabled Sweden to gain control of Baltic trade and acknowledged France as the preeminent Western power. The power of the Holy Roman emperor was broken, and the German states were once again able to determine independently the religion of their own lands. But this peace had come at an exorbitant price: the deaths by war or directly related disease and starvation of over eight million Europeans, and the setting back of the German economy and civilization by at least a generation. Indeed, without the enduring faith and sacrificial love of courageous seventeenth-century German men and women like those portrayed by Peter Erhart, Anna Ritter, Hans Mannheim, and others in this novel, it is difficult to imagine the survival and restoration of hope for so ravaged a land.

*Note: Sources for these summaries include *The Thirty Years War* (Peter H. Wilson, 2009, Belknap Harvard) in addition to information gleaned from a survey of pertinent English and German historical articles online.

ACKNOWLEDGMENTS

Many contributed their time, expertise, and spirit to the creation of this book.

I am especially grateful to authors William Greenleaf (*A Plague of Gods*) and Barbara Kyle (*The Queen's Lady* and other novels in her Thornleigh Saga series) for their invaluable reviews of the draft manuscript and insightful suggestions for overall story structure, plot, styling, and character portrayal.

Thanks also to Marshall White, Pat Ricucci, Kiffer Brown, and Tina Dow for their constructive beta reviews and critiques that inspired key aspects of the story, and to Vanessa Wells (Wells Read Editing) for her editorial suggestions and help with historical fact-checking.

When push came to shove in the final stages of development, the best team was there. Special thanks to: Shayla Raquel for her amazingly thorough copyediting, styling, proofreading, and author-friendly publishing support services; to Melinda Martin (Martin Publishing Services) for her meticulous work with the interior formatting; and to Monica Haynes (The Thatchery) for her captivating cover design. Together, they made the entire journey from draft manuscript to book release a joyful ride.

To David and Terry, my faithful encouragers and fellow believers: thanks for keeping me on task, motivated to finish, and focused on the One who made it all possible.

And last but not least, thanks and love to my beautiful wife Nancy, for enduring my frequent outbursts of authorial frustration and patiently supporting me in the heavy investment of time, attention, and effort needed to pursue the vision for completion of this work.

ABOUT THE AUTHOR

 Driven by a lifelong passion for military and religious history, Bruce Gardner researches and writes creatively about the impact of major wars on the lives and faith experiences of everyday people. Retired from a thirty-year career in national aerospace and defense systems engineering, Bruce is actively involved in church and community volunteer work. He lives with his family in northern California. He is the author of the epic historical novel, *Hope of Ages Past*, which was awarded the 2016 Chanticleer Chaucer Award for Best-In-Category and was also named by Kirkus Reviews as one of the best books of 2018.

CONNECT WITH THE AUTHOR

BruceGardnerBooks.com
Goodreads.com/AuthorBruceGardner

LEAVE A REVIEW

If you enjoyed this book, will you please consider writing a review on Amazon and Goodreads? Reviews help self-published authors make their books more visible to new readers.

AMAZON:
https://www.amazon.com/gp/product/B07CKQGMRF

GOODREADS:
https://www.goodreads.com/book/show/39924771-hope-of-ages-past

www.ingramcontent.com/pod-product-compliance
Lightning Source LLC
Chambersburg PA
CBHW030643120726
47905CB00001B/35

* 9 780999 881118 *